TWICE DEAD

BOOK ONE

TWICE DEAD

CAITLIN SEAL

Charlesbridge
TEEN

Published by Charlesbridge
85 Main Street
Watertown, MA 02472
(617) 926-0329
www.charlesbridgeteen.com

Library of Congress Cataloging-in-Publication Data
Names: Seal, Caitlin, author.
Title: Twice dead / by Caitlin Seal.
Description: Watertown, MA : Charlesbridge, [2018] |
Summary: Daughter of a sea merchant captain, seventeen-year-old Naya Garth is on
a trading mission in Ceramor when she is murdered, and resurrected by a necromancer
as one of the "undead," bound to her former body by mysterious magic runes, an
abomination in her homeland of Talmir—she has been effectively recruited as a spy
for Talmir, and soon finds herself embroiled in politics, kidnapping, and murder,
and facing the truth that she can never go home again.
Identifiers: LCCN 2017028989 (print) | LCCN 2017061790 (ebook) |
ISBN 9781632896483 (ebook) | ISBN 9781580898072 (reinforced for library use)
Subjects: LCSH: Magic—Juvenile fiction. | Death—Juvenile fiction. |
Wizards—Juvenile fiction. | Identity (Psychology)—Juvenile fiction. |
Conspiracies—Juvenile fiction. | Adventure stories. |
CYAC: Magic—Fiction. | Dead—Fiction. | Wizards—Fiction. |
Identity—Fiction.| Conspiracies—Ficton. |
Adventure and adventurers—Fiction. | Fantasy. |
LCGFT: Action and adventure fiction.
Classification: LCC PZ7.1.S33688 (ebook) | LCC PZ7.1.S33688 Tw 2018 (print) |
DDC 813.6 [Fic]—dc23
LC record available at https://lccn.loc.gov/2017028989

Printed in the United States of America
(hc) 10 9 8 7 6 5 4 3 2 1

Display type set in Java Heritages by Heybing Supply Co.
Text type set in Centaur by Monotype
Printed by Berryville Graphics in Berryville, Virginia, USA
Production supervision by Brian G. Walker
Designed by Susan Mallory Sherman and Sarah Richards Taylor
Jacket design by Shayne Leighton

For Matt, who supplied food and tea,
and believed in me even when I didn't.

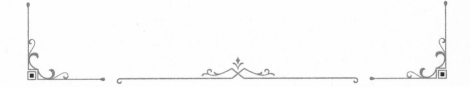

BELAVINE CITY

NORTH ROAD

EMBASSY
OF SILMAR

EMBASSY
OF TALMIR

EMBASS
OF THE
BANEM
ISLAND

EXECUTION
LOCATION

MARKET STREET

THE
PALACE

VISTEL
SQUARE

D·O·C·K·S

WAREHOUSE
DITRICT

BELAVINE BAY

MARKET STREET

THE RISEN LANDS

THE BANEN ISLANDS

LITH LOR

TAMIR

FAL VESH

AL DRAS

ENDRAN CITY-STATES

THE BLACKSPINE MOUNTAINS

PASS

MILAL

SURES

BELAVINE

CEROAMOR

RIORRICA

ROLSINA

BONE SWAMP

SILMAR

AVISINE

TEREVAR

BELANORE HILL

ALANCE'S HOUSE

SANMORE HILL

MERCHANT SELLENO'S HOUSE

CANSA HILL

THE GLASS SHOP

EAST ROAD

BITTER DREGS CAFÉ

LUCIA'S SHOP

BEIRDO HILL

SOUTH ROAD

Blando

CHAPTER 1

Naya stood on the deck of her father's ship, the *Gallant*, watching the crowded docks with a growing sense of unease. Any one of the brightly dressed strangers down there could be undead. She shaded her eyes against the afternoon sun as she turned to face her father. "I'm not certain I can—"

"You're ready." He stood beside her, arms crossed, scowling at the city beyond the port. He was a tall man with broad shoulders and dark eyes. His beard was trimmed neat and he wore his black jacket like battle armor.

A warm sea breeze blew across the deck, making the rigging creak above them. Naya touched the silver pendant hanging below her throat. "Yes, sir. I won't let you down."

The scowl left her father's face as he met her eyes. He squeezed her shoulder. "I know. Learn all you can here, and keep your wits about you. This city is full of liars."

"I will."

Her father looked like he wanted to say more. Instead he looked back at the city and his scowl returned. "Go. Creator guide you."

Naya clutched her oilskin document folder as she descended the gangplank to the docks. She stuck out her chin and tried to mimic the calm expression her father usually wore. *Find Master*

Selleno. Ensure that he signs the contract. Return to the ship. Simple. As for the undead, everyone said they looked and acted like ordinary people. If she ignored the walking corpses, they'd do her the same courtesy. Probably.

The smells of the market—flowers, strange spices, sweat— flooded Naya's nose as she shouldered her way into the crowd. The press of bodies trapped the afternoon heat, making her head spin as she searched for a street sign. Normally her father dealt with suppliers here by the docks. But Selleno was special. He owned some of the finest orange groves in all of Ceramor. The fruit would fetch a good price back home in Talmir. First, though, Naya needed to convince him to sign the contract, and the stubborn old eccentric refused to meet outside his house in the city's western hills.

Naya tightened her grip on the folder. Though she was already past her seventeenth birthday, this was the first time her father had let her go ashore alone to negotiate with a supplier. From her father's tone she guessed her task would be more complicated than just collecting a signature. Perhaps he worried Selleno would try to cheat them. Or maybe he expected her to negotiate for a better price. Whatever it was, it was obviously a test. If she passed, she could prove he hadn't made a mistake by taking on his bastard daughter as an apprentice.

A whistle shrieked. Naya stepped back just in time before a rune-powered tram barreled past. Her heart raced as she tucked a sweat-damp curl back into her braid. She would not fail.

People stared at her as she continued down the main road, past shops in tall buildings with large front windows displaying gowns and gentlemen's shoes. Naya hunched her shoulders. She could imagine what those strangers must be thinking: *foreigner.* Her tan skin and brown hair could have let her pass for local, but her clothing made her stick out like a barnacle on a well-scrubbed hull. The people here, in the city of Belavine, wore loose, bright-colored cottons. Men and women alike favored brass-buttoned vests that stopped just above the hips. Even the poorest embroidered their hems and cuffs with elaborate geometric designs that looked gaudy in comparison with the simpler fashions of her home.

A drop of sweat trickled down Naya's back and into the hem of her gray wool skirt. She fought the urge to unbutton the high collar of her blouse. Maybe it would have been smarter to concede a little to the local fashions. She'd likely have been more comfortable, and far less conspicuous. Safer. The people here had no love for Talmirans like her.

Naya pushed the uncomfortable thought away. Her father wouldn't send her into danger. And he hadn't offered an escort from among the crew. That meant he thought she could do this alone. Naya focused on the warm sun and the lively sounds of the market. So long as she got back to the *Gallant* before nightfall, she'd be fine.

Despite her initial unease, a smile rose on Naya's lips as she followed her father's directions deeper into the city. There was a thrill to exploring new places, even those that had been tainted by necromancy.

The streets narrowed when she left the main thoroughfare. The big glass windows were replaced by smaller storefronts and pushcarts manned by eager vendors selling everything from bruised vegetables to lamp oil. The faded wooden street signs were barely legible here. Naya had to double back twice before she finally found the right one.

As she rounded the corner, she noticed a man standing a few paces behind her. He turned away before she could get a clear look at his face, but something about him tugged at her memory. He had shaggy black hair and wore the oft-mended clothing of a common laborer. Naya frowned. She could have sworn she'd glimpsed the same man lingering near the docks. *No. Not just at the docks.* Hadn't he been standing outside the bookshop she'd passed a moment ago?

Goose bumps rose on her arms despite the heat. Was he following her? Naya stepped backward, keeping her eyes on the man.

"Watch——!" Something slammed into her. Next thing she knew, she was sitting on the cobblestones and staring up at a heavyset woman in a flowing green skirt and black vest. A shopping basket lay next to Naya, its contents scattered over the paving stones. The woman pursed her lips as she bent to collect her things.

"I'm sorry." Naya grabbed her folder and scrambled to her feet. Her palms stung. When she lifted them, she wasn't surprised to see beads of blood rising from the scrapes. *Wonderful.* She couldn't even deliver a simple contract without getting into trouble. What would Selleno think when she arrived with stained skirts and bloody hands?

"Are you all right?" the woman asked in the local tongue. She glanced at Naya's hands, and her brow wrinkled with concern.

"I'm . . ." Naya began in the same language. But the words died in her throat when she noticed the black runic tattoos encircling the woman's neck and wrists. She'd heard of marks like these. They bound the woman's soul to her formerly dead body. *She's one of the undead,* Naya thought.

Her skin crawled as she stumbled away from the walking corpse. "No. I'm fine." Before the corpse could do anything else, Naya hurried off. Her heart thudded against her ribs. *Fool.* It wasn't as though the corpse had done anything wrong. Naya could have avoided her if she hadn't been walking backward like a child scared of wraiths in the night. She paused, looking back the way she'd come, but the strange man was nowhere in sight.

She followed the road up into the city's rolling hills, turning right at an inn with a massive smiling fish carved over its door.

The road turned again, narrowing to a lane barely wide enough for two people to walk abreast. Tall, brightly painted houses rose up on either side, blocking out the sun. Naya glanced back over her shoulder at the empty lane. Her father had said Selleno's house wasn't far from The Happy Cod inn. This had to be the right way.

After a few minutes following the winding lane, her certainty wavered. The city below was laid out in a proper grid. But up here the streets looked like they'd been mapped by wandering cows. *Blind cows.* Naya glanced back down the hill. The shimmer of the bay was just visible above the rooftops. The street was empty, but she couldn't shake the feeling that someone was watching her.

Naya's fingers strayed to her pendant, running over the stylized bird embossed on the flat disk. Foolish. Her father would be disappointed if he saw her fear. Fear made you hesitate, and those who hesitated were overtaken by others bolder and smarter. Naya took a steadying breath, then continued on her way.

Her luck turned when she glanced down an alley to her right. It opened onto a wider street, and through the growing afternoon shadows she could just make out a narrow purple house. Pillars flanked the doorway, matching her father's description. Naya grinned as excitement washed away her unease.

Her shoes splashed through puddles spreading from a clogged gutter as she jogged into the alleyway. Finally. If she hurried, she could be back on the *Gallant* before dinner. With all her attention focused on the house, her mind barely registered the scrape of footsteps behind her. She felt a sting at the back of her neck. Naya reached up to slap whatever bug had bitten her, but her fingers brushed against something long and narrow protruding from her skin. *What in creation?* She stifled a gasp as she pulled the thing out and held it up to the light. A dart. It was fletched with tiny red feathers, and something dark and oily was smeared across the needle-sharp tip. Her stomach clenched.

Naya tried to turn, but her neck caught fire with pain. The sensation spread like swarming ants up her scalp and down the curve of her spine. Her jaw snapped shut so tight she thought her teeth might shatter. She tried to run, but her feet got tangled and she stumbled to her knees instead. She tried to call out but only managed a weak moan. The folder slipped from her stiff fingers. When she exhaled, her mouth filled with the copper taste of blood.

Naya tried to take a breath. Nothing. Her chest burned. She tried again, failed again. Numbness crept through her limbs, more terrifying than the pain. *No, this can't be happening.* She was dimly aware of her body collapsing to the ground. Dirty water splashed against her cheek and into one paralyzed eye. As the edges of her vision darkened, she saw a pair of scuffed boots with bronze buckles.

Then everything melted away.

CHAPTER 2

"It worked. Incredible."

Naya opened her eyes. The world blurred, then swam into focus. *What worked?* Her memories were fragmented and jumbled. There had been a song, persistent and alluring, but sung in a language she didn't recognize. She'd been standing on a black expanse, struggling against an icy tide that sought to suck her away.

No, wait, that wasn't right. She'd been on a street. She'd been doing something important. What was it? The details slipped away like fever dreams, so she narrowed her eyes and concentrated on the present. The ceiling was all wrong. It was too high, and too white to be the ceiling of her cabin on the *Gallant*.

Naya was lying down, so she raised her head. An older woman stood nearby, staring at her. The lines around the woman's eyes and mouth suggested she was somewhere past her fiftieth year. Sweat glistened on her forehead and her skin was flushed with exertion. Round glasses covered eyes so dark they were almost black. Behind the woman, shelves sagged under neat rows of jars with labels too small to make out. A window set in the right wall overlooked a cluttered counter next to the shelves, but it had been covered with heavy drapes.

Weak light shone from oil lamps and reflected off a strange

metal table pushed against the wall opposite the window. A man of average height and build stood next to it. He wore a dark, well-tailored suit and held his hands clasped behind his back. A wide-brimmed hat shadowed his face.

The woman with the glasses watched Naya with an expression of grim triumph. *What in creation did you do to me?* Naya tried to ask, but all that came out was a moan. She tried to draw breath. Couldn't. Tried again. Still nothing. Fresh panic ignited her thoughts. Her memories returned, indistinct at first, but growing clearer with every passing moment. She was in Belavine, a wealthy port in the country of Ceramor. She'd been looking for something for her father. Naya's head spun as she tried to recall the details. Why did she feel so strange? Her back seemed to barely touch the floor, almost like she was drifting.

"There. She's almost completely solid. Where's my book?" The woman turned to search the cluttered counter, oblivious to Naya's panic. Anger sparked in Naya's chest. Who were these people? The drifting sensation lessened. She pressed her hands against the cool stone floor as her anger grew.

The woman dug out a worn leather journal from a pile of papers. She grabbed a pen and began writing, stealing glances at Naya between sentences.

Naya tried again to take a breath, and this time air flooded her lungs. She sat up. The blanket covering her slid away. When she glanced down, a noise somewhere between a yelp and a scream escaped her throat. As if waking up in a strange room surrounded by strange people weren't bad enough, someone had taken her clothes. The rough wool blanket slipped through her fingers as she struggled to cover herself, but after a moment she managed to pull it to her chin. In the flickering candlelight her fingertips looked silvery-blue, almost transparent. Naya blinked and the illusion vanished.

The woman looked up. "Please, try to remain calm."

"Who are you? What's going on? Where am I?" Too late Naya realized she'd asked in Talmiran. Even using the familiar words, her voice sounded strange. She took another breath and repeated the question in Ceramoran.

The woman gave her a tight-lipped smile. "My name is Lucia Laroke, and this is my shop. I realize this is disorienting, but I promise that will pass." She wrote a few more lines in her journal. "Now then, would you please raise your right hand above your head?"

Naya clutched the blanket tighter. She looked again at the strange room. White chalk runes encircled the bare patch of floor where she'd awoken. An idea tugged at the back of her mind, one too terrifying to acknowledge. "Why?" she asked.

"It's a standard test. I need to gauge your motor functions." Madame Laroke spoke like a physician. Her calm tone pushed back against Naya's fear.

Reluctantly, Naya shifted her grip on the blanket and raised her right hand. Her memories were beginning to stitch themselves together. She recalled the alley and the stabbing pain in her neck. She'd been attacked. A mugging perhaps?

"Good. You can lower your arm."

What kind of physician left her patient to lie on a stone floor? And where had Naya's clothes gone? She scrambled to her feet, wrapping the blanket around her shoulders.

"Please, I had a folder with me. Where is it?" she asked.

"It has been taken care of," the man by the metal table said. Naya almost jumped in surprise. The man had stood so quiet and so still that she'd nearly forgotten he was there.

"You don't understand. I need to deliver it, and I need to get back to my father's ship. I can settle whatever accounts we have after—"

"I'm afraid your ship has already begun the return voyage to Talmir," the man said.

"That's impossible. What day is it? My father wouldn't leave without me." The panic growing in the back of her mind threatened to envelop her. She ignored it. Foolish little girls might panic when they woke in a strange place, but Naya wasn't a fool or a child. These people were obviously confused. They'd mistaken her for someone else. All she had to do was figure out where she was and what they had done with her document folder and her clothes. Then she could be on her way.

Madame Laroke stepped back and glanced nervously between Naya and the man. "There are a few more tests I need to run to make sure the runes have set properly. After that you're welcome to—"

"I believe your tests can wait until she recovers her senses." The man pulled off his hat, revealing an angular face with a long chin and thick black eyebrows. His hair was combed back and held in place with some sort of oil. His skin was smooth save for a few wrinkles around the corners of his eyes. Naya frowned. The man's features seemed familiar. "Do you know who I am?" he asked. Like Madame Laroke, he spoke Ceramoran, though his words were clipped by a faint Talmiran accent. Naya glanced at his feet. He wore slick black boots laced up the front—definitely not the boots she remembered seeing in the alleyway.

Naya stared at him. She was certain they had never met, but there was something about him. "You're Ambassador Valn," she said after a moment. Dalith Valn was the ambassador assigned to represent her home nation of Talmir here in Ceramor. Her father had always insisted she keep up with politics, and she'd seen a sketch of Valn in one of the morning newspapers back home.

Valn's job was to facilitate communications and trade between the courts of Talmir and Ceramor. He also worked with the ambassadors from Banen and Silmar, two neighboring countries that, along with Talmir and Ceramor, formed the Congress of Powers. Together they enforced peace in all the lands between the Banen Islands and the Blackspine Mountains. Each time the *Gallant* docked in Belavine, her father had met with the ambassador to get his signature on the ship's manifest.

Valn nodded. "Yes, I wanted to come personally to make sure you had recovered."

"So you know what happened to me?"

"There was an incident while you were traveling alone in the city."

"I was attacked." How did Valn know so much? And why was he here? She could understand why the ambassador would be concerned about an attack on a Talmiran citizen, but it hardly made sense for him to visit personally.

"Yes. I cannot begin to express how sorry I am that we could not reach you in time for a better solution."

"But I . . ." She remembered the burning in her chest, then the icy blackness and the song. It had felt like she was dying. But no, that was impossible. She felt fine now and there wasn't a mark on her. Except . . . Valn continued to stare at her. The clawing, biting panic finally tore loose as she realized what he was implying. "No," she whispered, but the confirmation was there in his eyes, and the pity.

"No. That's impossible." She looked down at her hands. *We could not reach you in time.* There were no runes on her wrists, but that didn't mean much. The undead could take different forms depending on the necromancer's whims. *She's almost completely solid.* That's what Madame Laroke had said. Naya had heard stories about the other monsters that necromancers could make, the things they'd let loose on the Talmiran Army during the war. "No," she said again.

"I'm sorry, child."

Naya shuddered, finally noticing the signs she'd let herself ignore. She didn't feel the need to breathe. Yes, she drew in air to speak, but when she wasn't talking her chest remained still.

When she pressed her fingers against her wrist, she felt no pulse. She should have had bruises on her knees and cuts on her hands from the fall. Her feet ought to have ached from the long walk up the hill. But she felt entirely fine—too fine, too normal to be real. A scream threatened to push its way up her throat.

"What did you do to me?" Her voice was ragged. She took one step back, then another. There was a door to her left, and another behind her. One of those had to be an exit.

"I resurrected you." The necromancer hurried to put herself between Naya and the side door.

"So I'm dead?"

"Not at all. You're a wraith—one of the best I've ever constructed."

Naya stared down at herself. The fingers holding the blanket were hers. Her right arm still bore the faded scar from when she'd fallen and cut herself as a little girl. But if what the necromancer said was true, then none of it was real. Wraiths were worse than other undead. The woman she'd collided with in the street earlier was an animated corpse. Such creatures were violations of nature, but at least they were corporeal. Wraiths didn't even have true bodies. They were just ghosts, spirits that sucked energy from the living.

The rough wool blanket prickled her fingertips. She didn't feel like a ghost, or a monster. She felt solid, and at least more or less like herself. She took another deep breath. This had to be a nightmare. Maybe she was still lying unconscious in the alleyway. Naya squeezed her eyes shut and willed herself to wake. Nothing changed.

"I realize you may consider the process distasteful," the necromancer said. "But there are a few things you should know. I've condensed the runes and scribed them to a network of bones in your left hand. I'm hoping this configuration will allow for greater flexibility in the bond's outer limits and—"

"Thank you, Madame Laroke, but I don't think now is the time to discuss the details of your work," Valn said, his words tinted with scorn.

The necromancer gave him a look Naya couldn't interpret. "Of course," she said.

Valn turned back to Naya. "I imagine you'll have many questions."

She did. Dozens of them banged against her tightly pressed lips. A part of her wanted to charge the too-calm ambassador, then wrap her hands around his shoulders and shake him until he told her it had all been a mistake. That she wasn't really dead and he hadn't really let this necromancer strip her bones and drag her soul back into the world. "Why would you condone something like this? If I really died, then why didn't you leave me dead?"

She didn't want to die. But surely it would have been better to face the Creator's judgment now than to live on as some twisted abomination. Necromancy was forbidden in her homeland. She would never be allowed to go back, not like this. Her old life, sailing the oceans with her father, was gone. Her old dream of someday joining the merchant guild and traveling the world, bringing home bright treasures and stories of strange places, was dead. The thought filled Naya with a nausea-like tingling.

"I'm afraid your situation is complicated," Valn said. "But I want to assure you that things are not as bad as they seem. I've made arrangements. And if you give your consent, I think you can have a most productive future here. Your ship's captain regrets he could not deal with this matter personally, but his business in Talmir could not wait."

The captain. Her father. He couldn't have left her. "What arrangements?"

Valn glanced at the necromancer, and Naya saw distaste in

the way his lips pursed. "Leave us. I need to speak to the girl alone."

The necromancer said, "I don't think that's best right now—"

"Go." Valn's voice was quiet, but there was a hard edge to his tone.

The necromancer scowled, then lowered her gaze. "Fine. Call me if she shows any signs of instability." To Naya she added, "There are clothes on the counter if you wish to get dressed. The fit won't be exact, but they should do for now."

Floorboards creaked as the necromancer retreated upstairs. Valn crossed to the back of the room and turned away, giving Naya the chance to dress. The clothes on the counter were foreign things, but at least the shoes Naya found on the floor nearby were her own. The skirt the necromancer had left her was patterned with interlocking rectangles and lines. The neckline of the shirt dipped uncomfortably low, and the red vest wasn't any help in covering what the shirt didn't. All of it felt too loose, and far too thin. Still, it was better than the blanket. "You can turn around," she said.

Valn turned, then strode to the staircase the necromancer had taken. He checked it, paused as though to listen for any conspicuous sounds above, then nodded. He met Naya's eyes. "How much do you know about your father's true work in this city?"

CHAPTER 3

Naya shivered. She wasn't cold, but something in Valn's voice made her want to snatch up the blanket and wrap herself in its comforting warmth. "My father is a merchant." Valn had switched back to Talmiran and Naya did the same.

"True, but Hal Garth came to Belavine for more than trade and profit, as I think you may have suspected."

"I . . ." She had wondered why they'd spent so much time in the Ceramoran capital. There were other ports they might have sailed to that offered the chance for similar profits, and her father had no love for Ceramor or its necromancers. "I asked, but he wouldn't say."

Valn nodded. "I'm not surprised. Why don't we sit?" He motioned to a pair of stools pushed up against the counter. Naya perched on one, trying not to look at the array of knives and chisels spread out nearby. Valn sat across from her. "You asked me before why I didn't let you die and go to your place by the Creator's side. Simply put, we could not afford to lose you. We have too few trustworthy assets in this city as it is."

"I don't understand."

"You've studied the Treaty of Lith Lor?"

Naya frowned. What did that have to do with anything? "Of course. The treaty ended the War of Betrayal, and it created the

Congress of Powers to ensure that no Ceramoran ruler could ever raise another undead army."

"Correct. When we signed the treaty thirty-two years ago, our King Lohen sought to eradicate necromancy entirely. But a few clever liars convinced the rulers of Banen and Silmar that it would be better to show mercy and set restrictions rather than outlawing the necromantic arts outright. They argued that the elimination of Ceramor's army, combined with the reparation payments, and the execution of the Mad King and his generals was punishment enough. So Ceramor's necromancers were allowed to continue their work under the watch of the other Powers. Ceramor was allowed the protection of our defensive alliances and a place in the Congress of Powers.

"Ever since she took her father's place on the throne, Queen Lial has fought to uphold Lohen's ideals and to protect her people from the threat of another undead army. But as memories of the war fade, our allies grow less willing to help us monitor the Ceramoran necromancers and enforce the restrictions. If the restrictions weaken, I fear it will only be a matter of time before the necromancers break the treaty to raise another army and march on Talmir. Your father and I are part of a group working in secret to find proof that Queen Lial can use to convince others of this danger."

Naya clutched the edge of her stool. "You're saying that my father is a spy?" She'd always known he had secrets. But she'd never imagined anything like this. It sounded absurd. And yet the more she thought about it, the more she realized it made sense. It would explain their frequent visits to Belavine, and the trips he made alone into the city. He'd made sure she learned to keep ledgers, barter, and gauge the markets. But he'd also taught her ciphers, politics, and languages. "What does all this have to do with me?"

Valn's expression softened. "Your father intended to bring

you into our work. The day you were attacked, you were sup-posed to meet with me."

"You're the merchant Selleno?"

Valn smiled. "In a manner of speaking. That house is a place where we can conduct our business without drawing suspi-cion." His smile fell. "Unfortunately, we cannot guard against all threats. We've had trouble with some of the locals, but until now they haven't been so bold as to kill in broad daylight. From what my agents uncovered, we know you were followed from the docks by someone who decided your father was asking the wrong sorts of questions. They went after you as a warning." He brushed his fingers over the counter, like he was trying to get rid of some invisible stain on the smooth black stone. "I'm sorry we couldn't protect you, but rest assured my people have dealt with the one responsible."

There was a finality in what he said that made her shiver. "If you and my father are trying to stop the necromancers, then why would you hire one to bring me back?"

"I understand your doubt. It was not an easy decision. But as I said before, our resources are stretched thin. If you can help us in our mission, then I think the Creator will forgive us this transgression."

Naya twisted the fabric of her skirt between her fingers. Her father had always hated such nervous habits. But she couldn't seem to stop. She felt like a lifeboat caught in a tempest, her ship already smashed by the waves. Horror spread through her as she thought about the way her fingers had seemed silvery-blue and nearly transparent when she'd first awoken. It was all so wrong. And yet Valn's words shone in her mind like the half-glimpsed beam of a lighthouse, a promise that shore and safety still existed somewhere within her reach. "Help how?" she asked.

"Your father meant for you to train under me, so we've al-ready made arrangements to explain your absence from the ship.

This attack changes things, but I've found a cover that should allow you to remain in the city without drawing unnecessary attention." He pulled a folded document from his coat pocket and handed it to her. "The embassy records will show that Naya Garth left the city at her father's behest to tour several orange groves and meet with various Ceramoran businessmen whose goods the *Gallant* might carry back to Talmir. Meanwhile, a Talmiran servant girl was crushed by a horse cart near the docks. The official report will say that Lucia Laroke witnessed this tragic incident and decided to revive the girl. The girl's old master, wanting nothing more to do with her, has agreed to sell her contract to Madame Laroke, who is in need of an assistant. As the ambassador between our countries, I will ensure this potentially delicate transaction is completed smoothly."

Naya stared at the document. It was a ten-year servitude contract for a girl named Blue, making the girl a slave in all but name to whoever held her papers. "Blue?" Naya asked, not liking the sound of the name. "Won't a Talmiran wraith draw too much attention?"

"Not so much as you might think. Over the years a few of our countrymen have, in the face of sickness or dire injury, abandoned their faith and traveled to Ceramor seeking a chance at resurrection. You will be seen as a novelty at first, but the risks are less than if we tried to pass you off as a native of somewhere else."

Naya's grip tightened, making the paper crinkle. Was Valn really asking her to become some necromancer's servant? A bitter voice in the back of her mind whispered that it fit. *After all, I'm just a dead girl whose father couldn't be bothered to stay in town after his daughter was murdered.* No, that wasn't fair. Her father had a mission. If he trusted Valn to act in his stead, then he wouldn't have wasted time loitering in the city.

Valn leaned forward. "I can tell that you dislike the idea,

but think for a moment. Who do you imagine will be more conspicuous, the merchant's daughter who ought to be dead, or one more servant? Which one of those two will be able to blend in among her enemies and gather secrets to help shape her country's future?"

Hope flared in Naya's chest. "You'll still train me as a spy?"

"Yes. We stand at a delicate point. In four months the Powers will convene for the Tenth Congress. Certain factions in Ceramor are gathering strength. Once they convince our allies to lift the restrictions, I believe they will seek to rebuild Ceramor into the terror it once was. We need the very best on our side if we're going to prevent that fate. Your father has told me you are decisive, hardworking, and loyal to your country. Will you join us?"

Naya tried not to hunch under the weight of the ambassador's praise. Would her father really say all that? Hal Garth was a great man. He'd dragged himself up from work as a dock boy to become one of the queen's most favored merchants. Naya worked hard to follow his example, but he'd never praised her efforts so openly. *Then again, maybe that's not why they want you, not really.* If even half the stories she'd heard about wraiths were true, then their strange forms would make them perfect for the work Valn described. And no one would expect a wraith to be working for Talmir.

Naya closed her eyes. After two years traveling aboard the *Gallant*, it was hard to see herself as anything but a merchant. But when she imagined gathering information to protect Talmir, she felt a tickle of the same excitement that had gripped her every time she'd stood on the docks and looked out at the open sea. Maybe if she proved herself here, her countrymen would make an exception to the rules that forbid creatures like her in Talmir. She took a deep breath. "I'll do it."

"Excellent." Valn stood. "Tell Madame Laroke to take you to the embassy tomorrow morning to file the necessary paperwork.

Celia will explain the rest to you then." Before Naya could ask who Celia was, Valn had already donned his hat and retreated to the door.

"Wait!" she called. But the only answer was the click of the latch closing. Naya stared at the writ of servitude and felt the dark menace of the foreign city pressing down on her.

CHAPTER 4

When the thump of shoes on the stairs announced the necromancer's return, Naya was still sitting on the stool with her knees drawn up and her eyes locked on the document. "So it's done, then?" the necromancer asked.

Naya nodded. "He says you're to take me to the embassy tomorrow." She scanned the writ one more time before setting it on the counter. She could hear the soft patter of rain outside. When had it started to rain?

"The embassy. Of course." The necromancer pushed her glasses up her nose. "I suppose there's no going back now," she added, almost too softly for Naya to hear.

Naya said nothing. The necromancer took a few steps toward her, then hesitated, smoothing an invisible wrinkle in her plain blue dress. Wisps of gray hair had escaped her bun. They hung lank around her face, making her look more like an exhausted schoolteacher than an evil practitioner of the dark arts. "There are a few more tests I should run. But I don't think any harm will come from waiting until morning."

Imagining what sort of tests the necromancer might subject her to made Naya's skin crawl. She looked away, but there was nowhere safe to cast her eyes that didn't remind her of what this place was—and of what she'd become. "Very well, Madame Laroke," she said softly. Her throat closed around the words, but if she had to get used to pretending to be this woman's servant, better to start now.

"Please, just Lucia is fine." Lucia wrinkled her nose. "I don't know what's usual for an indentured servant, but I'm not fond of formal titles. It will only draw more attention if people hear you calling me that."

Naya nodded. "Very well, Miss Lucia." Back in Talmir, no servant, indentured or otherwise, would ever call her employer by their first name. Were things different in Ceramor, or was Lucia just eccentric?

Lucia pressed her lips together like she'd just tasted something bitter. "Close enough I suppose. I need a few hours to recover from the singing. Until then I suggest you stay inside." She rubbed the bridge of her nose, and her mouth stretched in a half-suppressed yawn. "You're welcome to look through any of the books while you wait, but please don't touch anything else. Wake me if you experience any sudden changes. Oh, and your personal effects are in that pouch on the counter."

Naya's eyes widened at the mention of the pouch. Her fingers darted to her throat in search of her mother's pendant and found nothing. How could she not have noticed its absence? Naya snatched the bag off the counter. She turned it over and sifted through the more ordinary objects—coins, pens, ink, and a small knife—before she spotted the gleam of the pendant.

"Would you like help?" Lucia asked.

"No!" Naya fumbled the clasp in her haste to open it. Finally her fingers found the latch and she closed the chain around her neck. Her shoulders relaxed as the familiar weight of the pendant settled just below her collarbone. She glanced up to see Lucia watching her. Lucia looked like she was going to ask something, but instead she rubbed her eyes.

"Well, it seems we're in this together now. As I said, wake me if you experience any sudden changes."

Naya kept her eyes fixed on Lucia as the necromancer shuffled toward a door in the side of the workroom. She waited in tense silence until she could no longer hear the creak of the stairs. When all was still, she wrapped her fingers tight around the pendant. She closed her eyes and let the sound of the rain wash over her, trying to make sense of the strange nightmare she had fallen into.

As the steady drum of rain filled her ears, her thoughts wandered back to the first voyage she'd made with her father. It had been the summer just after her fifteenth birthday and her father had finally agreed to pull her from the academy and begin her apprenticeship. They'd sailed into a storm two days out, one strong enough to make the *Gallant* rock as it plunged into the troughs of the waves. Each flash of lightning had exposed new shapes in the churning clouds. Naya had ignored her father's warnings and sneaked from the cabin. She'd strapped her safety line to the mast and stood grinning into the sheets of rain. The pitch of the deck had made her heart leap, and the thunder had sung in her bones. She knew she should have been afraid. But after years of bowing her head and learning to navigate between the nobles' heirs, who knew she didn't belong, and the tutors, who only tolerated her because they feared her father, she couldn't be scared of a little storm. Naya opened her eyes and felt her smile fade as the empty workroom replaced the memory of the storm.

She walked toward the window. It was dark out—a few hours from dawn, if the clock on the wall told true. The window's rain-washed glass only showed her wavering reflection. The face that looked back was hers: hazel eyes, thin lips, expression tight with fear. The hair framing that face was the same curly brown mess it'd always been. She wrinkled her nose and saw the reflected monster do the same.

Naya shuddered and turned away. It wasn't right. Monsters should look like monsters.

She looked back at the workroom, with its shelves stuffed full of jars of who-knew-what and black-bound books. She paced the length of the room, her steps making no sound against the stone. Even just walking, she could feel the grace in her strange new limbs. Her skin buzzed with power that begged to be unleashed. It made her want to scream. It made her want to run laughing through the rain. All her life she'd heard stories about the twisted creatures the necromancers of Ceramor spawned from the remains of their countrymen. The stories varied, but one fact remained the same: the undead weren't human anymore, no matter how well they faked it.

Naya still felt human. She didn't feel consumed by monstrous urges, but would she even be able to tell if she was?

She bit her lip, then turned to face the door. The smart thing to do would be to wait here until morning. But as convincing as Valn's story had seemed, a part of her still couldn't believe it. She imagined her father waiting for her on the deck of the *Gallant*, staring out through the rain and wondering where she'd gone. Naya glanced again at the monster reflected in the window. If she stayed here with nothing to distract her save the unanswered questions darting through her mind like swallows, she'd go mad.

No. Lucia had trapped her soul in this form, but she wouldn't stay trapped in this room, waiting on the necromancer's pleasure. She would go to the docks and see for herself if the *Gallant* had truly sailed. With one final glance at the stairs, she hurried for the door.

The rain hit her, soaking her clothes and running off her skin. Naya breathed deep, savoring the smell of wet wood and stone. Between the pouring drops and the steady blue-white light of the rune lamps lining the street, the city looked almost like it had been plunged underwater. She hesitated on the doorstep, fear creeping up her throat as she stared out at the darkened streets of the strange city.

Then she laughed, the sound perilously close to a sob. She was already dead, already resurrected as a monster. What more could this place do to her? She shot a defiant glare back at the necromancer's shop, then hurried out into the night. Little streams gurgled in the gutters and Naya followed them. Finding the docks would be simpler than her search for Selleno's house. She needed only follow the water downhill, until she reached the coast.

The rain and dark dimmed Belavine's brilliant colors, and the houses loomed over her. Naya could barely see a dozen steps ahead. As she left the hills, the road got wider and flatter. The buildings here were bigger, but still mostly constructed from wood and coated in peeling paint. Many had iron grates shaped like vines or flowers covering the lower windows. Music and tipsy laughter rang out from an open door, and here or there she saw a slumped and swaying figure hurrying through the rain. She felt their eyes following her as she passed them. She shivered, quickening her pace.

Relief flooded through her when she finally heard the rumble of the tide grinding against the pebbled shore. She came to a wide road hemmed in on one side by what looked like warehouses, and on the other by the sea. Up ahead the bay curved gently. The lights of the docks and the ship lanterns floated above the water just a little ways ahead. In the dark she couldn't guess if any one of them was the *Gallant*. She broke into a run. For an instant her hopes soared. Maybe Valn had been wrong. Maybe the *Gallant* hadn't left yet.

As soon as she reached the glow of the dock lamps, though, she knew it wasn't so. A few small fishing boats huddled behind the seawall surrounding the docks. Farther out, four vessels sat at anchor. One was a big trading ship with three masts, a wide hull, and a high stern. But even from here the fat shape looked nothing like her father's narrow *Gallant*.

A sob escaped her lips. *No.* She ran toward the nearest dock.

"Hey, what the——?" someone shouted behind her in Ceramoran.

Naya spun, struggling to keep her footing on the wet ground. The speaker, a man almost entirely covered by an oilskin cloak, hurried toward her. He held a lantern in one hand. Bright light seeped from the runes carved in the metal plates behind the glass. When he got close, Naya saw a sailor's craggy face with a drooping black mustache peeking out from under the cloak's hood. "What do you think you're doing out here, girl?"

"There was a ship here from Talmir, the *Gallant*. Do you know when it sailed?"

The man's bushy eyebrows came together. "Aye, sure, just yesterday. They left in quite a hurry." He frowned. "Why're you asking 'bout the *Gallant*?" His eyes trailed up her sodden skirts to the too-thin vest and blouse plastered against her breasts.

Naya took a step back. "Yesterday? You're sure?"

"Course. Now listen here, I think you'd better be coming with me. Little thing like you shouldn't be out here on your own." He reached for Naya's wrist. Her mind flashed back to the alley, and she leapt away.

"Wait," the man called, but Naya was already sprinting back along the coast. When the light of the docks was far behind her, she glanced over her shoulder. Nothing. The man hadn't followed. In the distance she could still just make out the dark shapes of the ships at anchor. The sight of them wrenched at her chest.

A full day had passed since the *Gallant* had left for Talmir. So it was true, then. Her father had sailed without her. Abandoned her.

Naya wasn't sure how long she stood staring at the ships.

Cold rain soaked her clothes, but she didn't feel chilled. Numbness crept through her and this time she welcomed it. Her shoes squelched as she turned toward the necromancer-infested shore. Valn must have spoken true. Even if she'd failed to return to the ship on time, her father wouldn't have left without trying to learn her fate. His leaving was a message, and this business with Valn was her real test. Naya focused all her energy on that thought as she trudged back up the hill.

CHAPTER 5

By the time Naya found her way back to the necromancer's shop, the rain had worn itself down to a drizzle and dawn's glow shone through the clouds above the eastern mountains. Her steps had grown sluggish during the last half hour of walking. She wasn't winded. Her legs didn't burn, nor did her pulse pound. But a steady ache radiated from her left hand. The necromancer had said something about that hand, some nonsense about bones and bindings. Still, why should running make her hand hurt?

She'd examined her conversation with Valn a dozen times on the walk back up the hill, but it still didn't feel real. She was in Ceramor. Her father had abandoned her. She was dead. Naya reached for her necklace. As her fingers traced the design, a memory surfaced, worn around the edges like the pages of an old book, but still strong enough to make her chest ache.

It had been just a few weeks after her seventh birthday. Her mother lay in a narrow bed, covered up to her chest in rough wool blankets even though the air in the room was hot and stuffy. Naya sat on a stool by the bed, watching the incremental rise and fall of the blankets as her mother struggled for breath. "I don't understand," Naya whispered as she rubbed one finger along the withered flesh of her mother's thumb.

Her mother smiled. "Everything's going to be fine, little bird. Your father will—"

"He's not my father."

Little wrinkles appeared in her mother's brow. "He is. I know he hasn't been here, but he knows about you now and—" Her words were cut off by a fit of coughing. Naya scrambled for the water pitcher. When she returned with a wooden cup, fresh red dots speckled her mother's lips. Naya held her mother's head as she took the water in tiny sips. When she'd finished, she continued talking as though nothing had happened. "You're going to love the new house, little bird. You'll have your own room and the very best tutors and all the rhubarb jam you can eat."

"But why aren't you coming with me?"

Her mother lifted one hand to run her fingers over Naya's curls. "You heard the doctor. I can't be moving right now. But I'll see you again. I promise."

She'd died two days later, while Naya slept on silk sheets in a new house even bigger than the tavern where her mother had worked. The Dawning keepers had promised that if Naya was good, she'd see her mother again on the other side of death. The keepers spent their lives studying and preaching the Creator's word. They ought to have known as much as any mortal could about the afterlife. But Naya had seen death. There'd been only blackness and cold tides and the irresistible pull of the necromancer's song.

Naya closed her eyes and willed the memory away. The pendant dug into her hand as she imagined folding her fears into a tiny square, then placing that square inside a box. The box she locked and shoved deep under the big canopied bed in her room back in Lith Lor. Her father was the one who'd taught her the trick. He'd said once that bad memories could make you strong. They could burn inside and keep you warm when it seemed like the rest of the world had gone cold. But not all bad memories could be so used. Some were more like broken glass buried in your heel, bringing pain with every step. Those you had to lock away until time could grind them down and make them safe to touch.

Her father couldn't have known the dangers when he sent her into the city alone. He'd given her a task, and the only thing to do was finish it. She could not let the truth of what she had become be a spike of glass in her heel. She would lock it away and she would do what needed to be done.

Naya let herself back into Lucia's shop as quietly as she could. She passed through the shop's small front room, empty save for a desk and a few uncomfortable-looking chairs pushed against the walls. The workroom beyond was dark and quiet. Naya stood in the doorway, listening to the slow drip of rainwater from her soaked clothes. If she were to masquerade as the necromancer's servant, she would probably have to live here. That was not a comforting thought.

Suddenly desperate for light, Naya ran to the room's single window and jerked the curtain open. The heavy fabric caught the edge of a jar and knocked it over. Before Naya could catch it, the jar rolled off the edge of the counter and smashed against the floor. Naya winced at the sudden noise. The pale morning light showed glass shards and dried herbs scattered all across the floor. She'd just begun searching for a broom to sweep up the mess when she heard the creak of footsteps on the stairs.

Lucia came into the room, wearing a sleeping robe and a worried expression. Her eyes widened as she seemed to take in Naya's dripping clothes and the broken jar. "Why are your clothes wet?" the necromancer asked after several agonizing seconds of silence.

"I went to the docks," Naya muttered.

"The docks." Lucia repeated the word as though she were sounding it out, as though she'd never heard anything so absurd.

She took a deep breath. "What in the Creator's name were you thinking going out there? And what were you doing at . . . no, wait, never mind. I don't want to know."

Naya frowned. How much did Lucia know about her identity? Last night she'd seemed afraid of Valn. She'd followed his orders, but it was hard to believe a necromancer would willingly serve a Talmiran spy.

Lucia turned from Naya's scrutiny. "I'll find you something dry to wear," Lucia said before disappearing up the stairs.

She returned a few minutes later, wearing a fresh dress and carrying another bundle of clothes for Naya. Naya dressed while Lucia cleaned up the broken glass, and a few minutes later they departed for the embassy. Lucia locked the door behind them with a heavy iron key. As she did, Naya saw a faint blue glow shimmer between the door and the frame. It reminded her of the bluish tint she'd seen around her fingers earlier. She shuddered. Could it be that even the door was tainted by the necromancer's touch?

"This way," Lucia said as she turned west, down the hill, and toward the lower city. She'd spoken little since Naya's return. That was a relief, since Naya had no idea what to say to Lucia. Would the necromancer expect gratitude for what she'd done? Obedience? She would have to speak to Valn. There had to be another way for her to help that didn't involve masquerading as the servant of someone who made her livelihood damning souls. Naya tried to keep her expression even as Lucia led her out onto a wide street with tram tracks running through the middle. They joined a small crowd waiting at the corner.

Naya's eyes wandered over the people standing nearby as they waited for the tram. The man next to her was another walking corpse, his wrists and neck banded with runic tattoos. Naya stared at the flowing black lines and wondered what her father had thought when he learned his daughter had become a wraith. Had it been shame that drove him from the city?

She locked the horrible possibility away. If she let herself dwell on what might be, or on what she'd become, she'd go mad. Searching for a distraction, she noticed something strange about the undead man's tattoos. Blue light leaked out around their edges, like the light she'd seen on the door. She opened her mouth to say something, but her words were cut off by the rattle and screech of an approaching tram. The sounds of the wheels braking against the track set the humid air vibrating. As the tram approached, Naya was nearly overcome by the bizarre impression that something was pulling on her—draining energy from her limbs. Her vision blurred and her hand throbbed.

She started to slump, but Lucia grabbed her and pulled her up the steps into the seating area. Naya jerked her arm away as Lucia dropped two tin bits into the conductor's collection box. Her legs wobbled, but at least the draining sensation wasn't as strong inside the tram.

She couldn't help but gawk as they settled onto the wooden bench. They had rune-powered trains back in Talmir—huge steel constructions that rumbled through the countryside hauling coal, produce, and people toward the cities. The lines still didn't extend more than fifty miles from the capital, but the royal engineers had promised that soon any citizen would be able to ride from the northern coast to the Ceramoran border. Naya remembered watching the first of the big trains pulling into the new station in Lith Lor as a child. Compared with those, the boxy single-car trams of Belavine looked almost delicate.

Any impressions of delicacy vanished as the car lurched forward, picking up speed to swing around a bend in the track. Naya grabbed the edge of her seat so tight she could feel the wood digging into her fingertips. Lucia seemed unperturbed as they careened downhill. "We can take this to Market Street. From there it's only a short way to the embassy," she said.

Naya didn't reply. She was busy trying not to think about the way the city sped past, revealing glimpses of glittering blue ocean between the houses. Nobody else looked like they were swallowing a scream every time the tram whipped around a corner. Then again, the people of this country practically worshipped necromancers. Would they even care if they died in a crash?

The tram didn't slow until they reached the base of the hill and turned onto one of the wide streets Naya had crossed on her way to deliver the contract for her father. Salt air flooded through the half-open window and seemed to infuse her entire body. The day was already getting hot and she could smell the unappealing aromas of sweaty bodies, rotting fish, and refuse as she and Lucia stepped off the tram and joined the crowd on the street.

They'd gotten off at an intersection where the lines of shops ended and the rows of stately houses began. The buildings here were grander than the ones she'd seen in other parts of the city. Lucia paused in front of a white, three-story building with imposing mahogany doors. It stood out from its lime-green and purple neighbors like a dove among peacocks.

Two soldiers guarded the doorway, dressed in the blue uniforms of the Talmiran Army. The soldiers didn't move, but eyed Naya and Lucia warily as they approached. Naya tried not to stare at the rune pistols and longswords hanging from their belts. The weapons looked far more menacing than the clubs the Belavine city guard were allowed to carry.

On the door between the soldiers was a brass plaque reading EMBASSY OF TALMIR. A flag rode above the peak of the roof, the queen's crest set in blue and gold on a black field. A sudden wave of homesickness made Naya's eyes sting. This would probably be the closest she'd ever come to seeing her country again.

A black-clad servant answered the door before Lucia's hand could leave the bell rope. He was tall and hollow-cheeked, with unusually pale gray eyes. Gray flecks peppered his thinning hair. He bowed, then led them into a hallway with plush carpet and white walls.

The servant paused at a door near the end of the hallway. "Ambassador Valn will see you now."

Lucia eyed the polished wood as though it might bite. Naya moved to join the necromancer, but the servant grabbed her arm.

"You may wait in the kitchen."

Naya stared at the man. Surely she'd misheard. "I need to speak to the ambassador." Valn had sounded certain that resurrecting her had been the best, if not the only, option. But his faith had only spawned more questions in her mind.

"The ambassador has no need to speak to you."

Naya looked at Lucia, who pointedly avoided her gaze. "But why would he . . ."

"The kitchen is over there." The servant nodded at a smaller door at the very end of the hall. It was clear from his tone that he didn't intend to let her into the other room. He didn't even let go of her arm until Lucia had disappeared inside, closing the door behind her.

Naya looked once more at the door, struggling to squash the doubts bubbling up inside her. Valn's story made sense. It was the only thing that could explain her father abandoning her in a city corrupted by dark magic. *Keep your wits about you. This city is full of liars.* Naya forced herself to walk through the kitchen door, wondering which liars her father had meant to warn her about.

CHAPTER 6

The kitchen was quiet, the only occupant a thin-armed boy roll-ing dough on the back counter. He glanced up as Naya entered. "You looking for Celia?"

Celia. Valn had mentioned that name last night. "I think so."

"She's upstairs." He pointed to a door to the left. Naya opened it and found a narrow servant's stairway. She glanced back, but the boy had already returned his attention to the dough, and the man who'd directed her here was nowhere in sight. The stair let her out onto a second-floor hallway. Here the floors were simple wood, and the white surface of the walls was unbroken by paintings or other decorations.

"Hello?" Naya stepped tentatively into the hall.

A door opened to her left. "Who's there?"

"I'm . . ." Should she introduce herself with her real name, or the fake one Valn had given her?

A middle-aged woman stepped into the hallway. She was an inch or two taller than Naya and clad in a servant's outfit of black skirt, white blouse, and black vest. The few streaks of gray in her hair didn't match the graceful way she walked or the hard gleam in her eyes. Naya had to fight the urge to squirm when those eyes met hers.

"Ah, come in." The woman motioned Naya into a tiny bedroom with a battered desk and narrow bed.

"Are you Celia?" Naya asked.

"Yes. And you must be the dead girl."

Naya clasped her hands in front of her to keep her fingers from wandering toward her necklace. "Yes."

"He told you about our work?"

Naya met Celia's eyes. Obviously the woman was much more than a servant. "Ambassador Valn said I would be gathering information. But I have some questions about—"

Celia silenced her with a wave of her hand. "We'll deal with that later. First let me look at you." Celia crossed her arms over her chest. "You don't stand much like a servant."

Naya frowned. "I'm not a servant."

The blow came so fast Naya barely saw it coming. Her head snapped sideways, and tingling waves of force spread from her cheek to the rest of her body. It didn't hurt exactly, but it was far from pleasant. Celia flexed her fingers, looking like she was considering slapping Naya again.

"Wrong. You are whoever the job requires. From this second on you will start believing that with every scrap of your soul. Today you are Blue. You are a servant. You have always been a servant. And now you are very, very eager to prove yourself useful to your new master."

Naya's skin burned with anger. "What's wrong with you?"

Celia shook her head. "Ambassador Valn says I am to make an agent of you. He thinks you are smart and useful. He thinks that your condition will make you a valuable asset. But before I can make you useful, I must know you won't get yourself killed again by giving away your identity to every stranger you meet."

Naya rubbed her cheek. "And that gives you the right to hit me?"

"Yes. You must be able to hold your cover even when others

push you, even if they make you furious or afraid. If an[y] suspects your true identity, you won't just be risking your ow[n] safety. You will be endangering all our operations in this city. Our people. Do you understand? I do not care who you are or who your father is. If I cannot trust you, I cannot use you."

Naya glared at Celia. She wanted to stomp out the door, or slap the older woman right back, but damn it if either one wouldn't prove Celia right.

"No? Then return downstairs. I will tell Ambassador Valn that training you would be a waste of time," Celia said.

Naya could feel her body tensing, readying itself for another blow, or for her to lash out herself. Instead she closed her eyes, dragging out an old memory from among the locked boxes in her mind. Her mother stood silhouetted in the doorway of their tiny room, pleading softly. A man in a sweat-stained coat scowled at her from the hallway. He owned the tavern below where her mother scrubbed tables and served drinks. He liked to come upstairs in the evenings to remind them how lucky they were to have his generosity, that there were plenty of others in Lith Lor with no steady work who'd gladly take her place. Naya remembered watching from the far corner, waiting for her mother to snap at the man, to tell him it was no generosity for him to take more than half her wages for a tiny room that was hot in the summer and drafty in the winter. But her mother had taken the abuse without comment, even going so far as to thank the man before he left.

Sometimes, little bird, you have to bend to keep from breaking. Slowly, Naya felt her shoulders adopting her mother's hunch. When she opened her eyes, her gaze stayed fixed on the floor. "I'm sorry to have given you the wrong impression. If you give me a chance, I'll show you I can be useful."

Silence. She had to fight to keep her head down. Finally Celia huffed. "Well, it's not the best I've seen, but it's not the worst

lling to admit mistakes and you're willing to

ook up."

ed her head up and found Celia surveying her

one finger against her thigh. "So you were just

aya wasn't sure if that made her angrier or relieved.

. Ambassador Valn may be running this opera-
tion, but ... trusted me to manage the details. No matter how
much potential he thinks you have, I won't work with a fool
who can't learn."

"I'm not a fool."

"We'll see. How many languages do you speak?"

"I speak the court tongue, and some Banian. My Ceramoran
is fluent. My father said my accent is barely noticeable." Naya
straightened and met Celia's eyes. Now that she had gotten
through Celia's little test, there was something oddly comforting about the older woman's hard words and glares. She wasn't
interested in what Naya was, only what she could do.

"Useful, but too clever for a galley girl. Blue spoke
Ceramoran. Her master used her to translate sometimes, didn't
like sullying himself with foreign tongues. But her command of
the language was limited. No accent will make you stand out
worse than not being able to speak at all. Can you fake one?"

"I think so," Naya switched to Ceramoran, forcing herself
to clip her *r*'s and *s*'s, and adding a harsher note to the vowels to
emphasize her slight Talmiran accent. It felt strange after spending so long trying to learn the silky native accent. She sounded
foolish, but maybe that was the point. "I don't mean to pry, but
you're talking about Blue like she was a real person."

"So far as you're concerned, she is a real person. She is you
and you are her. That is all you need to know."

Naya opened her mouth again, but when she saw Celia's
scowl deepen she forced it closed and nodded. *I am Blue. I am a
monster with a stolen name.*

"Your accent is passable, but you sound like you're trying too hard. I'd recommend avoiding any long conversations until you can improve."

"So I'm going to be staying in Belavine for a while?"

"Yes. King Allence and his court won't be returning to his winter palace until after the Tenth Congress. Our work requires us to remain close to his government."

Naya ran her palms over the front of her skirt. "I understand. But what about the man who attacked me? Ambassador Valn said he'd been dealt with, but he also said there've been other attacks on Talmirans. What if he wasn't working alone? If someone sees me and realizes I'm still in the city . . ."

Some expression flickered over Celia's face but was gone before Naya could read it. "I wouldn't worry about that. Ambassador Valn has already seen to the issue. The odds of anyone recognizing you are very slim, especially if you keep your eyes down and act the proper servant." She seemed to consider this for a moment. "Still, it will be best for you to learn to change your face."

"Change my face?"

"Your body is energy, yours to control. You look the way you want to look. The sooner you learn to manipulate that, the better. Has that necromancer taught you to use your sight yet?"

"I can see, if that's what you mean." Naya's mind was still spinning as she struggled to keep up with the strange conversation.

"No, not ordinary sight. Wraiths can supposedly see the flow of aether. Even more important for our cause, you can see where aether has been redirected to power a rune binding. You must learn this skill. And meanwhile you must also practice being a good servant. Do whatever the necromancer tells you, no matter what you think of the task."

"How do you know so much about wraiths?"

"Only a fool shuts her eyes to something because she is

afraid. Regardless of what the keepers say of necromancy, it is powerful and that power must be understood." Celia glanced at a pile of papers on the small desk. "In ten days you will wait for me at the corner of Rillon and Wavecrest Streets at the fifth morning bell, provided you do not destroy your cover before then. I will evaluate your progress and we will see if you are worth the risk of training. Do you understand?"

Less than two weeks to learn two things she hadn't even known existed a moment before? Naya took a deep breath, then nodded.

"Good. Ask whatever questions you have now."

Naya clasped her hands to keep herself from fidgeting. She had so many questions, but one forced its way ahead of all the rest. "Ambassador Valn says my father sent me to join your work before I was . . . killed. Does he know what happened to me? Did he leave me any kind of message?"

Celia paused before answering. "I'm not privy to the details of Ambassador Valn's communications, but I would assume he notified Lord Garth before he sailed. As for messages . . ." She extracted a small key from her vest pocket and unlocked one of the desk drawers. "Your father left this for you." Celia pulled a folded sheet from the drawer. Naya's father's seal was stamped on the front, and below it he'd written her name in neat script.

Celia held the paper out. "Written and delivered before your death, so it will not answer your question, but perhaps it may offer some comfort in his absence."

Naya took the paper in shaking hands. "Thank you."

Celia nodded. "I've business to tend to now. You may stay to read that, but don't tarry long. I suspect Ambassador Valn will soon be done speaking with the necromancer." She paused by the door. "Though it should be obvious, don't tell her about your true mission."

"How much does she know?" Naya asked.

"She knows the story others will be told. You are a servant girl she resurrected, and Ambassador Valn has transferred your contract to her."

The letter crinkled under Naya's grip. Lucia knew more than that already. Or even if she didn't, Naya doubted it'd be easy to hide the nature of their work while living with the woman. "Does that mean I have to actually serve her? There must be someone else we can work with who isn't—"

"Isn't a necromancer?" Celia asked.

"Someone who isn't likely to turn against us the first chance she gets," Naya clarified.

Celia snorted. "I trust Lucia Laroke to follow her best interests, and the ambassador has ensured that those interests align with ours. She may not like it, but she'll play her part and hold her tongue."

Naya wanted to ask what sort of interest could be strong enough to make someone like Lucia work for Talmir. However, Celia's tone suggested the matter was closed.

"Anything else?" Celia asked.

"No. I'll learn what you asked."

"Good."

As soon as Celia left the room, Naya tore open her father's letter. Inside were scrawled several lines of jumbled nonsense, a cipher he'd taught her when he brought her on as his apprentice. She skimmed once over the words, letting her eyes pick out the pattern, then began to read.

> Daughter,
>
> If you are reading this, then it means you have reached Valn and our plan has entered its next stage. I have sent you to him to learn of our true work and to help enact the Creator's will. I apologize for not telling you of our plans, but I could not risk others learning the truth. The necromancers grow more dangerous by the day. We must

stop their plots before they can finish what the Mad King began. Valn
will explain what must be done. We will not meet again for some
weeks. In that time you must trust and obey him as you would me.
Know that what we do protects the people of Talmir from dangers they
refuse to see.

Naya read it again, then twice more to ensure she hadn't missed anything. *Trust and obey.* So Valn had told the truth. Her father really had meant for her to stay in Belavine and help protect the treaty.

She closed her eyes. If her father had a task for her, then she would do it. But everything about this felt wrong. Her father had never hinted that this trip was anything more than a contract negotiation. If their mission was so important, then surely he could have found a way to tell her something. And if he'd been working with Valn all this time, he must have known about the dangers growing in the city. Why hadn't he warned her? If he had, then she would have been more careful. Maybe she would still be alive if only . . . Naya locked the thought away before it could go further. Her father must not have known the extent of the danger. Valn had said none of the other attacks had happened while the sun was up.

She folded the letter, running over each crease with her fingers. If the necromancers were planning another attack, then they had to be stopped. It was an honor to be trusted with such a task. She repeated the thought as she made her way out of the embassy, trying to drown out her traitorous doubts.

She found Lucia waiting outside. As Naya walked toward the street, her foot caught on a loose stone and she almost stumbled into the necromancer. The aching she'd managed to ignore during her meetings with Celia returned full force. Her head spun, and not just from the dizzying horror of the past two days.

Lucia frowned as she caught Naya's elbow. "Are you all right?"

"I'm fine." In truth her limbs felt heavy and her vision was starting to blur around the edges.

Lucia clicked her tongue and extracted something from her bag. It was a delicate metal rod with tiny runes carved into the shaft and handle. Before Naya could make her sluggish body respond, Lucia grabbed her hand and touched the rod to it. The skin around the rod turned transparent, revealing what Naya assumed must be the bond Lucia had spoken of. Four bones floated in the space where her hand should have been—one in the bottom half of her thumb and three in her palm. Dozens of tiny runes had been carved into each bone. Their lines wove a complex pattern that blurred and twisted as she tried to trace their shapes. Naya shuddered. She pulled her hand away and was relieved when it returned to normal as soon as she broke contact with the strange rod. "What are you doing?"

Lucia examined the rod's now-glowing runes, then muttered something to herself as she stuffed it back into her bag. "That device is a reader, which allows me to measure the energy flowing through your bond. You're running dangerously low on aether."

"Aether?"

"Yes, the energy fueling your bond. You'll need to draw more in. It shouldn't be a problem here. Any one of them can give you more than what you need." She waved at the crowd.

"What are you talking about?" Aether was a type of energy, normally impossible to sense but collecting everywhere there was life. Celia had claimed wraiths could see aether, but what did Lucia mean by drawing it in? Naya's mind conjured the stories she'd heard as a child about wraiths sucking out people's souls to feed. Horror rose like vomit in her throat. "I won't. I can't."

Lucia only looked annoyed. "You have to. Every wraith has to. Honestly, I'm surprised you haven't done it instinctively yet."

The prospect of accidentally consuming the energy of those around her was even more horrifying. Naya took a step back.

Lucia scowled, then pulled a small silver watch from her pocket and glanced at it. "This is ridiculous. Come with me."

CHAPTER 7

On the tram ride back up the hill, Naya sat pressed against the window with her hands tucked in her lap, trying to look like the good little servant she was supposed to be. But even before her father taught her to brush elbows with the upper class, she'd never been good at holding in questions. "Where are we going?" she asked when the tram passed into a neighborhood she didn't recognize.

"To visit an old apprentice of mine. Hopefully he can show you how to use your binding properly."

"I thought *you* were supposed to help me," Naya said. It didn't seem wise to involve someone else, especially not another necromancer.

The tram rattled around a sharp turn. Lucia grimaced. "I'm not sure I can. You Talmirans are so . . ." Lucia made a vague gesture with one hand, then pushed her glasses up her nose. "You must understand that an aetherial body does not function the same as a physical one. Your thoughts affect what you are now as much as those runes I scribed. Every other wraith I've resurrected has drawn aether intuitively when they ran low. They didn't need to be taught any more than babies need instructions on how to breathe. You seem to be blocking that process, and until you stop, your bond will continue to destabilize."

"If you can't explain it, then I don't see why your apprentice would do any better," Naya said.

"Former apprentice. He's better suited to the task because he has firsthand experience in the matter, and he's always had a knack for explaining the core principles behind the theory of our work. I hope that will be enough to help you, because right now I feel like a fish trying to explain flight to a bird."

Three stops later they got off at a plaza shaded by a huge oak tree. They crossed the uneven cobblestones to an unremarkable two-story stone building set a little apart from its neighbors. A queer metal chimney poked out of the back, the air above it shimmering with heat. Above the door was a sign marking the place as a glassworker's shop. Naya peeked over Lucia's shoulder and saw an array of ordinary-looking plates, bowls, and glasses on display in the window. Her brow furrowed. This was where Lucia's former apprentice worked? Lucia pushed the door open, causing a bell to chime somewhere inside.

The place was set up more like a sitting room than a shop. Other than the pieces in the window, there wasn't much merchandise on display. Glass sculptures stood on pedestals and shelves around the edges of the room. Naya tilted her head, trying to make sense of their strange shapes. Before she could, a door at the back of the shop opened.

"I'll be with you in a moment," said a young man about her age. Naya pulled her attention away from the sculptures. The newcomer wore a heavy leather vest set with black metal plates carved with runes. Underneath, his chest was bare, revealing a lean figure with well-muscled arms and tan skin a shade or two darker than Naya's own. His brown pants were heavily padded and streaked with burns. He had dark hair that curled tight against his head, and dark-brown eyes set over broad cheekbones and a square jaw.

When he saw them, his welcoming smile froze. "Lucia."

Lucia cleared her throat. "Hello, Corten. It's good to see you again. How are you and Matius getting on?"

Corten's eyes shifted to Naya, then back to Lucia. "We're fine. Are you looking to buy some glass?"

"Ah, no. Not today." Lucia pushed Naya forward. "This is Blue. She's a recent patient and she's . . . well, she's Talmiran and she's having some trouble learning to draw aether. Normally I wouldn't want to bother you, but I hoped you could help her better understand what it is to be a wraith."

Corten's eyes widened. He glanced at Naya again, then shook his head. "I can't. Matius is working on a set of vases. He needs me to watch the front."

Some of the false cheer drained from Lucia's voice. "This is important. She needs someone to explain the basics of aether manipulation. You can describe those concepts better than I can. I'm sure if you told him what it was for, Matius would be happy to spare you for a few minutes."

Lucia and Corten stared at each other in silence. The air between them felt charged, though Naya couldn't guess the source of the tension. Finally Corten looked away. "And you expect me to believe there was no one else you could ask?"

"I am asking the person best suited to the task."

Corten rubbed the back of his neck. His eyes found Naya's, then darted away. "All right, fine. I'll ask Matius."

Corten disappeared through the shop's back door. He returned a couple of minutes later followed by a large bald man with a round face and eyes surrounded by laugh lines. Like Corten he wore singed pants and a vest covered in runed plates. "Lucia! Haven't seen you in an age. How are you?"

"I'm well. Sorry to barge in, but I need to borrow your apprentice."

"So I heard." The big man, Matius apparently, clapped Corten on the shoulder. "Course we're happy to help."

"Thank you." Lucia's smile brightened and she turned to Corten. "The chief problem is her aether. There's no issue with the binding, but she isn't drawing new energy. Teach her that, and I'll handle the rest."

The pain in Naya's hand was making it hard to concentrate. She tried to keep her eyes downcast while still stealing glances at the two strange men. Celia had told her to avoid speaking too much until she could get her accent right, and here Lucia was dragging her in front of a pair of strangers, one of whom seemed not at all happy to see them.

"We'll get her sorted out," Matius said.

"Thank you," Lucia said. "Now, if you'll excuse me, I have an appointment I'm already late for. Blue, please come back to the shop when you're done here. I have a few errands to run. I doubt you'll get back before I do, but just in case—take this." She handed Naya an iron key, like the one she'd used to lock the door earlier, before practically fleeing out the door.

"Well, a Talmiran wraith," Matius said after a moment of awkward silence. "Not every day you see that. Blue, was it?"

Naya nodded. They were both looking at her now.

"No need to be shy. You're among friends here," Matius said.

Friends. It had to be a joke, but the warmth in his tone suggested otherwise. Well, he certainly wouldn't consider her a friend if he knew who she really was. "Thank you," she managed to say. Her instincts screamed at her to be wary, but she was almost too tired to care.

Matius smiled. "No need. Corten, why don't you take Miss Blue outside for a bit? If she's low, then I can't imagine it's comfortable for her to be this close to the furnaces."

Corten, who had been staring at Naya like she was a puzzle waiting to be solved, blinked. "Right," he said. Then to Naya he added, "Give me a minute to get changed. You can wait outside if you want."

Corten hurried up a flight of stairs set into the wall on the right. With a smile and a nod, Matius retreated through the back door. Corten returned a moment later wearing a white shirt only marginally less singed than his pants. He gestured toward the door, and Naya followed him out into the shady plaza.

Corten shoved his hands into his pockets as he walked. "So your name is Blue?"

"Yes."

"And you're really from Talmir?"

Naya frowned, unease coiling in her chest. "Why are you asking?"

Corten looked away. "Sorry. I wasn't trying to be rude. It's just unusual to see a resurrected Talmiran."

"You say that as though there are others." Valn had claimed as much, but Naya still found it hard to believe.

"None that I've met."

Naya crossed her arms over her chest. "That's probably because most Talmirans are smart enough to stay clear of this cursed place."

Corten raised his eyebrows and Naya quickly lowered her gaze. *Fool. Hold your tongue.* She felt like her head was full of fog, and the ache in her hand wasn't helping.

"That's a little hypocritical, don't you think?" Corten asked.

"What are you talking about?"

"Well, you did accept Lucia's resurrection. If you'd died anywhere else, you'd just be dead."

"I didn't accept anything."

Corten frowned. "The necromancer's song isn't a command, it's an open door. You chose to step through it."

Naya felt a sudden chill. Corten had to be wrong. "I didn't," she said, taking a moment to go back over the story Valn had told her. "Last I remember, I was on my way back to my master's ship. I guess I wasn't paying enough attention while I was walking.

I remember hearing shouting, hoofbeats, and wheels rattling behind me. Then something knocked me over. Next I knew I was in Miss Lucia's shop and she was telling me that she'd purchased my contract and that I was to work for her now."

Corten frowned. "Your contract? What do you mean?"

"I'm indentured. Miss Lucia bought me while I was dead and then resurrected me to work for her."

"That can't be right. Lucia would never take on an indentured servant, especially not without giving them a choice."

"I'm not lying," Naya said, maybe a little too forcefully.

"I didn't mean—" Corten shook his head. "We'll talk about it later. Right now we need to get your aether stabilized. Come on. You'll be more comfortable sitting." He crossed the plaza and sat on a bench under the big oak tree. Naya hesitated, then perched on the opposite end of the bench.

"So, how much do you know about wraiths?" Corten asked.

"Not very much. I've heard stories but . . ."

Corten snorted. "Let me guess. You've heard we're evil monsters who suck the life out of children for kicks."

"We?"

Corten raised one hand and Naya watched, fascinated and slightly queasy, as his fingers glowed blue, then turned transparent. "Yes, we. You, me, wraiths."

A blush heated Naya's cheeks, followed quick by a flash of anger. She shouldn't have been embarrassed by Corten's brassy tone, or the way he stared at her. She didn't care what he thought. "Fine. If wraiths aren't like they are in the stories, then what are they like?"

"We," Corten corrected. "What are we like."

Naya glared at him. Corten actually had the gall to smile back. "It's not as bad as you think. We aren't monsters. Our bodies are just a little different from other people's. We don't need food or sleep. We just need to draw in aether to keep our bonds steady. You know what aether is, right?"

Saying they were a little different was like saying a whale was a little bigger than a minnow. "I know it's a sort of energy."

"Close enough. Most rune scribes classify it along with the other three types of energy: light, kinetic, and heat. We still don't know as much about it as we'd like. Aether is given off by all living things. It tends to disperse through environments like a gas. It doesn't fade like other energies, though it can be converted to them with minimal loss. You won't need to worry about the details of how it works. The runes in your bond will let you draw it and convert it into whatever you need."

"Miss Lucia said I was running out of aether. What happens if I don't draw more in?"

"Your bond fades and you die. It's painful, or so I'm told. Given that it's almost impossible to bring a soul back a second time, I really wouldn't recommend it."

Naya tried to imagine what it would be like to fade. Would it be like falling asleep, or like starving? The memory of the darkness she'd seen after the poison stole her breath was still with her, despite her attempts to lock it away. Her fingers balled tighter around her skirt. No matter how much she hated this new body, she didn't want to die again. "All right, so how do I draw aether?"

"It's like breathing," Corten said, unhelpfully.

Naya took a deep breath, then let it out. It didn't do anything to lessen the pain throbbing from her hand. "I don't feel any different."

"Breathing air won't do you any good. You need to stop thinking about yourself the way you were. Here, try this. Close your eyes. I want you to try to feel the world around you. This city has a pulse. All life connects to that pulse through the aether. Try to feel it, then when you do, breathe it in."

"I don't feel anything."

"You aren't trying." There was an edge of frustration to his voice now.

Naya glared at him. "How would you know?"

Corten took a deep breath and Naya saw, or thought she saw, something faint and blue swirl around him. "You're right. I'm sorry. I can't guess what this must be like for you. I know how your people feel about us. But trust me—no matter how strange this sounds, once you get the feel of the aether you won't lose it. Wraiths are naturally attuned to life energy."

He was right: he didn't have any idea what it was like. She knew what the people of Ceramor believed about necromancy. People here claimed to follow the Creator's teachings as set down in the Scrolls of the Dawning, just as her people did in Talmir. But the Ceramoran keepers twisted the words of the Scrolls to justify Ceramor's use of necromancy. They believed souls were bound to life because they had some purpose to fulfill. That purpose might be one great deed or a thousand tiny acts spread through a long and quiet life. But when accident or illness stole a life before its purpose was fulfilled, the necromancers argued, the soul should be brought back. They claimed that resurrections could only succeed if the soul still had business in this world, and that such miracles would be impossible without the Creator's blessing. Naya's father had called those arguments the pinnacle of man's hubris. Necromancy was a temptation made to test the faithful. Anyone could see mortals weren't supposed to have control over life and death. If they were, then there would have been a way to bring people back exactly as they had been, not as tattooed walking corpses or ghostly wraiths.

Corten didn't seem to understand that his explanations only made Naya's legs itch to run despite her exhaustion. She could make it to the docks, stow away on the next ship for home, and then start a new life somewhere in Talmir. But even as the idea blossomed, she knew how futile it was. Running wouldn't change what she was, and in Talmir she'd be hunted the moment her nature was discovered.

At least by staying she had a chance to protect others from suffering her fate. Naya forced herself to take a slow breath. "Fine. What do I have to do?"

"Close your eyes." She closed her eyes, uncertain. "Good. Now try to relax. Don't think about anything, just try to feel the city. Try to find the pulse."

Naya spread her fingers as she leaned back. The wooden bench was rough underneath her hands. Hot sun beat down on her face through the stagnant afternoon air. Both were reassuringly familiar—ordinary wood, ordinary sun. Despite the chaos of the past two days, despite all Corten's unnerving comments about energy and wraiths, some of the tension leached from her body. She thought about the blue wisps she'd seen glowing around the undead man's wrists, and the ones around Lucia's door. Runes could manipulate aether. Maybe what she'd noticed before was part of the special sight Celia had mentioned.

The square filled with the mingled sounds of the city: the distant rumble of the trams, children laughing and voices calling from some other street, footsteps. Now that she was paying attention, those sounds did have a certain rhythm to them. It wasn't a pulse exactly, but it resonated through her. She concentrated harder, trying to pin down the beat.

At first it was like trying to catch the words of a song sung two rooms over. But as she listened the beat grew clearer. Suddenly it became more than a sound. She could feel it surrounding her, like the very air was humming. Concentrating harder, she thought she could almost taste it—warm and sweet-salty. But it wasn't all the same. Inside the cloud she sensed thousands of subtle variations. A boy ran past, and she could sense his eagerness. His joy was sweet lemon in her mouth and warm paving stones under pounding bare feet. Intuitively she knew she could draw that energy in and make it her own, erase the weakness in her arms and legs and soothe the aching bones in her hand.

Naya's eyes snapped open. This wasn't right.

"What are you doing?" Corten asked.

"I can't do this, I'm sorry." She stood up. "It isn't going to work."

Corten stood and took a step toward her. "But you haven't even—"

"Please, just leave me alone." The sensations weren't going away. She could feel them pushing in from all sides now. The boy, and now an old man lying in the gutter somewhere far to her left. The sickness in him oozed like slime on her skin. Naya spun, scanning the edges of the plaza until she caught sight of the man. She took a hesitant step toward him, but then another sensation slammed into her. In one of the houses nearby a couple fought, their bitter anger making her vibrate with the need to be away from them. She covered her ears and stumbled sideways. What Corten had called the pulse assaulted every one of her senses. It intensified by the second. She tasted sorrow, like pepper and vinegar, and felt excitement like goose bumps on her skin. The worst part was that she wanted nothing more than to draw it in. There was power there, life, and the opportunity to lose herself in that chaotic surge.

Monster. Those lives weren't hers to steal from. Maybe aether really was excess energy. Maybe none of those people would ever miss what she took. But that didn't make her feel any less like a beast preying on them.

"Blue, you need to focus." Corten's hand was on hers. He was leaning in close, his fingers surprisingly warm against hers. "Don't get lost in it."

She took a step, and then another. She could feel Corten moving with her, but it was getting harder and harder to pick her own thoughts out from the maelstrom. Her legs wobbled, and the bones in her hand burned with hunger. Corten spoke, but his words were nonsense in her ears. If she didn't do something soon, the press of all those emotions would destroy her.

The last shred of her will snapped and Naya drew in a deep, shuddering breath. *I'm sorry. I'm so sorry.*

Naya opened herself to the wild, pulsing energy and gulped it in. For an instant it felt like the flood of foreign emotions would sear her away to nothing. Then the world snapped back into focus. Her exhaustion vanished, and the pain in her hand dulled to a barely noticeable ache. She was kneeling next to the bench. She could still sense the city's pulse, but her own thoughts were clearer now. Corten knelt in front of her, his gold-flecked eyes wide with shock.

"Well . . ." he said after a long silence, during which Naya struggled to gather her scattered wits. "I guess you don't do anything halfway." He stood up. After brushing off his dusty pants, he held out his hand. "I think maybe that's enough for today."

CHAPTER 8

Naya followed Corten back to Lucia's shop in a daze. Her body hummed with aether, and the city's energy swirled around her in a distracting mix of sensations. Sometimes she felt it brush against her skin, like heavy, damp mist. Other times it was a pale-blue light condensing around the rune bindings on door frames, lamps, and other undead she walked past. When the emotions in that energy were strong, they overwhelmed her every sense.

Corten was a single spot of calm in the shifting torrent. Though a faint blue outline sometimes glowed around him, she could sense nothing of his emotions.

A few blocks from the shop, they passed a grocer's where two men argued over an upturned cart of cabbages. Before, Naya would have walked right past without a second glance. But now she stumbled under the sudden force of their frustration and anger. It twisted at her and filled her mouth with the acrid tang of smoke and iron. Corten helped her to her feet, and after a few more steps the sensation faded. "How do you manage it? How can you pretend something like this is normal?" Naya asked, her voice shaking.

Corten's face was pinched with worry when his eyes met hers. "You need to stay focused. Try to concentrate on the physical world. You shouldn't be able to sense other people unless you're pulling aether from them."

The shop's front door was locked when they got back. Naya noticed the same faint glow around the edge of the door that she'd seen that morning. Now she realized what it must be—aether collecting around the door. Had Lucia guarded her shop with some sort of rune ward? Naya had heard of wealthy lords and merchants in Talmir who purchased wards that could produce a loud noise or light if anyone tried to break into their homes.

"Are you all right?" Corten asked.

Naya blinked, realizing she'd been staring at the door. "I'm fine." She pulled out the key Lucia had given her, but her hands were shaking so badly that it took her three tries to fit the cursed thing into the lock.

Once inside the shop, she shuffled through the tiny front reception room and into the workroom. When she turned she saw Corten standing on the threshold. His face was carefully blank and his stance tense. Naya didn't understand what had caused the tension between him and Lucia, but it was obvious he didn't want to linger. "You don't have to stay," she said. The energy she'd absorbed raged inside her, making her hands shake. At least the city's pulse felt weaker inside the shop.

Corten shook his head. "You shouldn't be left alone like this."

Naya clenched her teeth. "I'm fine."

"You're shaking."

Naya crossed her arms over her chest and tried to sort her own emotions from the storm inside her. One part of her wished Corten would just leave her alone. He was the one who'd made her do this. He hadn't warned her what would happen. For all she knew he'd done it on purpose to laugh at her suffering.

A more logical part pointed out that Corten's concern seemed genuine, and so far all he'd tried to do was help. "It's the aether," she said. "I feel like someone made me drink a dozen cups of tea." She paced to the far side of the room and turned back. "Or maybe a hundred." A hundred cups of poison tea stolen from the minds of the men and women around her.

Corten gave her a sympathetic smile. "That happens when you draw too much. It takes practice to learn your limits." He looked around the room and seemed to come to a decision. "I know something that should help." He walked toward the little furnace at the back of the workroom and motioned for her to follow. "Put your hand here."

Naya backed away. She'd noticed the rune furnace before. Such things existed in Talmir but were uncommon outside the homes of the wealthy or those with connections to the Academy of Magics. Her father had only managed to get one installed last year and at first she'd found it strange to see one in Lucia's otherwise modest shop. But she remembered her father once telling her that rune scribes in Ceramor weren't organized through a single institution the way they were in Talmir. Anyone with a bit of knowledge and the right skills could try their hand at carving runes. It made things like Lucia's stove, and the ward on the door, cheaper and easier to acquire, but also meant they lacked the sophistication and consistency of Talmiran creations.

Naya eyed the stove warily and saw a circle of wavering blue runes that seemed to glow from somewhere inside its metal belly. "What will it do to me?" she asked.

"It will draw out some of the extra aether." Corten held out his hand to her.

Naya looked from the furnace to Corten. A part of her still wanted to curl up in a ball and scream. Everything was happening too fast. And despite what she'd said to Celia, she wasn't at all sure she could become what Valn needed. But what other option did she have? She could feel her father's letter where it rested in her pocket. He was counting on her to help protect Talmir.

Naya locked away her fear and took Corten's hand. His fingers brushed against hers as he guided her to a spot on the furnace. The metal was hot against her palm, but not unpleasantly so. Corten turned the dial on the side of the furnace. A faint click sounded as the metal plates inside shifted. Moments later a second circle of pale-blue runes began to glow from within.

Naya felt a pull. It was the same as what she'd felt waiting for the tram with Lucia, only not as strong. The buzzing inside her lessened as she watched wisps of blue energy flow from her hand to the runes. She peeked through the window at the stove's front. The dial obviously worked the same as the one on her father's furnace. By turning it, Corten had shifted two rune plates together to create a second circle of heat runes. When those runes activated, they'd somehow begun drawing energy away from Naya's bones.

After a moment Corten turned the dial back down. The plates separated and the light faded from the second set of runes. Naya looked down at her hand, rubbing one finger over the spot where her bones rested.

"Better?" Corten asked.

Naya nodded. "I—"

The workroom door opened. Corten's head snapped up and the smile left his face. "Lucia."

Lucia paused on the threshold. "Corten, Blue. I didn't expect you back yet." She carried a parcel wrapped in brown paper under one arm. "I trust her aether is now stable?"

"She should be all right for a while. But I need to speak to you in private." Corten's tone became suddenly formal.

Lucia paused, her eyes darting between Naya and Corten. "Of course. Blue, why don't you wait here?" She smiled, but now that Naya was aware of the aether, she could feel Lucia's unease. Naya looked at Corten, but he avoided her eyes and followed Lucia up the stairs. What could Corten want to say to Lucia that he didn't want her to hear? He'd acted friendly enough. But what if he'd realized she wasn't what she claimed? What if he meant to warn Lucia? The two obviously weren't on good terms. But Corten must have still felt some loyalty to her, or he wouldn't have agreed to help. Naya needed to know what they were saying.

She snuck up the stairs, pausing halfway when she heard raised voices coming from the second floor.

"—against her will. What were you thinking?" Corten asked.

Lucia's reply was softer. Naya inched farther up the stairs, but before she could catch anything else, a door slammed above her. Naya scrambled back down the stairs, just making it into the workroom before Corten descended. He gave her a look she couldn't interpret, then headed for the exit. Naya tried to follow, but Lucia caught her arm.

"What are you doing?" Naya asked.

"You will be staying here," Lucia said with surprising firmness.

Naya pulled free. "You don't get to decide where I go."

Lucia pushed her glasses up her nose, her lips tightening with irritation. "I know. Your master has made me painfully aware of that fact. But I would have thought you'd have a vested interest in keeping this mad business a secret. Go after him now and you only risk poking more holes in the story we are trying to establish."

"Why? What did he say?"

Lucia shook her head. "He doesn't know the truth, but you seem to have given him the impression that I'm holding you here against your will. For now he's not a threat. But I suggest you steer clear of him in the future."

"If you're so worried about me speaking to him, then why did you send me there in the first place?" Naya asked.

Lucia rubbed her temples. "Because it was the natural thing to do. If we are to make others believe this farce the ambassador has concocted, then I must treat you as I would any other patient. Had I truly resurrected you and purchased your contract on a whim, and had I later found you were having difficulties adapting, then Corten would have been my first choice for assisting you. My other option was to risk your bond fading entirely. I think the ambassador would agree that avoiding that outcome was worth a small gamble."

Lucia's reasoning made sense, but it didn't satisfy Naya's doubts. "If having him teach me was the natural thing to do, then won't avoiding him now make us look more suspicious?"

Naya thought she saw a muscle under Lucia's eye twitch. "He's obviously angry with me, but he isn't the sort to spread rumors. Now that he's taught you what I asked, we'll both be better off if you keep your distance and avoid giving him any more reasons to ask questions."

CHAPTER 9

For the next four days Lucia kept Naya busy with errands and mundane tasks. Every time she wanted to snap at the necromancer, Naya reminded herself of Celia's warning. She swallowed her pride and did her best to adopt the manners of the quiet servant she was supposed to be. As she worked, she kept an eye out for Corten, but he didn't return after his fight with Lucia. That was probably a good thing. If he didn't come back, then he couldn't ask inconvenient questions. Still, Naya was surprised to feel a twinge of disappointment. She told herself it was only because Corten's explanations had been so much clearer than Lucia's. That, and it would have been nice to learn from someone who didn't so obviously distrust her. Lucia always seemed to be watching Naya when she thought Naya wasn't looking. And the answers she gave to Naya's questions were either so vague, or so technically complex, as to be useless.

Despite Lucia's reluctant help, Naya began to adjust to the aether and the extra sense that Celia had called the sight. She'd been seeing snatches of aether ever since her resurrection, but learning to spot it on purpose took practice. It was a matter of unfocusing her eyes, and convincing herself that what she was seeing wasn't impossible.

When she finally mastered the trick, the world lit up with a subtle glow that was both beautiful and frightening. Pale-blue energy drifted constantly from the living, concentrating to a brighter glow where it was drawn into rune bindings.

While the sight came easily enough, learning to change her features was another matter entirely.

"It's too complicated, especially given your rudimentary understanding of aether. Some wraiths never master the change," Lucia said when Naya asked.

Naya thought of several snarky answers but kept them pinned behind her lips. "You're a necromancer. Surely you of all people could explain it."

Lucia's eyebrow twitched, but her voice didn't betray the smoky anger Naya felt in her aether. "If you wish to master the subject, start with Sellencio's *Aether and Will.*" She gestured to a set of thick books near the top of one of the shelves.

Naya smiled, though it felt more like a grimace. "Ambassador Valn thinks it's important I learn this."

"Then you'd best start reading." Lucia turned her attention to refilling one of the many jars of herbs lined up on the counter.

"Or," Naya said, keeping her tone light, "perhaps I should go ask Corten for help."

Lucia froze. "Don't. There's no reason to involve him further." She took a deep breath. "I promise, Sellencio's works are as thorough an explanation as you could ever hope for."

Naya's heart sank as she eyed the massive books. She wanted to push further, but she wasn't sure what would convince Lucia to be more helpful. Maybe she could speak to Celia later about Lucia's uncooperative attitude. For now she'd learn what she needed with or without Lucia's help.

Naya spent her nights trying to master what Lucia wouldn't teach. She struggled through dense books, stopping every few hours to stare into a mirror and try to force her features to change. In some ways it reminded her of her days back at the academy. There she had stayed up late almost every night, reading until her eyes blurred and trying to ignore the loneliness that hung over her, as stifling as a heavy cloak in summer.

Though she didn't need sleep, she sometimes found her thoughts drifting into a dreamlike state. She imagined herself home in Lith Lor, or learning knots from the sailors on the deck of the *Gallant*. The familiar memories were a welcome refuge from the strangeness around her. In the last week it seemed everything had turned inside out and upside down. Her father was a spy. The Talmiran ambassador kept a necromancer under his thumb. And when Naya closed her eyes, she saw the smile of a boy who should have been her enemy.

She knew necromancy was wrong. The dead were supposed to stay dead. But the more she thought about it, the harder it was to reconcile that truth with the kindness she'd seen in Corten's eyes. He could have left her alone. Instead he'd helped her, and he'd seemed truly angry when he learned Lucia was supposedly forcing Naya to serve against her will. Those weren't the actions of a monster.

Two days before her meeting with Celia, Naya climbed onto the shop's roof to take a break from her studies. She was just settling down to watch the stars when she heard the front door open. Naya frowned. Hadn't Lucia already gone to sleep? She peeked over the edge of the roof and saw Lucia walking down the darkened street. Where could she be going at this hour?

Celia claimed they could control Lucia. But how secure was that control? Naya hesitated, then hurried to follow Lucia. Her new identity felt like such a fragile thing. If Lucia proved untrustworthy, then all of it would fall apart. She had to find out where the necromancer was going.

By the time Naya reached the front door, Lucia was already at the end of the street. On her way out, Naya grabbed a simple green shawl from the hook by the door and wrapped it loosely over her hair in a style common among the local women. It was barely any disguise at all, but until she learned to change her features, it would have to do.

Naya followed Lucia down their narrow lane, past the flower seller's shop, and onto one of the wider streets, where a few people still lingered outside restaurants and cafés. At night the aether around Lucia's shop usually settled into a sleepy haze so subtle Naya didn't notice it unless she concentrated. But here the air was alive with a peppery unrest that made the back of her neck itch. Men and women held animated conversations over tables scattered with empty glasses. Naya ignored the tightness in her chest as she hurried on, trying to keep her focus on Lucia.

The necromancer was obviously nervous, glancing back over her shoulder every couple of minutes and forcing Naya to stay far back or risk being seen. Lucia continued to the end of the street, then disappeared into a shabby-looking café. Naya hesitated, tugging her shawl a little tighter. She doubted it'd be easy to avoid detection inside, but if she turned back now she'd learn nothing for her trouble.

The café's front windows were small and showed glimpses of an interior dimly lit by the warm glow of a few scattered oil lamps. Naya wondered if the owners were too poor to afford rune lights or if they preferred the natural flicker. She could just make out Lucia sitting with another woman at one of the back tables. Naya took a moment to steady herself, then slipped inside before her doubts could send her running.

The café wasn't large, but even at this late hour more than half the tables were full. The lanterns left deep shadows in the room's corners, and though the aether was thin, the air was thick with a smoky haze that smelled of spices. Naya picked a table a little to the left of Lucia's, tucked away next to a partition separating the seating area from what she assumed was the hall leading back to the kitchen. She kept her shawl up and was careful to sit with her face turned away from Lucia's table.

"Can I bring you something, miss?"

Naya started and looked up to see a young waiter in a rumpled white shirt. No aether drifted from him, but when she concentrated she could see a faint blue glow outlining his limbs. *Like Corten*, Naya thought. The waiter had to be another wraith. She turned her gaze away. "Uh, tea," she said, immediately feeling foolish. The other wraith could probably sense what she was. He would know she couldn't eat or drink. But instead of asking why she would waste a perfectly good cup of tea, he only smiled and said, "Of course."

As soon as he was gone, Naya let her eyelids droop and focused on the hum of conversation around her. The books she'd read said wraiths didn't see and hear the same way the living did. Somehow, they perceived the world through their soul's connection to the aether. With proper concentration they could extend their senses through the aether to pick out details the living would miss. Naya let her concentration wander from the physical world, trying to sense the aether around her. Once she did, she realized with a start why the aether felt so thin: several of the people sitting around her were wraiths. Glancing around, she noticed glowing runic tattoos peeking out from the sleeves and collars of many of the other patrons. Aside from Lucia and her companion, hardly anyone in the room was living.

Naya looked more closely at the other patrons, grim curiosity overcoming her unease. The crowd varied widely in both wealth and age. They lounged in small groups over cups of tea and small glasses of amber liquor. She wasn't the only wraith who'd ordered a drink. She watched as a young woman a few years older than her raised a glass and touched it to her lips before setting it back on the table. The woman smiled, then laughed at something her companion said.

The waiter returned with a delicate white cup. "Your tea, miss."

"Oh, thank you," Naya muttered, hoping he wouldn't notice the way she'd been staring at the other customers. After he left, Naya leaned back in her chair. Wisps of steam curled off her tea. When she breathed them in, she could almost taste the rich, earthy aroma. Her throat tightened and her eyes prickled with the sudden threat of tears. Foolish, all of them. Pretending they were still alive wouldn't make it so.

She closed her eyes, trying to refocus her attention on the aether. She hadn't come here for tea. She was a spy. She had a mission. She needed to make sure Lucia wouldn't compromise that. With the aether so thin, it wasn't hard to pick out the nervousness drifting off Lucia. Naya homed in on it, trying to let her other senses follow the aether to its source.

"—told you it's nothing," Lucia said. Her voice was barely audible over the hum of other conversations, but Naya still felt a thrill as she picked out the words. She pushed back her chair so she could glance over at Lucia's table. The necromancer was holding a cup of something steaming. Across from her sat a slightly younger woman in a green silk dress. Her fine black hair was accented by a few strands of silver and fell in waves around a heart-shaped face. Her aether was tinged with grating frustration, mixed with a fierce, warm concern that somehow made Naya feel guilty for listening in.

"Lu, please. I'm worried about you," the other woman said. "You've been so tense lately." She reached over to lace her fingers with Lucia's.

Warmth and bitter sadness spread through Lucia's aether. She squeezed her companion's fingers. When she smiled, the expression didn't reach her eyes. "I'm fine, just busy. Were you able to find out anything?"

The other woman pursed her lips. "About the missing

Talmirans? I spoke to a few people, but all I've found out are rumors. It's troubling certainly, but I don't see how it's Council business."

Lucia sighed. "Perhaps it isn't." She was silent for a moment. "Please don't take this the wrong way, but it may be harder for me to meet in the future."

"What—" the other woman began.

"Haven't seen you around here before," someone said from Naya's left.

Naya turned. The young woman from the table next to hers had come to stand beside her. She planted one hand on her hip, the other holding her drink. She had a round face and a wide smile.

Naya tensed as frustration battled with a sudden flash of unease. She tried to recapture the string of Lucia's conversation, but the interruption had broken her concentration. The woman continued to stare at her, obviously expecting an answer. "I'm new," Naya finally said.

The woman's eyebrows rose as she registered Naya's accent. "Talmiran?" she asked, an edge creeping into her voice.

Naya cursed silently as a couple of the woman's friends looked their way. Their expressions were only curious, but Naya still wanted to flinch from their attention. Instead she forced herself to sit a little straighter. "What if I am?" she asked.

The woman tucked a stray lock of dark-brown hair behind one ear. "Sorry. I just didn't think your kind could be resurrected."

One of the woman's companions snickered. Naya's cheeks grew hot. "Well, we can be." She'd met the woman's type back at the academy. The best way to get rid of her would be to avoid giving her a reaction. Make the game boring enough and they would move on. Usually. Naya's grip tightened on her teacup. She tried to reach back into the aether and find Lucia, hoping the necromancer hadn't noticed her.

"Fascinating," the woman said, again breaking Naya's concentration. "Well, I guess Talmiran principles aren't as strong as all your Dawning keepers claim. Necromancy must not look so evil when you've seen the other side."

Naya stood up. "You have no idea what you're talking about. You—"

A hand gripped Naya's shoulder. Lucia's aether flooded into Naya through the touch. Though she looked calm, her energy stank of fear and anger. "Why don't we go home, Blue."

The woman in front of them gave Lucia a quizzical look. "Lucia?"

Lucia nodded politely, then dropped a few coins onto the table next to Naya's cup of tea. "It's Iselia, right? Nice to see you again, but my assistant and I will be leaving now." She tugged Naya's shoulder. Naya followed, unsure what else to do. She could hear the other patrons murmuring, could feel their stares against the back of her neck. So much for avoiding notice.

She pulled free of Lucia's grip as soon as they reached the street. "Are you trying to destroy our cover?" Lucia whispered.

Naya glared at Lucia. "No. Are you?"

"Of course not. But you shouldn't have followed me. You had no right."

"Oh? Then what were you doing there?" Naya asked.

Lucia glanced over her shoulder. They'd walked a ways down the street, and so far it seemed no one had left the café to follow them. "I was doing what I had to. If I cut all ties after your resurrection, it would only draw more suspicion."

"What does that have to do with you asking about missing Talmirans? And who was that woman you were talking with?"

"She's no one," Lucia said, perhaps a little too quickly. "Our conversation had nothing to do with you. You can assure your master that I'll hold to our deal. He's made his threats perfectly clear."

Hearing the grim note in Lucia's tone almost made Naya feel bad for the necromancer. She obviously didn't like their situation any more than Naya did. But that was all the more reason to watch her closely.

"Why ask about them if it doesn't have anything to do with our business?" Naya asked, trying to add a hint of Celia's stern certainty to her voice.

Lucia spun to face her, her teeth flashing in the beginning of a snarl. "Why do you care? Haven't you people demanded enough of me already? I brought you back from death. I've lied to everyone I care about to protect your secrets, and I've put up with your childish whining. But none of the ambassador's orders involve allowing you to prod into every corner of my personal life."

Naya shuffled back a step. Lucia's aether was dark and heavy. It seemed to settle over Naya's shoulders, dragging her toward the dirty pavement. Her own anger sputtered under the weight of those emotions, leaving her feeling trapped and afraid. She looked away from Lucia. "Just remember, if you betray us, the ambassador will find out."

The words had sounded more menacing in her head, but they seemed to do the trick anyway. Lucia wrapped her arms across her chest. "I know." She turned away, walking back toward her shop.

Unease and guilt warred in Naya's chest as she watched Lucia go. Despite her slumped shoulders and fear, the necromancer hadn't actually answered her question.

CHAPTER 10

When the day of her meeting with Celia arrived, Naya found herself wishing for another week, or even another dozen weeks, before she'd have to face the older spy's scrutinizing gaze. But ready or not, it was time to prove she could help with her father's mission.

Naya waited in the morning dark on a corner one block west of Lucia's shop. She wore a shawl over her hair and carried a big woven basket with sturdy handles. She kept her eyes down but extended her senses through the aether to ensure no one snuck up on her unannounced. After several minutes, footsteps tapped the pavement to her right. She felt the aether shift, like a cool breeze bringing the smell of snow on a winter's morning. For an instant it filled her with a sense of stillness and quiet confidence. Naya spun and saw Celia eyeing her from a few feet away. She was dressed as Naya was, in the plain skirt, blouse, and shawl of a servant. "You're early," Celia said.

"I wanted to make sure I'd be ready when you came." It was still at least a quarter of an hour before fifth morning bell. Even the most dedicated nighttime revelers had taken to their beds and the morning crowd hadn't yet surfaced.

Celia peered at her in the dim light. "I still see the face of a dead merchant girl."

"I haven't learned how to change my features yet." She'd sat alone every night with a mirror and tried to force her features into new shapes. Once or twice she'd thought she saw them shift. But every time the change reverted in the space of a blink.

Celia's frown deepened. "I see. Then maybe I was wrong in telling Valn you could be useful."

"That isn't fair. I've learned the other things you asked. I can use the sight now, and I know how to spot rune bindings. I'll learn how to change my face. I just need more time."

"And do you think our enemies will sheath their blades just because something isn't fair to you?"

"No, but you can't expect . . ."

"I'll expect what I please." Celia twitched her shawl tighter. "However, for what I intend today your face may not be such a great issue. Follow me, and keep your shawl up at least."

"Where are we going?" Naya asked.

Celia glared over her shoulder. "To the markets. Where else would two servants be going at this hour?"

"Okay," Naya said as she caught up with Celia. "Why are we going to the markets?"

"To buy provisions for our masters. And perhaps on the way we will pass certain residences and you may or may not note where they've scribed their rune wards."

They walked quietly for a few blocks. Naya gathered her courage. "There's something you should know," she said.

"Hmm?" Celia asked.

"The other night, Lucia went out. Late. I followed her and saw her meet with another woman at a café full of undead. Lucia asked the woman about the missing Talmirans. I wasn't able to hear everything they said, but it seemed strange."

"Ah. I see you didn't trust me when I said our master had the means to control her."

"It isn't that. I just . . . She's a necromancer."

Celia snorted. "Yes, she is a necromancer. And you are some-one who promised she could follow orders. I told you to keep your head down." She met Naya's eyes and her gaze softened. "It is useful to know Laroke is asking questions, but our master did not have you brought back so you could watch her. Do you understand?"

Naya nodded reluctantly.

"Good. Then come with me and we'll see if you've learned enough to be useful."

Celia led her to the end of the block, where they boarded a tram for the lower city. Naya's anticipation rose like a tide, washing away her doubts as the tram rattled down the hill. She was ready to prove her worth. She had to be.

More people boarded the tram as they approached the docks. By the time they reached the waterside, the car was nearly full and the sky behind the hills was gray with dawn. Naya had expected Celia to take her to Market Street, the wide boulevard where the city's most prominent shops were located. Instead they walked along the docks, past warehouses whose fronts were blocked by stalls selling salt, spices, pickled vegetables, and fish, all fresh off the ships. Naya peeked at the big trading vessels anchored in the harbor. The *Gallant* wasn't there. She hadn't expected to see it, but the certainty of its absence still brought a stab of disappointment.

They moved with the flow of the crowd, past other women dressed as they were and a few men who looked like butlers out placing orders for their masters' kitchens. Children wove through the crowd, some of the older ones hawking newspapers, and hungry-eyed beggars stared from the outer edges of the market. The air was pungent with the smells of food and rot and the ever-present scent of the ocean. Naya could feel energy building around her as people stomped their feet and shook off sleep, preparing for the day's work.

Celia stopped here and there, occasionally dropping a small parcel into her basket or into Naya's, but more often scheduling orders to be delivered back at the embassy. She paid from a heavy pouch stuffed with the triangular tin coins that were the most common currency in Ceramor. At one time Ceramor had used gold and silver coins like those common in Talmir. But those metals had grown scarce as the Crown struggled to pay off the debts imposed by the Treaty of Lith Lor.

As they neared the end of a row of stalls, Celia dropped a few coins into a beggar's cup. The grizzled old man smiled and grasped her hand in thanks. Naya just caught a glimpse of white paper passing from the man's hand to Celia's. Celia tucked the paper away without looking at it, then gestured for Naya to follow her down a side street.

"That building there. Tell me what you see," Celia muttered.

Naya glanced at the house. It was of average height with no balconies. Simple grates covered the lower windows, and the walls were painted a muted robin's-egg blue. It didn't look like anywhere important, but when Naya concentrated she spotted a double set of runes glowing on the doorway and the front stoop. They looked a little like the alarm runes warding Lucia's door. Naya described them as best she could, making sure to note the exact locations of the bindings.

"I see," Celia muttered after Naya finished describing the runes.

They continued down the street, and Celia picked out three more houses for Naya to examine. By the time Naya finished, Celia's lips were curled into something that looked like it might actually be a smile. "Well, it seems you can learn. The wardings on the Gallroth house are tricky to pick out, or so I am told."

"You already knew where they were?"

"Of course. You think me a fool who would give a test I didn't already have answers for? Follow me. These next houses we haven't been able to scout for some time. I am very curious to see what you can learn of their defenses."

The sun had risen above the hills by the time they finished their work. Naya squinted at the hazy blue sky. Not yet midday and already it was getting hot. "You did well," Celia said as they approached the corner where Naya would board the tram that would take her back to Lucia's shop.

Naya wrinkled her nose. She'd found runes at six of the seven houses Celia had taken her past. The last one had seemed grand, exactly the sort of place she'd expect would have magical defenses, but she'd found nothing. "I still think I must have missed something at—"

Celia cut her off with a wave of one hand. "It would have taken a week of careful investigation to learn what you've told me with a morning's watching. You did well."

A smile tugged at Naya's mouth in response to the unexpected praise. "Why those houses?" she asked. She half thought Celia would dismiss the question. Instead the older woman glanced around, then leaned in closer.

"Let us say that the residents are some of the more enthusiastic supporters of necromancy—financiers and politicians who would gladly see the Treaty of Lith Lor abolished. Our master was curious to know if any of them had increased their defenses since last we checked," Celia said softly.

"And have they?"

"They have indeed."

"Why?"

Naya caught a glint in Celia's eyes. "*That* is a very good question."

CHAPTER 11

Lucia wasn't at the shop when Naya returned, and the note she'd left on the door indicated she wouldn't be back until evening. Naya frowned as she read it. Lucia had barely spoken to her since the night Naya followed her to the café. She had to admit that nothing Lucia had done or said suggested she was trying to sabotage Naya's mission. That still left her with the question of what she had overheard. Celia hadn't seemed worried, but Naya could think of no good reason why Lucia would be asking about missing Talmirans.

Naya folded the note and tucked it into her pocket. Wherever Lucia had gone, there wasn't much she could do about it now. She'd have to trust that Celia and Valn were right about the necromancer.

Naya considered her options for the afternoon. She could go back to her room and try again to change her features. But if she spent another hour alone in that cramped space, she was likely to explode from frustration. She hadn't made much progress working on her own, and she doubted Celia would accept many more delays.

Perhaps it was time to get help from another source. Lucia had made it clear she either couldn't or wouldn't offer more help than what was in her books. But she wasn't the only person who knew about wraiths. Corten would probably know how to help her. Despite Lucia's warnings, the risk of seeing him again would be worth it if he could teach her to change her features.

Naya nodded to herself. Acting like a servant didn't make her one, and Lucia didn't get to decide who she spoke to. There were probably all sorts of useful things Corten could teach her. Naya's spirits rose as she hurried inside to drop off her basket and shawl. Corten had been reluctant to help before, but he'd seemed angrier with Lucia than with her. She'd find a way to convince him to teach her. And when Celia next tested her, Naya would impress the older spy with her skill.

She got lost only once trying to retrace her steps to Corten's shop. When she finally found it, she was surprised to see Corten sitting outside on the bench under the big oak tree in the plaza. He waved to her, but his smile was cautious. "Blue, what brings you here?"

"Miss Lucia is busy. I was wondering, if you have time, would you be willing to teach me more about aether?"

Corten rubbed the back of his neck. "Does she know you're here?"

"No," Naya said. Then with more force she added, "Does it matter?"

Corten smiled. "I guess not."

"Good. Miss Lucia's tried to help, but she can't teach me everything I need to know."

Corten's expression turned thoughtful. "What is it you want to know?"

Naya met his eyes. How much could she safely say? Was it even normal for wraiths to go around changing their features? "I can't believe all the old stories about the wraiths are entirely untrue. I need to know what I really am, but the books in the shop are too complicated, and Miss Lucia always gets frustrated when I don't understand things right away."

Corten smiled apologetically. "She always was better at performing resurrections than teaching." His smile fell. "I can guess what sorts of stories you've heard about us. We aren't the monsters your keepers want you to fear."

"Then what are we?" Naya asked, surprised to feel her throat tightening around the words.

"We're people."

Naya shook her head. "People eat. People sleep." People couldn't see the life drifting off their companions, or feel their emotions churning in the air.

Corten looked away. "Is that all you were before you died? A body that ate and slept?"

"Of course not!" Naya snapped, but she felt her anger sputter under the weight of the question. What was she really? Who was she? She'd been trying not to ask herself that ever since she woke in Lucia's shop. She looked away, wrapping her arms across her chest.

"We're more than our bodies," Corten said. "Necromancy proves that. It proves there's more to existence than just this one life."

"Does it?" Naya asked softly. She could almost feel the cold darkness of death, icy tides trying to drag her away. "What if it just shows us that darkness is all that's waiting?" Saying it out loud made the fear feel more real.

"You'll have to ask the keepers about that," Corten said. Naya looked up and saw him watching her with his hands shoved in his pockets.

"I'm asking you."

Corten's eyes met hers, then darted quickly away. "I don't know. All I know is that we're alive here and now, and we get to decide what we do with that." After a pause he added, "If you really want to know more, I'll try to help, but first I have to finish some things in the shop."

Naya hesitated. She didn't like the questions Corten asked. They left her feeling like the ground was crumbling beneath her piece by piece. But there were things she had to learn, and precious few people she knew could teach her. Besides, she'd seen a challenge in his eyes before he looked away. If she walked away now, he would think her a coward unwilling to face the truth. She tilted her chin up and forced a smile. "Just tell me what I need to do."

Corten looked at her again, like he was searching for something in her expression. Whatever it was, he seemed satisfied, because he motioned for her to follow. "Come on. I've got a batch of glasses to shape. Matius is at lunch. Once he gets back I'll ask if he can spare me for a bit." They stopped in front of a heavy door in the back of the room with the glass statues. "Your bones are in your hand, right?"

"Yes. Why?" Something about the shop felt wrong. The aether was too thin and she could sense something sucking away her energy. Some sort of rune device, and a large one judging by the strength of the pull.

Corten pulled his vest off the hook by the door and stripped off his shirt. Heat rose in Naya's cheeks and she tried not to notice the way his muscles flexed under smooth brown skin. Like most people in Ceramor, Corten seemed to have little concept of decency. Even on her father's ship, the sailors had kept their shirts on. And no Talmiran man would strip so casually in front of a woman who wasn't his wife. Naya fixed her eyes on one of the strange statues until she heard Corten clear his throat. She turned and saw he had finished cinching the vest. When he met her eyes, his lips twitched with a barely suppressed smile. Naya glared at him, the heat in her cheeks doubling.

"Try this on." Corten held out a thick leather glove. Like his vest, the glove was covered in heavy plates of some dark metal scribed with runes. "It'll be harder to draw aether while you wear it, so if you're low, you should breathe some in now."

Naya eyed the glove, but she couldn't see any aether coming from the runes. "Why do I have to wear it?"

"It'll keep the furnace from draining you. Otherwise you'll have to wait out here." He raised one eyebrow as he reached for the doorknob.

Naya shivered, then shoved her fingers into the glove. Almost instantly, the tugging sensation lessened to a tickle at the back of her mind. Naya's eyebrows rose and she flexed her fingers.

"Sorry it's a little big. All I had to work with were some old gloves of mine," Corten said.

Naya looked up. "You made this for me?"

Corten turned away, double-checking the ties on his vest. "I keep extra rune plates around as backups for when mine wear out and crack, so it wasn't any trouble to attach some of the smaller ones."

"How did you know you would see me again?"

Corten rubbed the back of his neck. "It probably sounds stupid, but I had a feeling you might come back. After what happened when you drew aether, I figured you would have questions." He met her eyes again, as though searching for something. "Anyway, it's not exactly comfortable in here for a wraith without some protection, so I decided there wasn't any harm in having something ready."

"Thank you," Naya said, trying to dismiss the strange tightness in her chest.

Corten nodded, then led her through a short hallway and into a room illuminated by the steady orange glow of three big furnaces against the back wall. Hollow clay and metal pipes nearly twice the length of Naya's arm leaned against the left wall, next to a metal table strewn with various tools. Naya could feel heat billowing off the furnaces. When she concentrated she could see aether flowing toward them to power the massive rune plates set into the sides of the furnace.

"So you make glass?" Naya asked.

"I make things out of glass." Corten walked to the far-right furnace, the largest of the three. He examined the rune dials, then opened the hatch to peer at something inside.

"Miss Lucia said you used to be her apprentice. How . . ." Naya trailed off as Corten's shoulders stiffened. He snapped the door shut and walked toward the leftmost furnace.

"How does a necromancer's apprentice become a second-rate glassblower?" Corten asked.

"I didn't say that."

He smiled, but not wide enough to hide the shadow in his eyes. "The dead can't sing souls back. After my accident I wasn't going to be any use to Lucia. I had to find something else to do with my time, so I picked this. Wraiths are especially good at this sort of work. We don't have the same limits as others. Here, watch." He reached into the furnace and pulled out a glob of molten glass, as calmly as someone else might scoop a handful of water.

"Are you insane?" Naya stepped forward, unsure what she hoped to do.

Corten grinned, then dropped the glass back in the furnace and showed her his undamaged hand. "Maybe, but not for that. I can feel the heat but it doesn't burn me. No flesh, remember?"

Naya shook her head. "It isn't natural."

Corten's grin faded and he turned back toward the furnace. "Better than dying before your time." He picked up one of the pipes and spun it in his hand.

Naya hadn't missed the bitterness in his tone. "For some-one who claims wraiths are just people, you don't exactly sound happy when you talk about what you are. And I've seen the way you act around Miss Lucia. If being a wraith is so wonderful, then why do you hate the person who brought you back?"

Corten's hands froze on the pipe. He didn't turn around,

and at first Naya thought he would ignore her question. When he spoke, his words were soft enough that she had to struggle to make them out. "I don't hate her."

Naya waited and eventually Corten turned to face her, his expression carefully neutral. "You Talmirans assume that just because we practice necromancy we see the undead as somehow superior to the living."

"Well, the Mad King—"

"Has been gone for more than thirty years. Allence is king now. He won't make his father's mistakes."

Naya looked away. King Allence was a sniveling, weak-willed man. Everyone knew the real power of the throne lay with his advisers. If they decided to fight the treaty, she doubted the king would stop them. "You still didn't answer my question."

Corten sighed. "Yes, I believe that necromancy is something truly good. I believe that we do the Creator's work when we help undo some of this world's chaos. But none of that changes the fact that I lost everything I was the day I died. I appreciate what Lucia did resurrecting me, but seeing her brings back the memory of that loss. You'll forgive me if that's a reminder I'd rather avoid."

Naya opened her mouth, then closed it again. Shame warred with anger inside her, magnified by the fact that she couldn't tell which one she had the right to feel. If Corten truly believed he'd lost everything, then how could he not see that necromancy was wrong? When she met his gaze, she saw hurt in his eyes, but no shame. He'd meant what he said.

Naya looked away. "If seeing her makes you feel that way, then I can't imagine talking to me is much better. Does that mean you want me to leave?"

"No. But if we're going to do this, you need to decide what you actually want. I can't teach you anything if you deny what you are."

What she wanted was to be alive again and sailing with her father to someplace far, far away from Ceramor. But she knew that wasn't going to happen. Naya met Corten's eyes. "I want to learn."

CHAPTER 12

Naya waited for Corten to finish his work. She watched as he pulled a fresh blob of glass from the furnace. With surprising grace he spooled it onto the end of a metal pipe and blew until it ballooned out to form a globe. He twirled another piece of glass and attached it to the bottom, forming a stem and base, before cutting off the top of the bubble and gently widening it to form the bowl of the goblet. He examined the goblet, then placed it next to several others already cooling on a rack in the far furnace. There was something calming about the dance of hand and molten glass. Naya's thoughts quieted as she watched the newly formed goblets fade from fiery orange to pale yellow. When Corten finished, she was surprised to find herself reluctant to leave.

"So, you wanted to know more about wraiths?" Corten asked after they had returned to the front of the shop and shrugged off their protective gear.

Naya nodded. "If I'm going to work for a necromancer, then I want to understand what she did to me."

Before either of them could say more, the shop's front door opened and Matius strode in. "Sorry I'm late. Sannesa made roasted prawns for lunch, and the children—" He paused when he saw Naya and offered her a warm smile. "Well hello. I was wondering when we'd see you again."

Naya returned his smile, reaching into the aether to figure out whether or not the expression was genuine. Nothing. *Another wraith, then.*

"Blue's asked me to teach her more about aether," Corten said.

"Has she now." Matius's smile widened as he looked between them.

"I know we've got that order of plates to wrap for Mistress Beronia but—"

Matius waved the comment away. "Bah, no. I can handle the plates. You've earned yourself a break. Go have fun."

Corten looked like he wanted to argue. Instead he glanced at Naya and nodded. "Right. Well, I'll try to be back in an hour or so."

"Take a half day if you like. The shop won't burn down without you," Matius said before heading up the stairs to the shop's second level.

Corten snorted, his expression a mix of wry amusement and frustration.

Naya raised her eyebrows. "Is something funny?"

Corten shook his head. "It's nothing. He just thinks I work too much. He's always trying to get me to go out and 'have fun,' as if . . ." He glanced at Naya, then let the words trail off.

"As if what?" Naya asked.

Corten remained silent for a moment. "As if that mattered." He shook his head. "Sorry, you didn't come here to listen to me complain."

"It's okay," Naya said. "You must really like the work. I'd think he'd be proud you're so dedicated."

Corten blew out a breath. "He doesn't see it that way. He says the way I shape glass is too mechanical and that unless I get out and find something to be passionate about, I'll never get any better. Matius pities me because he thinks I don't have any real friends. Which is stupid. Working glass might not have been my first choice, but at least it's something I can still do. And no matter what Matius says, I'm never going to get any better if I waste my time sitting around in some café." Corten rubbed the back of his neck. "Not that you're wasting my time now or anything. I mean . . . Creator, I need to stop talking. Why don't we go get some fresh air?"

Naya followed him to the door, sifting through what he'd said. Back at the Merchants Academy, she'd had some of the best grades in her year. It wasn't that she loved calculating sums or memorizing maps and languages, but studying had given her something to focus on. If she poured all her attention into exceeding her teachers' expectations, then she wouldn't have to think about the way her classmates avoided her like she had something catching. Naya couldn't imagine why Corten would have any trouble making friends, but she thought she'd seen an echo of that old ache in his eyes.

"So how have you been?" Corten asked as they passed the bench where he'd first taught her to draw aether.

Naya stole a glance sideways. Corten's tone was light, almost unnaturally so, as though their previous conversation had been about nothing more consequential than the weather. "I've been fine." Naya tried to think of something the galley girl Blue might say. "The aether isn't so bad now that I'm used to it, and the work Miss Lucia gives me isn't hard compared with working on a ship." Maybe she could come up with a casual way to ask about changing her features.

"What's that like?" Corten asked.

"Sorry?"

"Working on a ship. What's it like? I've never been out to sea."

Freedom. Adventure. Traveling with my father. Those were the things Naya had always loved. But what about Blue? Naya tried to imagine the girl she was supposed to be. "The work wasn't anything special," she said slowly. "I was in the galley mostly, scrubbing and fetching things for the cook. But I liked being at sea. Sometimes I'd go up after dinner and the sunset would color the waves orange and for a few minutes it would be like the whole world was glowing."

"Sounds like you miss it," Corten said, his tone soft.

Naya nodded. Her throat felt suddenly tight. She might never again sail with her father, or see the white cliffs of her home. Corten wasn't the only one who'd rather not be reminded of what he'd lost when he died.

They continued in silence along a wide road that ran across the city's hills. Naya began to see why she'd gotten lost on her first day. The city spread out and up from the ocean to cover five different hills. Lucia and Corten both lived on Cansa Hill. Behind them was Beirdo, the southernmost hill. Up ahead she could catch glimpses of Sanmore, Lennia, and Belanore. A high wall surrounded the city, with houses and farms scattered out beyond its borders.

Past the narrow strip of flatlands surrounding the port, the roads followed the geometry of the hills, twisting like rivers around obstacles rather than adhering to a grid. It was nothing like her home city of Lith Lor, where white houses rose in orderly rows along every street. That city was built on a flat clifftop overlooking the sea. Fresh breezes always blew through the streets, cooling the air and carrying away the less appealing smells of the city. Naya couldn't remember how many times she'd snuck away from the academy to sit on the cliffs and stare at the ocean, lost in dreams of the day when she could sail away and explore foreign places.

Corten paused at a plaza far wider and better maintained than the one near Matius's shop. A group of children played outside a small school on the far side, but otherwise she and Corten were alone. Through a gap in the buildings, Naya could see all the way down to the docks. Many-colored houses spilled down the slope. They looked like toy blocks piled up against the glittering edge of the bay. Even with her thoughts still filled with images of Lith Lor, Naya had to admit the view was impressive.

"I've been thinking about what you told me—about Lucia buying your contract, that is." Corten ran his fingers through his black curls. "Honestly, I half expected to hear you'd run away from her."

Naya crossed her arms and turned away from the vista. Corten's expression was tense. "Why would I run? Even if I could get away, it wouldn't undo what happened. And without knowing anything I'd never be able to hide what I am." There were days when the thought of fleeing was so tempting that Naya felt the presence of the docks like an anchor tied to her chest. But the things she wanted to run from couldn't be escaped with a change of location.

"So you do plan to run, just after I've taught you what you need?"

"What? No, that's not what I meant."

"Don't worry. I'm not fishing for information to help Lucia." Corten seemed to consider something for a moment, looking out at the bay. "I don't think what she did to you was fair."

"Why? I thought you said resurrecting people was doing the Creator's work." It was hard to keep the edge from her voice.

"It is. Usually anyway."

His words sent a chill through her. "What do you mean?"

Corten glanced around. "See those kids over there?" he asked with a nod to the group playing on the other side of the plaza.

Naya's brow furrowed. "What do they have to do with anything?"

"Can you sense the emotions in their aether? Without moving any closer, I mean."

"Of course," Naya said. When she focused, it wasn't hard to reach out and feel the bright joy swirling around the children. "Why?"

"You're sure?"

"Yes. What is this about?"

Corten shoved his hands into his pockets. "You shouldn't be able to distinguish their emotions from the city's pulse. There's a limit to how far away a wraith can reach. Your range is a lot farther out than it should be." He paused. More questions came to Naya's mind, but she held them back, waiting for him to continue. A part of her hoped he wouldn't.

"It could be I'm just making soldiers from mist," Corten finally said. "But I felt it when you first drew aether. You pulled so much so fast that I thought for sure you were going to crack your bond. I told myself maybe I'd imagined it, but then Lucia was acting so strangely, and if your range is really that much longer than mine . . ." He took a deep breath. "Then there's something I want to test."

Naya took a step back. "Lucia already tested my bond. She says I'm fine."

"Just bear with me. This won't take long." Corten pulled a palm-size metal disk from his pocket. "Do you know what this is?"

"Some sort of rune device?"

Corten nodded, then turned the outer rim of the disk to align the runes. The disk began to glow. Little wisps of aether drifted toward the runes like glowing mist curling into an open window. "I want you to try something." Corten held the disk out in front of him and pointed at one of the runes. "You know how rune devices tend to break after a while? That happens because the process of converting aether stresses the rune plates and causes them to warp or crack. No matter what you're converting the energy to—heat, or light, or kinetics—the more aether the device absorbs, the faster the binding breaks down."

Corten paused, and Naya nodded her understanding. He gave her a tense smile, then continued. "This is the taos rune." He pointed to a rune in the center of the disk, tracing the spots where its lines overlapped to connect with the other runes radiating out along the edges. "Taos is always the center of a binding because it's the only rune that attracts aether. It's also the weakest point. I want you to try pushing aether into it. See if you can break it."

Naya frowned. "How am I supposed to push aether?"

"It's not so different from drawing it in. It's like breathing in and out, just two halves of the same process."

Naya reached for the metal disk but Corten took a step back. "No, try doing it from there."

"Why?"

"Just try." Corten's fingers tightened around the disk.

Naya glared at him. He was hiding something, dodging her questions while demanding answers from her. Only her curiosity kept her from turning around and leaving him and his stupid disk alone. Could she break a rune binding without even touching it? She'd never heard of anything like that, but after her outing with Celia it was hard to deny that such a skill would be useful.

She focused on the rune Corten had indicated. Aether did seem to concentrate in the center of the disk. The runes around the outer edge glowed with ordinary white light, but the taos rune was illuminated only by the wispy blue of aether flowing through it. She drew in a breath of aether and watched it swirl away from the amulet. For a moment the runes dimmed, then more aether flowed toward them, like water filling a hollow. *Like breathing out, huh?* She breathed out and tried to imagine pushing the energy away. Her arms and legs grew suddenly heavy, and a tired fuzziness filled her head. Aether concentrated around the disk, but otherwise nothing happened. Naya scowled. She pushed out again, this time imagining the aether swirling in a tight spiral to collide with the taos rune. The energy continued to drain from her, making the world spin. Just as she thought she would have to give up or else collapse into a pile of nothing, the disk glowed brighter.

Naya tried to rally her efforts, but it was no use. She couldn't keep going. She dropped her focus and drew in more aether. Her weakness vanished, leaving only an uncomfortable twinge in her hand. When she looked up, Corten was still staring at the disk. "I couldn't do it," she said.

Corten shook his head. "Doesn't matter."

"What do you mean? If it doesn't matter, then why bother trying?"

"You may not have broken it, but you came close. Did you see how the light flashed brighter at the end?" Corten tucked the disk back into his pocket. He looked shaken. "Have you ever heard of the reapers?"

Naya fought off a shudder. "Just stories. Nightmare tales to scare little kids."

"Well, at least some of those stories were probably true. Near the end of the war, King Sallent tried to lift the old laws against experimentation. He commanded his necromancers to find new ways to bind wraiths, anything that could make the returned more powerful. The wraiths they brought back could do things nobody had seen before. They could manipulate aether at a distance, concentrate and convert it in ways normal wraiths never could. They could—"

King Sallent, the Mad King. "Stop," Naya whispered as she realized what he was implying. Reapers were the stuff of her people's nightmares. Wraiths that could muster the strength of a dozen men, roast soldiers in their armor with a thought, or create blinding light from empty air. "You're wrong. Even if the reapers did exist, the experimental runes were all destroyed. The Mad King's necromancers were killed." Naya wanted to run away or cover her ears, but Corten's words left her rooted in place.

"Maybe, but that doesn't mean the knowledge was lost," Corten said. "The way I've heard it, only a few reapers were successfully resurrected, and that was near the very end of the war. The man responsible for making them was named Renor Marotin. He died during the surrender, but the stories say one of his apprentices managed to flee south and evade capture. It took more than a year before the Talmirans finally caught her. Who knows what she did during that time? Maybe she passed on her master's secrets."

Naya shook her head. "So you think Lucia found this lost apprentice's notes and used them to make me a reaper? That's madness!"

"I don't know how she found the runes for a reaper binding. Maybe she didn't. Maybe you're something new. But what you just did isn't possible for an ordinary wraith."

Naya took a moment to steady her nerves, trying to ignore the horror of what Corten was suggesting. Was it possible? It could explain why Lucia was always watching her so intently. Naya had assumed it was because Lucia didn't trust Valn or his spies, but maybe she was more interested in tracking the results of her experiment.

She met Corten's eyes. As badly as she wanted to dismiss his claims, she didn't think he was lying. In the time she'd known him, he'd been kind to her. He'd helped her even when she'd lashed out at him. She didn't believe him cruel enough to make a joke of something so awful. "Let's pretend for a moment that I believe you. What you're describing would violate the Treaty of Lith Lor. Why are you telling me about it instead of turning me in?"

"Because it isn't your fault. You didn't ask to be this. Lucia just decided to use you because . . . I don't even know why. Maybe she thought it would be safer, since a Talmiran wouldn't notice the signs."

Naya's brow creased. "If that's true, then why risk sending me to you at all?"

"I'm not sure. Maybe she didn't think I'd notice either. Or she knew I wouldn't risk both your lives by turning her in."

That might explain why Lucia had sent her to Corten specifically, but not why she'd risked involving an outsider. Naya thought back to the conversation she'd overheard in the café. Lucia was definitely up to something.

Sunlight reflected off the brightly painted houses and the shimmering expanse of the bay. On the other side of the plaza, the children let out a shout as one girl held up a scrap of red cloth, triumph flooding off her in waves. Naya met Corten's eyes. "So, what are you going to do?"

Corten slumped onto the paving stones and ran both hands through his hair. "I have no idea."

CHAPTER 13

Naya stepped away from Corten. The bright sunlight had lost its warmth, and the children's laughter now sounded more menacing than joyous. A reaper. Could it really be true? If Corten had noticed, then would others see it as well?

"I have to go," Naya said.

"Wait!" Corten scrambled to his feet. He reached out, but stopped just short of grabbing her arm. "Blue, please."

Naya shook her head, backing away from him. "I shouldn't have come here. I'm sorry. This isn't your problem. Just forget you ever met me."

"I won't!" The certainty in his tone stopped her.

"Why?" Naya glanced around, lowering her voice to barely above a whisper. "You said it yourself—if you're right, then even being around me is dangerous."

"I know. But there's something wrong about all this. Let me come back with you. I know Lucia. I'll make her tell us why she did this. After that . . . I don't know, we'll figure something out."

"No!" She couldn't let him confront Lucia. Who knew what the necromancer might let slip? Naya squeezed her eyes shut. Celia had told her not to draw attention to herself, and here she was exposing secrets she hadn't even known existed. Creator, she had to be the worst spy who'd ever lived. "No," she repeated in what she hoped was a calmer tone. "I'm not sure how Miss Lucia will react if she finds out we know. Please, for now just promise me you won't tell anyone else about this?"

"I promise. But what are you going to do?"

"Nothing. I don't know. I just need some time to figure this out."

Corten took a step back. He still looked like he wanted to object, but after a moment he nodded. "Okay. Why don't you come by the shop tomorrow? We can talk more then."

"Tomorrow," Naya said, though her voice sounded small and far away in her own ears. She turned and hurried away before Corten could ask anything else. She felt numb as she walked back to Lucia's shop, her thoughts too tangled to sort through. Lucia was in the workroom by the time Naya made it back. She gave Naya a suspicious look as she trudged inside.

"Where were you?" Lucia asked.

Naya stared at the necromancer. "That's none of your business." Had this woman really risked her soul with forbidden experiments? The thought made Naya's insides churn.

Lucia pressed her lips into a thin line, then looked away. "Of course. My mistake." The aether around her was rough with frustration, but Naya didn't think she'd raised the woman's suspicion. No more than usual anyway. Naya retreated to the back of the workroom and pulled Sellencio's *Aether and Will* from its spot on the bookshelf. It took less than an hour of skimming to confirm what Corten had told her: no normal wraith should be able to push aether into a taos rune without touching it. That didn't necessarily prove she was a reaper, but it did prove Lucia had tampered with illegal runes when she created Naya's bond.

Why would she do such a thing? Why would Ambassador Valn support it? The simplest answer was that he wouldn't. It didn't make sense to violate the same treaty he was working to protect. And her father would sink the *Gallant* and himself with it before he agreed to something like this. That had to mean they didn't know about the illegal runes. Lucia had tricked Valn when she'd brought Naya back. She'd done it out of spite. Or she'd seen Naya's death as an opportunity to experiment on an unwitting victim.

Naya forced herself to draw in a careful breath of aether, feeling the steady pulse of the city around her. Fear chewed at the edges of her thoughts, threatening to consume her. She didn't dare report this to Valn. If he knew what Naya was, he might decide the risk of keeping her around was too great. It wasn't illegal to resurrect a Talmiran, but if anyone learned that their ambassador had been involved with forbidden necromancy . . . well, it would unravel all the work they'd done to protect the treaty.

Naya didn't want to risk the mission, but she also didn't want to die for it. Again. She'd have to find a way to keep the truth hidden. Lucia wasn't likely to expose them, not when it would put her own head on the chopping block. But how could she trust Corten with such a secret?

Naya was still grappling with that question when night fell. Lucia locked up the shop and retreated upstairs. Naya waited a few minutes before following. She paused on the stairs, listened, then reached into the aether. The energy around Lucia's bedroom was fuzzy with the beginning of sleep. Worry hung like bad breath, but Naya didn't sense anything that suggested the necromancer would be going out that night.

She slipped into her own room, a closet-like space with a slanted ceiling and only a chest and narrow bed for furnishings. Moonlight spilled in through the window's open shutters, casting the room in shades of black and gray. Naya paced from the door to the window, then back again. Possibilities and half-formed plans spun through her mind, but none offered a solution. She slumped onto the narrow bed with a growl of frustration, then froze when a flash of motion outside the window caught her attention. A moment later a hand appeared and knocked hesitantly at the glass. Naya stared at the window, wondering if she'd gone mad.

The hand knocked again, louder this time. Naya searched the room for a weapon, then snatched up the heavy book she'd brought from downstairs. She held it awkwardly in one hand as she approached the window. At first all she saw was darkness and the wall of the next building over. But as she scooted to one side she spotted a figure crouching on the roof next to the window.

"Corten?" Naya lowered the book. When she met his eyes, Corten's mouth turned up in a cautious smile.

Naya unlatched the window and swung it partway open. "What are you doing?" she asked. The initial shock of finding someone lurking on the roof outside her window was fast replaced by anger. She'd told him to stay away.

"I wanted to make sure you were okay?" His tone was hesitant, making it sound more like a question than an explanation.

Some irrational part of Naya wanted to smile at that, but she quickly pushed it down. "So you climbed onto the roof and started banging on windows?"

Corten looked away. "Not windows. Just one. This used to be my room back when I apprenticed with Lucia. I figured it was good odds she'd put you here, and I didn't want to knock on the front door because I thought Lucia would just send me away."

Naya stared at him. She wanted to hold on to her anger. Corten was a wraith, and a former necromancer's apprentice besides. She hardly knew him, but he held a secret that could easily destroy her. "Well, you can see I'm fine," she said briskly.

Corten smiled again, and there was something bright and earnest behind it when he met her eyes. Naya's anger sputtered.

"I'm glad," he said. "And I'm sorry about this afternoon. I was so caught up in figuring out what Lucia had done that I didn't really think about how it would feel for you to learn something like that. So, uh, I understand if you're scared, or mad at me, but I wanted you to know that I'm still willing to help."

"You'll still teach me?" Naya asked, searching his face for any sign of deceit.

"I will. My bond isn't like yours, but I know a lot about the theory behind necromancy."

"Why would you want to help me? You have to know you're only risking more trouble for yourself."

"Well, the more you know, the less likely you are to tip someone else off by accident."

That was a fair point. Still, his kind words seemed like such fragile things compared with the weight of the secret he held. And she doubted he'd be so keen to help her if he found out who she really was. But maybe if she was careful, she could keep that secret hidden. "Okay," she said.

"Really? Great. Then come with me."

"Now?" Naya asked.

"Unless you're busy." Corten raised a skeptical eyebrow.

"Where are we going?"

Corten smiled. "It's a surprise. Follow me." He stood and retreated farther up the roof, leaving room for her to climb out the window.

Naya hesitated a moment longer before her curiosity got the better of her. She pulled herself through the window and crawled out onto the roof. The shop was only two stories, and soon she and Corten were standing on the shallow roof looking out over the city.

"This way," he said, before jumping the gap to the next building.

Naya's eyes widened. "What are you doing?"

"Just trust me."

Trust him? He was insane, and she was even worse for letting him talk her into coming up here. Naya inched toward the edge and glanced down at the street below.

"Are you coming?" Corten's voice held the faintest note of challenge.

Naya glared at him, then sucked in aether and jumped. The distance wasn't far, and her body weighed little more than her clothes. But when her shoes hit the shingles of the next roof, she stumbled to one knee. Corten caught her arm before she could slide off.

"Careful," he said as he helped her to her feet.

Naya was grateful to the dark for hiding her expression. She kept her eyes locked on the roof as she stood. Then she noticed Corten's feet.

She frowned. "You're not wearing any shoes."

"Why would I?" Corten wiggled his toes. "My bones aren't in my feet. It's not as though the ground can really hurt me."

"But it's . . ." Naya trailed off. The sailors on her father's ship often went barefoot. But in cities people wore shoes. That was how the world worked.

"It's comfortable, and it's easier to keep my balance this way."

Naya looked down at her own shoes. They were practical enough, well-fitted with thick soles. But those soles also made it hard to feel the contour of the roof under her feet. She clomped and crunched with each step while Corten made almost no sound at all. Naya's fingers brushed the edge of her necklace. Humans wore shoes. Humans didn't go running on roofs in the middle of the night. But she wasn't really human anymore, was she?

When she looked up she saw Corten watching her, waiting for her to make up her mind. How was it that he seemed ordinary and strange all at the same time? By his face and dress it was easy to imagine him as one of the dozens of sailors who came and went from the ports back home every day. She could close her eyes and see him standing beside her on the *Gallant*'s prow, or climbing the thousand steps from the Lith Lor docks to the gleaming white city above. But she wasn't in Talmir, and Corten wasn't a sailor. He was a ghost, standing barefoot on a rooftop as though it were the most normal thing imaginable. He asked the impossible like it was nothing. *Trust me.*

Naya looked over his shoulder at the familiar roof of Lucia's shop. What other option did she have? She could go back, but she knew she'd spend the rest of the night wondering and worrying if he'd change his mind and go to the city guard. And she'd still be no closer to learning what she needed to prove herself to Celia.

Naya untied her shoes. She felt the kiss of the warm shingles against her heels and toes as she set the shoes to the side. She met Corten's eyes and crossed her arms over her chest. Despite everything, her lips turned up to answer his smile. "Let's go."

"This way." He ran, jumping to the next roof and scrambling over its peak.

Insane, totally and completely insane. But she didn't give herself time to think about it. She ran. The air tugged at her clothes with each jump. Corten wasn't sprinting, but his pace would have been suicidal for an ordinary human. Naya soon found herself falling behind despite her efforts. Her nerves wouldn't let her leap from one roof to the next without slowing to judge the distance across the next gap. But with each jump some of her fear faded. Up here she couldn't smell the stink of the city. With all the lights below, the stars seemed brighter up above. Freedom welled inside her, and for a moment Naya let it drown out all the worries that had haunted her since she woke in this strange city.

CHAPTER 14

Naya followed Corten's zigzagging path across the city roofs. When she finally caught up, he was standing on the roof of a large house. She could see the towers of the king's summer palace not so far ahead, and to her right the dark expanse of the bay. Corten sat down, patting the roof beside him.

"Why here?" Naya asked.

"If we're going to talk about something as illegal as reaper bindings, I figured we might as well do it somewhere private. And you have to admit the view's much better here than back at Lucia's." His tone was light, but the smile was gone from his face as he looked out across the city's roofs.

"What about the people inside?" It was a warm night, so it wasn't impossible to imagine that they'd have their windows open.

"Don't worry. We're above an attic. And if anyone inside wakes up, you'll probably be able to sense them before they hear anything important."

"Oh, right." Naya checked the aether and felt only the haze of sleep below her. She supposed she should have been happy about that. No doubt most spies would love to have the trick of sensing when others were nearby. As useful as the skill was, she doubted any Talmiran would be willing to die for it. She sat next to Corten, the exhilaration of leaping across the roofs fast fading. The view up here was beautiful, but she hadn't come for beauty.

"How far do you think Lucia went with the changes in my bond?" Naya asked.

Corten was silent for a moment. "I'm not sure. We could try some things out, if that's what you want. But we'd have to be careful. There's still a lot we don't know about how soul bindings work."

"What do you mean? I thought Ceramorans have been performing resurrections for decades."

"We know how to resurrect people, but a lot of that knowledge comes from ancient texts. We can follow the instructions, but we don't know why they work."

Naya's eyebrows rose, but Corten didn't look like he was joking. "That's terrifying."

"I think the mystery was what drew me to necromancy in the first place." Corten looked down at his hands. His shoulders hunched and Naya wondered if he was again thinking of what he'd lost. "Anyway," Corten continued, "some of the changes in the reaper bindings make them dangerous to use. The runes a necromancer carves act like a sort of tool set that allows the wraith's soul to draw aether and re-create their body. The reaper binding was an attempt to expand that tool set, figure out how to let a soul do more with the energy it can access. The problem is that there's this dissonance that builds up."

Corten paused and apparently saw the confusion in Naya's expression. "Sorry, I'm probably not explaining this very well. Take the way I look." He gestured at his face. "This is me. I don't have to think about looking this way any more than I would have had to think about how to wiggle my toes back when I had a body. But if I want to change something . . ."

Naya drew in a sharp breath as Corten's hair flickered from black to pale brown, then back again. "Holding on to a little change like that is sort of like carrying a rock in my fist," Corten continued. "It's not much work, but I have to pay attention or I might drop it. The kind of things the reapers could do would be more like trying to lift a boulder. Go too fast or lift too much and you're liable to crack your bones."

"And that's bad?" Naya asked.

"Very."

Naya wrapped her arms around her chest. Did she even want to know what changes Lucia might have made to her? Talmirans had fought and died to keep this sort of power out of the world. But what if she could use it to help defend the treaty?

What if. What if. The questions multiplied, making her head ache. She met Corten's eyes. "Let's start with something small. How did you make your hair change like that?"

Corten shook his head. "That isn't small. Feature shifting isn't something every wraith can do, and even those who can are careful how they use it."

"Why? I thought all wraiths were resurrected with the same bonds. Shouldn't they all be able to do the same things?"

"In theory, sure. But just because someone is born with two hands doesn't mean they'll become a master artisan. Remember what I said about a wraith's bond being a set of tools? Well, having the tools and having the skill to use them are two different things. We know that the way a wraith looks is tied to their will."

"I've already read about that," Naya cut in. "Wraiths are supposed to be able to exert their will to change the way they look. But I've tried that and it never works."

"Let me guess: Lucia had you read Sellencio?"

Naya nodded. "I think she only gave it to me because she thought I wouldn't get anywhere with it."

"Sellencio's explanations aren't wrong, but face shifting is about a lot more than just conscious will. How you look now is less tied to the physical body you lost, and more to how you see yourself. Your perceptions determine the body you shape intuitively for yourself. In order to change that, you have to be able to let go of the idea that your body is unchangeable. You have to be able to look in a mirror and expect something different."

Naya stared out at the horizon, where the ocean seemed to swallow the stars. Could she let go of what she'd looked like before? She tried to imagine looking in the mirror and seeing a face she didn't recognize staring back. She turned back to Corten, examining his face. "You can change more than your hair?"

Corten nodded. "I can, but it takes a lot of effort. It's not something I like to do."

"So this is what you looked like when you died?"

"More or less." Corten rubbed the back of his neck. "It's been more than a year now, so I guess I look a bit older."

"You guess?"

"Most wraiths age, unless they're trying not to. But I don't know if how I look now is how I would have looked if I'd kept my body, or just how I think I should have looked."

Naya wrinkled her nose as she tried to sort that one out. How could someone even know what they'd look like as they got older?

Corten smiled. "See what I mean? This is why I said it's not a small thing. In order to change your face, you have to start thinking about yourself in a completely different way."

Naya gave up on trying to imagine an older version of herself. "Still, I want to learn it."

"So you can run away from Lucia?"

Naya shook her head. "I told you before. I'm not running. Can you teach me or not?"

Silence fell between them, then Corten sighed. "All right. Let's start with thinning. It takes some of the same mind-set as feature shifting, but most wraiths find it easier. Here, watch."

Corten lifted one hand, and after a moment his fingers faded to a wispy, transparent blue.

A shock of instinctive fear raced down Naya's back. She pushed it away. "I remember something like that happening just after I woke."

"That's common. When a soul is first called back, it can take time for it to adjust to the rune binding." Corten brushed the edge of a shingle and his fingertips seemed to sink into it.

Naya pressed her own hand against the roof. It felt rough, and undeniably solid. "How did you do that?"

"I reminded myself that my hand wasn't made of flesh and bone anymore."

"That's it?"

"Essentially."

Naya glared at her hand. She tried to drag up the memory of what her fingers had looked like when they'd slipped through the blanket. Her chest tightened. *Monster.* It had been one thing to agree to Celia's demands. But if what Corten said was right, then the only way she'd learn to change her body was by embracing this new form. She wasn't sure which was more frightening: the prospect of failing and being tossed aside by Valn and Celia, or what she might become if she succeeded.

Corten brushed the back of her hand, then carefully lifted her stiff fingers. His touch was warm and sure and it sent a shiver through her. He pressed his palm lightly against hers so the tips of their fingers just barely touched. Naya froze, trapped by the touch, torn between the urge to pull away and the desire to lace her fingers through his.

"Relax," Corten said. His hand turned transparent again. The pressure of his fingers against hers lessened until all she felt was a faint warmth, like the glow of a hearth in a cool room. Naya tried to let the rest of her body relax, but it was hard to focus on anything beyond that faint touch. It should have made her afraid. Naya met Corten's eyes, and the warmth against her palm seemed to flare hotter.

He doesn't even know your real name. Guilt settled over her like a rain-soaked cloak. Corten wasn't a monster, no matter what the Talmiran keepers taught. But what was she? Was she callous enough to use him, even knowing he would hate her if he ever found out who she really was? *Not callous, practical. Valn is trying to keep the peace. Would Corten be any better off if Talmir and Ceramor went to war?* No, he wouldn't. Just because he might not agree with her methods didn't mean she wasn't doing the right thing.

Naya imagined her will hardening like a crystal. Peace was more important than any trade deal she could have hoped to negotiate while sailing with her father. If war came, then thousands of others would die like she had. She wouldn't stand by and let that happen. She would become whatever she must to preserve the peace.

She focused on her hand. *Not flesh and bone. Something more, something stronger.* Her skin shimmered. At first she thought it only a trick of the starlight. Then slowly her hand faded until she could see Corten smiling through it.

CHAPTER 15

"Again." Celia's voice snapped like a whip, the sound reverberating off the stone walls of the basement.

Naya drew in more aether. If she'd had a body, she suspected it would have been drenched in sweat. As it was, the bones in her hand ached dully. She tightened her grip on the training knife.

Celia didn't look the least bit tired as she moved to attack again. In her right hand the spy wielded a thin club like the ones carried by the city guard. In her left she held manacles made of thick salma wood. The wood was near black, with knots and whorls of dark gray running through it. It was polished smooth, but somehow the surface seemed to suck the light in rather than reflect it.

Naya braced herself, trying to watch both the manacles and the club at the same time. Celia swung at Naya's head with the club. Naya ducked the blow and felt the rush of wind from the near miss. She tried to slip inside the older woman's guard, stabbing with the knife.

Celia stepped back, causing Naya to lose her balance as she stabbed at empty air. Celia raised the club as though to swing again at Naya's head. Naya saw the opening and turned her stumble into a lunge, slashing at Celia's chest. But at the last instant Celia turned the blow, striking at Naya's knife hand. The club slammed into her wrist, sending ripples of force through her whole body.

Naya concentrated on the point of impact. She imagined her arm not as flesh but as raw energy. Her wrist turned transparent and the club swung through it like a cool breeze. Naya's triumphant grin froze in place when she heard her knife clatter to the floor—having fallen through her now incorporeal fingers.

She hesitated, torn between retrieving the knife or moving back out of Celia's range. The moment of indecision proved damning. Celia shifted forward and locked the manacles around Naya's left wrist.

Freezing pain shot up Naya's arm, and her fingers went rigid. She hissed through her teeth, trying to pull her wrist free. She thinned the flesh of her arm, but no matter how hard she tugged, her arm remained bound in the manacle. Somehow, the salma wood blocked aether, locking her in place. Or at least that was the explanation Celia had given. The cuffs felt nothing like the rune plates Corten used for protection near the furnaces, and Naya had come to dread their icy touch.

Celia frowned as she unclipped the restraint. "Better, but you still think too much. If someone corners you during a job, you must be ready to defend yourself. King Allence can't afford to equip all his guards with salma wood, but most will have at least some training in how to fight your kind. You have to stop moving like your body is made of flesh and blood. What does it matter to you if I hit your head? Your bones are in your hand. That is what you should be protecting." Celia pointed the club at Naya's left hand for emphasis.

Naya scowled, rubbing her wrist until the cold faded. "I know. I'm trying." Celia's other lessons had come easily. In the weeks since her resurrection, Naya had mastered the hand signs and codes used by the Talmiran spies. She'd learned to follow without being seen, and a dozen other small tricks besides. But when sparring, it didn't seem to matter how hard she tried. She was always too slow.

"That's enough for tonight, I think," Celia said.

"I can keep going."

"No." Celia waved one hand dismissively. "I want you fresh for tomorrow night."

"Tomorrow?"

Celia nodded. "I have a job for you."

Excitement danced down Naya's spine like a shiver. "What is it?"

Celia walked to the crate containing their supplies and extracted a paper-wrapped bundle. She tossed the package. Naya caught it and unwrapped one corner, finding a set of dark clothes. "Meet me tomorrow night after first bell at the usual spot. Wear that. I will give you the rest of the details then."

Dozens of questions sprang to Naya's mind, but with an effort she held them back. "I'll be there."

"Good," Celia said, the word clearly a dismissal.

Naya glanced around the sparse basement, part of the safe house owned by the imaginary merchant Selleno. "Has there been any word from my father?"

Celia tossed the last of the training gear into the crate. "No. Perhaps next week."

Naya bit the inside of her cheek. The answer was always the same, but that didn't take the sting out of it. "Are you sure there's no way to get a message to him? I just want to—"

"No. I've told you already. We won't risk our network with unnecessary communications. Things are fragile enough as it is."

"I know, but—"

Celia gave her a sharp look. "The answer is no. You should be focusing on your own work."

Naya swallowed an angry reply. "I am."

"Good. I need you focused. Tomorrow there will be no room for errors."

A few minutes later Naya slipped out the back door into the alley behind the house. Light rain misted down, cool and refreshing on her face. She tucked the package under her arm and drew in a steadying breath of aether. Four weeks had passed since the night she'd met Corten on the rooftops. Four more weeks of silence from her father. Naya tried to tell herself it meant nothing. He was busy. Communications were too risky. But the stale excuses did nothing to ease the ache in her chest.

She started walking. *Focus on something else.* The paper bundle crinkled with each step she took. From the note of warning in Celia's tone, tomorrow night's job would be something new. Perhaps the older spy had finally decided to trust her with work more important than spotting rune wards on houses.

Naya paused at an intersection and peered up at the stars. The compass star was still a good three fingers above the horizon, which meant her training with Celia hadn't gone as long as she'd thought. She still had a few hours left before dawn. Good.

Naya jogged the last few blocks to Lucia's shop. She slipped inside quietly to drop off Celia's package, then headed toward the glass shop. When she got there, she found Corten waiting in the usual spot under the old oak tree. She slowed before he could see her, her chest tightening with familiar doubt. *Turn around. Leave him to wait. Forget about him.*

They'd met here most nights over the past weeks, sometimes so she could practice manipulating aether, other times to explore the city. Corten had lived in Belavine for years, and with his help Naya no longer felt lost wandering its twisting streets and rooftops. It'd gotten easier and easier to pretend around him—easier to forget about all the lies that lurked between them.

She stepped into the plaza and waved. This couldn't go on

forever. She knew that. Her secrets were too big. But when Corten returned her wave, she felt some of the tension in her shoulders ease.

"You're out late," Corten said as Naya sat down on the bench next to him.

"So are you."

"Funny thing. No matter how hard I tried, I just couldn't sleep."

"Strange," Naya said, matching his somber tone even as a smile pulled at her lips. At first the long nights had terrified her. Now sitting with Corten under the stars felt like its own sort of magic.

"So, what do you want to do?" Corten asked. "I don't have any projects for Matius. There's a night market in Vistel Square, or we could go down to the shore."

Naya grinned. "If I didn't know any better, I might think you were considering wasting time on something fun."

"I find myself more willing to give Matius's theories a try. Creator knows, it's not like I can get any worse at glass shaping if I take a few nights off." Corten tilted his head back. Above them the wind played through the leaves, nudging them aside to reveal glimpses of starlight. "Besides, I'm running out of things to teach you."

Naya's chest tightened and she looked away. "There's plenty I still don't know." She stood. "We can go out later, but for now there's something I wanted to show you."

"Oh?"

"Come on. I need to borrow your mirror."

They headed into the shop and up the stairs to Corten's room. The space was comfortably cluttered, with a shelf of books against one wall and a desk and bed in the opposite corner. A singed shirt was draped over the back of the chair beside the desk. Naya leaned against the wall by the door while Corten rummaged through the desk drawers. He came back with a square mirror a little larger than Naya's spread fingers.

Naya accepted the mirror. "Close your eyes," she said.

Corten raised his eyebrows. "I've seen you practice feature shifting before."

Heat crept into Naya's cheeks. "I know. Just do it."

Corten shrugged, then closed his eyes. Naya drew in aether, staring at the face in the mirror. She'd mastered the basics of feature shifting more than a week ago. Since then she'd been practicing in private, hoping to surprise him with her progress. *Let go of what you think you should look like.* The frizzy hair and hazel eyes weren't really hers. They belonged to a dead girl who'd been too weak to defend herself. Naya didn't have to be that girl anymore. Valn had given her a new name, and now she'd made herself a face to match. Her face tingled, then blurred. Her nose changed shape, becoming more rounded, while her cheekbones grew more pronounced. Her hair smoothed and darkened to black while her eyes became a brighter green.

Naya smiled. Those looked like the kind of eyes that would make a person pause. Green eyes were more unusual than brown in Ceramor, but not so uncommon that they'd make her truly stand out. She set the mirror down. "You can look."

Corten opened his eyes, then blinked. "Wow."

Naya grinned. "What do you think?"

"You look really different."

"Do you like it?" She tried to keep her tone casual.

Corten looked away. "I guess."

Naya's smile drooped. "You guess?"

"It's nice. Impressive. But you look like someone else."

"Well, that is the point."

"Why? There's nothing wrong with your real face."

Naya crossed her arms, annoyed, and angry at herself for being annoyed. She shouldn't care what he thought. But she'd worked for hours to get the nose right, and she'd hoped at least he'd be excited to see her succeed. "Well, I guess it's good to know you don't think I'm deformed."

"That's not—"

"Never mind," Naya cut in. "I just wanted to show you what I've been practicing." She let go of the new face—Blue's face—and felt her features shift back.

Corten shoved his hands into his pockets. "Sorry. I didn't realize you'd been working so much on your own."

"I wanted to surprise you," Naya muttered. What was wrong with him? It was one thing if he didn't like the face, but he looked almost angry.

"You managed that." Corten kicked at a bit of crinkled paper on the floor. "So were you going to tell me before you ran away, or were you just planning to disappear?"

"What are you talking about?" Naya asked. "I'm not running away."

"Then why do you need that?" Corten gestured to her face.

Because I'm a spy and my master ordered it. The words felt so small and simple that they might easily slip out, unraveling everything. She tried to imagine how this must look to him. For weeks now he'd been helping her test the limits of her bond. He'd taught her things no ordinary servant would need to know, and he'd never asked questions. He hadn't confronted Lucia even though she knew he wanted to. Was he angry because he thought she would run away after all that, or because he thought she'd do it without telling him?

Naya looked up and saw hurt written in the tightness around Corten's eyes. "I'm sorry," she said. "I should have told you what I was practicing. You said before that I had to accept what I'd become. I've been thinking about what that means. I know I wasn't exactly open-minded when we first met, and I said some things I wish I hadn't, so I guess I wanted to show you I'm trying to become someone new." It was true, even if it wasn't the whole truth.

Corten's shoulders relaxed. "Oh." Silence settled between them. "So, you really are planning to stay in Belavine?"

Naya smiled. "I really am."

"Have you talked to Lucia about . . . you know?"

He was talking about the illegal runes. Naya looked down at her hand, thinning her aether until she could see the carved bones. "There's no point. She hasn't tried to tell me, so she'd obviously rather keep it a secret."

"Who cares what she wants? She made you a reaper. If you're going to keep working for her, then you have a right to know why she took that risk."

"I'll ask her. Just not yet."

"Why not?"

Naya scowled. She could feel the weight of secrets and her father's silence bearing down on her. "Because I'm not sure if it matters. It's not like knowing will undo anything."

"But—"

"Can we please not talk about this right now? Let's just go to the night market, or the shore, like you said. I know I have to deal with her at some point, but right now I don't want to think about the future. I want things to be simple. Just for a little while."

"Simple." Corten blew out a slow breath. "All right."

"Thank you." Naya turned and started down the stairs.

"Blue?" Corten called behind her.

"What?"

He was standing at the top of the stairs, light from his bedroom outlining his lean frame. "Just promise me that if you do decide to leave, you'll tell me."

She reached up and squeezed her mother's pendant until it dug into her palm. "I promise."

CHAPTER 16

Naya got back to Lucia's shop just before sunrise. Corten hadn't brought up the future again, but Naya had still felt the question lurking in every silence that fell between them. She heard Lucia descending the stairs to the shop and pushed her worries aside. Tonight she would meet with Celia. She needed to make sure she was ready.

Naya flexed the fingers of her left hand, imagining the rune-carved bones hidden there. Changing her features wasn't the only thing she'd learned since she'd begun practicing with Corten. She concentrated on the air just above her hand, imagining aether pooling in her palm. Aether was potential, energy waiting to be focused into something new.

So Naya focused. After a moment the pale glow of aether was replaced by ordinary light. Pain prickled through her bones, but she ignored it. The light was absolute proof of what she was: a reaper, capable of weaving aether into other forms of energy with nothing more than thought. It was terrifying, inhuman. But a part of her thrilled at the power.

She stared at the light, making it glow slowly brighter until the pain in her bones grew to something she couldn't ignore. Reluctantly, she closed her fingers and snuffed out the light. So far she hadn't dared try anything more than creating tiny lights or bursts of heat. She could think of dozens of ways she might use the reaper's powers. She'd even debated telling Celia what she knew, but something always held her back. Just because Celia's views on necromancy were more pragmatic than those of most Talmirans didn't mean she'd risk working with a reaper.

The bell on the front door chimed. A moment later Lucia called up the stairs. "Blue! Come here!"

Naya scowled, then arranged her features into the mask of an obedient servant and headed for the workroom. She found Lucia standing next to a thin woman in a simple dress. One of the woman's arms was wrapped in a kitchen towel. She held it out reluctantly, flinching as Lucia peeled the towel back to reveal a nasty burn across the back of her hand and wrist.

Lucia clicked her tongue. "You should have come to me sooner. Come on. Let's get this cleaned up." To Naya she said, "Get me the ointment in the blue jar, third from the left on the top shelf."

Naya fetched supplies, then stood back as Lucia smeared ointment over the burn and bandaged it. "You'll want to change that twice a day. Add another layer of the cream when you do, and come back right away if anything looks off."

The woman smiled, revealing a gap where one of her front teeth should have been. "Thank you. I promise we'll pay as soon as Javen's next wages come."

Lucia returned the smile. "Don't worry yourself over it."

After the woman had thanked her again and left, Lucia turned to Naya. "When you're done here, there are some jars in the back room that need rinsing."

Naya nodded and started cleaning up the scrap bits of bandage. She'd been surprised when she first learned Lucia worked with the living more often than she did with the dead. Naya had gotten used to it, but she still didn't like watching the necromancer treat the injured. She didn't like watching the way her patients smiled and laughed with her. In these moments Naya felt the tension in Lucia's aether ease. She couldn't reconcile this smiling woman who treated coughs and scrapes with the one who'd risked Naya's soul experimenting with dangerous runes. There was too much of a contrast between them.

The shop's front bell rang again a few minutes later. Lucia frowned. "Seems we're in for a busy day."

Before Naya could respond, a wave of dark emotions slammed into her. The scissors she'd been holding clattered to the floor as the stench of panic and guilt made her stomach heave. She gripped the edge of the worktable.

"What—" Lucia began. Then her expression hardened. "Aether," she muttered. "I'll be right back." She hurried to the front of the shop.

Naya focused on the way the worktable's smooth surface pressed against her fingers, on the lingering smell of ointment, on anything that distracted her from the aether. What in creation was going on? A man shouted something, and the fear in the aether grew stronger. Naya took a step back.

"Blue, come here!" Lucia shouted before Naya could flee for the stairs. She considered pretending that she hadn't heard. "Blue!" Lucia shouted again.

Naya clenched her teeth and inched toward the front room. She found Lucia speaking with a middle-aged couple. A man with a pot belly, curly brown sideburns, and small eyes stood close enough to Lucia that his breath stirred her gray-brown hair. Beside him was a small woman with broad features. Her bottom lip trembled and her eyes were fixed on Lucia with a feverish intensity. In her arms she clutched a limp, blanket-wrapped form. A child's foot dangled from one end. Naya froze, her eyes locked on the foot.

"I will not make promises I cannot keep. After the fall you described, it may be difficult to find bones still whole enough to hold a bond," Lucia said calmly. "You may take her elsewhere if you wish, but time will be your greatest enemy now."

"They say you're the best," the man said, his voice rough with emotion. "Can you do it or not?"

"I will do everything in my power, but we should—"

"Just take her," the woman interrupted. "Please. If there's still a chance, just take her."

"I will. Of course. Blue, please take the child."

"What?" But before Naya could say anything else, the woman was pressing the blanket-wrapped thing into her arms. It felt cold, heavy, and terribly stiff.

Lucia directed her into the back room and shut the door behind them. "Set her down on the table there."

Naya could only stare at the flat metal surface. Horror rose inside her, steady as a crawling tide consuming the shore. She couldn't seem to think past the weight of the bundle in her arms.

"I said set her down!"

Naya lurched forward and slid the corpse—the girl—onto the table. The blanket caught on the corner, pulling away from her head. Thankfully the child's eyes were closed. Tangled brown hair spread out around her once-pretty face. At first glance she might have been sleeping. Then Naya noticed the way her features drooped to the right where her skull had caved in.

"Move." Lucia pushed Naya to one side. She pulled back the blanket, exposing the rest of the girl's broken body. The girl still wore a knee-length blue skirt and a blouse with bits of lace around the collar. There was blood on the lace, and one of the girl's arms lay bent at an impossible angle. Gently, Lucia prodded the girl's limbs and torso. "Right femur still seems whole," she muttered. "Good—that's good." She caught Naya's gaze.

"Go back and talk to the parents. Tell them I should be able to salvage enough bones to make the binding. It will take one day to extract the bones and make the carvings, and another for the singing. Answer any questions they might have. I need you to keep them calm and keep them from interrupting me."

"Me?" Naya's voice was tiny. Lucia didn't answer. She was already halfway across the room, gathering tools from the drawers under the counter. "I don't have any idea what to tell them."

"I don't care what you tell them. Just keep them calm and keep them out of my way. I don't intend to lose this girl."

But she's already lost. That was what Naya wanted to say, except the words wouldn't come out. Lucia crossed the room with absolute certainty, assembling her tools next to the girl's body. Naya tried to remember the death rites the keepers back home had chanted, the ones that would guide a soul to its final place in the light. But in the weeks since she'd come to Ceramor, everything had gotten muddled in her head. She couldn't find those words, which had once rung with absolute truth. All she could think about were the dark tides she'd plunged into after the poison dart had found her neck.

Naya spun away from the corpse and walked numbly toward the front room. There she found the girl's parents waiting in a set of chairs by the door. The girl's father rose as soon as he saw Naya. "What does she say? Can she bring Jesla back?"

Naya stared at them. The girl's mother clutched a handkerchief in her white-knuckled grip. The father stood tall and stern, but there was an unhealthy pallor to his features. In their eyes shone a strange mix of grief and hope. "Miss Lucia thinks there are still enough bones to make a bond, but it will take a couple of days."

"Should we . . . Should we go back there?" the woman asked.

Naya's mind conjured images of the tools she'd tried so hard to ignore, the knives and scrapers and jars of acid. "It would probably be better if you didn't." She kept the shake out of her voice, but only just.

The man licked his lips. "Of course." All the bluster had gone out of him. "When it happened, we wanted to go with something less extreme. But Master Essuran said with the damage to her head he couldn't hope to bind her soul and body back together."

"Not that we have anything against wraiths," the woman said, giving Naya a look that suggested she at least guessed what she was. Naya could only nod in reply. They were both staring at her now, silently, like they expected some sort of answer from her. But she had nothing to give them.

"I think maybe it would be better if you waited at home." The girl's parents shared a hesitant glance, so Naya added, "If you leave your address, Miss Lucia can send someone to get you when she's done."

"Shouldn't we . . ." the woman began, but her husband was already standing.

"No, Silvia, the girl is right."

Naya retrieved a pen and paper from the reception desk and recorded the address.

"Two days, you said?" the man asked.

"Yes."

Finally they left. Even after they were gone, the aether in the room still stank of their guilt and worry. Naya wrapped her arms around her chest, her mind filled with the vision of the girl's foot dangling from the blanket. It was the first time she'd ever seen anyone dead. How absurd. She lived in a city full of resurrected. She was dead herself. She shouldn't be bothered by a corpse. But there had been something so obviously missing from the girl. Without it she'd just been meat and bones. Had Naya looked like that when Valn brought her to Lucia?

"Blue, come here. I need your help," Lucia said through the door.

Naya thought again about the knives. She imagined them cutting into the dead girl, prying out the bones that would re-make her. She couldn't go back into that room. She couldn't watch it happen.

CHAPTER 17

Naya fled the necromancer's shop. She stumbled into blissful sunlight, sucking in deep breaths of aether and smothering her terror under the flood of mundane life. The afternoon looked exactly like every other she'd seen since waking in this strange city. People went about their days smiling, or frowning at their troubles, oblivious to the dark work going on just steps away.

Naya started walking and her feet eventually carried her to the oak-shadowed plaza across from Corten's shop. She couldn't remember deciding to come here. But the familiar sight of heat shimmering from the vents above the workroom eased the tight pain in her throat. The bell on the door chimed as she stepped inside. Naya blinked, waiting for her eyes to adjust to the dim light. The runes from the furnace tugged at her bond, but this time it didn't seem so bad. Maybe it could purge her of the grieving family's aether. Maybe if she stayed long enough, it would suck away the memory of the dead girl's mangled skull.

"Blue?"

Corten stepped out from behind the counter. His smile fell, replaced by a look of concern. Naya's lip trembled and her eyes burned with tears she couldn't shed. She dropped to a crouch, wrapping her arms around her knees and hiding her face. She tried to breathe, tried to push the image away.

She heard the soft brush of a footstep, and then Corten's hand was on her shoulder. His touch was hot, even through her shirt, as though his hands were made of the molten glass he shaped. The tightness in her throat doubled. She leaned forward until her forehead rested on his shoulder. Corten tensed, but after a moment his arms wrapped around her. He smelled of singed cloth and orange-scented soap.

"Talk to me. What happened?" Corten asked softly.

"Lucia's doing a resurrection."

A long pause. "That is her job."

"I know, but I couldn't stay. She's just a little girl, and I couldn't watch it." She pressed her lips tight to hold back a sob. "I'm sorry. I'm an idiot. I don't know why I came here." She broke from his embrace and turned away. She thought she'd finally gotten used to Ceramor's strangeness. That she'd shaken off the horror of her own death. Apparently not.

"Would you look at me?" Corten asked.

Naya drew from the quiet swirl of the shop's aether, sensing the tug of the furnace and the subtle gap of Corten's presence behind her. When she turned he was standing close enough that she could see the little flecks of gold in his dark eyes. Those eyes caught hers and held them, and Naya was struck again by a sudden urge to tell him everything. Maybe if she explained it just right, she could make him understand. She knew it was madness, but still the thought left her giddy.

Corten took her hand. His grip was gentle, as though he worried she might shatter. "I know things are complicated between you and Lucia. After what she did, I'm not surprised you didn't want to watch another resurrection."

Naya rubbed her stinging eyes. "It isn't that." She hadn't been thinking about the reaper binding when she'd run. Now a shudder passed through her. "You don't think she'd do it again?" Perhaps she should have confronted Lucia before now. If Lucia tried to resurrect more reapers, someone would surely notice.

"No," Corten said quickly, but there was a hint of worry in his eyes. "She wouldn't do that to a little girl. She's not . . . She's always been cautious. I still think there's something else going on here."

That was not a conversation she wanted to have. Naya stood a little straighter and tried to wrestle her face into a smile. "You're probably right. I'm sorry. I shouldn't have barged in like this."

"Right. Because you can see how terribly busy I was," Corten said with an exaggerated wave at the otherwise empty shop.

Naya glanced around. "Where's Matius?"

"In the back. He got a commission for a pair of custom statues and made it clear I wasn't to bother him until he's done." Corten rubbed the back of his neck. "If you wanted to stay for a while, I wouldn't mind the company."

"I do want to stay." The words slipped out before she could remind herself of all the reasons why it was a bad idea.

Corten's smile brightened. "Great." He shifted his weight from one foot to the other. "So, uh, what do you want to do?"

She thought about the way his arms had felt encircling her, and the clean smell of heat and soap on his clothes. His hand was warm and smooth in hers, and she could feel the strength lurking behind his gentle grip. She imagined him pulling her close. What would it feel like to bury her fingers in his hair, to wrap herself around him and never let go?

"Blue, I . . ." A question lurked in Corten's eyes, one so big it made her feel like she was teetering on the edge of a vast cliff.

Naya squeezed her eyes shut. *Blue.* The name hit her like a wave of cold seawater, bringing reality in its wake. Blue was the one he wanted to comfort. She was the ghost who could make him grin as they danced across the rooftops. She was also a lie. Naya stepped back and let go of Corten's hand. "You said Matius is working on a sculpture?" she asked, latching on to the first safe topic she could come up with. "Are all of these his?" She gestured at the glass figures lining the walls.

Corten blinked, then looked quickly away. Naya told herself it was only her imagination that painted the shadow of disappointment across his eyes. "Most of them. Do you want to take a closer look?"

Naya nodded. She'd been to the shop more than a dozen times since she'd met him, but usually they'd spent their time out in the city, or in Corten's small room on the second floor. At first glance the sculptures looked nonsensical. But as Naya examined them she saw the way their curves came together, the light runes carved in the bases illuminating the flowing shapes. "Are any of them yours?"

"A couple," Corten said after a pause.

"Could I see them?"

He turned away. "If you want. Just . . . don't expect too much." He led her to the back of the room and gestured at two smaller sculptures sitting on a shelf. The first was a simple sphere with blurs of colored glass in the middle that looked vaguely like a flower. The second was a bird, its half-furled wings tinted blue.

"That one's nice," Naya said, pointing at the bird. "Is it a duck?"

Corten let out a humorless laugh. "It was supposed to be a gull, but I guess it doesn't look much like one. And you don't have to lie. I know they're awful."

"They're not . . ." Naya started to say, then stopped when she saw the tension in his jaw. "If you hate them so much, then why have them out here?"

"Matius insisted. He's got this speech about how I need to develop my own style and celebrate my successes." His voice had deepened in approximation of Matius's. "And I'm trying, but some days I feel like my mother was right. Maybe I should stick to plates and glasses."

Silence fell as they stared at the duck-gull. "What's she like?" Naya asked.

"Who?"

"Your mother. I've never heard you talk about your family. They're not . . . ?"

"Dead?" Corten snorted. "No. But they've been distant ever since I lost my apprenticeship with Lucia."

Naya frowned. "That's horrible."

Corten picked up the bird, running his fingers over the glass. "It's complicated."

"Sorry." Naya looked away. "I shouldn't have brought it up." She recognized all too well the careful lack of inflection in his tone. Her family had never been simple either.

"It's all right." Corten said. "My parents aren't cruel. I just couldn't be what they wanted anymore after I died."

"What do you mean?"

Corten shrugged. "My family can trace their bloodlines back to the founding of Ceramor. I'm their eldest son, so I was supposed to carry on that bloodline as soon as they found me a suitable heiress to wed."

"Oh," Naya said, realizing the implications. Corten had lost not just his ability to sing souls back when he died, but also any chance he had at children. "But still, you're their son."

"It's not as though they disowned me. And in a way it was a relief not having to live up to all that anymore. My parents named my brother Bernel the family heir. Ever since, my mother's been sending letters hinting how lovely it would be if I would just come home. I think she sees me having a wonderful future as Bernel's secretary. I still don't really know what I want to do, but I know I'd rather die again than spend the rest of my life managing Bernel's appointments. So I decided to stay in Belavine, find something else I could be good at." He flicked the sculpture's beak. "Or try to be good at, anyway."

Naya leaned toward him, bumping his shoulder gently. She smiled when his eyes met hers. "Well," she said, "I'm sure if a duck and a gull ever had a chick, it would look exactly like that. Perhaps you're just ahead of your time."

Corten's laugh sounded a little forced, but it helped lessen the tight feeling in Naya's chest. "I'll keep that in mind." After a moment his expression grew serious. "I know you aren't comfortable with necromancy. But whatever you saw back at the shop, you have to know that Lucia is doing it to help that little girl."

"Like she was helping me?" Naya couldn't keep the bitterness from her tone.

Corten rubbed the back of his neck. "I've watched Lucia resurrect dozens of people. I don't know why she used those runes on you, but she didn't just do it on a whim. Unless she's become a different person since I worked with her, the only thing on her mind right now is how she can get that girl back to her family."

"I know," Naya said. That much had been clear from the look in Lucia's eyes.

Nothing in Ceramor was as simple as she'd once thought. Naya still wasn't sure why Lucia had made her a reaper. But Lucia obviously cared deeply for her other patients. And Corten and Matius were nothing like the monsters she'd once feared. Still, that didn't mean her father and Valn were wrong to protect the treaty. The last war had proved how dangerous necromancy could be when a country treated its dead like weapons. If Lucia was willing to experiment with reaper bindings right under the nose of the Talmiran ambassador, then how many others would do the same? How much worse would it get if the treaty restrictions were lifted?

The furnace room door opened and Matius strode out. "Corten! That back rune plate finally gave out. I'm going to need you to go talk to Anessa and see if the replacement is ready yet." He noticed Naya and smiled. "Well hello, Blue. How are you?"

"I'm well," Naya said, relieved at the interruption.

"Good. What brings you our way this fine afternoon?" His eyes flickered to Corten as he spoke. Something about his tone brought a flush to Naya's cheeks. The memory of Corten's arms around her resurfaced, and she was suddenly very glad Matius hadn't come out any earlier.

"She was just—" Corten began.

"I came to look at the sculptures," Naya finished quickly.

"Oh?" Matius's brows rose. "Did you see anything you like?"

"I . . . Yes, actually." Naya took the bird from Corten's hands. "This one."

"I see." Matius's face broke into a wide grin.

"You don't have to do that," Corten said, shoving his hands in his pockets.

"Bah. My apprentice is a terrible salesman. Don't listen to him." Matius plucked the sculpture from Naya's hands. "Give me a moment and I'll wrap this for you."

"How much is it?" Naya pulled out her small coin purse, painfully aware of how light it was. She'd only had a few tin bits on her when she'd fled the shop.

"No charge," Corten said, not meeting her eyes. "If you really want it, then take it. Call it a gift."

Matius pulled a sheet of brown paper from under the counter. "Corten, I will still be needing you to go ask after that rune plate."

"I should get back to Lucia," Naya said in response to Corten's glance. She tried to keep a smile on her face even though her insides rolled at the thought of going back.

Matius finished wrapping the bird and handed it to her. "Well, hopefully we'll be seeing you again soon."

"Are you sure you're all right?" Corten asked as he walked her to the door.

"No, but running away won't help. Besides, you have work

to do." And she still felt dizzy and uncertain from what had happened—what had almost happened—when they'd been alone. She imagined Celia scowling, and some of her calm returned. She couldn't let herself get distracted. In just a few hours she would need to be ready for whatever the old spy had planned.

"I'll see you later?" Corten asked.

"Yes. And thank you," Naya said, gesturing to the paper-wrapped bird. "Whatever you think, I really do like it."

"You're welcome." Corten looked like he wanted to say more. Instead he ducked his head and shoved his hands back in his pockets. "When you get back, make sure Lucia eats something. She always forgets when she's carving a new bond."

"I will."

Naya took her time getting back to the shop. She wandered the neighborhood until the light began to fade, trying hard not to think about Corten and all the lies she'd told him, or about the doubts that threatened to spread like cracks through her soul.

Before returning, she armed herself with a bag of fresh rolls from Lucia's favorite bakery, a wedge of cheese, and a pair of oranges. She steeled herself at the door, half expecting to find the workroom drenched in blood and bits of cut-up flesh. But it looked mostly the same as when she'd left. Lucia had covered the girl's body with a blanket. Naya skirted past it to where Lucia sat on a stool at the back counter.

Papers covered in runes and diagrams were spread around Lucia. At their center lay a bone that looked like it might have come from the girl's leg. Lucia's tools made tiny scraping noises as she cut the runes layer by layer. Naya set the package of food outside the circle of documents. "Would you like me to make you some tea?" she asked.

Lucia spared neither Naya nor the food a glance. "No."

"Then should I—"

"Please, I'm in no mood for your charade. You can't help. It was foolish of me to ask earlier. For a moment I forgot our situation. All I ask is that you stay away until the singing is done. This girl's life has nothing to do with your master's schemes."

Naya's smile disappeared and her insides went cold. She hadn't seen Lucia like this since the night at the café. "Corten said you'd need food. It's over there."

"Corten. So that's where you went. I told you not to drag him into this mess. He's suffered enough."

The cold in Naya's stomach flashed hot. This was what she got for trying to be nice? "I didn't drag him into anything. You sent me to him. I only went back because you wouldn't teach me what I needed to know. Oh, and by the way, he figured out your little secret. He knows what you did to my bond, and he wants to help me."

The scrape of Lucia's knife stopped, and silence filled the room. "Just go," Lucia said softly.

CHAPTER 18

Naya ran back to her room. Lucia's words burned at her, all the worse for the twisted scraps of truth in them.

She tore the paper off the glass bird and stared at it. The black eyes were a little uneven, but there was something charming about the way the corners of its beak turned up, like it was smiling. She closed her eyes and imagined Corten's fingers moving over the glass.

If she was using him, it was only because she had to. Lucia and Corten were Ceramoran. They couldn't see the dangers. Corten insisted that King Allence wasn't like his father and that Ceramor's people only wanted peace. But her murderer hadn't wanted peace. And in her trips with Celia she'd seen rune wards going up on houses across the city. The loudest supporters of necromancy were turning their homes into fortresses. Why do that if peace was all they wanted?

Naya set the bird down carefully next to the trunk at the end of her bed. She changed into the clothes Celia had provided—black pants and dark-gray shirt, along with a light hooded jacket and a cap. Naya ran her fingers over the supple fabric. It was unusual for women to wear pants in Belavine. She'd seen a few women down around the docks wearing them, but these weren't dockworkers' clothes, and they weren't the sorts of things Blue could be seen wandering around in. After a pause she undid the clasp on her necklace and tucked it away in the bottom of the trunk.

She pulled out her tiny hand mirror and watched as her face shifted into Blue's features. Once she was sure she hadn't messed anything up, she opened her window and pushed back the shutters. The night air pressed pleasantly cool and damp against her face. She tucked her now-black hair under her cap and pulled the cap low on her forehead. After taking a moment to double-check her disguise in the mirror, she crawled out onto the roof. From there she jumped to the next building, and then the next.

She reached the meeting spot several minutes later. The street was dark and deserted save for a couple strolling along the far end of the block. But after a moment she picked out a familiar flow in the aether: cool and tightly controlled. Celia.

She found the older spy lurking between two houses, frowning as Naya approached. Naya formed the hand signal Celia had taught her so she could recognize Naya despite the new face. Celia nodded once in response. She was dressed similarly to Naya but managed to look far more comfortable than Naya felt.

"Did the necromancer see you leave?" Celia asked.

"No. She's doing a resurrection. I doubt she'll spare a thought for me until it's done."

"Good. We cannot afford her questioning your absence— not tonight."

Excitement shot down Naya's back like a shiver. "Why? What are we doing?"

"We discovered one of King Allence's advisers plotting to forge a secret treaty with Banen to ensure they'll vote against us at the next meeting of the Congress," Celia said. "At first we assumed these plans were only in the beginning stages. But it seems our enemies are moving quickly. Our target has suddenly scheduled a visit to the Banen Islands. Ambassador Valn believes this man intends to meet with his allies to formalize the deal. We will ensure he doesn't reach his ship."

Naya's eyebrows rose. The Banen Islands lay far to the northwest. Their navy was twice that of Talmir's. If the rulers of Banen were swayed to the necromancers' cause, the Silmarans would likely follow. It would be the beginning of the encirclement her father had always feared. "Our allies wouldn't just betray us like that, would they?"

"I can't say. Our job is only to make sure that deal never gets signed. Assessing loyalties is for Ambassador Valn and his colleagues."

"But won't they just send someone else? Won't people notice if one of the king's advisers goes missing?"

Celia's frown deepened toward a grimace. "They will notice, yes. But we suspect King Allence may not yet be aware of the treaty. Removing the writer will slow the process, if not kill it outright. Ambassador Valn has deemed the risks acceptable."

Naya felt like she'd been plunged from a rocking deck into icy waves. But this was what she'd been waiting for: a chance to prove she could be trusted.

"I have a task for you," Celia said. "But if you do not feel you are ready . . ."

Naya squeezed her hands into fists. "I'm ready."

"Good. Then follow me and do exactly as I say. I wanted to wait before trying you on this sort of work, but we no longer have the luxury of time. Our target has to be gone by morning, and our resources in this city are stretched thin."

Celia led her through the twisting streets, keeping to the shadows. Naya tried to match her teacher's casual stride as they traveled downhill toward one of the wealthy neighborhoods near the summer palace.

After perhaps twenty minutes, they found two dark-clad figures waiting for them in an alley. Their faces were covered by hoods and black scarves so only their eyes showed. Celia produced a pair of similar scarves and wrapped one over her nose and mouth before handing the other to Naya.

"This is the dead girl?" one of the other spies asked.

Celia nodded. Naya struggled to keep her expression neutral as she wrapped the scarf. *The dead girl.* Was that all she was to the other Talmirans? She didn't need to see their expressions to know the answer. Suspicion and tension radiated off of them like the sharp-sour reek of sweat.

"I need you to find the rune wards on the house there with the balcony." Celia pointed toward a house across the street that was surrounded by green lawns and a tall, spiked iron fence.

Naya concentrated on the aether, burying the sting of the other spies' doubts. Action was the simplest way to prove her loyalty. "There's one on the fence. The runes repeat along the upper spikes, but it looks like the central binding is five feet from the left corner, buried maybe four inches down." The six-foot iron bars surrounding the front yard glowed bright with aether. Whatever the ward was, it was powerful.

Celia cursed softly. "Jer, Ral, how fast can you dig those?"

The one who'd called Naya "the dead girl" scratched his chin through his scarf. "Maybe a couple of minutes. More if our friend there has been tampering with the dark stuff."

"Do it cautious," Celia said. "I'll keep watch up the street."

"And the girl?"

"Stays here. We'll need her for the door."

"What door?" Naya asked. Having to feel the others' disdain was bad enough. She wouldn't let them talk about her as though she weren't there.

The third agent raised his eyebrows and gave Naya an evaluative look. "Celia, doesn't she—"

"Enough," Celia cut in. "We've got a great deal to do and precious little time to do it in. Blue, I'll explain your part when we come to it. Keep your senses open and let me know if you feel anyone else coming." Celia passed Naya a familiar palm-size bone disk scribed with runes. If Naya activated the runes, it would cause the paired disk in Celia's pocket to vibrate, alerting her that Naya had found a threat.

Naya drew more aether as the three agents inched forward. She tasted something sharp and coppery and her nose wrinkled. "Wait!" she whispered.

The others froze. Naya squinted, trying to pick out the source of the unsettling emotions. "Someone's watching us from the other side of the street. There. I think it's coming from that carriage."

Celia relaxed a fraction. "One of ours. Don't worry about him." Before Naya could say anything else, the others darted toward their designated tasks. The two men crossed the street and crouched next to the fence to dig down to the runes powering the wards. Once they had them exposed, they would hopefully be able to damage the central runes enough to disable them without triggering the ward. Naya tried to smother her unease as she searched for other signs of life. Everyone else nearby seemed to be sleeping, but she couldn't make out anything more than a street or so away. Beyond that was only the steady pulse of the city, beating against her, threatening to drown her if she let it.

Finally, one of the men across the street flashed a hand signal indicating their work was done. Naya hurried to meet them. Celia returned, then motioned for the group to follow her over the fence. No lights came on in the house when they vaulted the iron spikes and dropped into the soft grass. No one shouted at them from the street. Nothing was out of place in Celia's plan. So why did Naya's dread only grow as they approached the house?

"Other runes?" Celia asked, pausing just before the front step.

Naya's brow furrowed. "Strange. There's something on the windows, but the door looks clean."

Celia crept forward. One hand dipped into her pocket and returned with a delicate set of lock picks. In the space of a few breaths, Naya heard the muffled click of a latch turning. Celia tried the knob but didn't look surprised when the door wouldn't open. "I was afraid we'd find this. He must have installed a dead bolt inside. Blue, I'm going to need you to reach through and turn it. One of our watchers thinks there may be a salma wood plate, but it should be thin enough for you to push through."

Naya tensed. "I thought salma wood was impenetrable to aether."

"If it's thick enough. But I've been told our friend here doesn't have the funds for anything that could completely keep you out."

Naya eyed the door warily. If it was made partially of salma wood, that could explain the lack of runes. But why bother with something so expensive if it wasn't thick enough to stop her? She could feel the other spies' impatience like an itch on the back of her neck, so she pushed the question aside.

She peeled off her jacket and scarf and rolled up her sleeves as far as they would go. Even with her new face, she felt instantly exposed. She pressed her right hand against the wood and concentrated until her arm faded. Her fingers sank a half inch before pressing against the icy barrier of the salma wood. Naya hissed through her teeth as needle pricks of cold spread up her arm. Every instinct told her to pull away from the pain. Instead she pushed harder.

Pain flashed through her bones, an echo of the chill spreading past her shoulder. Naya gasped, then felt her fingers slip reluctantly past the barrier. The pain intensified as her wrist, then her forearm, disappeared past the door. Before she could lose her nerve, she forced her face through the barrier as well.

The room beyond the door was dark, and the freezing pain made it hard to think. Naya searched for the doorknob and spotted a latch just below the keyhole. She reached out, her fingers passing right through the brass. *Damn it.* It felt almost like the wood was sucking the life from her. She drew in more aether and grunted with effort as the tips of her fingers solidified. Slowly, the lever turned. The grinding of the tumbler vibrated in her head. The click when it finally snapped into place sounded loud enough to wake the whole house. Naya pulled herself out of the door, stumbling down the front step and gasping in aether. Her right arm tingled and the bone in her hand ached, but the fresh surge of aether smothered the pain.

Celia tried the knob again, and this time the door opened. She nodded to the others, then paused, frowning at Naya. "You've lost your face."

Horror shot through Naya as she imagined herself faceless, a wispy monster like the ones that had haunted her nightmares as a child. But when she reached up, she found her cheeks and nose solid. It was Blue's face she'd lost. The shock of the door had broken her concentration, and her features had reverted to their old shapes. Naya tried to restore the change. For a moment her skin prickled, but the feeling was followed by a stab of pain in her hand. Naya bit back a frustrated curse. "Give me a moment, I'll get it back."

Celia shook her head. "We don't need you for the rest. Wait round the other side, by the carriage. Keep yourself out of sight," she whispered.

"Please, I can still help you."

"No." The look in Celia's eyes made it clear that further argument would be pointless. "If all goes well, we will meet you there."

CHAPTER 19

Naya watched her mentor disappear into the house. Disappointment welled inside her. *Stupid.* She didn't even know what the rest of the plan was. Those other spies had probably trained for years. And here she was sulking like a child because they wouldn't let her tag along. Naya reached for her mother's necklace, then remembered she'd left it at Lucia's shop. She put on her coat and scarf, then crept around the edge of the house, toward the carriage and the man whose aether bore the copper tang of blood. She could just see him, a slouching figure waiting on the other side of the fence.

Seconds crawled by and the yard remained silent. Naya slunk a little deeper into the shadows beneath a wide stone balcony and tucked her hair back under her cap. She closed her eyes and tried to sense Celia and the others. The aether inside the house had the hazy feel of people sleeping. Woven into that, though, she sensed a peppery tendril of adrenaline. That had to be Celia and the other agents. But when Naya reached further, she sensed another group somewhere else in the house, also watching, also anticipating an attack. *Guards?*

Her eyes snapped open. There wasn't any fear or anger, so the two groups hadn't noticed each other yet. Did Celia know about the guards? She hadn't said anything, and none of the spies had been armed with anything more dangerous than a short knife. If they didn't know, then Naya had to warn them. She pulled the signal disk from her pocket but froze before turning the outer edge. If Naya used the disk, Celia would likely assume whatever threat she'd found was outside. Naya had to get inside.

She made it two steps before a muffled shout sounded from somewhere in the house. Naya froze. The carriage driver turned like a hound catching a scent. A long moment later a crash came from above as someone kicked the balcony doors open. The carriage driver sprang from his seat and bolted for the fence. Someone else shouted, the sound transforming into a scream of pain.

"Below!" Celia called out from the balcony. The top of her head appeared over the railing, and her eyes met Naya's as she shoved something large and white over the edge of the balcony. Naya lunged forward, holding out her arms to catch the thing. She had just enough time to register its size—it was bigger than she was—before it slammed into her. Some part of the thing scraped against her face as she caught it, dragging her scarf down. She collapsed to her knees, and her left hand ached as her body burned aether to keep from crumpling further under the sudden burden. When she looked down, horror mingled with her shock. A body. Only his face was exposed, the rest of him wrapped up in what looked like a repurposed bedsheet. He was an older man with a bristling gray mustache and a pudgy face that sagged, expressionless.

The body groaned, and Naya fought back a yelp of surprise. He was alive.

"Bring him here, damn you!" the carriage driver shouted. He was doing something to the latch on the back gate. Naya started toward him, legs unsteady with her burden. She'd only covered half the distance when she heard someone running toward her from the front of the house. She turned to see a boy in a dressing gown rounding the corner. By his unshaved face he looked to be Naya's age, or perhaps a bit younger. Sleep-mussed hair fell partway over his eyes, and he held a sword out before him.

"Stop!" The boy looked almost comical as he raised his weapon high and charged at Naya. His arms were spindly, the muscles shaking under the weight of what looked like an antique blade more suited to hanging on a wall than cutting people down.

Naya took a hesitant step back, more confused than frightened by the sudden assault. Who was this boy? And where was Celia? Had the guards gotten her? Naya knew this wasn't the time for such questions. She needed to do something. Lights were coming on in the house, and in the houses nearby. She took another step backward toward the gate, the weight of the body making her stumble. The boy was almost upon her.

Something pulled hard at the aether just behind her, and the snap of breaking metal cut through the night. Hot blood splattered Naya's cheek.

She blinked, and then her eyes locked on the gaping hole that had appeared in the boy's chest. She had to clench her jaw to keep from screaming. The carriage driver ran to her, the runes on his pistol dull where the metal plate had snapped. "Help me with him," he snarled as he grabbed Naya's shoulder and shook.

She blinked, staring at the weapon. She'd never seen one up close. How could something so small do so much damage? The carriage driver cursed under his breath, shoving Naya one more time before trying to haul the unconscious man from her arms. The motion dragged her back to the present, and she looked up at the driver. He had a lean face, the bottom half of which was covered by a black scarf. His eyes locked on hers, cold and determined. Fear lanced through Naya's chest. She shifted her grip so the driver could grab the old man's legs.

With the driver's help she hauled the old man into the cab of the vehicle.

The driver slammed the iron gate shut behind her and pulled a thick metal rod with a reinforced handle from his pocket. Heat runes glowed as aether rushed into the rod. The tip ignited a dusky red, and the smell of hot metal filled the air as he pressed the device to the gate's broken latch, melting it in place.

"Run," he said.

"But what about—"

"Just run. The rest isn't your business." He jumped into the driver's seat and whipped the horses forward. Naya glanced back. She saw movement in the front yard and thought she caught a glimpse of a dark shape scaling the fence near the front of the house. From the sound of things, the whole house had been roused by the chaos. Someone she didn't recognize was running toward the back gate, toward her. Naya forced her tired legs to move. She sucked in more aether, then picked a road leading opposite the direction the carriage had gone. She wasn't sure if anyone else had seen it pull away, but if they came after her, she didn't want to risk leading them back to their target.

Dark buildings flashed by. Naya tried to keep the bay on her right as she fled. Her world narrowed to the slap of cold stone against her feet and the next bend in the road. Left, right, straight: no questions, no looking back. All she had to do was keep running. Keep running and—her foot caught on a loose stone and she tumbled forward with a cry. The fall sent another painful jolt through her hand, and for a while all she could do was lie there, waiting for her vision to stop blurring.

Slowly, her mind refocused. Cool paving stones pressed against her. Waves slapped softly on the shore not far to her right. The air stank of fish and rotting vegetables. Naya dragged herself to hands and knees, then leaned back against the rough brick wall of a warehouse and carefully drew in more aether.

The pain in her hand faded a little. She glanced back the way she'd come. So far as she could tell, the nearby streets were silent and empty.

She'd done it. She'd gotten away. She'd gotten the man into the carriage. That had been the goal, hadn't it? She should have felt happy, or at least relieved. But her mind filled with images of the boy, his chest a bloody gaping hole. She wanted to throw up, but there wasn't anything to throw up, no relief for the sickness pulsing through her. She rubbed her hands against her pants, trying to wipe away the worst of the blood and grime.

The carriage driver had shot the boy without hesitation. The scene played again and again in her head. Blood spurting out, hot and metallic. The look in the boy's eyes. The cloud of fear surrounding him as he fell. Who was he? She shouldn't feel sorry for him. He'd been her enemy. He'd been attacking her, no matter how pathetic that attack had seemed at the time. And besides, someone would surely have him resurrected. It wasn't as though he'd stay dead.

Of course, he might not have died at all if she hadn't been so useless. If she'd gotten the old man out faster, then maybe the carriage driver wouldn't have shot the boy. Or if she'd managed to warn Celia about the guards, maybe they could have escaped without waking anyone. Naya extracted the bone rune from her pocket and glared at it. *Too slow. Always too slow.* With a growl of frustration, she forced aether into the runes. Her bones ached in protest, but she ignored the pain, drawing more energy and feeding it into the runes. The bone disk vibrated harder and harder until it exploded with a loud crack. Shards flew in every direction, snagging her clothes and bouncing off the wall behind her.

Naya stared at her palm. A few of the shards had embedded themselves in her hand. Shame singed her cheeks as she thought about what might have happened if she'd been holding the disk in her left hand instead of her right. She let her palm turn transparent, and the shards clattered to the stones.

She closed her eyes, trying to figure out what to do next. As she did, a new fear whispered for attention. She touched the scarf that had fallen around her neck when she'd caught the old man.

The boy had seen her face. Not Blue's face, but the one she wore every day while working in Lucia's shop. If they resurrected him, and she was certain they would, he would tell everyone about the girl he'd seen. The city guard would spread the description, and sooner or later Corten and Lucia would hear it. The thought of Corten learning what she'd done hit her like a kick to the stomach.

She couldn't let that happen. Naya pushed herself to her feet, leaning against the rough wall. She tried to force the sickness back. She needed to stop panicking and think. Had Celia and the others gotten out? She knew she'd seen at least one other person fleeing. If they were still free, then they would probably scatter among the network's safe houses. Naya only knew of the one at Selleno's house, and it didn't seem a good idea to run around the city looking for others. The earliest she could hope for information would be tomorrow. By then someone should have reported back to Valn at the embassy.

She examined her dirty clothes. She needed a plan. She couldn't undo what had happened at the house. Something had gone wrong inside. Someone had sounded an alarm, and that boy had seen her face.

But it would be a couple of days before anyone could resurrect him. Even then there was a chance the boy wouldn't be able to give a clear description. It had been dark outside the house and he'd had only a few seconds to see her before the bullet stopped him. She had to get to safety, then get in touch with Valn or Celia or someone before the boy was resurrected. They would know what to do.

Naya looked up at the stars, which were just visible through a ragged layer of high clouds. Celia had gotten out or she hadn't. The mission had succeeded or it hadn't. The boy would remember her or he wouldn't. She locked the image of him, confused and scared while his life pumped out through his gaping chest, away in a box. Then she imagined shoving that box into the farthest corner of her mind.

CHAPTER 20

Naya walked back to Lucia's shop, feeling as tired and miserable as she had when she'd first learned her father had abandoned her in Ceramor. Then, a block from her destination, she sensed something strange in the aether. She paused. Normally aether drifted and swirled through the city like a fine glowing mist. But here it flowed purposefully toward Lucia's shop.

The singing. How had she forgotten? Inside the workroom, Lucia would be using her magic to tear a hole between the living world and the void. Through the song she'd guide the dead girl's soul toward the rift, then bind the girl to her bones. Naya took a step back. The pull of the rift would probably be even worse inside. She didn't want to feel the touch of death's black tides, didn't even want to think about it. Especially not when she'd seen someone else thrown into that place only hours ago.

Naya steadied herself against a nearby wall. Singing or no, she needed to get inside and change out of these clothes—then destroy them—before anyone came looking for her. She gathered her courage and hurried on. She unlocked the back door and eased it open, peering into the dark hall that connected the stairs and the workroom.

Inside, Lucia sang. The rising and falling notes formed

strange chords that seemed to linger in the air. Naya didn't recognize the words, but she could guess their meaning. *Come, come to me.* She clenched her jaw and slunk toward the stairs. As she passed the workroom doorway, she glimpsed Lucia sitting cross-legged on the floor. Flickering oil lamps illuminated the runes chalked on the stone in front of her. In the center of those runes, the portal between life and death made the air shimmer and writhe. The color leached from Naya's sight as she tore her gaze away from the scene. The portal's tug was like a thousand tiny hands clutching at her. It was as though something lurking on the other side had noticed her and sought to pull her back through.

Five steps between her and the stairs, then three. The tug lessened as she started to climb. By the time she got to her room, it was no worse than a persistent whisper. Unsettling but hopefully not dangerous. Naya flexed her sore hand, winced, then began peeling off her soiled clothes.

She passed the night in a half trance, drawing in aether in sips and running her fingers over the glass bird Corten had given her. She tried to keep her thoughts from straying back to the night's chaos, instead imagining gulls calling above the sunny docks where she used to play when she was small.

Lucia's song stopped sometime around midmorning. For a long while there was silence, broken only by the soft sounds of Lucia moving in the shop below. Naya listened with growing frustration. She needed to get to the furnace and burn her bloody clothes, but she couldn't go downstairs with Lucia there.

Voices murmured below. Another minute dragged by and the stairs creaked.

"Blue?" Lucia asked through her door.

Naya considered not answering, but antagonizing Lucia further seemed pointless. She had bigger things to worry about. "What?"

"Come here, please." The last word sounded hesitant, almost apologetic.

Naya glanced down at herself. Even after changing, she half expected to see flecks of blood stuck to her hands and her hair—or maybe smeared onto the fresh clothes from the old. But she'd been careful. Her skin and dress showed no sign of the night's activities.

Lucia stood in the hallway, holding the hand of a pretty young girl. "This is Jesla," Lucia said. "Jesla, this is Blue."

The girl cocked her head to one side as she stared up at Naya. Naya struggled to reconcile the curiosity in the girl's expression with the inanimate, battered corpse of the day before. "Hello," she managed, not sure what else to say.

"Hello," Jesla said.

"Jesla is adjusting very well, but I want you to keep an eye on her for a few hours while I rest."

"I said I don't need—" the little girl began.

"Once I've recovered," Lucia continued over the objections, "I can send a messenger for her parents." Lucia's eyes drooped. She must have been awake since the girl's body was brought to them. "Will you do this?"

Anger kindled in Naya's chest as she remembered their last conversation. "Are you sure you trust me getting involved?"

Lucia's lips pressed thin, as though she were struggling to hold back her reply. Naya waited, almost eager to hear her yell. But when Lucia spoke, her tone was soft and carefully devoid of emotion. "I misspoke last night. We all do what we must. Right now this girl should not be alone."

Guilt dampened Naya's anger. Lucia was obviously trying to hide her exhaustion, but she looked ready to drop.

"I can watch her." It would give her an excuse to stay inside for a few hours. Maybe by then she could figure out what to do next.

"Thank you. Jesla, be a good girl and do as Blue tells you." Lucia let go of Jesla's hand and gave her a gentle shove toward Naya. Then she was off, shutting the door to her bedroom firmly behind her.

Jesla rocked from her toes to her heels and back again. Lucia had clothed her in a smock-like dress. Too big by half, it fell all the way to the floor and hung lopsided over one shoulder. She stared expectantly at Naya, who felt the sudden, almost irresistible urge to look at her own feet. What was she supposed to do with the girl now? "How are you feeling?" she asked after an awkward silence.

Jesla shrugged, continuing to stare at her.

"Okay, well, if you start feeling bad, let me know and we can wake Lucia."

Jesla nodded, then after a pause said, "Blue is a pretty name."

"I . . . thanks." Naya tried to think of something else to say. She'd never been much good with children.

Jesla picked at a stray thread on her oversize dress. She was probably still buzzing with energy from the initial binding. How much had Lucia explained to her? How much would she already know from growing up among wraiths and other resurrected in Belavine? More important, what was Naya supposed to do with the girl until her parents could take her home? She might not know much, but the necromancer's shop didn't seem like a good place for a child.

"Is that your room? Can I see?" Jesla peeked around Naya's skirt. Her eyes fixed on the glass bird sitting next to the chest. "What's that? Can I hold it?"

"No!" Naya said, more loudly than she'd intended.

Jesla's eyes widened and her lower lip trembled. "Sorry," she mumbled.

Naya cursed herself silently. "It's fine. Why don't we go downstairs?"

Jesla's brows furrowed as she glanced at the stairs. "Okay."

They walked together down to the workroom, but Jesla paused in the doorway. "Is something wrong?" Naya asked.

Jesla shook her head, making her brown curls swing. Naya stepped into the workroom, but Jesla didn't follow. She stared at her feet, one hand twisting the fabric of her dress. "Do you think my mama and papa are coming here?" she asked.

Naya crouched in front of the girl. "Miss Lucia said she'd send for them when she wakes up, remember?" Maybe Naya could send for them now. The girl seemed fine, and Naya needed to get in touch with the others and learn what had happened last night. Valn and Celia still treated her like a child, giving her only whatever scraps of information they thought were relevant to her next task. She had to figure out how to change that. If she'd known more last night, maybe she could have stopped things from going so wrong.

"Oh, okay," Jesla said, still sounding unhappy.

Why had Lucia demanded they keep the girl here, anyway? She'd said something about possible complications. But if the girl needed watching, why not summon her parents to keep her company? Not that Naya wanted more strangers in the shop, but having them there would have surely lessened the girl's unease. Naya was beginning to regret saying yes to Lucia's request. Last night's memories rattled in the back of her mind, threatening to break their locks and trap her. She wanted to curl up and hide, or run to the embassy and demand answers. But Jesla was staring at her expectantly. Naya couldn't just leave her alone. "Is there anything you want to do?" she asked.

Jesla looked up and Naya followed her gaze to the bookshelves. "Read me a story?"

Naya bit her lip. She knew those books contained anatomical diagrams, runes, philosophical debates about the void and the energy of souls. "Why don't I tell you a story instead?"

"What kind of story?"

"An adventure story?"

"Like with battles and stuff?" Jesla asked, excitement glimmering in her eyes.

Naya smiled. "This one has pirates."

Jesla seemed to consider this for a moment, then nodded. "I like pirates."

The stools by the counter were too tall for Jesla, so Naya led her to the stairs and they both sat down on the first step. Jesla squeezed in right next to Naya, her brown eyes wide and expectant.

Naya leaned back and tried to remember the old stories her mother had told when she was little. "Today I'm going to tell you the story of Lady Elza Thorn. She was a great explorer who lived a long time ago. Her ship was the *Dancing Bird*, and she and her loyal crew sailed all over, discovering new places and having many adventures. This story is about her greatest voyage, when she found the lost islands of Shal Rok and defeated the pirate king Andres, winning his ships and his heart." Naya was surprised how easily the words resurfaced from the fog of memory once she began. Her mind conjured up the dense jungles of Shal Rok, the fire of the sea battles, and the gleam of buried treasure as brightly as it had when she'd been young.

She'd just gotten to the part where Elza strode across the deck of Andres's flagship to accept his surrender when there came a knock at the door. Naya looked up, blinking. The knock came again, loud enough to rattle the door in its frame. It was not the sort of knock that announced good news.

Jesla must have seen some of Naya's apprehension. "Do you think it's my parents?" she asked uneasily.

Naya stood and gave Jesla a reassuring smile. "Maybe. Wait here a minute." She reached into the aether as she approached the door, but she couldn't sense anyone on the other side. Naya frowned. *Could it be?* She pulled open the door and saw Corten standing outside, one hand raised to knock again.

"Blue? Thank the Creator. Can I . . . Who's that?"

Naya turned to see Jesla peeking out from behind her. "This is Jesla. She's the patient I told you about earlier."

"Who are you?" Jesla asked.

"I'm a friend of Blue's." Corten's eyes met Naya's, and the worry in his face made her insides go cold. "I need to talk to you."

"Jesla, would you mind waiting here while I go talk to my friend?" Naya asked.

"What about the story?"

"I'll tell you more later," Naya said. Corten glanced over his shoulder like he was looking for someone, or like he was worried someone might have followed him.

"I guess." Jesla glared at Corten suspiciously, but she didn't try to follow them as they retreated upstairs to Naya's room.

"What is it?" Naya asked, thinking she knew and praying she was wrong.

"Have you gone outside at all today?" Corten asked. Naya shook her head.

Corten dragged his fingers through his hair. "Right. Well, somebody kidnapped Salno Delence last night."

Naya raised her eyebrows in what she hoped looked like mild curiosity. "Who?" She'd heard that name before, but Blue wouldn't know about the most notorious politician in Ceramor. From everything she'd heard, he practically ran Ceramor from behind the throne.

"He's one of King Allence's advisers. His house was attacked last night. Delence's son was killed and Delence is missing. The city guard think at least one of the kidnappers was a wraith." Naya's heart sank. Delence's son. That explained the fervor in the boy's eyes when he'd attacked.

Naya reached for her necklace. "Why are you telling me this?" Could he already suspect her involvement?

"The king sent guards to question wraiths all over the city. Matius and I already had to deal with half a squad inspecting the shop and asking questions. It's only a matter of time before they come here." His expression darkened. "I know you haven't kept it a secret that you're from Talmir, so—"

"I didn't do anything!" The words tasted bitter. But if Corten put the pieces together now, she was doomed.

Corten raised one hand. "I never said you did. But think about how this looks. You haven't been in the city very long, so maybe you haven't seen it. But whenever something like this happens, everyone always blames us. They assume because we can reach through walls or disguise our faces, we're all untrustworthy. We have to talk to Lucia. They might search the shop. If she has any notes about your bond, we need to make sure she hides them or, better yet, destroys them."

He didn't suspect her. He'd come to warn her, to protect her. The realization made her feel both horribly guilty and relieved at the same time.

"Blue, did you hear me?"

Naya nodded, but she wasn't thinking about Lucia's notes. Now that her initial terror was fading, something felt wrong. Why hadn't anyone else come to warn her about the search? Could the other agents not know what was going on? It seemed unlikely. *I need to get to the embassy. Need to find out what happened to Celia.* But first she had to get rid of those clothes. If the guard showed up and found them, they'd arrest both her and Lucia. Naya wasn't about to let that happen.

The beginning of a plan tickled the back of her mind.

CHAPTER 21

"I'll make sure Lucia's ready when the guards come. You should go," Naya said to Corten.

Corten shook his head. "Believe me, you'll need help if you're going to convince her to destroy her diagrams. Lucia might be a genius, but she's an idiot when it comes to stuff like this."

"No. I don't want you to get in more trouble. I can handle Lucia. We'll be fine." Naya smiled, hoping she looked confident. Corten's eyebrows scrunched up with doubt, so she continued. "Please. You've already done more than enough by warning me. I don't want you getting into trouble if anyone finds you here."

"You're sure?"

Lucia's accusations echoed in her mind. "Certain."

Corten tugged at his curls again. "Fine. But come get me if anything happens. What about that girl downstairs?"

"I'll make sure she gets home. Her bond seems stable and I know where her parents live."

She could tell by the look in his eyes that he still didn't like it, but at least he let her pull him down the stairs and back out onto the street. He paused in the doorway, his gold-flecked eyes very close to hers. "Blue, promise me you'll be careful."

The concern in his voice was almost enough to break her,

but Naya braced herself against the pain. She could feel the thing that had been building between them, like aether drawn toward a rune. It was more than friendship that fueled his worry. But whatever he thought he felt for her couldn't be true. The girl he saw was made of lies.

"I will." She pressed one hand against Corten's chest. No heartbeat, but she did feel a steady warmth through his shirt. She closed her eyes, trying to hold on to the feeling. "Go. I'll send you a message this evening," she said. Then she pushed him gently out the door and shut it fast.

Naya found Jesla in the workshop, passing her hand back and forth through a table leg with a look of baffled concentration. Naya ran upstairs and retrieved her soiled clothes. The bloodstains were barely visible, but the front of the jacket and pants were still smeared with muck from her fall. Besides, the outfit was different enough from the rest of her clothes that it would draw suspicion even if she managed to get it clean. She balled up the black fabric and tucked the bundle under one arm.

Jesla looked up when Naya rushed into the workroom. "What's that?"

"Just something left over from Miss Lucia's work. Don't worry." The girl's eyes fixed on the bundle as Naya shoved it into the furnace and wrenched the dial on the side. The runes glowed and little flames licked at the edges of the cloth. Remembering what she'd done to the signal rune, Naya pushed a little of her own aether into the stove. She felt the runes straining as the plates glowed brighter with heat and aether, and eased back before they could break. The flames licked higher, consuming the bloody clothes. Good enough.

She found Jesla standing behind her, peering at the stove. "Will you tell me the rest of the story now?" Jesla asked.

Naya shook her head. "We'll have to save it for later. Are you still feeling all right?"

"Yes, but that thing feels all suckey. I don't like it." Jesla pointed at the little furnace, which still tugged at the room's aether.

"Well, how about I take you back to your parents?"

"But what about Miss Lucia?"

"Don't worry. I'm sure she'll be happy to have you back with them. And she can come check on you herself when she wakes up. Don't you want to see your family?"

Jesla's lips puckered into a pout and she looked down at her toes. "I don't want to go back."

"What? Why not?"

"They'll be mad at me." Jesla kicked at the floor with one bare toe.

It took Naya a second to guess what she meant. "You mean your parents? They won't be mad. They'll be happy to see you."

"Nuh uh."

"Why would they be mad at you?"

"Because I fell. Papa said I wasn't allowed to climb the tree outside my window. But the other night the stars were so bright, and I couldn't sleep." She was picking at her dress, not looking at Naya. "See, I'm really good at climbing. But the bark was kind of slippery, and it was dark, and I think one of the branches must have broke, because it wasn't there when I reached for it. And then I fell."

It must have been a tall tree to have broken her body so badly. Naya crouched down so her eyes met Jesla's. "I met your parents when they brought you here, and I'm certain they won't be mad at you. I think they'll be very happy to have you back."

Jesla looked skeptical but didn't argue as Naya prepared to leave. She scrawled a hasty note and left it on the table where Lucia would find it. *Gone to buy groceries. Back soon.* She intentionally misspelled a couple of words, crossing them out and rewriting them. If the guards came while Lucia was still asleep, the note would explain her absence. She considered going upstairs to warn Lucia, but she didn't want to risk the necromancer trying to stop her. She needed to get to the embassy and figure out what was going on. Besides, Lucia had never struck her as stupid. Any evidence of her illegal work would surely be hidden in a safe place.

While her clothes burned down to ash, Naya retrieved Jesla's address and led her to the door. Jesla dragged her feet and tried at every opportunity to distract her and pull away. Naya's nerves were frayed nearly to breaking when they finally reached Jesla's house. The building was tall and narrow, scrunched between its neighbor on the right and a plaza on the left with a huge oak tree. The branches of the tree grew out to brush against the side of the house. Naya felt Jesla shy away from it as they mounted the steps to knock on the door.

Jesla's mother answered after the third knock. Dark bags shadowed her eyes, making her look as if she hadn't gotten much more sleep than Lucia. But her exhaustion vanished under a brilliant smile when she saw Jesla. "Oh, Oslyn, come here. It's Jesla. She's back."

Footsteps pounded down the stairs and the big man Naya had met before appeared in the doorway. His curly brown sideburns were wet. Dark stubble covered half his jaw, with bits of soap still clinging to his chin. "Jesla, my girl." He grinned.

Jesla tensed, probably still waiting for her parents to scold her. But in an instant her father swept her up in an embrace. Naya saw the split second when his face twisted as he registered his daughter's nearly weightless body. Then his smile returned. Naya took a step back, feeling strangely hollow as she watched the reunion. Jesla was laughing now, and tears dampened her mother's cheeks.

Jesla's mother turned to Naya. "Where is Madame Laroke? We haven't had the chance to thank her."

"Sleeping." Naya struggled to keep her tone light. She needed to leave before her own troubles disrupted the family's happiness.

"Is everything all right, dear?" Jesla's mother asked.

"Of course. There shouldn't be any problems. But if something doesn't seem right, you should take her back to Lucia. She'll come in a bit, after she wakes, to make sure everything is well."

"Would you like to come inside?"

"Yeah," Jesla said from her perch in her father's arms. "You haven't finished the story yet."

Naya blinked her burning eyes. "I'm sorry, I can't. I have to get back to my work." She turned, pretending she didn't hear Jesla calling out as she rounded the corner. The family's smiles cut more sharply than any knife. Had her father ever smiled at her like that? No, of course not. But theirs had never been that sort of family. Naya wiped reflexively at her dry, stinging eyes. Then she turned her steps and her thoughts toward the Talmiran Embassy.

Lucia would be furious at her for leaving, and for taking Jesla back without her permission. But she could deal with that later. Naya stopped in an alley not far from Jesla's house. Once she was certain no one was watching, she closed her eyes and took a deep breath of aether. She pressed the tips of her fingers lightly to her face. She'd never tried changing her features without a mirror before, but it couldn't be that different. After a moment the skin under her fingertips went uncomfortably soft. She tried to imagine Blue's face, the sharp features and green eyes that she'd chosen for herself. Her skin shifted, then grew firm again. She ran her fingers over her nose and lips, and then through her now-black hair. Close enough. At least she was pretty sure nobody would recognize her. On the way to the embassy, she stopped at Selleno's house. But the old couple who stayed there to maintain the facade hadn't seen any of the other spies since the previous day.

As Naya left the house, she tried to figure out what had triggered the feeling of dread now lurking in the place where her stomach should have been. Maybe it was that it should have been Celia, or Valn, who had sent her a warning about the guards. Maybe it was hearing that the man she'd helped kidnap was Delence. He'd publicly supported the Treaty of Lith Lor for years. If anything, he should have been an ally in the upcoming talks. The only thing she knew for certain was that she couldn't sit in Lucia's shop waiting. She needed to figure out if Celia had gotten away. She needed to know they hadn't failed, and what it was exactly they hadn't failed at.

Even with her face changed, she couldn't banish the tingling feeling on the back of her neck, as though someone were watching her. The streets were alive with talk of the attack on Delence's house, and the wraith the guards hunted. By the time Naya stepped off the tram and onto Market Street, her unease was growing with every passing minute. She'd never imagined word would spread so fast. Every casual glance from a stranger held an accusation. *Spy. Liar. Kidnapper.*

Within sight of the embassy's white-pillared front, Naya started to relax—until she saw a familiar figure walking toward the gate. Broad shoulders covered by a fine black coat, he strode down the street as though he owned it.

Her father.

In her shock Naya tripped, almost crashing into a wealthy-looking woman in a purple silk dress. She barely heard the woman's curse. All her attention was focused on the *Gallant's* captain as he crossed the street. The crowd seemed to part around him, deferring to the aura of command that hung about him like a cloak. Naya could only stand with her mouth hanging open as a servant ushered her father into the Talmiran Embassy.

CHAPTER 22

It couldn't be coincidence that her father had returned today of all days. Why hadn't anyone told her he was coming? Naya ran across the street, stopping a few feet from the embassy's front steps. Her heart screamed for her to follow him inside. She wanted to tell him she'd done everything he'd asked. She wanted to see him nod, maybe even smile, and say he understood. But even if it weren't for the guards out searching for wraiths, she couldn't risk drawing attention to herself by waltzing through the embassy's front entrance. Instead she followed along the side of the big white house until she found a servant's door near the back. A boy, maybe the one she'd seen in the kitchens the day she met Celia, was hauling burlap sacks from a delivery cart parked near the door.

"Excuse me." Naya grabbed the boy's sleeve before he could reach for another sack. A man stood a few paces away, next to a pair of sleepy-looking donkeys hitched to the front of the cart.

"What?" The boy pulled his sleeve away and looked her up and down nervously.

"Is Celia here?"

The boy's eyes darted to the man minding the cart, then back to the door. "What's it to you?"

"Could you give her a message for me?"

"What's the message?"

"Tell her Seamstress Talla has some questions about the embroidery on the new tablecloths," Naya said, using one of the many codes Celia had taught her. Celia would recognize it and know Naya needed information.

The boy pulled his arm away, looking down at his feet. "All right. Maybe I'll tell her in a bit."

Naya saw the cart man watching them more closely now over his donkey's flicking ears. He'd probably make a fuss if the boy tried to leave before he'd finished unloading the delivery. "Do you need any help with those sacks?" she asked the boy.

Between the two of them, they had the last of the bundles unloaded in just a few minutes. With the cart rattling away, the boy disappeared inside. Naya waited by the door, trying not to look impatient. After what felt like hours, the door cracked open and Celia peered out cautiously. An ugly bruise darkened her forehead, just above her left temple. "What are you doing here?" Celia demanded.

Naya tried to remember the words she'd rehearsed silently on the walk over. But all that came out was "I need to speak with my father."

Celia glanced over her shoulder. "You can't. You shouldn't be here."

"Why not? King Allence has guards out questioning wraiths. If they find me—"

Celia made a cutting motion with one hand. "It will be a thousand times worse if they find you here."

"Then what am I supposed to do? What am I supposed to say if the guards question me? Please, just let me speak to him." She wondered what would happen if she tried to force her way past the older spy. Celia had always bested her when they'd sparred. But as her anger built, Naya felt the potential of the illegal runes like a hum in her bones.

"Go back to the shop and wait for orders. I'm sorry, but noth- ing good will come from it if Captain Garth finds you here now."

"What do you mean?"

Celia met Naya's eyes. "Go."

"No! Wait——" Naya lunged forward, her body slamming into the door a half second after it closed. She jerked the knob, but of course it was locked. When she focused, she saw a faint shimmer of runes around the frame. Could she break them? She took a step back, glancing down the narrow street to check if anyone was watching. No one yet, but there were enough people around that someone was bound to notice if she tried to smash her way inside. Naya reluctantly uncurled her fingers from the doorknob.

Celia's warning wasn't without merit. If the Ceramoran guard realized she was here, it would only draw more suspicion. Except . . . Naya wasn't wearing her old face. Nothing about her appearance would connect her to the Talmiran wraith who worked at Lucia's shop. And unless she did anything unusual, no one who looked at her should be able to tell what she was. No one living anyway. And once she was inside the embassy, the risk of discovery would be even less. The embassy grounds were protected. If the city guard tried to force their way in, the Congress of Powers could declare it an attack on Talmiran soil.

Naya turned away from the door. What had Celia meant by claiming nothing good would come from Naya meeting her father? Fear wound tight around her middle. Did Valn mean to blame her for the chaos during last night's job? Or was some- thing else going on in the embassy that Celia wanted to keep her away from? Either way, Naya couldn't leave knowing a measly wall was all that separated her from her father. She closed her eyes, trying to imagine the layout of the embassy from her last visit. Valn's office was on the other side of the building, near the back. Her father would almost certainly go there.

Naya skirted the hedge surrounding the back garden, and

stopped outside the corner where she thought Valn's office was. The narrow alley between the embassy and its nearest neighbor was empty for the moment. Naya pressed her back to the wall. She could wait for her father to leave, follow him back to the *Gallant*, and speak to him there. But there was so much he hadn't told her, and Valn had kept his secrets as well. She wanted to know what they had to say to each other.

Naya closed her eyes and leaned against the building. She focused on the aether, trying to ignore the wall. The pulse of the city grew louder. The rough wood against her back became a distant thing as the chaotic energy pressed against her. Naya sifted through it, searching for her father's energy as she'd searched for Lucia's in the café all those weeks ago.

When she found him, she almost recoiled from the rage rolling off him like black smoke. Valn was near him, his own energy a mix of anger and impatience. A moment later she caught the strange echo of their voices through the wall.

"—and how was your journey?" Valn asked.

"Don't waste my time with that act. I want to know what the hell you were thinking," her father answered, each word snapping like the lash of a whip.

"I assume you're speaking about our friend Delence? I can assure you I have it under control. His son was an unfortunate casualty. We can't stop his resurrection. But—"

"Not that," her father said. "That I can understand. Though it sounds like you nearly botched the mission all the same. I'm talking about what you did to my daughter."

Silence for a moment, then Valn spoke again. "Well, I'm not sure what else you expect me to say on the matter. You've read my report. The point was for her to disappear as all the rest did. I've arranged all the necessary documentation to prove our story."

"You're telling me that after all your talk of recruiting a wraith, she just conveniently dies?"

"You were the one who insisted on involving her. Her death was unfortunate, but I can assure you I haven't done anything that wasn't necessary to our success." After a moment Valn added, "As I recall, you didn't have any problem with what happened to the others."

"They were expendable. She was never supposed to die. You were supposed to keep her safe, hide her, and train her so she would be ready to support our plans when the time came."

In the silence that followed, Naya had to fight to keep from shrinking away. She sensed grief in her father, but it was crushed under a flood of rage and disgust. Naya couldn't block those emotions without drawing her focus back to the physical world. She felt them in her chest as though they were her own. They scraped and oozed across her skin. She tasted them in the air, an acrid, salty mix that made her want to retch.

Valn broke the tense silence. "You'd do well to consider the advantages here. The reaction so far has been exactly what we planned. Rumors about the other disappearances have spread throughout the city. No one will fault us when we call for an investigation. And as I said before, I have all the documents in order should anyone else start looking before we're ready to make our next move. Your daughter was eager to help, once I explained the situation to her. Her condition is manageable. And she'll be quite useful for the next stage of our plans."

Another silence. When her father spoke again, his voice was raw with emotion. "My daughter is dead. That thing you created is not her."

"I understand your concerns," Valn said. "But is this really the time to be debating theology? Whatever she is, she can still—"

"No," her father interrupted. "What you're proposing isn't an option. We can't afford to have anyone notice the connection between you and that necromancer. This only works if the Congress of Powers believes that King Allence is responsible."

"I'm aware of that, and I would appreciate it if you dropped the theatrics. What we're trying to achieve here is so much bigger than one dead girl. I've valued your financial support and the messages you've passed to our friends in the navy, but I won't let your overdeveloped piety destroy everything we've worked for."

Her father snarled, and there was a loud crash as something fell to the floor. "No one is more loyal to our cause than I am. But I won't sit by while you defile my daughter's memory by pretending that thing is her."

"Fine," Valn said after a pause. "I'll make sure she's disposed of. You should make your accusations tomorrow. I expect you won't have any problem putting on a convincing show for the court? These letters should explain why it's taken you so long to begin searching for your poor missing daughter and—"

Naya pushed away from the wall. She couldn't stand to hear any more. Her father's disgust flowed through her like poison. *That thing.* He'd never been soft on her. But she'd believed Valn when he said her father knew what had happened, that he understood. It had all been lies.

She stumbled down the alley and into the wide street in front of the embassy. Bright colors and smells assaulted her. She started walking, not caring where she was going. She only knew she had to get away. She couldn't listen while Valn and her father discussed her like she was some dog to be commanded or put down depending on their needs. She'd thought she was being clever by learning what Corten had to teach. She'd thought that if she fought the necromancers, it would prove that death hadn't changed her loyalties. But it didn't matter what she did. Valn had only ever seen her as a tool, and to her father she was even less than that.

The road under her feet began to slope upward. Naya walked with her eyes on the ground. She hugged her shoulders, trying to stop her father's words from echoing through her head. *That thing.* She stumbled through a gap in the crowd. Someone shouted. Naya glanced up. She barely registered the blur of red before the tram hit. The world tumbled, up and down reversing as pain seared through the bones in her hand. Her back slammed against the paving stones. Screaming metal and the stench of oil surrounded her. Then the tram passed, its brakes bringing it to a jerking halt that probably sent more than a few passengers flying forward against the rows of wooden seats.

Naya heard shouting as she struggled to regain her bearings.

"Somebody fetch a doctor."

"Creator, did you see . . ."

". . . right there. What could she have been thinking?"

When she raised herself onto her elbows, she saw people rushing toward her. She stood up before they could reach her. Her body felt strange, like it was still rippling from the force transferred by the tram. But the pain was already fading as she drew fresh aether. Her bones hadn't been anywhere near the wheels when the tram passed over her. The people inside were probably hurt worse by the sudden stop than she had been. A man's hand clamped around her wrist, and Naya felt suspicion rather than concern in his aether.

"Hold on now," he began. Naya broke away. "Hey!" the man shouted.

"I'm sorry," Naya called back. She ducked and wove through the crowd, turning into an alley, then onto another street. Everyone who'd seen her back there would realize she was a wraith. With the guard, and now maybe Valn, hunting her, the last thing she needed was to draw attention to herself. She reached up to touch her face and was relieved to find her features hadn't been shocked back to their old shape. Her clothes hadn't fared as well. Her vest and skirt were torn, and something black had smeared across one of her shirtsleeves.

Naya started walking. She checked back over her shoulder but didn't see anyone following. She slowed to a more casual pace. She was acting too conspicuous. She needed to get away from here, find someplace quiet where she could think. She kept walking uphill, away from the bustle of the market district.

She eventually stopped in a plaza near the crest of Lennia, one of the hills in the northern sector of the city. Two girls tossed a ball in the plaza's center. A group of old men lounged in the shade on the far side, smoking from deep bowled pipes and mending a pile of old clothes. Afternoon light shone golden and the aether was soft with a sense of quiet peace that helped muffle the pain in her chest. Naya sat on a bench, trying to look as small and inconspicuous as possible.

Her hands began to shake, and something between a laugh and a sob pushed its way up her throat. She should have seen this coming. She'd known how her father felt about the undead. His hatred was as deep and cold as an ocean rift. Still, she'd wanted to believe that he could see past it. Maybe if she spoke to him, he could. There had to be something she could do or say that would prove she wasn't a monster. But that fragile shard of hope was almost more painful than the memory of his disgust.

Naya squeezed her eyes shut, trying to focus on something other than the pain. Valn had told her they were working to block Ceramor in the upcoming treaty negotiations, to maintain the status quo and stop the necromancers from enticing their neighbors toward corruption. But the plans she'd overheard hadn't sounded like they had anything to do with the treaty negotiations. What had been the point of kidnapping Delence? And what had Valn meant when he said her father hadn't cared what happened to the others? Had he been talking about the other Talmirans who'd supposedly gone missing in the city?

Naya rubbed her temples, dread and exhaustion warring

inside her. She had too many questions and too little information. "What do you know?" she whispered to herself.

She knew her father now wanted her dead. She knew Valn had given in to his demands and agreed to have her killed, and that the city guard was hunting her. They might not know enough to tie her to the kidnapping yet. But if they searched Lucia's shop and found evidence of her illegal binding, they'd kill her and Lucia without a second thought.

Naya opened her eyes. One glance at the sun told her hours had passed since she'd hauled Jesla from the necromancer's shop. It felt more like a lifetime. She couldn't just sit around waiting for someone to hunt her down. She didn't know what to do next, but she wouldn't let Valn discard her like a broken tool. She'd helped him because he'd made her believe they were protecting Talmir. But even that might have been a lie. Naya watched as a young boy joined the two girls in their game of catch. Running would be her smartest option. She could leave Belavine, head out to the orchards and villages that speckled southern Ceramor. No one there would know her. If she kept moving, maybe Valn's spies wouldn't find her.

But she'd been a part of whatever her father and Valn were plotting. She'd helped them kidnap Delence. She couldn't bring herself to leave without knowing what was really going on. Naya glanced again at the sun. Would the guards hunting Delence's kidnapper already have searched Lucia's shop? Even if they'd come and gone, the shop was the first place Valn would send people to look for her. That was reason enough to avoid it. But on the other hand, Lucia was the one person Naya could think of who might have the answers she sought.

The decision settled like a hard lump in the pit of her stomach. She stood up. No more following blindly. It was past time she found out what Valn was really up to.

CHAPTER 23

Naya found Lucia pacing in her workroom, a piece of paper clasped tight in one fist. When she saw Naya her scowl flickered to confusion. "Who are you? We're closed."

For a moment Naya wondered if Lucia had lost her mind, but then she realized what the necromancer must be seeing. She concentrated and felt her face shift back to its original features. It was like relaxing a muscle she hadn't realized was tense.

Lucia's scowl returned in an instant. "Ah," she said, the single syllable flat and heavy with scorn. "So you decided to come back." Her voice got louder with each word. "What were you thinking, leaving like that? Where is Jesla?"

Naya stepped back, trying to get out of reach of Lucia's wrath. "I took her home. She's fine. Listen, we have bigger problems."

"Bigger problems?" Lucia raised her hands above her head, looking like she wanted to throw something at Naya. "What do you suppose would happen if her bond became unstable? She could fade before her parents bring her back to us. Perhaps life is cheap for you Talmirans, but here—"

"I was trying to protect her. Would you just listen? Something's happened. I need you to tell me everything you know about Valn's plans." The words stuck in her throat but she forced them out.

Lucia paled. "I know nothing of that."

Naya stepped toward her. "Don't lie. I've seen how scared you are of him. You know something. So tell me or I'll tell him you've been experimenting with the war runes." Naya prayed the threat wouldn't ring hollow.

She hadn't thought Lucia's eyes could go any wider. "Tell him . . . ? But . . . are you saying you don't know?" Lucia laughed humorlessly. "Creator. Tell him all you want. Valn was the one who brought me those runes."

At first Naya was sure she'd misheard. "That's insane. He wouldn't."

"Why do you think I was working for him? He knows my history. He came here with your body and demanded I make you a reaper. He said if I didn't comply, he'd expose the truth about me. He'd also go after Alejandra. And everyone I'd ever resurrected would be investigated. I couldn't risk getting them into trouble like that."

What truth, and who was Alejandra? Naya shook her head. "That's impossible. Where would Valn get those runes? And why would he ever want to use them?"

"I don't know. I have been trying not to know since you arrived here."

Naya frowned. "Please. I think Valn might be planning something terrible, and I think you know more about what's going on than you're saying."

"Is that a joke? Why in creation would I know more than you? You're the one working with him."

Naya balled her hands into fists. "Not anymore. I thought we were trying to protect the treaty, but things have changed." She sensed a flicker of doubt in Lucia's aether. "I heard you that night at the café. You were asking about the missing Talmirans. Why?"

Lucia's nostrils flared. "Because someone has been trying very hard to make everyone think a necromancer killed them."

"But you think it was someone else?"

Lucia crossed her arms over her chest. "Seven Talmiran sailors have gone missing in the past five months. Anywhere else that wouldn't mean much. People would assume they'd abandoned their contracts, or met with some mundane trouble. But around here Talmir screams dark magic when one of your people so much as skins their knee. This time they've decided to stay quiet. I wanted to know why."

Naya felt the puzzle pieces in her head shift, then click into place. "Valn said they were ready to start the investigation," she said, half to herself. "And King Allence—" Before she could finish, someone banged on the door hard enough to rattle it in its frame.

"King's business! Open this door!" a deep voice shouted from outside.

"What the—? What did you do?" Lucia demanded.

Naya glanced to the door and cursed under her breath. "That must be the guard. They think a wraith kidnapped Delence. They're interrogating everyone."

"Salno Delence? He's been kidnapped? Why didn't you say something?" The knock came again, even louder this time.

Naya wanted to scream in frustration. "Just please tell me you keep your notes somewhere safe. Corten said they searched the glass shop. If they find evidence of my bond, then we're both doomed."

Lucia stared at the door. The crumpled note fell from her fingers. "So this was his plan. If Delence is gone, then . . ." She spun toward Naya. "If you're serious about protecting the treaty, then you have to go. Now. Valn will have me no matter what, but you still have a chance. Find Corten, tell him what you know. If I'm right, then Valn is dragging us toward another war. The Necromantic Council must be informed. Corten will know who to talk to." The door banged open in a cacophony of splintering wood. A bell on the counter, probably linked to the door's alarm ward, clanged frantically for a few seconds before going silent.

Naya stepped back as she sensed the guards advancing into the entryway, their aether filled with deadly intent. "If I run, they'll assume I'm guilty. And what about you? I can't—"

"I'll be fine. Go tell Corten what you know."

The workroom door burst open and a group of four men dressed in the red-and-white uniforms of the city guard marched in. Their leader, a man with a perfectly waxed mustache and oiled black hair combed back from a broad forehead, swept the room with a look of obvious contempt. "We are here on orders of His Majesty the King regarding the disappearance of Salno Delence. Are you Lucia Laroke?"

Lucia cast a despairing glance in Naya's direction. "Yes."

"Our information tells us you are harboring a Talmiran wraith."

"Information about my patients is confidential." Lucia stepped between Naya and the guards.

The man with the black hair smiled, showing the barest hint of teeth. "I'm afraid some questions have been raised about this girl's identity. I'm going to need to confiscate your records. And the two of you are going to come with us to answer questions regarding the disappearance of Lord Delence."

"I told you, you don't have any right to that information. Now get out of my shop and don't come back unless—"

"Sir," said one of the guards, hand moving toward his weapon, "this woman is resisting a direct order from the king. I fear she may become violent."

"Violent?" Lucia sounded confused. Naya glanced between the necromancer and the guards. Their eagerness infused the aether, making it buzz against her skin. This wasn't just another search for them. They'd come here expecting to find what they were looking for.

"Detain these two, then search the shop." The guards moved forward. To Lucia and Naya the black-haired guard said, "Please raise your hands above your head. No harm will come to you so long as you cooperate."

"Go!" Lucia said again. But Naya didn't move. She was sick of running, and she didn't like the idea of leaving Lucia to face the guards alone. As impossible as it seemed, Lucia hadn't sounded like she was lying when she said Valn had given her the runes.

She needed to get rid of the guards. She needed space and time to figure out why Valn and her father would want to frame the Ceramoran king for the disappearance of Talmiran sailors. Lucia had said war, but that couldn't be right. Naya took a step forward, raising her hands slowly.

"Wait—there's been a misunderstanding," she said. "Lucia Laroke was here all night performing a resurrection. We don't know anything about what happened to Delence."

The guard's smile widened a fraction. "This girl's features match the description, do they not?"

The man next to him, burly, with a nose that looked as if it'd been broken more than once, nodded. "Yes, exactly so." He walked toward her, then in a voice barely above a whisper said, "Come now, there's no need to get feisty. Play along and you'll be safe with us. You've done your job well and Ambassador Valn will protect you."

Naya froze. She'd never guessed Valn's network had infiltrated the city guard. He must have sent these men to dispose of her as he'd promised her father. He couldn't know she'd overheard his conversation, so he probably assumed she'd come quietly. But why would he want the guards to take Lucia? A shiver ran through her. Maybe Valn meant to get rid of anyone who could tie him to Naya's resurrection.

They couldn't go with the guards. But if Naya refused, she'd only be revealing that she knew about Valn's plans to destroy her. "I'll go with you," she said. "But Lucia isn't involved. There's no need for you to take her too."

"I'm afraid you're wrong there. Madame Laroke still has her part to play." One of the guards near the back slid his club from the leather loop on his belt.

Naya looked between the four men and saw her death written in their hungry eyes. They might pretend to be her allies, so long as she cooperated. But if she tried to run, they'd stop her. Rage boiled through her. She'd trusted her father, trusted Valn. She'd given up everything for their cause. She'd made her father's hate her own and believed him when he told her the undead were monsters. In return, he and Valn had sent strangers to kill her.

"My patience is running thin, girl," the black-haired guard said.

Naya took a step back. Four guards, all armed with clubs. She couldn't fight them. She might still be able to escape, especially if she could make it to the roof. But that would leave Lucia in the guards' clutches. Naya forced the rage down. She slumped her shoulders and widened her eyes, staring up at the man with what she hoped was an innocent expression. She needed time. Maybe if they thought she was cooperating, she could buy enough time to figure out how to get them both free.

"You're right. I'm sorry. Please take us to Ambassador Valn."

The black-haired guard grunted. "That's better." He jerked his head. His companions surrounded Lucia and Naya and escorted them outside. A black carriage with barred windows waited in the street. Naya could just see the silhouette of someone sitting inside. Another guard maybe? A shudder ran through her. If she got into that carriage, she didn't think there'd be any getting out.

Naya tensed as one of the guards inched closer. The sense of someone looming behind her brought back memories of the day she died. She could almost feel the prick of the dart in her neck and the terrifying numbness that had spread through her. Valn had claimed they'd dealt with her killer. But he'd never said who had done the deed. And hadn't there been a note of accusation in her father's voice when he asked about her death? The panic turned to anger as the truth hit her. Of course. Valn hadn't just organized her resurrection. He'd had her killed.

"Keep moving," one of the guards said. A hand pressed against Naya's back and something inside her snapped.

She spun and shoved the guard hard in the chest. "Don't touch me!"

Aether flared through her bond, and with it came raw power. She dug her toes into the gaps between paving stones. She could feel the aether shifting inside her, changing. A rush of impossible strength surged down her arms, then through her hands to the guard's chest. The guard's eyes widened as he flew backward. The bones in Naya's hand felt like someone had thrown them in a fire. But the sensation was somehow distant, like the pain belonged to someone else. Lucia screamed behind her.

When Naya turned she saw two guards hauling Lucia into the carriage. Lucia kicked and writhed, but it was clear she was no match for her captors. Another guard stood between Naya and the carriage. The scrape of boots behind her told her that the one she'd knocked back was already trying to get up. Fear was building in the aether around them as people all along the street hurried to hide in shops and houses.

Naya clenched her left hand into a fist, holding it close to her body as Celia had taught her. She feigned left, then ducked right, sliding past the guard before he could do more than swing clumsily with his club. Naya evaded the blow and reached out to drag the guards off Lucia.

"Run!" Lucia shouted. She managed to kick one of her captors in the shin, and the man snarled a curse.

Before Naya could reach Lucia, someone grabbed the back of her shirt and twisted hard. Her collar dug into her throat, and for an instant her body forgot that it didn't need to breathe, forgot that she couldn't actually choke. Her hands went to her neck as she stumbled backward. Before she could think of how to free herself, more hands were on her wrists. Naya tried to let them pass through her. Fingers slipped through her arm and someone shouted. Then the grip on her shirt tightened and ice shot through her wrist as a salma wood shackle snapped into place.

"Get her other hand!"

The world slowed around her. One of the guards hit Lucia hard with his club and she fell back into the carriage, dazed. The guard in front of Naya fumbled for a second set of shackles. Naya's eyes met Lucia's. The necromancer mouthed a single word. *Run.*

Naya's lips curled back from her teeth. The bones of her left hand flared hot even through the icy pain of the shackle. Her shirt tore and the pressure on her throat eased. Cold brushed her right hand but she jerked it back in time to avoid getting caught in a second shackle. She spun, coming face-to-face with the guard holding the shackle locked to her left wrist. His face had gone red with effort. Naya focused on her right hand, imagining the heat runes on the furnace in Lucia's shop. Again she felt the aether inside her change. Her bones ached and warmth spread across her palm, blossoming until it felt like she was cupping a handful of molten glass. With a shout, Naya grabbed the arm of the guard holding her.

The guard shrieked. The smell of charring meat rose off his skin. His grip on the shackle's chain loosened as he flinched away. Naya pulled the shackle free and ran. Pain arched through her bones with every step, and ice crawled up her arm from where the shackle still dangled around her wrist. She heard the carriage door slam and risked a glance back. Two of the guards still ran behind her.

Naya led the guards down a dead-end alley stacked with wooden crates. She scrambled up the crates, then leapt to grab the balcony of a nearby house. Her left hand slipped, the fingers rigid with cold and pain, but she managed to haul herself up. From there she climbed, fingertips scraping half-rotted wood and crumbling mortar, until she reached the slate roof. She heard the first creaks as the guards tried to climb after her, then a crash as the rain-wet crates collapsed under their weight. She spun, hoping to catch sight of Lucia. But the street in front of the shop was already empty. She could try following the carriage, but what would be the point? She couldn't free Lucia by herself. Even if she somehow managed that, they'd be chased by half the city guard in no time. The men below her cursed as they disentangled themselves from the wood. One of them blew three sharp blasts on a whistle. Better to be gone before they found a way to follow.

Naya picked a direction at random and started jumping along the roofs. She kept her head low, trying not to draw attention. When she could no longer sense anyone following, she slumped down on the roof of a house squashed between two taller neighbors. She pressed her back against the wall of one of those houses, where the long evening shadows would hide her. Despair pushed up her throat and made her eyes burn. She'd run, and now Valn had Lucia.

The wood behind her was cool and solid, and a gentle breeze tickled her cheek, carrying with it the smells of the ocean. Her thoughts wandered, wanting to drift away from the pain and failure. Maybe if she closed her eyes, she could fade into the pulse of the city, let its beat wear her down until there was nothing left.

No. She squeezed her left hand into a fist, concentrating on the pain. If she faded now, she'd be letting Valn win. Naya tugged at the shackle. One thick wooden cuff wrapped around her wrist, while the second dangled free on its metal chain. She tried to pry the cuff off but the latch was locked tight. She tried to force her wrist through the cuff, as she'd done with the salma wood plate in Delence's door. But either the cuff was too sturdy or Naya was too exhausted from the fight to manage that trick.

Naya glared at the cuff. She tucked her thumb down, trying to scrunch her fingers small enough to slip it off. The wood jabbed into her, refusing to budge. Naya let her head fall back against the wall.

How had everything gone so horribly wrong? All she'd ever wanted was to become a merchant, to sail the world and make her father proud. Instead she'd become a spy for a man whose schemes she didn't understand, her father wanted her dead, and the only people who might be willing to help her were those she used to think of as monsters.

Lucia said Corten would help, but Naya wasn't so sure about that. Just thinking about telling him the truth made her feel sick. She'd lied to him for weeks. He'd hate her, and he'd have every right to. Even if he didn't try to turn her in on the spot, what could the two of them possibly do?

Still, she had no one else to turn to. She needed to figure out what Valn meant to do with Lucia. And she needed to know the truth. Had her father sent her here not to help stop a war but to start one? Naya looked up, trying to get her bearings among the jumble of rooftops.

That was when she saw the man standing on the other side of the roof.

CHAPTER 24

Naya and the stranger stared at each other across the shallowly slanted roof. The man's expression was hard, and a wicked-looking knife gleamed in his right hand. Naya stood up. Why hadn't she felt him sneaking up on her? She reached out to taste his aether, and shuddered. The man's energy was rushing into the knife. She couldn't feel his emotions. Both the blade and the hand gripping it seemed to warp and shimmer in the dying light. "What do you want?" Naya asked.

"You should have accepted Ambassador Valn's invitation." The man stepped forward. He was dressed like an ordinary laborer but moved with a predatory grace that suggested he was nothing of the sort. "It would have been easier that way."

"How did you find me?" Naya tried to take a step back but ended up pressed against the wall of the taller building behind her. She could try climbing to the next roof, but that would mean turning her back to him.

"Your life belongs to us. You can't hide," the man said. He had a sharp nose, dark eyes, and a scar bisecting one cheek. Those eyes looked familiar. Naya recognized him with a start. He'd been the one driving the carriage the night of the kidnapping. "If there's even a scrap of humanity left in you, then you know what you must do. Submit. We can make this easy, peaceful. There's no need for more violence."

A snarl rose in Naya's throat. "You people are the real monsters. Get away from me."

The man tightened his grip on the knife. "So that's how it is." His boots pounded against shingles as he closed the distance between them in three swift strides. Naya screamed at her legs to run, but her whole body felt weak and her eyes were drawn to the knife. Blue-white runes glowed across the blade as the man raised it to slash at her.

Naya tried to grab the man's arm, but he was faster. At the last second he twisted the blade to slice through her wrist, less than an inch from the network of fragile bones that held her bond. Pain—worse than anything she'd felt since dying—seared out from the cut. An inhuman shriek sent the man stumbling backward. It took Naya a long second to realize the sound was coming from her. Red mist flooded her vision. She stumbled, trying to put the rest of her body between her hand and the knife.

What was going on? Aether seeped from her hand, the tips of her fingers going hazy despite the chilling influence of the salma wood. No normal knife should have been able to do that. The man's eyes narrowed and he attacked again. Naya ducked sideways, feeling the terrifying presence of the wall behind her. The knife sliced the side of her shirt. The man smiled. He caught the dangling shackle, pinning her. Naya tried to gather heat in her hand, to strengthen her limbs as she had earlier. But the knife was eating the aether all around her, and the best she could manage was a weak flicker of warmth in her palm.

The glowing runes crawled over the blade as the man's aether poured into them. Those runes had to be the reason the knife could hurt her. If she could break them, maybe she could draw enough aether to get away. She gasped in as much as she could and tried to channel it toward the brightest rune on the knife.

She imagined raw energy crashing into the runes like water. *Break.* The runes glowed brighter for an instant, then the hungry blade plunged into her chest.

The pain stole her thoughts and her sight. The knife was ice inside her, and the ice was spreading. Claiming her. The blade twisted as the man pulled it back for a second blow. This shouldn't be happening. He hadn't touched her bones once, but somehow she could feel herself unraveling. Naya screamed again. She reached out, no longer thinking about maintaining her physical form. She pulled at the man's aether. Most of it was going toward the knife, powering it even as her life drained into the blade. But the man was young and strong. The knife couldn't eat up all his energy.

Something glowed in the center of her darkened vision. A dense source of energy. Maybe enough to save her. Naya drew in a deep breath.

This time it was her attacker's turn to scream. Naya's vision came back all at once. The stranger stood above her. He stumbled backward, eyes wide. Naya leaned against the wall, trying to control the burst of strange energy. It didn't feel like any aether she'd ever pulled. It surged through her. It fought her, trying to tear its way back out even as it renewed her. She was no longer just Naya, clinging to the wall as death's tides tried to drag her under. Now she was Marcus, staring down at the thing, the monster he'd come to kill. It was disgusting—a bluish-white glow that barely resembled a girl.

He'd almost had it, but then something had gone wrong. His whole body burned. His grip on the knife was weakening. But the runes on the blade still glowed. He could still finish this. Finish it before the monster did.

Naya fought free of the man's confused thoughts. She concentrated on the energy, bending every fragment of her mind toward containing it. She heard the dark tides on the other side of death swelling around her, but she focused all her energy into the blade. This time the runes cracked. The air around the blade darkened, then twisted, reminding Naya of the portal Lucia had created for Jesla's soul. The blade's hungry draw faltered and Marcus's fingers jerked. The knife clattered to the roof and slid away. Marcus reached up to claw at his chest. He stumbled, then collapsed.

For just an instant Naya felt a terribly familiar burning in her own chest. Her vision darkened, then flashed with a collage of foreign memories. Marcus's father teaching him how to ride a farm nag. Years later a tavern brawl gone wrong. Blood on his knife and guards with shackles and wicked grins. Valn smiling and offering his hand. Then dank city streets, and the feel of the dart tube as he aimed death at the neck of the girl walking down the alley. Naya screamed as the memories blurred and darkness swept away her thoughts.

When her mind cleared and her vision returned, the last of the sunset's glow was just fading from the western sky. The assassin lay unmoving on the roof in front of her as she dragged herself to her knees. Gasping in aether, she let her eyes wander up to the first dim stars appearing in the evening sky. She welcomed the pain humming through her body. It kept her from reaching out and checking the man's aether. She didn't want to confirm what his empty eyes already told her.

"I didn't have a choice," she muttered. It didn't make her feel any better. Her voice sounded more like wind than human words. Hearing it brought back the memory of how she'd looked in Marcus's eyes. *He was right. I am a monster.* But this time fury smothered the old disgust at what she'd become.

No. She'd seen the truth in Marcus's memories. Valn had ordered him to kill her and he'd done it. He'd helped make her this way. And when his master decided he was done with her, Marcus hadn't hesitated to try killing her a second time. Only this time she'd had the tools to fight back. Naya dragged herself to her feet, nearly falling right back down from the pain.

She wasn't sure how she made it off the roof and through the twisting streets to Corten's shop. Every step hurt. The houses vanished and she was left in a fog of twisting aether. She couldn't block out the flood of foreign sensations streaming through the aether. Even the grass and trees seemed a pressure against her pain-scorched body.

With her thoughts clouded, the once-familiar streets became a labyrinth. It was Corten's furnaces that finally drew her to safety. Among the shadow houses the three sets of runes shone like molten beacons. It took several tries before she could make her fingers solid enough to fumble the doorknob open. Naya heard the faint tinkle of the shop bell. Then the floor rushed up to meet her and blissful, painless darkness swallowed her.

CHAPTER 25

When Naya opened her eyes, she saw only gray light. She blinked, and the world came grudgingly back into focus. Corten was leaning over her, his eyebrows furrowed with concern. Naya drew in aether slowly. She was lying on a bed in a room with a white ceiling. An aether lamp shone in the far corner, and outside the window was darkness. She frowned, struggling to pull together tangled strings of thought and memory.

"What happened?" she managed to whisper.

The relief in Corten's eyes made her chest ache. "I was going to ask you the same thing. When you stumbled in here, I thought for sure you were dying. You should be dead."

Her fuzzy thoughts sharpened and she remembered why she'd come. "I am dead." Naya tried closing her eyes, then eased them open again. It didn't seem to make any difference for the needle stabs spreading from her hand.

"I mean really dead."

Naya sat up halfway, then flopped back down on the thin mattress with a poorly suppressed moan. The chill was gone from her wrist. When she glanced down she saw the shackle lying discarded on the floor next to her bed. Corten followed her gaze. "I picked the lock," he said, sounding almost apologetic. "It took a while. I mean, I knew the theory, but I'm not very good at that sort of thing and all I had were some wires Matius uses for drawing details in glass, so . . ." He trailed off, rubbing the back of his neck.

She wanted to ask why he knew anything at all about picking locks, but the shackle was a harsh reminder that she had bigger things to worry about. She glanced at the stuffed bookshelves and cluttered desk and realized she must be lying in Corten's room. "I don't remember coming here."

"You were barely conscious when I brought you upstairs. It's not surprising you don't remember it. That can happen if you put too much stress on your bones."

"How long have I been here?" Naya asked.

Corten glanced at the clock on his desk. "About five hours."

Five hours? It had felt like only an instant. She didn't have time to be lying around like this. Valn was probably still hunting her, and Lucia was trapped in his clutches, or dead. She forced herself to sit up.

Corten put a hand on her arm. "You shouldn't move more than you have to."

Naya shook her head. "I've already wasted too much time lying here. There's something I have to do."

"What? Blue, what's going on? What happened to you?"

Naya squeezed her eyes shut. *What happened? What happened is that I've been lying to you since I met you. I ignored all the things I should have seen because I wanted to believe my father was a good man. Thanks to me Lucia's probably dead. And now I'm about to drag you into a mess I barely understand because I don't know anyone else who will help me.* It all felt like too much, so for the moment she decided to keep things simple. "I was attacked," she said, not meeting Corten's eyes.

"Who attacked you?" Corten spoke softly, as though calming a frightened animal.

"A man. He had a knife. I think it was a wraith eater." She'd never seen one of the weapons, but her father had told her stories of the men and women who'd wielded them during the last war.

Corten's grip on her arm tightened. "Are you sure?"

"I think so. When he stabbed me, it felt like the knife was trying to tear my soul away. I thought I would die, but then I found another source of aether. It was stronger somehow, harder to control. I . . . It's hard to remember exactly what happened, but I drew it in, and when it was over the man was dead."

"I don't think that was aether," Corten said. Naya saw the fear in his eyes and her chest tightened.

"Then what was it?"

Corten shook his head. "You can't kill someone by drawing their aether. But you can kill them if you draw out their soul."

Fear flooded through her. "I thought that was impossible."

"Not impossible. Just very difficult. It would probably shatter my bones if I tried to hold another soul. But you're . . ."

"A reaper," Naya finished.

"You didn't know," Corten said. His hand slid down her arm and he squeezed her fingers.

Naya shuddered. "What happens to a soul if a reaper draws from it?"

"I don't know. I'm not sure if anybody does." Corten shook his head. "But you shouldn't worry about that right now. If you think you can walk, then we need to get you back to Lucia's shop so she can fix your bone."

"Fix my bone?" Naya asked, trying to pull her thoughts away from the horror of what she'd done.

"Yeah. I examined your bones while you were unconscious. I'm not sure if it was the knife or the strain of touching another soul, but one of your bones is cracked."

Naya flexed her hand. The sharp ache she'd felt ever since she'd fought the assassin wasn't going away. "I thought you said that if any of my bones cracked, I would die."

"The crack is small. So far the damage hasn't been enough to destroy the bindings on your soul. But we don't heal the way the living do. If we don't replace that bone soon, the crack will spread. That's why we have to go to Lucia. Do you think you can walk there?"

"We can't go to Lucia. The guard already took her."

"What?" Corten's grip on Naya's fingers tightened. "You said you'd warn her."

"I tried. There wasn't time."

Corten's eyes darted around the room, then fell on the shackle lying next to the bed. "Don't tell me they were the ones who attacked you? They aren't supposed to be armed with wraith eaters."

"Yes. No. I mean, the guard did come to Lucia's shop. They didn't even pretend to search the shop. They just broke down the door and tried to arrest both of us. I tried to save her but they put her in a carriage and I couldn't . . . I ran."

Fear and confusion flickered over Corten's face before his expression settled into a determined scowl. "We'll have to find a way to get you out of the city."

"No! I won't run again." The words came out far louder than she'd intended.

"You don't have a choice. From what you described, it sounds like the guard already assumed you were involved in the kidnapping. They'll have searched Lucia's shop. Even if they didn't find evidence of what you are, you won't be safe here so long as they're looking for you. Any wraith who gets taken into custody has to have their bond examined for abnormal runes. I don't know if anyone else can fix Lucia's work, but for now we'll have to leave the city. We can go east. My parents have friends in Riorrica. I'll find someone there to help us."

The guilt felt like a giant fist squeezing her chest. "I can't run. What happened to Lucia is my fault. It's all my fault. I have to do something before this gets any worse."

"It's not your fault."

"It is! You don't understand. I'm not who you think I am."

"Blue—"

"Would you please listen? That isn't even my real name."

"I . . . What? What are you talking about?"

Naya drew a shuddering breath. Her eyes burned with tears she couldn't shed, and she wished more than anything that she could hold back what she was about to say. "My name isn't Blue. It's Naya. Ever since I died, I've been working as a spy for the Talmiran Embassy. I helped kidnap Delence. When the guards came for Lucia, they were looking for me."

Corten's expression froze. "No. That can't be right. You're confused. That crack must be worse than I thought. Or . . ."

"It's true." Naya's throat felt like it was trying to close in on itself, but she forced the words out. "When Ambassador Valn recruited me, he told me we were working to protect the treaty. But I overheard him talking to my father, and I think it's something bigger than that. They had me killed just so they could make me a wraith. I think they might have killed others too. Lucia thinks Valn is trying to start a war. She said we have to warn people and that you would know who to talk to. Please—I never wanted to get you tangled up in this, but I didn't know who else to go to."

Corten sat in silence. Naya closed her eyes, not wanting to see the look on his face. When he finally spoke, the words sounded flat and cold. "You're serious."

"I'm sorry," Naya whispered.

Corten pulled his hand from hers. "You lied to me? About everything? Creator, all that time I thought you—" The legs of his chair scraped the floor as he stood. He paced to the window. "Now you want me to help you? Why should I trust you? Either you're lying now or you've been lying since the day I met you."

"Why would I lie now? What would be the point?"

"I have no idea, but this is ridiculous. Nobody wants another war. And even if the Talmirans tried to start one, we still have our alliances with Banen and Silmar. They won't let Talmir get away with attacking us." But Corten didn't sound so sure anymore. He rubbed the back of his head.

Naya leaned forward. "I know it sounds absurd, but it's true. You asked me once to trust you, and I did. I don't deserve it, I know, but I need you to trust me now. Please." The last word came out as a whisper.

Corten closed his eyes and rubbed the bridge of his nose. "What you're asking is madness."

"Please. I don't know what to do. I don't want anyone else to die."

Minutes slipped past and Corten continued to stare at her. Naya forced herself to keep her eyes on his. She wouldn't be the first to look away.

"Damn it. Fine," Corten eventually said.

"You believe me?"

"No. But I can't just leave you here alone, and if something is really going on here, then the Necromantic Council needs to know about it."

CHAPTER 26

"Wait," Naya said. "I know we have to tell someone, but I don't see how getting the Necromantic Council involved will help." Lucia had told her to go to the Council, but that didn't mean it was a good idea.

Corten let out an exasperated breath. "They've got resources, and given what you told me, they're the only ones who will be willing to help Lucia at this point."

"But they're—" Naya swallowed what she was about to say when she saw the expression on Corten's face.

"They're what?" Corten asked.

According to Celia, the Council was a secretive mob of agitators and criminals always looking for ways to subvert the treaty. "They're being watched," Naya said. "Valn has spies keeping track of all the major leaders." Many of the houses whose runes she'd tracked had belonged to suspected members of the Necromantic Council.

"They won't be watching everyone," Corten said. "Do you feel like you can walk?"

Naya swung her legs over the edge of the bed and stood. It hurt, but at least she didn't fall over. "Where are we going?"

"There's something we need to pick up before we meet with

the Council. And on the way there, you're going to tell me everything you know about the Talmiran spies, and everything they
think they know about the Council."

Naya looked down at her clothes. Her skirt was ripped and
filthy from when the train had hit her. Her shirt and vest were
even worse, with holes and slashes showing where her attacker's
knife had pierced her. "Do you have anything else I can wear?"

Some emotion flashed across Corten's face, too quick for
Naya to identify. "Sure. Give me a minute to find something."
He dug through his chest, then handed her a bundle of clothes
and turned so he faced the desk.

Corten's spare pants were an inch too short. His shirt was
too broad around the shoulders, and the vest too tight across her
chest. Despite the distracting ache in her hand, Naya felt every
brush of the fabric as she put on the borrowed clothes. The
smell of orange-scented soap and old smoke enveloped her. It
was comforting despite the way Corten kept watching her out
of the corner of his eye, like she was a rabid dog that might bite
him at any moment.

Naya turned away from him and concentrated on Blue's face.
The ache in her hand pulsed brighter, and a wave of dizziness
threatened to send her to the floor. But after a moment she felt
her features shift as Blue's face settled into place. It would have
been better to wear an entirely new face. But with pain throbbing through her bones like a heartbeat, she didn't trust herself
to hold on to less familiar features.

"What about Matius?" Naya asked as Corten led her to the
door. "Won't he wonder where you are?"

"I'll leave this downstairs," he said, holding up a folded slip
of paper. "It should be enough to keep him from getting suspicious. I don't want him involved in any of this. He has a family."

"So do you," Naya said.

Corten hunched his shoulders. "Their lands are way out in

the southern foothills. I'm hoping that's far enough to keep them out of this mess."

Outside, the streets were turning gray with dawn. Naya walked beside Corten, telling him everything she could remember about the Council from her conversations with Celia. When she finished, Corten nodded. "I think I know who we can go to."

"Who?"

"Earon Jalance."

Naya thought for a moment, then shook her head. "I've never heard of him."

"Good," Corten said.

Naya's toe caught in a gap between two paving stones and she stumbled. Corten grabbed her arm, stopping her fall. When she looked up, her eyes met his. For a moment the world seemed to slow. Then Corten looked away. His fingers uncurled from her arm like she was made of salma wood. "Is it getting worse?" he asked.

Naya gritted her teeth. "No. Don't worry about me." She turned away, not wanting to see the hard set of his mouth. In doing so she spotted a familiar street sign and her brow furrowed. "Why are you taking me back to Lucia's shop?"

"Because we'll need your extra bones if we're going to repair your bond," Corten said.

"I thought you said no one would help with that."

"Jalance might, if we tell him what's going on. And if he can't do it, he should be able to connect us to someone who can. But that won't matter if we don't have your bones and Lucia's notes."

Dawn had fully broken by the time they reached Lucia's shop. There they found two guards leaning against the frame of the broken door. Naya watched Corten as he glanced from the guards to the rooftops, then down to the narrow alley where the shop's side door was located. "We'll need to figure out a way to distract those two if I'm going to get inside," he said.

"How?" Naya's bones throbbed, but she tried to keep the pain from her voice.

"You've got a key to the back door, right? If you keep them looking the other way, then I can sneak around back and get your bones."

Naya shook her head. "I mean how do you expect me to distract them? And what if they've got more guards around the side?"

"I don't know. You're the spy. Isn't that the sort of thing you're supposed to know how to do?"

Naya glared around the corner of the house they hid behind. She tried to remember every piece of advice Celia had given her, but the older spy's lessons had always been about how to avoid attention—not draw it. "Why don't I try getting inside?"

"No," Corten said. "You wouldn't know what you were looking for. Besides, I'm not giving you the chance to run off with your bones."

"I'd have a better chance of getting in."

"With your bond so damaged you can barely walk? No. We'll both be better off if you stay here."

Naya swallowed her retort. The scorn in Corten's tone made her want to sink under the paving stones. She peeked around the corner for a better look at the guards. "You're sure my bones are in there?"

"Yeah, assuming no one has taken them."

Naya's fingers tapped against her leg. By now Valn probably knew the assassin had failed. Like the guards who'd come for Lucia, these could be working for him. He might have left them here on the off chance she came back. Then again, yesterday she'd managed to fight her way through four guards, and the man with the wraith eater. Did Valn know about her injury? Was he underestimating her? Or were the two men part of a larger trap? Naya flexed the fingers of her left hand and winced at the pain. Trap or no, she couldn't afford to stay injured. She needed those bones.

Naya let her eyes unfocus so she could concentrate on the aether. The city's pulse beat in time with the pain in her bones. Underneath the flood of raw sensations, she could just feel the icy tides of death lapping at her calves, ready to drag her down if she let them. She tried to ignore the unsettling sensation as she searched for a trap. The street was emptier than it should have been this time of day, and there was a nervous sweat-stink in the aether. She tried to extend her reach to see if any more guards lurked by the shop's back door, but the world blurred and she had to grab the nearby wall to keep from falling over. She concentrated on the feel of rough wood against her fingers, and slowly the city's pulse faded back to a murmur.

"What is it?" Corten asked softly. He was leaning against the wall and obviously trying to act natural. But his eyes kept darting up and down the street.

"It's nothing. I'm fine." She pushed away from the wall. She'd just have to rely on more mundane sight. The two guards stood with their backs to the wall of Lucia's shop, almost lounging. But their eyes followed everyone who walked past. It would take something spectacular to keep them distracted long enough for Corten to get in and out. As her gaze focused on a pair of women hurrying away from the bakery down the street, Naya realized she knew exactly what could draw the guards' attention. But the only thing spectacular about the idea was how spectacularly foolish it was. She scoured her mind for a better solution, but with her hand aching she didn't dare risk anything complicated.

"Get ready to run," she said to Corten.

"You have a plan?"

"Yes." *No.* She sucked in a deep breath of aether. "Do you know the café by Lisala Plaza?"

"Sure, but what—" Corten began.

"I'll meet you there if this works."

"Wait. What are you planning?" He reached for her wrist but Naya pulled away, walking then running toward the guards before her courage could fail. Each step was agony, but if this worked, the pain would be worth it. She felt her face shift and blur as her hair curled back into its old tangled shape.

"Hey!" she shouted. "You're looking for me, right?" Both guards turned, obviously shocked. Naya's expression twisted into something between a smile and a grimace. She could sense growing curiosity behind her from the shopkeepers and their few customers. Some of them recognized her, or would soon. Maybe, if she was lucky, she'd have a chance to do more than just distract these two. She hoped Corten was ready.

One guard stepped forward. His cheeks were pox-dimpled, and he had a gangly look that made Naya suspect he wasn't much older than her. "Stay right there." He reached for the club strapped to his belt. This close she could sense the fear in his aether without trying. Maybe she'd been wrong about a trap.

"These men are liars," she shouted. "They're working for Talmir. They're trying to frame Lucia Laroke. Their masters kidnapped Delence and dragged Lucia from her home." She pointed at the guards and willed herself not to glance at the open street Corten would have to cross.

The second guard advanced with a scowl. He was an older man with thickly-muscled arms and a hard look in his eyes. "Everyone, stay back! This girl is dangerous and obviously mad."

Naya sensed movement to her left. She risked a glance and spotted a third guard leaving the alley, his club already drawn. Corten stood behind him, his back pressed to a nearby building and his eyes on the retreating guard. Naya stepped back, hoping to draw the guards away from the shop. "I'm not mad. The Talmiran ambassador—"

The older guard swung his club at her. Naya stumbled back and felt the wood brush through the tip of her nose. The ground seemed to tilt, and she fell on her back with a cry of pain. Before she could stand, an old man in a bright-red vest grabbed the guard's arm.

"Hey now, there's no need for this to get rough," he said.

It took Naya a moment to recognize the man's craggy features. He was the flower seller who owned the little shop next to Lucia's. And he wasn't alone. A half-dozen others had inched closer to the scene, including the broad woman from the bakery down the street. Bright curiosity was starting to overshadow their fear. Many of them had probably known Lucia for years. She'd treated their colds and scrapes. They wouldn't want to believe she was a criminal.

"Sir, this isn't any of your business," the guard said. He tried to wrench his arm free, but the old man's grip held. The younger guard was looking uncertainly between him and Naya, while the third guard approached from the left. Past him, Naya couldn't see any sign of Corten. Hopefully he was already inside.

Naya drew in more aether, trying to ignore the growing pain in her hand. She shoved herself to her feet. The younger guard reached for her, but his movements were hesitant and slow. Naya ducked under his arm and ran. After a few steps she glanced back over her shoulder and was relieved to see the guards following, shoving through the growing crowd of onlookers. The baker shifted her weight, knocking one of the guards with her hip and causing him to stumble. A tiny smile touched Naya's lips despite her pain.

She knew that with her bond damaged she couldn't outrun the guards for long. She wove through the neighborhood's now-familiar streets. She could still hear the commotion of the guards chasing her when her strength wavered. She squeezed into a narrow alley and collapsed into a shadowed doorway. She tucked herself into a ball, letting her limbs fade to wispy aether and trying to be as tiny and silent as possible. When the pain in her hand lessened, she extended her senses through the aether. The energy around her still felt bright and sharp with excitement, but no one nearby seemed to have spotted her. Naya leaned her head against the splintered wood of the doorway and breathed a silent prayer of thanks. Her limbs felt heavy, but she knew she had to keep moving. Once she had changed her face back to Blue's, she hurried out of the alley and headed toward the café.

She found Corten lingering near one of the outdoor tables in front of the little café. He had a bulging satchel slung over one arm that looked like the one Lucia had carried with her whenever she'd gone out. The look on his face was one of barely suppressed panic. Was he worried she'd been caught, or did he think she'd used the chance to run?

The glare he gave her when she approached didn't tell her which it was. Naya was too tired to argue when he grabbed her elbow and steered her into the shadow of the café's small awning.

"What in creation were you thinking?" Corten whispered.

"You said you wanted a distraction. It worked, didn't it?"

"Only because you got lucky. If they'd caught you . . ."

"But they didn't." Still, his words jarred her. He wasn't wrong. A month ago she'd never have attempted anything that risky. "Just tell me you got what we need."

"I did. Not that it makes what you did any less insane."

Naya smiled. She still felt tired, but the stabbing pain radiating from her hand had lessened to a dull throb now that she'd stopped moving. She let the calm of the café's patrons wash over her. They'd actually done it. They'd gotten her bones out of Lucia's shop, right under the noses of Valn's men. She stared at the innocent-seeming bag. "They're in there?" she asked.

Corten nodded, looking uneasy. Then his focus shifted to something behind her. "I think we should get moving."

Naya followed his gaze. Two women were sitting at one of the outside tables, whispering and stealing glances in their direction. She caught the word *wraith* and felt a chill. "Did they recognize us?" she asked, keeping her voice low.

Corten shook his head. "I don't think so, but look at your skin."

"My skin?" Naya looked down at her hands. Her skin was still the caramel brown she'd chosen for Blue. Except . . . She drew in a sharp breath. As she watched, the color shifted subtly, patches lighting to its old hue and becoming faintly transparent. She concentrated and the patches vanished. The sense of being watched felt like a sunburn tightening her skin. "What's going on?"

"It's called fading," Corten said. "Common side effect of a damaged bond." He grabbed her wrist and tugged her back onto the street. "Try to keep your head down. We need to get you to Jalance before those guards catch up with us."

Naya let him pull her along. She glanced again at the two women and saw them scowling back at her. Her stomach twisted like she'd eaten something foul. "Why are they looking at us like that?"

"They saw you fade. They know you're a wraith." Corten tugged her down a side street and out of view of the two women.

"Oh, right." Naya looked down at the paving stones. The suspicion and fear in their eyes probably weren't so different from the way she'd stared at the undead when she'd first come to Ceramor. Wraiths could change their faces. They could look like anyone. These people knew a wraith had kidnapped Delence, and apparently that was all it took to make her suspect. "Maybe we should go back to your shop. You said you can't sing souls back anymore, but couldn't you carve me a new bone?"

"No." Corten shook his head. "It would take me at least a week to pick through Lucia's notes, and even then I don't know if

I could re-create her work. Jalance has more experience than me, and he should be willing to help once we explain what's going on."

"Are you sure we can trust him? What if he decides he's better off turning us in?"

"He's part of the Council. Even if he refused to fix your bond, he wouldn't give us up to the Talmirans."

"But—"

Corten spun on her, and Naya nearly crashed into him. "Look," he said, his voice almost a growl, "I agreed to help you. But if you're going to second-guess everything I say, then I'll warn the Council myself and you can find someone else to fix you."

Naya took a step back. "I'm just trying to help." She couldn't blame Corten for his anger. But she also couldn't follow him blindly. She'd done more than enough of that with Valn and her father.

"Fine," Corten said. "But unless you have a better idea, this is what we're doing."

They could try rescuing Lucia on their own, but even Naya knew that was twice as crazy as going to Jalance. Even if they could figure out where Lucia was, she doubted the two of them alone could rescue her. Not to mention they'd still have to find a place to hide while Lucia did her work. For now Corten's plan was the best they had. That didn't mean she had to like it.

CHAPTER 27

Naya tried to keep up as Corten led her toward the palace district. But even moving downhill, her feet dragged. After a few blocks, Corten gave up on her. They waited at the next tram stop, where Corten exchanged a pair of coins for two seats near the back of the small car. As the tram started down the hill, Naya closed her eyes and focused on keeping her body solid. Every bump and jolt rattled up from the wood bench to shake her aching hand.

"Are you all right?" Corten asked as they rounded a tight turn.

She was not all right. She was starting to think capture by the city guard and a hasty execution would be far preferable to another second on this cursed tram. "I'm fine."

Corten looked like he wanted to say something else, but he only snapped his mouth shut and turned back to the window.

"I'm sorry," Naya said after a moment of silence.

"For what?"

"Helping them, lying to you, all of it. I know it doesn't change anything. But still I . . ." Her throat closed around the words.

Corten's shoulders stiffened, and his continued silence hurt almost as much as her fractured bone.

By the time they reached their stop and walked the last few blocks to Jalance's house, Naya was dizzy with pain. She had to lean on Corten just to keep upright.

"Ready?" Corten asked when they reached the door.

His plan was simple. They would ring the bell and claim to be patients. When they were alone with Jalance, they would explain the truth behind Lucia's capture. There wouldn't be any hiding what Naya was once the necromancer started work on her bond. But Corten seemed convinced Jalance would keep her secret for Lucia's sake.

"I'm ready."

Jalance's house was two stories, painted pale yellow with white trim. It had not two but three major rune bindings around the front door. More runes protected the upstairs windows and balconies. Doubt slowed Naya's steps as she recalled Celia's warning about the necromancers and their supporters increasing their defenses. The men and women of the Necromantic Council were bound to have their own plots. Was it wise to give herself up to the people who, only a week ago, she'd been trying to undermine? What was to say this stranger wouldn't use her exactly as Valn and her father had?

Corten pulled the bell rope and a servant answered after the first ring. She looked a couple of years older than they were and wore an immaculate white-and-black uniform cut to show the rune tattoos circling her wrist and neck. Her dark hair was pulled up in a tight bun that accented the sharp angles of her face. "Are you here to call on Lord Jalance?" the servant asked, her eyes widening a little as she looked at Naya.

"Yes, please, my friend's bond is fractured. She needs help." Corten's tone held an impressive mix of desperation and near panic.

"Is she a patient of His Lordship?"

"No. She was visiting the city from Riorrica, but there isn't any time to send her home. Can't you see how badly injured she is? We need to get her inside."

"Oh, well. This is a bit unusual. I'll need to consult with Lord Jalance," the servant said. "You can wait in the parlor if you like."

The parlor was richly furnished, with a deep-blue couch to one side and a handful of portraits hanging on the walls. Blue-and-white upholstered armchairs guarded two of the corners, and a stately writing desk sat under a curtained window looking out to the street. Everything looked expensive, but as Naya sat she noticed the colors were faded and the fabric worn thin from years of use.

Corten caught Naya surveying the room. "Jalance's family owns a small silver mine to the east. He's registered as a necromancer, but he hardly ever performs resurrections. Most people who don't know him well think he studied necromancy just because he enjoys being controversial."

"That could explain why Celia didn't connect him to the Council," Naya said.

"Maybe. Or maybe your friends just aren't as good as they think."

Naya turned away. "They're not my friends."

Silence fell between them, interrupted a moment later when a man strode into the room. He was unusually tall for a Ceramoran, almost as tall as Naya's father. Unlike Hal Garth, though, he had a thin frame emphasized by the hard lines of his black suit. He was perhaps in his late forties, with dark-brown hair swept back over his head and a neatly trimmed mustache on his upper lip. He carried a dark wood case under one arm.

"Corten?" The man paused and looked Corten up and down. "What in creation are you doing here? I was told I had a patient waiting."

"It's my friend, sir. Her bond's been badly damaged."

"I can see that." The man offered Naya a shallow bow. "I am Earon Jalance."

"Blue," Naya said with a nod.

"A pleasure, Miss Blue. Who did you say performed your original carving?"

"We didn't." Corten said. "Is there someplace more private the three of us could speak?"

Jalance's frown deepened. "She shouldn't be moving unnecessarily. You know that."

"I'm not that bad," Naya said.

Jalance raised one eyebrow. "Well, you still seem to have some fire in you at least. However—"

"Please, sir." Corten shot a warning glance at Naya. "My friend was resurrected only recently. She's still adjusting, and I'm sure she'd be more comfortable if we could do this somewhere private."

Naya nodded, trying to look meek. The servant had left them alone in the parlor, but the big double doors were open and it wouldn't be hard for someone to peek through the windows and see them. "If that's all right?" Naya asked.

Jalance tilted his head to the side in an almost birdlike gesture. "Well, of course we can move to my office, if that will make you more comfortable. Though I can assure you none of the house staff will bother us regardless of the room."

He led them upstairs to a much smaller, more sparsely furnished room. The desk, unlike the one downstairs, was battered from long years of use. It seemed ready to collapse under the heavy books stacked haphazardly on top of it. "Please have a seat." Jalance shut the door and motioned to a set of plain wooden chairs. Naya sat down in one, her unease growing as the necromancer set his case next to the desk and turned to face her. "Now then, I'm going to need a full description of how the bond was damaged and who carved the original bones. If the damage isn't too severe, then we really must see to transporting you home."

"That isn't an option," Corten said.

"What do you mean?"

Corten shifted so he stood between Jalance and the door. "We haven't been entirely honest with you, sir. For that I'm sorry, but the situation is dangerous and I wasn't sure what else to do."

"What are you talking about?" Jalance's previously worried expression darkened. "If this is some sort of prank, I can assure you it isn't the least bit amusing."

Corten glanced at Naya, and she saw his fingers tremble before he closed them into fists. But his voice was steady when he spoke. "I wish this were only a joke. Believe me. I think once you hear who wrote this girl's bond, you'll understand."

Jalance licked his lips. "Who?"

"Lucia Laroke."

Naya expected Jalance to look scared, or for the clouds of anger growing behind his eyes to darken still further. Instead he just appeared confused. "Lucia? I thought you said her binding was done in Riorrica. If Lucia performed the binding, then why haven't you taken the girl to her?"

"Wait—you mean you don't know yet?" Corten asked.

"I cannot say what I know or don't know, since you've yet to give me any clear indication what this conversation is about."

Was Valn intentionally keeping Lucia's arrest a secret? Why? "Lucia's been taken by the guards. They'll say it has to do with Delence's kidnapping, but it's a lie. She wasn't involved," Naya said.

"Absurd. Should Lucia have been arrested, I'm certain I would have been informed." Jalance's tone was stiff, his eyes hard.

Naya prayed the silence didn't mean Lucia was already dead.

"It's true, sir," Corten said. "I was in her shop just this morning. There were guards standing watch outside, and the front door was splintered, like someone had forced it open."

Jalance's expression stilled. "You're sure?"

A knock at the door cut off Corten's reply.

"What?" Jalance shouted.

"My Lord?" It was the servant who had let them in. "There's a message for you. They say it's very urgent, but if you're busy . . ."

"No, give it here." Jalance stood and brushed past Corten to open the door. The servant handed him an unmarked white envelope. Inside was a single sheet of paper. Jalance's eyes widened as he read it. He stared at the note, then up at Naya and Corten. His steps were almost mechanical as he crossed the room and sat down on the chair in front of the desk. "This is absurd," he muttered.

"Sir? Is that about Lucia?" Corten asked.

"No, not Lucia. Some mad Talmiran petitioned the king, claiming necromancers kidnapped his daughter. As if any necromancer would be so foolish."

Naya's body went rigid. "Is the man's name Hal Garth?"

"How would you know that?" Jalance asked sharply.

Naya clenched her fists, physical pain smothering the stab of hearing her father's name confirmed. Whatever sorrow he felt over her death obviously wasn't enough to stop him from using her to further his plans.

She met Jalance's eyes. "My real name is Naya Garth. Hal Garth is my father."

"Your father?" Jalance stood up and looked between her and Corten. "What is going on here?"

Naya repeated the story of how Valn had used her death and manipulated her into helping him kidnap Delence. She explained her suspicions about what Valn intended, and Lucia's claim that the ambassador was trying to start another war. Halfway through her story, Jalance slumped back in his chair, his fingers twitching to brush at his already smooth mustache.

"And you trust her? You believe this . . . this account?" Jalance asked Corten when she'd finished.

Corten didn't answer right away. He sat staring at his hands, making Naya wish she could read his aether like she could that of the living. "I didn't at first," he admitted. "I didn't want any of it to be true. But there were signs I should have noticed, and when I saw Lucia's shop ransacked I couldn't keep pretending."

"Well, this is something. There is certainly something going on here." Jalance tossed the now-crumpled note onto his desk. "This business with the kidnapping . . . I don't suppose you can tell me where Delence is, or if he is even still alive?"

"No, I don't know if he's still alive. But I don't think they would have done things that way if they meant to kill him," Naya said.

Jalance shook his head. "I suppose whether or not he's alive matters little at the moment. The palace has been in an uproar ever since he vanished." He rubbed his temples. "The timing of this Hal Garth's proposal isn't accidental. He means to take advantage of our weakness."

Naya's fingers drifted toward the pendant on her neck. By some miracle she hadn't lost it in the fight with the assassin. "I heard my father and Valn saying something about making sure the king was blamed. I think they were talking about the missing Talmirans. They said they had all the evidence in place."

Jalance went pale. "If Talmir could convince the rest of the Congress that King Allence ordered kidnappings for necromantic experimentation, it would doom us. The other Powers would turn their backs on us. It would give Talmir the freedom to call for another purge."

Naya's thumb rubbed a slow circle over the bird on her pendant. If they could prove something like that, it would make everyone think King Allence had violated the treaty. Any chance to pass a vote lifting the restrictions on necromancy would die.

It would force the leaders of Banen and Silmar to admit the Talmirans had been right in their suspicions.

Could her father push it even further than that? They might execute the king under the same laws she'd feared when Corten discovered she was a reaper. King Allence didn't have any children, and she doubted the Congress would let Ceramor decide the path of succession on its own. If such things came to pass, it would weaken Ceramor's position, but it wouldn't necessarily mean war. Maybe Lucia had been wrong.

"But Hal Garth can't prove anything," Corten said. "If Blue—sorry, Naya—comes forward and tells them who she is, then it all falls apart."

"My father might not know I'm still alive," Naya said slowly. A wave of exhaustion hit her as she realized it'd been less than a day since Lucia's arrest. It felt more like a lifetime. "Valn probably only found out a little while ago that his assassin failed. What if he hasn't told my father yet? He might be hoping he can still finish me off before I can do anything." Could it be that simple? All she would have to do to stop her father was come forward with the truth. Naya's fingers wrapped tight around the necklace, making the metal bite into her hand. Tell the truth and sign over her life and Lucia's in the process.

Jalance stood up. "I cannot say. But I for one am certainly not going to make any decisions based on these speculations." He took a step toward the door.

"Where are you going?" Naya asked. She stood up, then had to grip the edge of her chair to keep from falling back down.

"A few key members of the Council are meeting to discuss Captain Garth's accusations. As absurd as they sound, they aren't something we can ignore. I intend to figure out what's really going on here."

"Wait, her bond—" Corten began.

"Has not worsened since she arrived here and is not likely

to fade in the time it will take me to meet with the Council. I am sure I can leave her in your competent care." There was an undertone to those words that Naya didn't think she was meant to hear.

Corten stood for a moment, staring at Jalance. Then he nodded and, with maddening calmness, sat back down. "Of course."

"Are you going to tell them about me?" Naya asked. Jalance was already halfway to the door.

"I don't know yet," Jalance answered, surprising her. "That will depend, I think, on what I learn from the others. Regardless, we will discuss this further when I return."

CHAPTER 28

After Jalance left, Naya heard the soft click of a key turning in the lock. She cursed and jumped to her feet. When she tried the knob, the door wouldn't budge. She squinted, examining the keyhole, then felt in her pocket for the set of picks Celia had given her.

"What are you doing?" Corten asked.

"He locked us in."

"So?"

"So why would he do that if he intends to help us?"

Corten's eyebrows rose. "You just admitted to helping kidnap Delence, and you're surprised someone locked you up? What did you think would happen? Jalance isn't going to act on your word alone, or even mine for that matter."

Naya glared at Corten. What was wrong with him? How could he be so calm?

"If you could unlock that door, where would you even try to go?" Corten asked.

Naya opened her mouth, then shut it again. She didn't have any idea where she intended to go, only that the thought of being locked up was unbearable. The room spun a little, and she had to grab the door frame to keep from stumbling. "I have to do something."

"I think you've done enough," Corten muttered.

Silence fell between them. Naya pressed her forehead against the door. Her eyes burned with the memory of tears. "I know. I'm sorry I got you stuck in all this."

"It isn't your fault," Corten said. But he didn't sound like he meant it. "Lucia's the one who sent you to me. And I'm the fool who fell for everything you told me."

Naya turned. "You're not a fool. Please, Corten. You were the one who . . ." The ache in her throat swallowed the words before she could say them.

Corten's shoulders drooped. He turned away from her and snatched a book off the desk. "Can we please not talk about this?"

Naya stared at his back. If he felt her watching, he ignored it. Eventually her dizziness got the better of her and she slumped down in one of the chairs.

Time seemed to thicken in the little room as they waited for Jalance to return. Waiting, with nothing to do and only the pain of her bond to distract her, was torment. But when Naya finally heard Jalance's key turning in the lock, she found herself dreading the answers he might bring almost as much as she'd hated the delay. Jalance glanced at her, then at Corten, as he walked into the room. His suit was as neat as it had been when he left, his hair still brushed back with the same immaculate precision. Yet something in the way his eyes fell on her, and the hesitant motions of his hands as he shut the door, gave the impression of a man badly rumpled by his experiences.

"What happened?" Corten asked. He abandoned the book and sprang to his feet.

"It would seem you were telling the truth, or at least one version of it," Jalance said. "No one has heard from Lucia since her last resurrection, and several of her neighbors saw the city guard break into the shop. There's been no official announcement of her arrest, though, and I didn't want to make myself too conspicuous by asking around the guard. We have allies there, but it will take time to contact them discreetly."

He pressed his knuckles into the small of his back and winced. "I did, however, manage to talk to a couple of other members of the Council who were close to Lucia. Alejandra's in a fury. I think she was half-ready to march on the palace herself and demand Lucia's release. She confirmed some of your claims. She's apparently been helping Lucia investigate the recent disappearances, and she's convinced the Talmiran Embassy means to frame Lucia for your disappearance, and possibly for the others who've gone missing as well."

"This doesn't make any sense," Corten said. "Naya's been living with Lucia for weeks. Everyone in the neighborhood knows she's Talmiran. She hasn't exactly been acting like she was kidnapped. Anyone with half a brain will be able to see they're lying."

"Valn has documents to support my fake identity," Naya said. "He could deny anything I say and claim the real Naya died in Lucia's experiments." No one here had known her before her death. Why would anyone believe her over Valn and her father? "Besides," she added, "if they find out about my bond, they probably won't care who I am."

"What do you mean?" Jalance asked.

Naya gripped the edge of the desk. So far she'd kept quiet about the illegal runes. The secret felt even more dangerous than her work with Valn. But if Jalance was to help fix her fractured bone, he'd need to know the truth. "Lucia resurrected me using the old war runes. She claimed Valn gave them to her, but I'm still not sure if that's true."

Jalance's eyebrows rose. He looked to Corten, who nodded. "That," the necromancer said slowly, "was a rather critical detail to omit."

"I wasn't sure you'd help us if we told you right away," Naya said.

Jalance's expression grew thoughtful. "I thought all the copies were destroyed in the purge. If Talmir kept them . . . Corten, are you sure we're dealing with the war runes?"

Corten nodded. "Either that or Lucia figured out how to make a copy. The things Naya is capable of fit all the stories I've heard."

Jalance rubbed the bridge of his nose. "Lucia, you fool," he muttered under his breath. "Who else knows about this?"

"I don't know," Naya said. "Valn and his people never mentioned it to me. If he knew, I would have thought he'd try to use the extra power." A new realization dawned on her, and cold settled in the pit of her stomach. "When the guards came for me and Lucia, I burned one of them. I'm not sure if anyone else saw, but they might have figured out what it means."

"Then we should assume Valn knows. Are there records?" Jalance asked.

Corten shook his head. "I think I found all the diagrams when I took Naya's bones."

"Good, well at least we have that. I can't imagine she would have been foolish enough to keep more copies," Jalance said, but his distant tone and the sour-worry taste of his aether didn't match the words. "Let me see your bond, girl."

From his case he extracted a slender metal rod with a rune-covered handle, similar to the one Lucia had used to examine Naya's bones. Lucia had said once it was called a reader. When it touched the back of Naya's hand, the aether around her bones thinned. The bones looked almost as they had before, the smooth curves shining blue from the glowing runes. Now that Naya knew more about rune bindings, she could appreciate the complexity of what Lucia had created. Every inch of the bones was carved in flowing runes, their shapes overlapping in patterns that seemed to shift the longer she stared at them. She could also tell there was something very wrong. The runes flicked, fading in one spot only to flash too brightly somewhere else. And along the bone in her thumb, she could just make out a faint line. The crack was so fine she might not have noticed it had the runes around it not been far darker than their fellows.

Jalance stared at the runes for an uncomfortably long time, then leaned back. "It's true," he muttered. "This changes things. Your bond is proof of Lucia's treason."

"If the ambassador forced her to use those runes, then it's the Talmirans who broke the treaty, not her," Corten said.

"Perhaps." Jalance was staring at Naya's hand, but now there was a hungry gleam in his eyes, and a thread of eagerness leaking out into the aether. "The war runes were the pinnacle of our field. To see them restored . . ." He shook his head as though to clear it.

"Those runes were banned for a reason," Corten said.

"Of course," Jalance said, though there was still something hungry in the way he looked at Naya. He turned to Corten. "You say you recovered her notes, and the spare bones?"

"Yes," Corten said.

"Good. I'll need to see them if I'm going to work on the bond. I never had the opportunity to work with any reapers before the ban, but I imagine it won't be too hard to sort out Lucia's diagrams."

"What about my father?" Naya asked.

Jalance tapped the reader against the edge of his desk. "I'm not sure yet. You've given us an advantage by coming here. If we can find a way to expose his lies, then perhaps we can unravel this mess before it gains further momentum." He slipped the reader back into its case. "Regardless, we'll need more information before we can act. I'll request a general meeting of the Council. With all of us together, we should have enough eyes and ears to sort this out. In the meantime I think it's best you two stay here."

"What—why?" Corten asked.

Jalance smiled apologetically. "Ambassador Valn's agents will no doubt be searching for anyone who might be harboring our young friend here. It shouldn't take them long to learn of your connection, if they haven't already."

"Won't it draw attention if I suddenly vanish?" Corten asked.

"We can use that to our advantage. You're Matius's apprentice, correct? I'll get someone to send word to him. He can spread the news that you left in the company of a young woman. With any luck Valn will think the two of you have fled together."

"And what if Valn doesn't believe it?" Naya asked.

"Matius and I aren't part of your Council," Corten said. "You don't have the right to use him like that."

Jalance's expression hardened. "Miss Garth obviously seems to be involved in the ambassador's plans. From what you've told me, those plans put all of us—necromancers and undead—at risk. If that risk is as great as Lucia guessed, then we all need to do our part. That means Matius will say whatever the Council tells him, and you two will stay here until we decide what to do next."

Corten continued to scowl but didn't argue further. Jalance gave him a thin smile as though that settled the matter. He turned to Naya. "Follow me. I have a place where you can rest safely until we know how best to fix this mess."

Naya was surprised when Jalance led them out to a small back garden. The garden was overgrown with late-summer flowers. A tall hedge surrounded it, and a heavy gate was set in one corner. Two big trees stood at opposite ends of the hedge, their leafy boughs casting dappled shade and obscuring the view of the nearby houses.

"You want us to hide in your garden?" Corten asked.

Jalance offered him a conspiratorial smile and motioned to a cluster of paving stones near the base of one of the trees.

He knelt, pressing his palms against two of the smaller stones and rotating them an inch to the right. Something below clicked, and a large flat stone popped free of its mortar a few paces in front of them. Jalance lifted the stone, and it swung up like a trapdoor, revealing a set of hidden stairs.

"If you'll come this way." Jalance started down the stairs. Naya exchanged a wide-eyed look with Corten, then followed. The stairs were steep, descending about fifteen feet before stopping at a heavy wooden door. Jalance unlocked it with a small silver key he extracted from a chain around his neck. "I haven't had any trouble with the guard yet. But if they do come looking, they won't find you here."

The room beyond the door wasn't large, perhaps ten feet deep and a little more across. The walls were almost entirely lined with bookshelves. A single chair and desk like the ones in Jalance's office had been wedged into the corner, and a thin bedroll lay on the ground beside them. Jalance crossed the room, activating aether lamps set between the shelves.

"What is this place?" Naya asked.

"My vault. I own several rare books that others find controversial. I keep them here where I can enjoy them without sparking any uncomfortable questions."

"What kind of books?" Naya asked, remembering the hunger in Jalance's eyes when he'd examined her bones.

"History, poetry, a few theoretical texts on necromancy. After the first purge many Ceramorans were bitter about how the war ended. The treaty stripped our army, limited trade, and gave Talmir a dozen tools for tampering with our affairs. Delence convinced young King Allence and several other powerful members of the court that it would be best to quietly censor the loudest dissent so as not to give Talmir an excuse to push for even tighter restrictions."

"And you think he was wrong?" Naya asked.

"I do. Every concession we make willingly only weakens us. Delence was naive to think he could convince the Congress of Powers to treat us as equals. What your ambassador did is proof of that. Maybe if Delence and the king hadn't been so eager to roll over, we wouldn't be in this mess."

Naya's brow furrowed. "I'm not sure that's true." Valn had said the other Powers believed Ceramor's show of good faith and that they would soon give in and lift the restrictions. Had that been another lie? If so, then why had they kidnapped Delence?

"How long do you intend to keep us down here?" Corten asked, snapping Naya out of her thoughts.

"Hopefully not long," Jalance said as he headed for the door. "It will take a day or two for me to sort through Lucia's notes. I'll update you on anything I learn from the rest of the Council regarding Valn."

The door's hinges squeaked as it closed behind him. The sound made Naya think of a prison cell creaking shut. She glanced at Corten and saw her own uncertainty mirrored in his eyes.

CHAPTER 29

Naya hugged her shoulders, staring at the closed door. Had they done the right thing coming here? Corten seemed to trust Jalance, but she couldn't make herself feel the same. She turned and saw Corten leaning against the bookshelf opposite her. He stared back warily.

"What is it?" Naya asked, if only to break the silence.

"Nothing." Corten glanced at the door, then back at her.

Naya let her arms fall to her sides. "Then stop looking at me like that."

"Like what?"

Like I'm a monster. "Like I'm going to run. I'm not."

Corten pushed away from the bookshelf and took a step toward her. "You seemed ready to earlier. And you'll have to forgive me if I don't exactly trust everything you say. Everything you told me before today was apparently a lie. Maybe you're still lying. Or maybe you're just having second thoughts."

"I'm not!"

Corten looked away. Naya didn't need to feel his aether to see the bitter anger and hurt written in his expression. Hurt she'd caused. Still, it was a struggle to keep her own anger down. "You don't know what it was like to wake up in that room and realize I was dead. Valn gave me a chance to help the people I cared about.

I thought that if I protected the treaty, I'd be helping keep the peace. I swear I didn't know Valn was involved in anything else."

"That doesn't excuse what you were doing. You used me and Matius and Lucia. You put us all in danger just so you could keep protecting your stupid treaty. Did it ever occur to you how many people here have been hurt by Talmir? Didn't you ever wonder if maybe there was a better way of doing things? All those times you came by the shop and I thought . . ." He gritted his teeth. "I should have trusted Lucia. It never made sense that she'd take on an indentured servant like that." He paused, one lip curling in a grimace. "You must have thought it was hilarious, twisting all of us around like that."

"It wasn't like that."

"Then what was it? The way I see things, you could have stopped coming to me weeks ago. Most of what I taught you, you could have learned just as well from Lucia. You didn't really need my help. So why didn't you leave me alone?"

Naya's chest ached with grief and anger. "What do you want me to say? What could I ever say that would make this right? I'm sorry? Well, I'm sorry it took me so long to see the truth. I'm sorry I believed all my father's lies about the undead." Her voice rose. She knew she should stop talking, but the words tore free. "I'm sorry for lying to you. And you're right. I should have stayed away from you. I should have let you live your life. But I couldn't. Because you were kind and smart, and you wanted to help me even after you knew I was a reaper. When I was with you, I felt like I could forget about everything else. I was falling in love with you, and I couldn't just leave."

Silence fell between them. Corten's eyes went wide. He opened his mouth, then closed it again.

Naya reached toward him. She didn't know what she meant to do, but she needed something from him, anything more than that shocked look on his face.

Corten backed away. "No," he said softly. "I can't."

Naya suddenly wished the ground would open up and swallow her. She squeezed her eyes shut, not wanting to see his shock transform to anger or disgust. A moment later she heard the soft squeak of hinges. When she opened her eyes, Corten was gone.

Naya stood perfectly still, staring around the empty room. Her hand throbbed, but she welcomed the distraction. *I can't.* He couldn't what? Couldn't love her? Couldn't bear to even be in the same room as her? Creator, why had she said that to him? She should have made something up or just kept her mouth shut.

Did she really love him?

She did.

She wasn't sure when it had happened. But how else could she explain the warmth that had filled her whenever he smiled, or how spending time with him had felt like coming home? What else could justify the way the squeak of that door closing could hurt so much more than the pain of a cracked bone?

Minutes inched by and the silence in the little room seemed to deepen toward something ominous. Where had Corten gone? What if he'd fled into the city? What if the guard captured him and—

No! Corten wasn't a fool. Even if she could somehow go find him, she doubted he'd want her help. She spun, staring at the shelves in search of anything that could distract her. Her eyes caught on an old history book and she pulled it free. Jalance had said the vault was full of books that had been banned during the purges, and as she read the title, Corten's words echoed in her mind. *Did it ever occur to you how many people here have been hurt by Talmir?* She'd always assumed the restrictions set into the Treaty of Lith Lor were the only way to protect Talmir and Ceramor from another war. But she'd been wrong about so many things she'd thought she'd known. How well did she really understand the complicated web of politics that balanced the Congress of

Powers? Not enough to see through Valn's plans. Naya flipped the book open. Powerful people had feared these books enough to want them banned. Perhaps among their pages Naya could find some insight into the truth.

One book soon became a pile. She flipped page after page, pausing on whatever caught her eye. She read about the famine and disease that had swept through Ceramor after the war, made worse by the reparation payments the other Powers had demanded. There'd been hunger in Talmir during the reconstruction, but nothing so bad as what Jalance's books described. One text told of dozens being sent to the headsman's block during the purges, and whole neighborhoods burned under the aegis of destroying dangerous magics. Somehow, all that had been done in the name of peace. She'd never questioned it before. After all, the Mad King had started the war. His armies had decimated southern Talmir. The treaty had been an act of justice, one approved by the other Powers and accepted by Ceramor. Was it still just? How could anyone find who was in the right when both sides had done so much evil? Naya tried to fit the scraps of history into what she knew of Valn and his plans, searching for anything that might give her a new perspective on the problem. But it only left her feeling uncertain and small.

Naya slammed the book she'd been reading shut and set it on top of her pile. The room felt suddenly suffocating. Surely by now Jalance would have found out something. Why hadn't he come to speak with her?

She looked around the silent room, then made her decision. But when she opened the door, she found Corten waiting on the stairs leading to the garden. He sat with his eyes closed and his head resting against the wall. If Naya hadn't known any better, she might have guessed he was dozing.

Corten's eyes snapped open. He stared at her, his expression tired. "Where are you going?"

Naya's face flushed and she couldn't meet his eyes. Had he been waiting out here this whole time? "I just want to go up and see what's going on," she said. "We should have heard something by now."

Corten stood. "I don't think that's a good idea."

"Then you don't have to come with me. I just want to know if Jalance has learned anything."

Corten's jaw tensed. But after a moment he gave her a brief nod and stepped to the side of the stairs. They stood staring at each other. Naya wanted to ask why he'd waited out here. But he didn't say a word about their previous conversation and she didn't want to be the one to bring it up.

Not trusting her voice, she nodded in thanks, then jogged up the narrow stair. After a moment fumbling in the dark, she found the switch to open the hidden trapdoor. Fresh, cool air brushed her cheeks, and the musty smell of the underground vault was replaced by the rich scents of wet earth and crushed leaves.

It was dark in the garden, and the grass and flowers glistened with spent rain. A storm must have blown in while they were stuck below. When Naya closed her eyes, she could hear the unsteady patter of drops falling from the wet leaves above.

"What now?" Corten asked, making her jump.

Naya turned and saw him standing at the lip of the open stairway. "I thought you said this was a bad idea," she said.

"It is. But I wasn't going to let you come out here alone."

He'd probably only followed her to make sure she didn't try anything foolish. Still, the hard edges in his face had softened and Naya couldn't squash the hope that blossomed in her chest. She started toward the house, straining all her senses to see if there was anyone around who shouldn't be.

The house was quiet, and the only aether she could detect had the fuzziness of people sleeping. The back door was locked, but after a minute of fumbling with her picks she felt the bolt turn. She opened the door and glanced back. Corten was standing behind her with his arms crossed. "This is a bad idea," he said again.

Naya forced herself to meet his eyes. "Maybe. But I can't fix anything by waiting around and hiding."

She stepped through the doorway, and after a moment Corten followed. The hallway was dark and still. Naya crept through it, retracing her steps to the house's main stair. What aether she could sense seemed to be coming from above. Her feet made no noise on the stairs as she climbed to the second floor.

Partway down the hall she sensed aether coming from what proved to be a well-furnished bedroom. Inside, Jalance lay sprawled on a massive bed set against the far wall. His mouth hung open and his hair had tangled free of the paste that had contained it. Seeing him like that sent a fresh surge of anger through Naya. He'd said he would bring them news. Instead he'd apparently come home and gone to sleep. She stomped forward, then grabbed Jalance's shoulder and shook him.

His eyes snapped open. He broke her grip and rolled away faster than she would have thought possible, fumbling for something on the nightstand. When he turned to face her, he was holding a long knife in a white-knuckled grip. Confusion wrinkled his brow when he saw Naya, but he didn't drop the knife. "What are you doing here?" he demanded.

Naya hesitated. Some small part of her whispered that any sane person would have had the decency to wait until morning. But their situation wasn't exactly ordinary. "You said you would bring us news."

Jalance was looking past her. "Corten, do you have any idea what time it is?" he asked. The sharp panic in his aether was fading, replaced by smoldering anger.

"Late, I would assume," Corten said, his tone surprisingly

light. "There's no clock in your vault." He crossed the room to stand beside Naya. "Sorry to interrupt your sleep." Despite Corten's initial reluctance, it seemed Naya wasn't the only one who'd grown impatient at being left waiting for so long.

Jalance tugged at the collar of his sleeping robe, then set down the knife. "I didn't come for you because I didn't have anything significant to tell you. King Allence has agreed to provide assistance in investigating Garth's claims. Valn has asked that they also investigate the rumors of missing Talmiran sailors. Because the supposed crimes were committed against Talmirans, the treaty gives him the right to lead the initial investigation. But so far he hasn't done anything public."

"What about Lucia?" Corten asked. "Does anyone know what happened to her?"

"Not yet. The Council will be meeting tomorrow night to discuss what sort of action we'll need to take. Hopefully I'll have more information for you after that."

Naya caught the implication behind his words and frowned. "I want to go to that meeting," she said.

"No," Jalance said. "I've only just begun examining Lucia's notes. I won't be able to repair your bond before the meeting. Besides, we can't risk having you captured. You're too valuable."

Naya's jaw tightened. "Either you take me to that meeting or I'll find someone else to help me."

"That's absurd. You're wanted by half the city and you can barely walk. You need my help."

"Actually, it would be good to have Naya at the meeting," Corten said. "She knows more about Valn's organization than any of the rest of us, and she was there when Lucia was taken. The others will probably want to question her before they make any decisions."

Naya. That name still sounded strange coming from him, all the more so because she hadn't expected him to take her side.

Jalance rubbed the bridge of his nose. "We're already taking a risk in calling this meeting. The city's wound tight, and it seems Valn has managed to gain himself a foothold among the guard. I don't need you drawing more trouble."

"I won't," Naya said. "If I move carefully, I think I can keep myself from fading. No one will notice me."

Jalance drew a slow breath. He held it for several seconds, then let it out in a puff. "Fine. You can come. But you must do as I say." He picked up an engraved pocket watch from his nightstand and grimaced when he saw the time. "Now, would you please leave me be? I need rest if I'm to sort through that chicken scratch Lucia calls handwriting."

CHAPTER 30

The next morning Salina, the servant who had greeted them when they'd first arrived, brought Naya a fresh set of clothes to replace the shirt, vest, and trousers she'd borrowed from Corten.

Corten glanced at the bundle and closed his book with a snap. "I'm going to get some air. Let me know when you're done," he said before retreating up the stairs to the garden.

Naya's brow furrowed as she watched him go. Since they'd returned to the vault, he'd spoken little. When he did talk, he acted like their previous fight had never happened. Naya wasn't sure if she should be relieved or worried. Though she couldn't sense him through the aether, his presence in the room had felt like a constant tug on her heart all through the long hours of waiting. She wanted to talk to him about the books she'd read, or find some way to make him see that, despite the mistakes she'd made, her intentions had been good. But she wasn't sure good intentions were enough. And every time she tried to speak, her voice failed her.

Naya dressed, running her fingers over the smooth cotton. The new clothes—a dark-green skirt, a matching shirt, and a black vest with brass buttons—were of good quality but not extravagant.

"You're really from Talmir?" Salina asked as Naya fastened the last button.

Naya tried to hide her frown. "Yes." Jalance had claimed he was keeping their presence here a secret.

Salina's expression brightened. "Really? I've never met a Talmiran wraith before. I didn't know you people could be resurrected." She must have seen something in Naya's expression, because her cheeks flushed and she glanced away. "Not that I believe the stories about how you don't have souls. That's just silly. But my father said that when the necromancers tried resurrecting your soldiers during the war, your souls always resisted the song."

Salina's chipper tone made Naya's insides twist. She'd heard those same stories, except then they'd been about brave soldiers who managed to resist the call of corruption even in death. "How did you know I was Talmiran?"

"I figured it out on my own. Everyone on the streets is talking about the missing Talmirans, and Lucia Laroke's been arrested. People are saying that she had a Talmiran wraith living with her. But now that wraith's gone missing, and since you're hiding . . ." She paused for a breath, then shrugged. "Also, there was your accent. I didn't hear you say much, but you didn't sound like you were from here."

"Wait," Naya said, "they've announced Lucia's arrest?"

Salina nodded. "It was all over the papers this morning."

"Is Jalance upstairs?" Naya asked.

"Not at the moment. He went out around dawn to pay a few calls. He said to tell you that he'll come speak to you when he gets back."

Naya struggled to keep the frustration out of her voice. "Do you have a copy of that newspaper?" she asked.

Salina took a small step back. "I think there's still one in the drawing room. I'll bring it down."

When Jalance returned a few hours later, Naya was waiting for him in the garden with the newspaper. Jalance stopped a few paces away from her and frowned. Naya felt anger leak into his aether, though she could tell he was trying to suppress it. "I told you to stay inside."

"You also told me you'd bring any news as soon as you heard it," Naya said. "Why didn't you tell us about Lucia's arrest this morning?"

The fingers of Jalance's right hand twitched. "Because I went out to see if anyone knew more about the issue."

"Did they?"

Jalance brushed at the front of his jacket, then glanced around the yard. "I would much prefer it if we didn't discuss this in the open."

Naya felt his unease like something crawling against the back of her neck. Suddenly the leafy trees and thick hedge seemed like weak protection from the forces seeking her. "All right," she said.

Corten was waiting for them in the vault. He stood as soon as he saw Jalance. "Naya told me about the arrest. Has there been anything else?"

"Nothing we can act on."

"What about the investigation?" Naya asked, stabbing at the newspaper with one finger. "King Allence is still helping the embassy. We have to warn him that Valn is the one behind all this."

"Even if we had that kind of influence, there isn't much the king can do. On paper Valn's still acting within his rights according to the treaty. And other than your word, we don't have any proof that he's behind the disappearances. Anything King Allence does to block the investigation will only draw suspicion toward the Crown."

"If he doesn't block it, he's just giving Valn the opportunity to plant whatever evidence he wants," Naya said.

"I am aware of that." Jalance's words were clipped with anger. "But the situation is delicate. King Allence is accustomed to following Delence's orders when it comes to Talmir. He's never had a strong will, and right now all he probably wants is to make this problem go away as quickly as possible. If we try to make him see what's really going on, he's more likely to have us arrested than to listen."

Naya crossed her arms. A part of her suspected Jalance was right. But that didn't dampen the sense that they had to do something. "What if we sent a message to the courts at Banen and Silmar? Ceramor might not have all the rights the other Powers do, but they're still protected by the defensive alliance. If we let the other rulers know what Valn's trying to do, then maybe they can help us."

Jalance shook his head. "It's more than a week's journey to Banen on a fast ship, longer if the winds don't cooperate. It's a little faster to reach Silmar, but it would still take days for a message to reach anyone significant. And even then we still have the same issues of credibility. It might be different if we had someone with access to the longscribers in the king's message room. But as things stand, we have to assume Valn will have his say before we can get a message out."

"Longscribers?" Naya asked.

"They're rune devices," Jalance said. "The Congress leaders started using them just a few years ago. A longscriber consists of a set of paired bone disks. If you tap out a message using one half of the pair, then the other half will mimic the movements even if it's hundreds of miles away. The disks are fragile and tricky to use, but they're the fastest and the most secure way to send a message."

"And the king has one?" Naya asked.

Jalance nodded. "He has at least three, one for each of the other Powers. But as I said, we don't have any contacts in the palace who could access them. The embassies representing the other Powers likely have longscribers connecting back to their own governments as well, but we face the same problem of credibility with them as we would at the palace."

"So Valn's manipulating the investigation to frame King Allence, but we don't have any way to prove it to the king or to get a message out to the other Powers. Is there any good news?" Corten asked.

"Some. The Council has allies among the city guard. They're working to figure out how far Valn's influence extends. Captain Terremont is working with Valn, and we suspect he may be in on the plans to frame the king. Terremont commands the guards in the city's northwest sector, but three squads of his men have been reassigned to the investigation. They've been involved in all the arrests so far, including Lucia's."

"How many people have they taken?" Corten asked.

"Three other necromancers, one of whom they've already released."

Corten's expression brightened. "They let someone go? Who?"

"Marsco Ceravace. He was taken shortly after Lucia. We're not sure yet why they released him. Alejandra is looking into it. Hopefully she'll be able to bring him to tonight's meeting."

The rest of the day Naya tried to draw hope from Jalance's words. But with each passing hour her unease grew. By the time Salina came to fetch them, Naya was practically humming with the need to escape. Even Corten looked relieved as they climbed the stairs up to the garden.

Jalance waited for them in a carriage outside the garden gate. Naya's hand throbbed with each step as she climbed into the carriage. "Have you heard anything new?" she asked Jalance as she slid onto the bench across from him and Corten took a seat next to him.

Jalance shook his head. "No, but I'm sure those at tonight's meeting will know more."

The carriage stopped a few minutes later in front of a large house with an elaborate iron balcony overhanging its double doors. "This is where you scheduled the meeting?" Naya asked.

"Of course not. Stay inside. The driver will take you around and I'll meet back up with you in a few minutes," Jalance said as he stepped out of the carriage.

"What—" Naya began, but he was gone before she could finish the question. "What is he doing?" she asked Corten instead.

Corten glanced out the window, a furrow appearing between his eyebrows. "I'm not sure."

The carriage began to move again, turning at the end of the street. A minute later the driver stopped next to an inn. Naya bunched her fingers in her skirt and craned her neck to peer out the window. "I don't see him," she said. "Maybe we should get out."

"I'm sure he's fine," Corten said.

"That's not what I'm worried about."

Corten propped his elbow on the window and rested his chin on his fist. "If Jalance was going to betray us, he could have done it while we were sitting in that vault."

"How can you be so calm?" Naya asked.

Corten made a snorting sound that might have been a laugh. "Oh, I'm terrified, just not of Jalance."

"Of what, then?"

Corten met her eyes and his gaze turned thoughtful. "I'm scared of what we'll find at this meeting. There's a reason Matius and I have steered clear of the Necromantic Council. Jalance's views on Talmir are mild compared with what most of the Council thinks. A lot of the older ones lost friends and family during the war, or during the purge. I'm worried about what they might try to do."

"Then why did you insist we go to Jalance for help?"

"Because I knew we couldn't get to Lucia on our own and I didn't know who else to ask."

Naya forced her fingers to untwist from the fabric of her skirt. "Well, thank you," she said after a long pause. "I'm not sure how I could have gotten anyone to believe me without you."

Corten turned back toward the window. "This city is my home. I'm not going to let Valn ruin it."

Silence fell between them, but it was interrupted a few minutes later by the carriage door opening. Jalance shuffled inside, followed by another wealthy-looking man with broad shoulders, thinning hair, and a round gut. The shirt under his black jacket dipped just low enough to show the ring of runic tattoos encircling his neck.

"Well," Jalance said cheerfully, signaling the driver by knocking once on the ceiling of the carriage. "That should be enough to confuse anyone who might have been watching us. If we're lucky, they'll assume I've gone out to share a cigar with an old friend and won't think to look further."

"Who's this?" Naya asked, eyeing the new man warily.

"Antinole Salavastre." The man extended his hand, the gesture awkward within the confines of the carriage. "And what's your name, my dear?"

"This is the girl I told you about," Jalance said.

"Ah." Salavastre withdrew his hand. "A pleasure. I didn't realize you'd be joining us tonight."

Naya wasn't sure what to say to that, so she just nodded. Jalance took the silence as an opportunity to draw Salavastre into a conversation about the prices of various metals used in forging rune plates. It was the sort of conversation Naya's old self would have listened to eagerly, hoping to pick out details about the local market. Now she found her thoughts wandering.

She turned toward her window, watching Salavastre out of

the corner of her eye. He was undead. But unlike her and Corten, he still had a body. When she used her sight to view the living, she saw them wreathed in aether, the aura of energy shifting with their emotions. Aether drifted from the tattoos on Salavastre's wrists, ankles, and neck, but the emotions in it were shadows, almost overwhelmed by what she felt flowing from Jalance. She wondered why that was. From what she'd heard, undead with bodies led lives far more normal than those of wraiths. They could eat and sleep, though like wraiths they lost the ability to bear children.

Her thoughts were interrupted by the jolt of the carriage stopping. "We're here," Jalance said, his expression serious. Naya followed him out onto a dark and grungy street. Blocky warehouses rose in front of them, the lines of their roofs visible where they blotted out the stars. Drunken laughter drifted from one of the streets behind them, and up ahead she could just make out the murmur of waves against the shore.

"This way." Jalance led them down one of the wide streets running straight between the warehouses. Naya walked slowly, wary of the dull throb still pulsing from the cracked bone in her hand. In the dim light it was hard to tell if her skin was fading.

They came to an intersection, and Naya's neck pricked with the sense of being watched. She checked the aether but couldn't sense anyone outside of their small party.

A clump of shadows moved away from the wall of a nearby warehouse. Naya tensed, catching the gleam of eyes from under what she'd assumed was a pile of rags. "Spare a coin for the damned?" a woman's voice asked.

"Alas, I have only fellowship to spare," Jalance whispered. "Tonight we're all damned."

Naya thought she saw a flash of teeth. "Welcome. Quite a crowd tonight," the woman said as she huddled back under her rags.

Jalance motioned them forward. "Guards?" Naya asked under her breath.

"Watchers. Wraiths mostly. There will be more on the roofs. If anyone unwelcome arrives, they'll give us the time we need to clear out."

They turned at the next cross street, and Jalance stopped in front of an unassuming metal door set in one of the warehouses. He knocked—three quick raps, then a pause, and two more knocks. Naya drew in a sip of aether and felt the dense pulse of many people's emotions mingling.

Jalance's smile sharpened. "Now, Miss Garth, if you'll follow me, I'll introduce you to the Council."

CHAPTER 31

Neat stacks of crates filled the cavernous warehouse. Jalance led them down a narrow aisle to a spot where the crates had been shifted to form a circle of empty space. Here a crowd had gathered, its members dressed in everything from fine silks to rough sailcloth.

Elbows jostled ribs as people shifted to clear a path for Naya's small group. Jalance walked with his head high and his mouth set in a confident smile. Aether pressed in against Naya. Fear, excitement, and anger swirled together, making it impossible to tell one person's emotions from the next.

The crowd surrounded an improvised platform. On it stood two men and a woman. Naya was sure she'd never seen the men before, but the woman looked familiar. She appeared to be in her middle years, with almond-shaped eyes and black-and-silver hair spun up in an elaborate bun. Her lips were painted a bright red and there was something unnerving about her smile. *The café.* That was where Naya had seen her. This was the woman Lucia had snuck out to meet shortly after Naya's resurrection.

"Marsco was obviously terrified," the woman was saying. Her voice was edged with exasperation as she answered some question Naya hadn't heard. "He claims the guard spent hours questioning him and examining the records of everyone he's resurrected in the past four months."

"That's why you should have brought him here," one of the men said. He was bald and his sleeves were rolled up to show muscular arms and wrists banded with rune tattoos. "We need to know exactly what they asked."

"What good will that do?" the second man asked. He was the youngest of the three and had a rich voice that made Naya want to listen even though his simple clothes and bland face gave him the look of a shop clerk.

"A moment," Jalance said, stepping up onto the platform.

All eyes turned to him. "Ah, Earon, I'm glad you were able to join us," the woman said.

"Alejandra," Jalance said with a nod.

"We were just discussing Marsco's release," the younger man said. "I personally think this is the best sign we've seen since this mess began. It's possible we've misjudged the severity of the situation."

"Ranal here thinks we shouldn't dare interfere with our fine Talmiran lords," Alejandra said. "Apparently Marsco's release is proof of their good intentions and we should all go home and sit on our hands until they decide who to lock up."

"Better than risking more bloodshed on the word of a self-proclaimed spy," the younger man, Ranal, said.

"You think the girl is lying?" the bald man asked. "So far all the evidence supports her story. It'd be risky to dismiss that and hope for the best."

"Her story provides one possible explanation," Ranal said. "But we'd be fools if we didn't consider other possibilities."

"At this rate we'll all be long dead before you run out of possibilities to consider," the bald man grumbled.

"Don't misunderstand me, Denor," Ranal said with a glance at the bald man. "I know we've all suffered under the Talmiran oppression. But does it really make sense that they would risk their position in the Congress of Powers just to institute another purge? And if this is a trap, then what's to say the girl isn't part of it? Even if her intentions are good, someone so young could easily be misled. Perhaps they sent her to spread false information, to bait us into doing something that would allow them to destroy the Council."

A chill spread through Naya. "That's not true." The words left her mouth before she could stop them, and she felt the crowd's eyes turn toward her. She wanted to shrink under that collective gaze. Instead she forced herself to step up onto the platform next to Jalance.

Alejandra raised one eyebrow. "I take it you're the Talmiran spy?"

"I was."

"You shouldn't have brought her here," Ranal said, scowling at Jalance.

"I thought you would want to hear her story from the source before you made any decisions." Jalance's voice was calm, but standing next to him, Naya could feel his unease.

"You have something to say, little spy?" Denor asked.

Naya drew in a small breath of aether. With the full weight of the crowd's attention on her, she suddenly wished she hadn't argued to come here. "I swear, I wasn't lying when I told you about Valn's plans. If you sit back and wait, you'll only be giving him exactly what he wants."

"And what is that, exactly?" Ranal asked. "Dalith Valn's been ambassador here for five years. If anything, life has gotten better for our communities under his watch. Do you even understand what you're involved in, girl? Why should we trust the word of a child who claims to be both a spy and a traitor?"

"I'll vouch for her," Corten said, his voice ringing over the growing murmur of the crowd. Naya's lips parted as she stared at him in shock. Corten looked surprised himself, but his expression soon shifted to one of determination.

"Who are you?" Ranal asked.

"He's Lucia's old apprentice," Alejandra said. Her expression turned calculating as she surveyed Naya and Corten.

"I've known Naya the longest out of anyone here," Corten said. "It's true she was a Talmiran spy, and you have every right to question her. But I think she's being honest when she says she wants to help."

"Corten—" Naya began, but she was interrupted by a burst of noise from the crowd behind them. A figure in a red-and-white guard's uniform shoved her way through to the platform. Naya took a step back, ready to run. But no one around her seemed frightened.

"Officer Selmore, what's happened?" Denor asked, his voice snapping sharp as a whip.

Officer Selmore paused, smoothing one hand over the front of her uniform. She was a small woman with short hair and lean features. "Sir, I've found information regarding the captured necromancers."

"Well then? Speak up!" Denor said.

Officer Selmore snapped a quick salute. "Sir, I managed to gain access to Captain Terremont's office when he was called away to deal with some sort of emergency regarding the prisoners. I found a stack of papers on his desk. They were signed confessions claiming Dalton and Elmaron have confessed to kidnapping and murdering Talmiran sailors to perform necromantic experiments. Their confessions implicated Laroke, and . . ." The guard licked her lips. "And they claim all of them were acting under the king's direct orders."

There was a moment of stunned silence in the room. "Did anyone see you?" Denor's voice was soft, but it carried easily through the big space.

"I don't think so. I left everything as it was. It was near the end of my shift, so I told my captain I was feeling ill and got an early dismissal."

"Well," Alejandra said drily, "it seems the girl was telling the truth."

Ranal shook his head. "We can't jump to conclusions," he said, but there was a high note in his voice now that undermined the former tone of authority.

"What we can't do," Denor said, his voice gaining strength, "is continue to act like cowards." His shoulders straightened and his eyes took on a new sharpness.

"He's right," Alejandra said. "We can't risk letting them execute our own over false charges."

"We still don't know they're false," Ranal said. His lips curled into a condescending smile. "You're hardly an impartial authority on this, Alejandra. I think maybe you're letting your feelings for Lucia blind you. For all we know—"

"We know she isn't a murderer," Alejandra snarled. "Would you have us sit by while they kill her?"

"I would not," Denor said. "Ranal, I understand your desire for caution. I agreed to follow Delence's lead and try to show the world we are not the monsters Talmir fears. But the events of the past week have proved something. No matter how much ground we give, Talmir will always want more. Even when we give them no excuse, they will still seek to destroy us."

Naya could almost feel the crowd's attention focusing on Denor. "I died protecting the people of this city," he continued, "and as thanks I was stripped of my rank and thrown out of the city guard. All because the Talmirans don't think someone like me is human enough to trust with a weapon."

He let his eyes sweep over the crowd. When his gaze met Naya's, he stopped. "Tell me, little spy, did your masters treat you any better?"

Naya froze as their attention focused on her again. The room grew quiet, so quiet she could hear her father's words echoing in her mind. *That thing.* She thought about how Celia had kept the truth of their work hidden. How the other spies had scorned her. How Valn had had her killed. "No," she said. "They'll never see us as anything but monsters."

Murmurs rolled through the crowd, and Naya felt the anger in their aether rise. Denor nodded. "Then I say, enough!"

"Enough!" Voices echoed through the room.

Denor's voice rose to a shout. "I say we show this upstart Talmiran ambassador that we're not afraid to fight back. This country is ours, and those northern bastards have no right to decide what we do with it."

The cheers were louder this time. Anger pressed against Naya like heat from a roaring fire. Ranal's forehead glistened with sweat. He took a step back from Denor but didn't raise his voice in protest.

"Tomorrow," Alejandra said, her voice cutting above the din. "Valn's making an announcement at the palace tomorrow. If we go after him there, we can rescue the prisoners before he executes them."

Again the crowd cheered. Naya exchanged a wide-eyed look with Corten. She saw his lips move, but the words were drowned out by the excited voices around them.

CHAPTER 32

The planning began almost at once. Alejandra and Denor drew Naya aside, along with an older wraith and two undead who seemed to have some sort of authority. They asked question after question about Valn, about her father, about his spies and what he knew. Naya's voice came out flat. She tried to answer their questions but her thoughts were muddled. When they finally finished interrogating her, she stumbled away, finding a corner between two stacks of crates where she could sit without being disturbed.

She closed her eyes, feeling the aether like a current around her. The pain in her hand throbbed stronger, and when she opened her eyes the tips of her fingers looked partially transparent. The Necromantic Council was planning an attack on Valn. The suddenness of it made her head spin. She'd succeeded in convincing them of the threat. But the fiery anger she'd felt resonate through the crowd's shouts scared her. Was this what she'd wanted? Denor's speech hinted at much more than stopping Valn. How far would they try to push? How far could they push before Talmir decided to send in their army, treaty or no?

"So is it Blue, or Naya? I've heard both and I wasn't sure," a female voice said from somewhere nearby.

Naya looked up. "Sorry?" A young woman stood in front

of her. She had a round face framed by thick brown curls and stood with her right fist planted on one generous hip. The stillness in the aether around her marked her as a wraith. Something about the woman seemed familiar, but Naya couldn't place it.

Her question had sounded casual, but it left Naya groping for an answer. Who was she really? Blue was the wraith, the one who'd made a place for herself in Ceramor. But she'd never been more than a mask, and telling Corten the truth had shattered her. "Naya's fine. Do I know you?"

"*Know* might be too strong a word, but we have met. Remember? At the Bitter Dregs?"

Naya shook her head. "I don't know what that is."

"The café. You were there with Lucia."

The woman's familiar features clicked into place. She'd been the one who'd noticed Naya's accent. Naya winced, remembering how badly she'd handled that mess. "Oh, that café."

The woman nodded. "The Bitter Dregs is one of our meeting spots. It's usually only Council regulars in there, so when I went to talk to you, I figured you were just a new face. Felt a little bad for goading you, after you left." Her smile widened as though they were sharing a private joke. "Didn't realize I was chasing off a Talmiran spy."

"You didn't chase me off," Naya snapped. "I was keeping an eye on Lucia. Once you made her notice me, there wasn't any point in staying."

"My mistake," the woman said. Naya hoped she would leave it at that, but instead she stepped closer, leaning back against the crate next to Naya. "My name is Iselia, by the way."

"Nice to meet you," Naya said without much conviction. Lucia had mentioned that name before she'd dragged Naya out of the café. Iselia had been quick enough to bully her before, and Naya wasn't sure what the woman wanted from her now. She wondered where Corten was. She'd lost track of him when Alejandra pulled her aside for questioning. She needed to speak to him, needed to know what it meant that he'd spoken for her, and if he still thought she'd done the right thing in coming here.

"You've made quite a ruckus tonight," Iselia said. "Even the inkers seem ready to fight."

"Inkers?" Naya asked, curiosity overcoming some of her wariness.

Iselia traced a finger around one wrist. "Bodied, inkers, whatever you want to call them. It's always easier for them to slip back into their old lives, so it's easier for them to pretend like there aren't any problems that need fixing. People like us, though . . ." Iselia paused, holding up one hand. Her eyes turned thoughtful, and after a moment her fingers blurred and flickered. "Even the folks who are used to necromancy tend to get nervous when they find out you're a wraith. All the propaganda your people spread only makes it worse. Until tonight we haven't had enough folks willing to take a risk to make any sort of difference. I guess we owe you thanks for that. You finally got them scared enough to act."

"But what if it doesn't work?"

Iselia shrugged. "Better that we try to fight than to just lie down and let them stomp all over us." She pushed away from the crate and glanced back at Naya. "Besides, it's a little late now for second guesses."

Naya watched Iselia disappear into the crowd. It had thinned in the last hour or so as people left to begin preparations. Naya stared at the faces around the outer edge of the gathering, wondering what their stories were.

She watched a pair of young men talk, their hands moving to punctuate their words. One had tattoos binding his soul, the other could have been a wraith, or one of the living. She couldn't tell from here. Something tugged at her chest, and she realized that despite her fears she wanted to be a part of this. She would never be Ceramoran. But maybe she could still find a place here. They could rescue Lucia, and Naya could apologize for how she'd treated the necromancer. They would stop Valn and her father, and somehow—somehow—they'd find a way to make everything right.

Naive fool, her father's voice seemed to whisper in her mind. *These people will always be your enemies.* Naya ignored it and shouldered her way into the crowd. It took a few minutes to find Jalance standing on the edge of a conversation. "Can I talk to you?" Naya asked.

"What? Oh, yes." He rubbed one hand over his face. The skin around his eyes was puffy with fatigue, and he looked less self-assured than he had before. "I suppose we should get going? It seems all the plans are set. I'm sure Antinole and Corten are around here somewhere."

Naya grabbed his arm. "I need you to fix my bond before the announcement tomorrow," she said, dropping her voice so it wouldn't carry.

Jalance licked his lips. "I don't think that's wise."

"I intend to go with them tomorrow. I can't do that unless you help me. If you can't do it yourself, then tell me who can."

"You'll be worse off going with someone else. Lucia's work is complicated. I think I've figured out the trick of it, but I can't make you any guarantees."

"Fine. So long as you can get it done by tomorrow." Given the madness they were all about to sign on to, guarantees seemed a distant luxury.

Jalance closed his eyes and pinched the bridge of his nose. "If I start the carving tonight, then yes." In a lower voice he muttered, "It isn't as though I was likely to get much sleep anyway."

After Jalance left to find Antinole and Corten, Naya sought out Alejandra. She found her among a group examining a rough map. When Naya made her a proposal, Alejandra's companions frowned, a few shaking their heads. Naya met Alejandra's gaze, ignoring all the rest. After a moment the older women smiled and extended her hand.

Naya found the others, and they returned to the carriage. They dropped Salavastre off at the inn they'd stopped at before, then continued on to Jalance's house. They spoke little, and when they reached the garden, Naya descended into the vault while Corten went to help Jalance with the carving.

Naya waited alone for the rest of the night and into the next day. Her thoughts danced in nervous circles, playing out the attack plan, and what might come after.

When Corten finally returned, Naya sprang to her feet. "Is it ready?"

"We finished the carving," Corten said.

"Good. What do I need to do?"

"Jalance has the new bone in his lab. I can take you there, but you know you don't have to do this, right?"

"What are you talking about?"

Corten took a hesitant step forward. "You don't have to go with them. Give us a few more days to check the carvings and make sure we got everything right. You being there tonight won't change whatever's going to happen."

"You can't know that," Naya said.

"None of us know what's going to happen. The Council's never tried anything this direct."

"That's why I have to be there." Naya moved to step around him, but Corten grabbed her sleeve.

"Wait," he said. "Before you go through with this, there's something I need to say."

Naya froze. The faint touch of his fingers on her sleeve seemed to send static dancing up her arm. "What is it?"

"It's about what you said before. About how you felt. I'm not . . ." Corten paused and seemed to steady himself. "There's still a lot I don't understand. But I respect what you're trying to do. So I think I'd like another chance to get to know you."

"You do know me."

"I knew Blue. But she was just someone Valn made up. I'm still not sure what parts of her were real and what parts were lies you told to get me to trust you."

Naya shook her head. Her throat felt tight and dry. "I don't know either. When I was around you I sometimes felt like Blue was real, and the life I lived before Belavine belonged to someone else. Now I'm scared that everything about me is built on lies—mine or the ones other people fed me. What if there's nothing good left underneath all that?"

Corten paused. "I think that whatever else you are, you're strong. You were brave enough to tell me the truth eventually, and you're willing to risk your life to help fix things now. That's something."

Naya met his eyes and felt some of the tightness in her chest ease. It was something. A place to start. "Thank you," she whispered.

Corten led her back into the main house, then down to the basement. She hadn't seen this part of the house before, and at first she was struck by the difference between this workroom and the one in Lucia's shop. The floor was tiled with smooth black stone. Tools hung on the walls, and Naya saw a few jars of liquids in a neat row on the counter. There were none of the herbs and medicines that Lucia kept. Apparently Jalance's work didn't extend to tending the more minor ailments of the living.

Stranger than the grimness and tidiness of the space was the stillness in the aether. Nowhere in the room could she feel the tug of aether flowing through runes, and she had to stretch her senses to detect even a whiff of the mingled emotions of the city above.

In the center of the room, the black floor had been chalked

with a triple circle of runes. There was a gap in the outermost circle, facing the door. "What's that?"

"An isolation binding," Jalance answered. "Once I complete the outer circle, those runes will dampen energy transference. It's probably unnecessary. But given the experimental nature of Lucia's work, I thought some extra caution was in order."

Probably. Naya didn't like the doubt in his tone when he said that word. *Probably* he'd gotten the runes right and the bone would fit her bond. *Probably* she wouldn't explode like a feast-day sparkler. It was far too much uncertainty, but right now *probably* was all she had time for.

Jalance turned to retrieve something from the other side of the room.

"Sure you don't want to wait?" Corten asked Naya. "If this goes badly, I don't know if Jalance will be able to sing you back."

"I'm sure," Naya said, surprised to find her voice steady.

"Here we are," Jalance said. He carried a narrow silk bundle in both hands. The silk rustled as he pulled it back with a flourish, revealing a carved arm bone. Sharp runes spiraled around the bone. They were bigger than Naya was used to seeing, and they looked strange without the glow of aether behind them. But after a moment she recognized the familiar pattern of Lucia's design. The bone was beautiful, too beautiful to have come from a corpse. Naya tried to imagine it wrapped in blood and flesh and skin but found she couldn't.

"It's your left humerus. I must say, the carving came out better than I could have hoped." Jalance gave her a smile that seemed at odds with the nervousness tainting his aether.

He instructed her to sit down inside the circle, then placed the bone in front of her. Jalance and Corten stood outside the circle, both looking too nervous for Naya's comfort. "Once I seal the circles, all you will need to do is push a little of your own aether into the new bone," Jalance said.

"That's it?"

"That will begin the integration process. You'll experience some disorientation at first, but the important thing is not to fight it. Once you fill the new bone, it should take over for the damaged one in your thumb. The runes on the old bone will fade as your aether rebalances. After that we can extract it safely from your bond. Ready?"

Naya drew in a deep breath of aether. "Ready."

Jalance bent to chalk the final rune. "Oh, I almost forgot. Once the new bone has settled, you'll want to smear one of the inner runes of that circle to break the isolation binding."

Naya nodded and Jalance completed the circle. All at once the world outside vanished. Naya gasped, her voice sounding strangely flat. It was so dark she could barely see the white sheen of the freshly carved bone.

Had something gone wrong? Naya reached toward the barrier, but it was like trying to force her hand through wet sand. She jerked her fingers back. She searched the floor and spotted the rim of the chalk circle. *Focus!* The darkness was probably just part of the barrier; she could dispel it by marring the runes. Realizing that took the edge off her fear.

Naya allowed herself a single calming breath, then reached toward the bone. A gentle hum resonated through her arm as her hand drew close. Then her fingers brushed the surface and the floor lurched beneath her. The runes flared, Naya's fingers disappeared, and then the sleeve of her shirt collapsed as her arm vanished. Blackness crawled over her vision as her remaining aether rushed into the bone. She wanted to scream but had no mouth, no lungs. Her body pulsed and shifted as it tried to make sense of itself and reshape itself around the new runes.

Inside the new bone waited all the pain of her first death, the ice that had filled her veins, and the desperate panic. It made her want to push the bone away. It wasn't hers anymore. It had been too long. She wasn't that same girl anymore. Whatever had connected her to the bone was gone, and trying to force it back now would only tear her apart.

But rejecting the bone would be as good as giving up, on Lucia, on Corten, on everyone Valn and her father intended to hurt. If she did that, she would be letting them win.

Naya pulled, trying to draw her body back together. She visualized herself as she had been, and how the bones would fit back into that form to make her whole. For an eternity it felt like it wasn't working. Then slowly the balance shifted. She sensed something that might have been fingers, then an arm, legs, her head—her body condensed into parts. Her eyes opened, and she again saw the circle, and darkness beyond.

Naya blinked. Had it worked? The pain in her hand had lessened to a dull ache. She tried to suck in aether but came up with only a tiny trickle. She must have already drawn all the energy on this side of the barrier when she'd touched the new bone. The hunger for aether grew inside her, clawing at her.

She still had enough presence of mind to reach for the clothes that had fallen away when she'd been sucked into the new bone. She dressed quickly, then used the edge of her skirt to brush away some of the chalk circle. The air felt strangely thick, but after a couple of tries the barrier vanished. Naya gasped in aether, reveling in the way her vision focused and her exhaustion faded.

She only half heard Jalance's shout of success. Corten hurried toward her, his expression a mix of excitement and concern. "Are you all right? Did it work?"

Naya stood, flexing her fingers and toes. "I think so."

Jalance's eyes shone eagerly as he ushered her out of the circle. But his expression darkened after he sat her down and checked her bones with the reader.

"What is it?" Naya asked. When she looked at Corten, a cold lump settled in the pit of her stomach. "What?"

Jalance examined the runes again, then tossed his reader onto the table. "Creator mar that woman," he muttered. "Something's gone wrong."

"So it didn't work?" Naya asked, not bothering to keep the frustration out of her voice.

"Not exactly," Jalance said. "The bone activated. It's in the right place. But there's some sort of dissonance between it and the bones Lucia carved. Instead of draining, the damaged bone is sucking aether from the new one, far more than it should need even if it were functioning properly."

Naya clenched her hands into fists to fight the sudden shake in her fingers. "What does that mean?"

"I'm not sure. I've never seen anything quite like this. But with the energy flowing that way, we can't safely remove the old bone. It could be it will still settle out on its own. But as things stand now the binding is unstable. Depending on what's causing the instability, the runes might respond erratically. They could flicker and cause more fading, or the uneven aether flow might cause the binding to overload and snap."

"Can you fix it?" Naya asked.

"Possibly, given time to analyze the problem."

Time they didn't have. They had less than two hours before she was supposed to meet the others at the palace. "What's the worst thing that can happen if we don't fix it?"

"If your bond snaps, you could explode," Corten said, his dry tone making the words sound all the more absurd.

"Explode?" Naya raised her eyebrows and glanced at Jalance.

"Unlikely, but not impossible," Jalance admitted. "The crack doesn't seem to have widened at least. But as I said, I've never seen anything like this before."

Naya flexed her hand. "I don't feel like I'm going to explode." The ache hadn't left her hand, but the fresh aether had soothed it to a tolerable level.

"Still," Corten said, "maybe it would be better if you stayed here."

"No." Naya drew in more aether. "You said it's possible the old bone will still settle out on its own?" she asked Jalance.

"Possible, but I agree with Corten. You'll be safest waiting here."

"No," Naya repeated. "I'm the only reaper the Council has. I won't hide while other people risk their lives to stop Valn. I'm going to the palace."

CHAPTER 33

King Allence's summer palace was located on a wide street just a few blocks from the Talmiran Embassy. Naya had walked past it more than a dozen times but had never been beyond the high stone walls. Now the gates stood open, allowing people to trickle in toward the hall where Valn would make his announcement. Naya clutched at the front of her skirt as she joined the small crowd waiting to pass through the gates. There were fewer people here than she'd expected. Were others afraid to come? Or did they still not understand the threat lurking behind Valn's investigation? Naya slowed until she fell into step just behind a woman in a yellow silk gown and a man in a brown suit.

Her hand and arm ached, though she wasn't sure if it was from the damaged bone or because of the strain of holding a new set of features. Valn had had plenty of time to spread her description, and she wasn't sure who among his spies might be lurking in the crowd. At least some of them would be able to recognize Blue's face. That wasn't a risk Naya wanted to take.

As she approached the guards flanking the wide gates, she willed herself not to reach up and double-check the contours of her face. She'd made her hair a dull brown and given herself a weak chin and pale cheeks scattered with a few pox scars. Hopefully the plain features would help discourage anyone from taking notice of her. The couple ahead of her passed the guards, the man giving them a brisk nod. Naya scurried to follow, reminding herself to breathe with each step. *In and out. Don't be afraid. You're just an ordinary girl come to listen to the speech.*

"Excuse me, miss!"

Naya froze, fear buzzing from her toes to the tips of her hair. She willed her expression to remain calm as she turned, schooling her features into a mask of dim curiosity.

One of the guards strode toward her. "You dropped this," he said.

Naya recognized the slim wooden case in his hand. She felt at her skirt's pocket, then muffled a curse when she found the tear. "Thank you," she mumbled as she accepted the case back from the guard. She quickly tucked it into the waistband of her skirt, hopefully before he could notice the shake in her fingers.

The guard nodded once, barely giving her a second glance before returning to his post. Naya continued down the path. The back of her neck itched with the certainty that, at any moment, the guards would realize who she was. It was only after she crossed half the distance that she got the courage to look up from her feet.

A wide gravel path led from the gates to the palace proper. Gardens spread out all around her. Ancient-looking trees shaded a tiny pond to her right, and to the left was what looked like a hedge maze. The palace loomed ahead, the last rays of evening light making the pale-gray stone walls seem to glow.

No one else bothered her as she made her way through the big double doors and down a short hallway to the grand reception room. Naya paused by one of the stone pillars near the back, scanning the crowd. The Council's leaders had decided it would be best for everyone to enter separately. That way they were less likely to draw attention.

After a moment she spotted Alejandra. Naya pushed forward and touched the older woman's elbow. "It's me," she said softly.

Alejandra glanced at her, then nodded. She looked far calmer than Naya felt. "Turnout is a bit thinner than we might have hoped," Alejandra said.

"Is that going to be a problem?" Naya asked, keeping her voice low.

"Probably not. Are you ready?"

"Yes."

Alejandra smiled. "Good. I saw Officer Selmore a moment ago. She's in position."

Naya nodded, continuing to watch the crowd. The king's audience chamber was a long, rectangular room with pillars running down each side and a raised platform with a throne at one end. People stood in loose clumps, most of them clustered near the throne. Corten would be somewhere in that crowd, along with Iselia and most of the others Naya had seen at the meeting. Between the shifting bodies, Naya could just make out a line of guards separating the crowd from the platform. Valn would likely have chosen people loyal to him for that post. The Council would have to break through quickly if they were going to take Valn captive during the speech. Naya hoped any fighting would be brief and that Corten would have the good sense to stay far back from the worst of it.

She drew in aether, her head swimming for a moment with the heavy mix of fear and excitement. The new energy dulled the pain in her hand like the cooling balm her mother used to rub on her scrapes when she was little.

"And so it begins," Alejandra said, interrupting Naya's thoughts.

Valn walked across the platform at the far end of the room, flanked by four men wearing the formal uniforms of the Talmiran Army. Naya frowned. There still wasn't any sign of King Allence or any of his advisers. Had Valn already detained them? Surely he didn't have the manpower to move against them before he'd even made his announcement.

"Come," Alejandra said, tugging at Naya's elbow.

Naya reluctantly turned from the stage, following Alejandra. They found Officer Selmore standing at attention against the left wall, next to a set of doors leading deeper into the palace. Behind them, Valn began his announcement. "Thank you all for coming. I understand that this investigation has been a great source of anxiety for the people of Belavine. The increase in violent attacks near the docks is a danger to all of us, and I appreciate your support in finding and punishing those responsible. Long ago the people of Talmir and Ceramor lived as one, and in my role as ambassador here I have hoped to rekindle that sense of brotherhood. So it is with a heavy heart that I bring you the initial findings of my report. The necromancers of Belavine have betrayed the sacred restrictions of the Treaty of Lith Lor by performing profane experiments on unwilling victims. Worse, my men have found evidence suggesting—"

"Lies!" someone shouted from within the crowd. Valn ignored them, but more voices joined the chorus, and the shouting quickly drowned out his speech.

"That's our signal," Alejandra said as she started walking toward Officer Selmore.

Naya followed, doing her best to appear calm. She need not have bothered. The guards around them were all focused on the growing chaos near the front of the room. Officer Selmore nodded as they reached her. A moment later Officer Rossen, another guard loyal to the Council, joined them. Rossen was a young man with a narrow frame and hazel eyes that looked too big for his face. He gave Naya a nervous smile when she met his eyes.

"Okay," Officer Selmore said softly, "let's do this quick."

The rest of them nodded, and she opened the side door. She

went through first, followed by Alejandra, then Naya. Officer Rossen came through last, shutting the door behind him.

The noise of the crowd dimmed to a murmur, then disappeared as they followed Officer Selmore down a series of hallways. Fine portraits glared down at them from gilt frames, and Naya was grateful for the plush carpet that muffled their footsteps. Selmore had planned their route to minimize the chance of unwelcome confrontations. Still they paused at every intersection, giving Naya a chance to check the aether for anyone nearby.

After several long minutes, Selmore stopped at a heavy wooden door. "This is it," she said. "These stairs lead to the dungeons. I didn't get an exact count, but given how many guards Valn assigned to the main hall, I don't think there will be more than two or three on watch below. Could be we can convince them to let us through. If not, we'll need to disable them before they can call for help." She met Naya's eyes. "I don't have the key, so this is where you come in."

Alejandra's smile was shark-like. There was something hungry in her aether, and underneath it a bone-cracking worry that Naya assumed was for Lucia. "You heard her. Show us what you can do."

The others stepped away, giving Naya room to crouch beside the door. There were no runes around the frame, but the iron knob was locked tight. Naya pulled the small case from her waistband and extracted the lock picks she'd hidden there. She slipped the picks into the lock and closed her eyes, feeling her way through the pins one by one. Celia's voice echoed in her mind. *Keep your hands steady. Don't rush.* She wondered what the old spy would think of how Naya had chosen to use her lessons.

She'd just gotten the second pin set when Officer Selmore let out a sharp hiss of breath. "What's going on here?" an unfamiliar voice called from the end of the hallway.

Naya's eyes snapped open and she stood, using her skirts to cover the lock. A group of five guards strode toward them, their aether humming anticipation. She'd been so focused on the lock she hadn't felt them coming.

"Sir," Selmore said. "These two were identified as suspicious persons wanted for further questioning. Officer Rossen and I were escorting them to the cells."

"How unusual," said the man who'd spoken. He had a hard face with a nasty scar bisecting his lower lip. "You two are supposed to be keeping watch in the main hall. And so far as I know, no one has given you a key to the lower levels."

Naya's throat tightened as she felt certainty flowing like cool water through the guard's aether. He knew Selmore was lying. She exchanged a glance with Selmore, who gave her a fraction of a nod. Naya drew in aether and reached for the knife hidden in her sleeve. They were outnumbered, but given the guards' expressions, she doubted they'd be able to talk their way out. From the corner of her eye she saw Alejandra's hand disappear into her pocket.

Before Naya could attack, the guard with the scar snatched something from a holster on his belt. Naya's eyes widened as the gaping barrel of the rune pistol swung up. The guard pulled down the hammer and a heavy click sounded as the first of the two rune plates slid into place. He pointed the weapon at Alejandra. "Move and I'll blow her head off," he said in a conversational tone.

The aether in Naya's bones hummed, begging for release. But all she could think of was Delence's son running toward her with a sword, and the way his blood had gushed when the carriage driver shot him. Alejandra was staring at the pistol. Sweat glistened on her forehead. Her hand was wrapped so tightly around something in her pocket that the muscles of her arm stood out like narrow ropes beneath her skin. No one moved.

"Good," the guard said. "Now, Officer Rossen, would you kindly relieve Officer Selmore and her companions of their weapons?"

"What?" Selmore snarled, turning to look at Rossen.

Rossen avoided her gaze. "Sorry," he mumbled, unslinging his club and starting toward them.

"You're working with them?" Officer Selmore asked, staring at Rossen as though he'd grown a second head. "What about your brother? What do you think these bastards will do to him?"

Rossen flinched, then licked his lips. "Come on, Lila, you've got to see it. The Council's gone too far this time. They're going to get us all killed. I had to do something. They said if I helped, they'd make sure Jebel wasn't harmed and—"

"Move it along, Rossen. This isn't story time," the guard with the scar said. Naya saw one of his companions pull out a set of salma wood cuffs and start toward her. Seeing the cuffs snapped her out of her terror. The guard with the pistol was only a couple of feet away from her. As Rossen and the man with the cuffs moved in to disarm her, Naya let the aether flow into her legs. She bent her knees, feeling the energy change and imagining the power in her legs compressing like a spring, and then she lunged for the guard with the pistol.

She slammed into his arm, knocking it to the side. Runes pulled sharp and sudden on the aether, and a crack resounded so loud it seemed to ripple through her. The guard staggered as Naya wrenched the pistol down, trying to pry it from his grip. Someone screamed behind her. From the corner of her eye, she saw Officer Selmore swing her club at one of the other guards. The guard with the scar grunted as Naya managed to pry two of his fingers free of the pistol. Too late she saw another guard swing at her hand with his club. She jerked her hand back, but one of her fingers snagged in the pistol's trigger guard. The club slammed into the back of her hand.

Blinding pain arched through her body, turning her vision white. She stumbled and felt the cold press of salma wood snapping closed around her wrist. She tried to flail away, but her limbs felt weak and useless. More salma wood snapped around her other wrist, locking it in place. Naya sagged against the icy restraints. People shouted and jostled around her, but their words fled her mind before she could make sense of them. Someone yanked on the cuffs, hauling her forward until she was stumbling down a steep flight of stairs.

CHAPTER 34

After the stairs, the guards dragged her down a long hallway and into a brightly lit room. Naya's vision refocused as they shoved her into a chair and locked her manacles to a set of hooks on the arms. A guard she didn't recognize stood beside her chair, his eyes focused on the far wall. She craned her neck but couldn't see any sign of the others.

Then the door opposite her opened and Valn walked into the room. His suit was as neat and black as it had been the day he'd taken her name and convinced her to join his cause. His face was set in the same mild, unreadable expression she remembered. If the attack in the main hall had unsettled him, he hid it well. Naya lunged forward, or tried to. She barely made it an inch before the restraints jerked her back into the chair.

"Please, let's try to be civil." Valn smiled, but his eyes remained cold.

"Let me go," Naya snarled.

"You know I can't do that." He stepped closer. "I must admit I was surprised to hear you'd come. I'd expected you'd have the good sense to flee, but I should have known Hal Garth's daughter would be too stubborn for that."

"Don't compare me to him," Naya said. Valn recognized

her. That must mean she'd lost her hold on the face she'd been wearing.

"Oh? What happened to the girl who would do anything to make her father proud? Ever since you first slipped my men, I've been wondering what made you betray your mission." He paused, then shrugged when Naya didn't answer. "I suppose it doesn't matter. Thanks to the intelligence Officer Rossen provided, my troops made short work of your little revolt upstairs. I should be thanking you, really. The attack adds weight to our claims that I never could have manufactured alone."

Naya flexed her fingers. She didn't think the cracked bone had gotten any worse, though it was hard to tell through the icy pain from the salma wood. "Why are you doing this?" she asked.

Valn regarded her thoughtfully. "Your father would say we are fighting a noble battle to stop the necromancers from spreading their foul magic."

"But you don't care about stopping necromancy. You had me killed, just to turn me into a wraith."

Valn blinked, then smiled again. His pale lips didn't curl quite far enough to expose teeth. "Aren't you full of surprises? You're right. I don't share your father's devotion to the old laws of Talmir. I don't believe in throwing away a useful resource just because aspects of it may be distasteful." He said it so casually, as if deciding to kill her had been no more difficult than picking what to eat for breakfast.

"No matter how much your father denied it, we needed a reaper for our plans to progress smoothly. A normal wraith couldn't have pushed through that salma wood door Delence installed in his home. Also, your existence is undeniable proof that the necromancers of Ceramor have violated the treaty. Your arrival in the city fit perfectly with our time line, and your father assured me you shared his zeal for protecting Talmir. In this at least I'm sorry to see him proved wrong."

Naya twisted against her bonds. The numbness was spreading, but maybe if she kept him talking, she could find some way to slip out. "The necromancers aren't the ones who've been murdering Talmirans. You did that. You're a traitor and a liar!"

Valn's eyes widened as something sharp and painful shot through his aether. "We all have to make sacrifices. I did what was necessary to protect my homeland."

"How could killing your own people be necessary?"

Valn closed his eyes. After a moment his features regained their smooth calm. "You must understand, the balance between Talmir and Ceramor is a delicate one. The Mad King's war wasn't the first time we've fought. Our two countries have always been uneasy neighbors, and there have always been disagreements over how far our respective borders extend. The cost of maintaining an army we can muster quickly to repel any attack along our border's length is significant. And so long as we must maintain defenses to the south, we cannot spare the resources to compete with the Banian Navy at sea."

"That's why we have the treaty," Naya said. "Ceramor doesn't even have an army, and if they did somehow attack us, Banen and Silmar would come to our aid."

"True, but the balance of power is shifting." Valn's voice took on a tone that reminded Naya of her teachers back at the Merchants Academy. "When we first met I warned you that our allies' support of the treaty restrictions was weakening. The other Powers think Ceramor isn't a threat anymore. But the Ceramoran people haven't forgiven us for our last victory. The treaty kept them weak, and the hardships it caused have only added more fuel to their anger. Whether it's over necromancy or something else, another war is inevitable. The only questions are when and who will strike the first blow. If we continue to wait, we risk losing our advantage."

"You're planning an invasion," Naya said with growing

horror. "You made it look like the Ceramorans broke the treaty, so Banen and Silmar wouldn't retaliate against you."

"So far as they will see it, Talmir has every right to land troops. We will argue that King Allence's involvement in the recent deaths and the attack tonight were already acts of war."

Naya turned away from him, sickness churning inside her. She'd helped him. Even given everything she'd done to fight, she still somehow had helped him. "You're disgusting," she said. "Do you have any idea how many people will die because of what you've done?"

"Fewer will die now than if we hadn't acted. You said it yourself: Ceramor has no army. Any defense they offer will be easily destroyed. I've spent years building alliances here. Once we've taken martial control, those allies will step forward to form a new Ceramoran government, one more willing to follow our lead." Valn leaned forward, his gaze intense. "Everything I've done has been for our queen and the good of Talmir. I had hoped you'd be able to see that. I had hoped you could find some peace in knowing that your death will help save so many of your countrymen."

There was something about the look he gave her that was almost pleading. And when she drew in aether, she sensed the barest hint of uncertainty. Maybe deep down he really did regret killing her. Now he was asking her to tell him it was all right, that she understood why he'd done it. Naya sat a little straighter in her chair. "I. Will. Never. Forgive. You." As she spoke the words, she imagined each one like a dagger thrown at his chest.

Valn leaned back, then turned away. "I'm sorry to hear that. But I would still beg you to think of the bigger picture. I assume you know what has to happen next?"

Naya clenched her jaw. "Let me guess: you're going to kill me. Again."

"The executions will be tomorrow," Valn said, as though they were talking about the weather. "Again, I'm sorry. I had hoped we could continue working together. I'm sure you're try-ing to come up with ways to fight me, but I'd like to propose an alternative. If you cooperate, and refrain from any undignified and futile displays of protest, then I will do everything in my power to help this city's undead during the transition. I won't be able to save all of them, and of course there will have to be strict bans on any further resurrections, but I think I can make the queen see the value in sparing those who submit."

For a moment Naya was too shocked to answer. Her throat tightened. "Why would you help the undead?"

"Why wouldn't I? Everything I've done here has been to minimize the damage of the coming conflict. But if you continue inciting violence among the undead, you'll only make it harder for me to justify sparing them once our troops take the city."

Naya drew in a deep breath of aether. The energy felt thick and heavy with determination, mixed with that same sour threads of regret. Valn's expression gave no hint of whether he was lying. He was a murderer who got others to do the dirty work for him. But he also didn't share her father's rage. If he thought granting mercy to the undead would make it easier to build his puppet government and dominate Ceramor, he might actually do it. Her thoughts turned to Corten, to Jesla. "You really expect I'll trade a handful of lives for all those deaths your war will cause?"

"I expect you'll refrain from a futile show of resistance to save those you can. War is coming. Nothing you do or say will stop that."

Naya's hands shook. He was wrong. There had to be some-thing they could still do. But even as she thought it, her shoul-ders sagged. The cold from the salma wood cuffs had spread past her elbows. She was trapped, and everything she'd tried so far had only made things worse.

"I'll give you time to consider your options." Valn motioned for the guards to follow him. "Bring her, if you would."

The guards detached Naya's shackles from the chair and used the chain to drag her to her feet. They led her down a hall lined with heavy doors. The whole place stank of old sweat, rotting straw, and other, worse things besides. The oily reek of despair in the aether infected her, mixing with her own emotions and making her sag against her shackles. The guards hauled her to a stop in front of a door with no window.

"Celia told me you had little trouble forcing your way through the salma wood plate inside our old friend's door, but I know you can't break through this." Valn withdrew a large key from a chain around his neck and used it to unlock the door. "I'm going to have one of my men remove those cuffs. Every guard in this dungeon is equipped to deal with wraiths. Even if you were to fight your way out of this cell, you would not make it out of the palace. Do you understand?"

"Yes."

One of the guards unlocked her shackles. Naya barely had time to register the relief of warmth seeping back into her arms before she was shoved into the cell. She stumbled forward and collided with the far wall. Behind her the door slammed shut, plunging the cell into darkness. Naya jerked her hands away from the wall. It nipped at her skin with the frostbite chill of more salma wood. She tried to press through it, but the chill only intensified.

"Who's there?" someone asked from just to her right. The voice was ragged, but Naya recognized it all the same.

"Lucia?" She spun toward the sound.

"Blue? I thought that was you. What are you doing here?"

Naya blinked, then squinted, but the dark was absolute. She raised one hand and felt it brush a sleeve, felt the arm under that sleeve wince away. "I, um, came to rescue you."

Lucia seemed to consider this new information for a moment. "Ah . . . I don't suppose this was part of that plan?"

"No." Naya fumbled forward until she reached what she

thought was the door. She pressed her hands against it. The smooth wood was as icy and unyielding as the walls. "Is this whole place made of salma wood?" she asked, marveling at what that must have cost.

"I believe so," Lucia said.

"Why would they put you here? You're not a wraith."

"I wondered that myself." She coughed. "There are only a handful of cells like this in the whole kingdom. I suspect Valn wanted to protect against the chance that the Council would decide to send a team of wraiths to rescue me. Unlikely, of course. As for you, well, there's nowhere else they could safely put you. I suppose it was simpler to leave me in here than to move me."

Naya sat on the floor. It, at least, didn't have the same unyielding chill. But when she let her hand sink down experimentally, she ran into another barrier of salma wood.

Lucia cleared her throat. "Do you know what's going on outside?"

"War," Naya said. She drew in a breath of aether and let the despair sink in.

CHAPTER 35

Bit by bit, in response to Lucia's prodding questions, Naya revealed what had happened since they'd separated.

"Alejandra," Lucia said, her voice going rough around the name. "Were you able to see what happened to her? Is she still alive?"

Naya closed her eyes, replaying the chaos of the brief fight. "Last time I saw her, one of the guards had her pinned to the wall. She was struggling, so I think she's still alive at least."

"Then they'll have her down here somewhere."

"I'm sorry," Naya said.

"I doubt there's anything you could have done to stop her from coming. Alejandra's always had a habit of rushing into things."

Lucia's voice held a note of tender sadness that sent heat rushing to Naya's cheeks. "I didn't realize. Do you love her?"

Lucia remained silent a moment, then sighed. "Yes. I suppose it's not so damning as being an undead Talmiran, but it's still not the sort of thing we like to proclaim."

"Why?" Naya asked.

Lucia made a snorting sound. "Because most people here still see relationships like ours as selfish. After the war, one of King Allence's advisers began a campaign to 'rebuild the population.'

The treaty stripped our weapons, but I think he had some vague hope that if we just had enough babies, we could eventually protect ourselves by numbers alone. It was stupid of course, but it gave an excuse for others to scorn people like Alejandra and me. Never mind that we both had far better things to do with our time than make babies."

They sat in silence for a moment. "In Talmir no one would have minded. Not so long as you married," Naya said.

"Oh, of course. Well, it was such a comfort to know Valn didn't scorn my private life while he forced me into treason and threatened the woman I love."

"I'm sorry," Naya said again. "I should have realized sooner what was going on. I should have figured out a better way to stop him."

Lucia sighed. "And I should have taken Alejandra and run rather than letting him threaten me into resurrecting you. Yet here we are."

Silence fell, and it felt heavier for the darkness around them. "Why didn't you run?" Naya asked.

Cloth rustled against wood as Lucia shifted. "Does it matter?"

"It does to me. Corten talked about you like you were this pillar of morality. I don't think he'd have believed you would use the old war runes if he hadn't seen the evidence himself."

"That boy," Lucia said softly, "is too trusting for his own good."

"I know." Naya hugged her knees tighter.

"Well," Lucia said after a long moment. "I suppose if we're both going to die tomorrow, there's no harm in one more person knowing the truth." She paused, as though considering her next words carefully. "The short answer is that Valn knew who I was during the war. Even if we'd run, he could have caused all sorts of trouble by exposing my identity."

"Who were you?" Naya asked.

"Isabela Cerones, apprentice to Renor Marotin. Valn came to me because I'm probably the only person still alive who'd ever resurrected a reaper."

Naya drew in a sharp breath and heard Lucia chuckle in response. The laugh transformed into a cough. "I suppose you think I'm lying, given the show the Talmiran Army made of purging everyone involved in the research."

"I . . . Corten told me there were rumors that some people escaped the first search, but I thought they were all caught."

"That's mostly true. I was an apprentice when the Mad King's war began. My master and I were drafted to design the reapers. But we finished our work too late to make any real difference. My master was sent to the front lines to perform resurrections, while I remained at our research center on the border. After the Battle of Nel Hill, only a handful of us made it out before the Talmirans broke through into Ceramor. The others were caught by patrols in a matter of days, though I didn't know it at the time.

"I ran south as fast as I could, sleeping in ditches and stealing food whenever I had the chance. Eventually I made it down to Rolsina, by the Silmaran border. By then the city was already thick with refugees who'd fled the fighting in the north. The Talmirans still searched there of course, but I managed to avoid them."

Naya sat in stunned silence. "If the Talmirans knew you escaped, then why would you ever start practicing necromancy again? Wouldn't that just draw attention?"

"Current circumstances do point to that conclusion," Lucia said drily. "But at the time it felt like the only option. I lived on the streets in Rolsina for almost a year, begging to keep myself alive, stealing when that wasn't enough. I probably would have gone on like that until something killed me. But one day I overheard someone say my name. At first I thought that was the end. I was too exhausted to keep running. Yet the man was telling his companion I'd been found and executed. I could hardly believe it. But I found the announcement in the newspaper the next day."

Lucia paused, then let out a tired sigh. "I still don't know if the Talmirans believed that whatever poor soul they caught really was me, or if they just needed to execute someone so as not to look like they'd failed. Either way, someone else died and I was given a second chance. I decided I had to use it to help people, and necromancy was the only thing I knew. I changed my name and found someone to forge the documents I needed to make my identity official. Once that was done, I joined a group of refugees traveling back north to Belavine. I'd heard rumors that the necromancers here were working to preserve what they could of our art. It was a risk, but I wanted to do whatever I could to help. Everything was going well until . . ." She trailed off.

"Until Valn found you," Naya said.

"Yes. I still have no idea how he figured it out. So many years had passed that I thought I was finally safe. But when he came to my door, he knew my real name. He had one of my old research notebooks. It seemed impossible. I hadn't taken anything with me when I fled, and I assumed everything else had been destroyed. But apparently that wasn't the case."

Naya tried to absorb what Lucia was saying. "Where would Valn have gotten your notes?"

"I don't know. He seems a bit young to have taken part in the purges, though it isn't impossible. Creator knows, I wasn't much older than you are now when that all began."

Naya scowled. "Why hide the runes all this time? And why wait until now to use them?"

"Perhaps it took him this long to make his plans. Or perhaps there's some other factor at play. It doesn't seem to matter much now. I doubt you or I will live long enough to learn the truth."

Naya squeezed her knees tighter against her chest. "I won't let him kill me again."

Lucia didn't answer. Naya closed her eyes, even though it made little difference in the dark. She hated waiting and not knowing what was going on. The attack on Valn had failed, but what had happened to everyone from the Council? What had happened to Corten? Hopefully he'd been able to escape. But even if he was free, she doubted he'd be able to stay that way for long if the Talmiran Army managed to take the city. A heavy weight settled in her stomach. If she gave Valn what he wanted, maybe he could protect Corten.

"You said Jalance repaired your bond," Lucia said, startling Naya from her thoughts.

"He tried. It made things a little better, but he said there was something wrong, something about the old bone draining energy from the new."

"Interesting. Are your original bones still causing you pain?"

Naya flexed her fingers. "Not anymore, and I feel sharper than I did before."

"Hmm," Lucia said, satisfaction buzzing through the word. "Then it must have worked."

"What worked?"

"Your bones are healing."

Naya stared in the direction of Lucia's voice, her eyes straining to pick out some sign of the necromancer's expression. "I thought that was impossible. Corten said a wraith's bones can't heal."

"It was impossible, or at least that's what everyone thought. One of the biggest challenges we faced when designing the reapers was that the new abilities put too much stress on the bones. The fractures were tiny, but they accumulated quickly. The few reapers we successfully resurrected had to have new bones carved after nearly every battle, which was hardly ideal. We'd tried all sorts of solutions—reinforcing the runes, adding duplicates to reduce strain—but the cracks kept forming. I thought that if we couldn't prevent them, then maybe we could find a way to repair them without continually carving new bones. I've been playing with the theory since before the war's end, but your bond was the first chance I had to really test it. From what you've described it sounds like the crack you suffered was severe. The new bone Jalance carved must have taken some of the strain off the cracked area. If the pain's gone, then it's possible the bone is already healed."

"So you did experiment on me," Naya said. It seemed stupid to be angry about it now, but she couldn't stop the emotion from leaking into her voice.

Lucia coughed. "Yes, well, if Valn was going to force me to break the treaty and possibly destroy my own life in the process, I wanted to at least learn something from it."

The answer was so absurd it startled a laugh up from Naya's chest. "Some good it does if the secret dies with us."

"You said Jalance has my notes."

"He does, but I'm not sure he actually understood them. After he added the new bone, he said the repairs could cause my bond to snap. For all I know I could explode before Valn gets the chance to kill me."

"Explode?" Lucia snorted. "That's—oh. Oh!"

"What?"

Cloth rustled as Lucia shifted closer. "Come here. I have an idea."

CHAPTER 36

The walls of the cell muffled sound as well as aether. So there was no warning before the door finally opened, dazzling Naya with a sudden flood of lantern light. "Cuff them both," Valn said from somewhere behind the light. Naya's instincts screamed at her to run. Instead she held her hands forward and let the guards clamp the wooden cuffs over her wrists.

One of the guards locked a more mundane set of iron cuffs around Lucia's shaking wrists. A greenish bruise marred one of her cheeks, and the lines around her eyes seemed far deeper than Naya remembered. Lucia met Naya's eyes and dipped her chin in a slight nod.

Naya looked away, not daring to let any sign of hope show on her features. Lucia's plan was more than a little mad, and more likely to get them killed than provide a means of escape. But it at least meant they'd die fighting, instead of going passively to their execution.

Naya's eyes stung when she thought of Corten. Was she throwing away her best chance to help him survive the coming conflict? But that help was such an uncertain thing. Besides, Corten and the rest deserved better than the future Valn offered. She had to believe they would find a way to keep fighting.

The guards dragged them down a different hall from the

one Naya remembered, through a series of twists and turns, and eventually up a narrow stair. They came out into another hall, this one furnished with rich carpeting and paintings on the walls. Valn paused. "I trust you've considered what we discussed?" he asked Naya.

Naya ignored Lucia's curious glance. She let her shoulders slump. "Yes."

"Good." Valn patted her shoulder the way someone might pat a favorite dog. "I don't expect you to understand, but I am sorry. I wish this could have ended differently for you."

Naya's skin crawled, but she bit her lip and nodded. With her hair falling over her eyes, at least she didn't have to see his face. The guards gave her shackles a jerk and led her outside. Naya hunched, looking as pathetic as possible. They were somewhere near the back of the palace, outside what looked to be a servant's entrance. Evening light glowed against the high stone walls. Two black carriages waited just a few steps from the doors, surrounded by guards.

Naya risked a glance at Lucia as the guards shoved them into the first carriage. Two guards flanked the necromancer, and two more held chains attached to the loops on Naya's restraints. A fifth guard already sat in the carriage, glowering at all the rest. He had a jutting chin and a star insignia decorating the breast of his uniform. He watched Naya through narrowed eyes as the others dragged her into her seat. Lucia was pushed onto the bench across from Naya, her shoulders hunched to make room for the burly men to either side. After a moment the driver whipped the horses, and the carriage jerked forward.

Heavy shutters covered the windows, so Naya could only guess at their direction as they rattled along in silence. Her head buzzed with tension and it wasn't long before she started wishing they would reach their destination. She'd had more than enough of waiting in a dark cell.

She sensed the gathered crowd just before the carriage stopped. Anger. Fear. Disgust. She wondered what had happened while she'd been locked up, and what stories Valn might have spread. *No, don't think about that.* The people out there had come to watch her and Lucia die. But if she was careful, and smart, maybe she could put on a very different sort of show.

The doors opened, letting in the noise of the crowd. Shafts of sunlight peeked between the buildings as the sun sank toward the ocean. Naya caught a glimpse of masts silhouetted against the sunset and felt her heart wrench. She turned away. The crowd was packed into a wide square she remembered from her travels with Celia. A makeshift wooden platform rose from the center of the square. Naya's knees locked, but the guards only pulled harder on the chains, forcing her to stumble forward.

The crowd pressed tight around the platform, rich and poor alike craning their necks to see the convicted necromancer and her creation. Naya wished she couldn't sense their aether. She didn't want to feel the mix of raw emotions that hung in the air like swamp gas. Two men in shackles were dragged from the second carriage by more guards. Naya didn't recognize them, but from their hopeless expressions she guessed they must be Dalton and Elmaron, the other necromancers Valn had arrested. The guards forced them up the steps to the top of the platform. Naya's eyes gravitated toward the objects dominating its center, and the two masked men who stood beside them. One of those men had his hands wrapped around the haft of a heavy-looking ax. A plain wood block and a wicker basket sat next to him, their intended use as obvious as it was horrifying.

The second man held a mallet and stood next to a table made of dark salma wood. There were shackles where Naya's arms, ankles, and neck would no doubt be secured. A shudder ran from her hair to her toes as she imagined what would happen. They would strap her in. The mallet would fall, crushing her bones. The runes anchoring her soul would shatter, and then she'd vanish into the void on the other side of death.

It took all her will not to pull against her manacles. A scream strained at her throat but she clamped her teeth together. She forced one foot forward, then the other. She wouldn't give them the satisfaction of seeing her fear.

The guards would have to take the manacles off to get her onto that table. She would have one chance. Valn climbed onto the platform, wearing a grim expression as carefully tailored as his suit. "People of Belavine, as many of you know, last night I was attacked while attempting to reveal the findings of my investigation. Those behind the attack were radicals who sought a return to the horrors of the Mad King's reign. These necromancers"—he gestured at Lucia and the others—"murdered Talmiran citizens while trying to rediscover the secrets of the war runes. They did so under the direct authority of King Allence."

Angry voices rose from among the crowd. Naya stared out at them. Several well-dressed people stood near the front. Their expressions didn't match the cloud of fear and anger she felt. Instead they looked almost eager. Were they allies of Valn, or ordinary citizens who believed his lies? She spotted movement behind them, then her eyes widened as she recognized a familiar face. Iselia was pushing through the crowd. Naya opened her mouth, wanting to call out, but before she could, two of the guards shoved her onto her back on the salma wood table. The wood was like a block of ice underneath her. She tried to keep listening to Valn's speech, but the cold made it hard to focus. Instead she closed her eyes and hoped the guards would think her resigned to her fate.

Cold encased her legs as they locked her ankles to the table. The urge to panic tightened like a hand around her throat, but she kept herself still. The noise of the crowd rose, and something thudded against the platform nearby.

"Liar!" someone shouted.

Valn's voice rose to a boom as he tried to speak over the crowd. "—reinforcements under Talmiran command and with the authority of the Congress of Powers will arrive shortly to maintain order while we continue—"

Naya pushed away the distractions, waiting until . . . There! Warmth spread through her left wrist as the shackle on that side opened. Naya sucked in aether, taking the crowd's fear and anger as fuel. She wrenched her wrist free of the shackle before the guard could secure it to the table. The guard's eyes widened and he opened his mouth to shout. Naya concentrated all the force of her enhanced bones into the palm of her hand and shoved. The guard stumbled, hitting the man behind him and knocking him off the platform. Another guard started toward her.

Naya let the aether of her arm go transparent, exposing the bones of her binding. According to Lucia, a wraith's bones weren't that different from other types of bindings. They could be overloaded to cause an explosion of energy. Normally it would be suicide. But the bone Jalance had carved was a duplicate to the one in Naya's thumb, unnecessary now that the old bone had healed. Hopefully.

Her fingers wrapped around the new bone in her arm. She pulled.

The pain was white-hot. The sky went black. The shouts of the crowd became the roar of death's tides. Then the bone, its ties to her soul already weakened by the dissonance between the new runes and the old, tore free of her arm. One of the guards reached for her, trying to pin her back against the salma wood table. Naya ducked under his arm. She concentrated, and shimmering heat pooled in the palm of her left hand. She let her arm pass through the guard's, then slapped him hard across the face. His cheek blistered at her touch, and he shrieked as he stumbled backward.

Naya twisted, her ankles still caught in the restraints. One half of the manacles was locked around her right wrist, but, with the other half dangling free, it was more annoyance than hindrance. Valn was standing near the edge of the platform. She met his eyes and saw his mask of calm fracture. She drew in every scrap of energy she could, then forced it into the new bone, concentrating on the runes Lucia had described while they'd waited in the darkness. Naya's head spun and the edges of her vision blurred. Just as she felt the energy overflowing, she threw the bone at Valn.

She had an instant to savor the shocked look on his face before the bone exploded. The blast hit her like a train. It caught the edge of the table, flipping it and her sideways onto the platform. Her senses dimmed, then snapped back into hazy focus. Her body rippled from the explosion's force, and her whole arm ached. For a moment the dark tides roared in her ears, but Naya drew more aether and the sound faded.

She bent forward and was relieved to find the bindings on her ankles held shut by sturdy clasps rather than locks. She unlatched them. Blissful warmth flooded back to her toes as she rolled away from the table and got unsteadily to her feet. A few steps to her right lay Lucia, who was trying to stand up but failing. Her wrists were still shackled and there was something wrong with the shape of her right arm. Blood dripped from a cut on her forehead.

Smoke rose from the far edge of the platform where Valn had been standing. One of the prisoners sat next to the headsman's block, staring in blank horror at the ax lying embedded in the platform next to him. Naya couldn't see the other. The executioners and the guards were recovering slowly from the blast, some showing injuries even worse than Lucia's. Fights broke out in the crowd near the platform as people tried to flee the chaos. Before anyone could stop her, Naya grabbed Lucia and hauled her to her feet. Lucia snarled a curse but managed to stumble after Naya as she ran to the edge of the platform.

Naya's toes hit the edge and she froze. Anger and fear roared in the aether around her. "Naya!" a familiar voice shouted, barely audible in the chaos.

"Corten?" Naya scanned the crowd, then spotted an arm waving frantically above the sea of people, not far from where she stood.

Lucia groaned, leaning more of her weight against Naya. Naya looped one arm under the necromancer and hauled her over her shoulder. Lucia screamed as her arms bounced against Naya's back, then fell limp. *Don't you dare die*, Naya thought. She scanned the crowd again, but Corten was gone.

Unsteady footsteps creaked on the boards, and someone behind her snarled. Naya spotted an opening to her right. She jumped from the platform and pushed into the crowd. The mass of people was packed tighter than a school of cod trapped in a net, all of them trying to push their way out, but many seemingly unsure which direction out was. She heard more people fighting, the sound of fists against flesh and guards shouting behind her. Here and there she caught flashes of familiar faces, men and women she'd seen at the meeting of the Necromantic Council. Things looked a little less tight to her right, so she headed that way. Lucia's weight pressed against her shoulder, but among the crowd the aether was so thick she almost didn't need to breathe it in to feel the energy infusing her.

"Naya!" A hand grabbed her arm and she spun, nearly losing her grip on Lucia. It was Corten. He wore a brimmed hat pulled low to shadow his face. The shoulder of his shirt was torn, and a button had been ripped from the bottom of his red vest, but otherwise he appeared unharmed. "Is that Lucia?"

"She's alive," Naya replied, sagging with relief at the sight of him.

"Good. Follow me." He grabbed her hand and they shoved through the thinner edge of the crowd. A man clawed at Naya's shirt. Corten swung a clumsy punch and managed to catch the man on the chin. Naya twisted free, pushing toward what she hoped was the edge of the crowd. After a few steps she glanced back and was relieved to see Corten just behind her.

Members of the guard were trying to form a perimeter around the square, but the gaps in their line were wide and there were still too many people trying to force their way out. Naya and Corten passed within ten feet of a guard shouting orders over the heads of the crowd.

Corten led her through side streets, behind gardens and shops. The streets darkened as somewhere to their left the sun slipped below the horizon. When they were fairly certain none of the guards had followed them, they paused between two high garden walls, far from the light of the streetlamps. Naya eased Lucia down onto the pavement. She was still unconscious, but the cut on her forehead had stopped bleeding and her aether didn't feel like it was fading.

Naya turned around. "We should—" Before she could finish the thought, though, Corten's arms wrapped around her and his lips pressed against hers. The touch sent a shock through her entire body. His skin was fire on hers, burning through her like lightning through a tree. It seared away everything but the sensation of his body against hers.

"I'm sorry," Corten gasped as he pulled away. "I'm sorry, I know I shouldn't have. But I thought you were dead. When we realized the announcement was a trap, I thought—"

Naya pressed her mouth to his, silencing the protest. His lips felt soft and warm and so wonderfully real against her own. For a moment she lost herself in a burst of fierce joy, reveling in the fact that they both had somehow survived.

"It's all right," she said when she finally found the will to pull away.

"Yeah," Corten said. He looked a little dazed. The soft smile that spread across his face made her want to kiss him all over again. But the not-so-distant sounds of the crowd reminded her they were far from safe.

"How did you get away?" she asked. Her mind was still reeling from their escape, and from the kiss. Had Corten really kissed her? Had she really kissed him back?

Corten's expression turned serious. "Got lucky. I was near the back when Denor led the charge against Valn. As soon as we moved, another couple dozen guards jumped us from the side entrances. They had wraith eaters and pistols. It wasn't even close to a fair fight. The crowd panicked and rushed the doors. We still aren't sure how many made it out—a lot of people are hiding. When the morning paper announced the execution, Iselia and I got everyone we could together. After what happened at the palace, we weren't sure what we could do, but none of us felt right standing by while Valn killed innocents."

"Thank you," Naya said.

Corten's smile was tight. "I'm just glad you had your own plan. I doubt we could have gotten to you without that distraction."

A shout came from the next street over, and both of them turned toward it. "We should move," Naya whispered. "We need to get Lucia somewhere safe."

Corten nodded. "I know a place. Come on."

The address Corten led her to was only a few blocks away, but still they had to stop twice to avoid other groups fleeing the foiled execution. Their goal proved to be a small second-floor apartment on a quiet street. The floorboards creaked as Naya hauled Lucia up the narrow stairs, expecting at any moment for someone to come barreling down on them.

Corten knocked in a quick pattern. Apparently they were expected, because the door opened almost immediately. An old man with rumpled clothes and sad eyes motioned them in, then relocked the bolts as soon as they were through.

"Who is it, Granpap Fredricel?" a woman's voice called from the next room.

"More stragglers," the old man, Fredricel, said as he helped Naya ease Lucia down onto a couch. Two others stood in the room, a gangly boy of perhaps fifteen whose aether marked him as a wraith, and a slightly older girl with a nasty scrape along one cheek. By the similarities in their features, Naya guessed they were siblings. "I don't suppose you stole the key to those manacles?" Fredricel asked.

"No," Naya said. "But if you have anything I can use as a pick, I should be able to get them off."

Fredricil nodded. "I'll see what I can find, and we'll need something for that broken arm." He turned to open a small closet. "Jessin, we've got a patient for you to look at," he called through an open doorway leading to what looked like a kitchen.

Footsteps came from the kitchen and a moment later Iselia walked in, followed by a balding man wearing cracked spectacles. The man, who must be Jessin, hurried over to Lucia. Iselia gave Corten and Naya a tight smile. Her clothes were torn in spots, as though she'd been fighting, but her thick curls still tumbled artfully over her shoulders. "You actually got them out." She looked at Lucia, still lying unconscious on the couch, and her smile fell. "Did you see anyone else?"

Corten shook his head. "I think Dalton and Elmaron got away from the platform, but I lost track of them in the crowd. Velicia was leading a group toward them, I think. They were still at it when we got away. Has anyone else come by?" Naya searched her memory. She was fairly certain Alejandra had introduced her to a broad-shouldered woman named Velicia at the Council meeting.

Iselia shook her head. "Just what you see. I got here with Lestare and Marecen just a couple of minutes ago. Osvolen was near us for a while, but we got separated in the crowd and I haven't seen him since."

Fredricel returned from rummaging through the closet with a set of tarnished, woman's hairpins. "Will these do?" he asked.

"Yes, thank you." Naya set to work, first carefully unlocking the cuffs around Lucia's wrists, then the one that still dangled from her right arm. She let out a small sigh of relief as the icy salma wood clattered to the floor.

"Okay," Naya said, trying to infuse the word with confidence. Now that they were out of danger, the joy of escape was fading. "What do we do now? Does the Council have a plan?"

"What do you care?" the girl with the scraped cheek asked. She stood protectively next to the boy, her arms crossed and her aether bitter with anger and loss.

"Now, Marecen . . ." Iselia began.

"No!" Marecen said. "I saw her at the meeting, the same as all of you. But I still don't see why any of you trust her. She's Talmiran, for Creator's sake! She's the reason Denor and Alecia are dead."

"Denor is dead?" Naya asked. Her voice sounded small as she struggled to recover from the onslaught of Marecen's anger. Denor was the one who'd asked her if she thought that the Talmirans would ever see the undead as people. She'd seen sympathy in his eyes when he'd looked at her.

"We still don't know that for certain," Iselia said.

"I saw one of those Talmiran bastards shoot him in the chest. He's gone." Marecen glared at Naya. "He put all the best fighters at the front, so when your ambassador sprang his trap they were the ones who got caught. Seems pretty convenient to me that you showed up just in time to lead us all into that trap and cripple the Council."

"Rossen was the one who sold you out, not me," Naya said.

"And we're supposed to believe that on your word alone?" Marecen asked.

The boy—Iselia had called him Lestare—put a hand on his

sister's shoulder. "They were trying to kill her. Why do that if she was still working for them?"

"We assumed they were going to kill her," Marecen said. "But maybe that was all an act. We'll never know now that you fools rescued her."

"That's quite enough," Fredricel said. "I know you're all frightened, but what's done is done. Right now we need to figure out the best way of contacting the others and protecting ourselves from what's to come."

"Fine," Marecen said. "But give me one good reason why we should let her stay."

Naya forced herself to meet Marecen's eyes. The girl's anger pressed in on Naya through the aether. A part of Naya wanted to shout at Marecen. She'd been prepared to die to stop Valn. Wasn't that enough? Then again, she might have felt just as angry if she were in Marecen's position. "I know you have plenty of reasons not to trust me," she said, trying to keep her voice even. "But I swear I'm on your side. I know how Valn's spy network functions, and I know what he's planning."

"Good. See? We're all on the same side," Fredricel said. "Why don't you lot stay here. I'm going to see who else made it out of that riot."

"You shouldn't go back out there," Iselia said, planting her hands on her hips. "What happens if the guards catch you, or if you get stuck in a crowd and your knee goes out?" Her tone was scolding, but there was real worry in her eyes.

"The guards won't be interested in an old man like me, and my knee will hold out just fine, young lady," Fredricel said. He donned a floppy brimmed hat, then gave them all a reassuring smile before ducking out the door.

A moment of tense silence fell before Iselia turned to Naya. "Well, Miss Spy, I guess it's time for you to start talking."

Naya nodded. "Okay, but this could take a while."

Naya tried to ignore Marecen's continued suspicion as she told them everything she could remember about Valn's plans. The six of them sat in a loose circle next to the couch where Lucia slept. Once Naya finished telling them what she knew, she let the others talk, hoping one of them might have a fresh idea for how to solve the problems she'd been gnawing at ever since she'd learned of Valn's plans. Corten's fingers found hers as the conversation wore on. The touch and the memories it kindled were a balm against her growing frustration.

"We have to fight," Iselia said, for what Naya guessed was the dozenth time. "Anything else is just stalling."

Corten shook his head. "If we fight now, we lose. We have to start evacuating the undead. If we flee south, maybe we can rally enough support to do something productive. There's still a chance Banen and Silmar will side against Talmir."

"What if they don't?" Marecen asked. "This is our home. And we can't very well leave everyone behind and hope the Talmirans don't kill them."

The conversation was interrupted by the sound of the front door opening. Six sets of eyes turned toward it. Lestare's hand went to the kitchen knife tucked under his belt, and Iselia reached for something behind the couch.

"Just me," Fredricel said as he shuffled into the apartment.

Iselia scowled. "Granpap, you were supposed to knock."

Fredricel waved the comment away. "Knock. It's my house, you know."

Iselia crossed her arms and opened her mouth to say something else, but Corten interjected. "What did you find out?"

Fredricel eased into an old rocker by the door. "Nothing good. Captain Terremont still seems to have control of a couple of squads of the city guard, along with eight Talmiran soldiers from the embassy. They've got rune pistols and wraith eaters and who knows what else. Talked to a couple of lads in Vistel

Square, said they saw the guards take Valn back into the palace. Guess they mean to hole up until reinforcements arrive."

"What about the rest of the guard?" Lestare asked.

"Scattered. Some are still patrolling the streets, trying to keep folks calm. I think Lieutenant Astenda has set up at the guard station past Hillside Street. She probably isn't taking orders from Valn, but that doesn't guarantee she's on our side either."

"Did you find anyone else from the Council?" Iselia asked.

"We've got about ten folks holed up at Velicia's shop off Market, and apparently a few more at Jalance's home. They'd sent out runners to try finding more, but I didn't want to wait around for them to get back." He shifted in his chair, scratching the back of one elbow. "It's looking bad," he muttered. "No one knows what's happened to the king or the rest of his advisers. Some folks are saying they're still in the castle or that they've already fled the city or that Valn had them all killed."

Grim silence fell. Naya looked around the room, then realized everyone else was staring at her. "What?" she asked.

"You're the one with all the inside knowledge," Iselia said. "You've been sitting there all clammed up. How about a little insight?"

Corten's fingers squeezed hers and Naya squeezed back. She met the others' eyes even though she would have rather sunk away through the floorboards and out of sight. "I'm not sure. I—" Everything she'd tried so far had gone horribly wrong. She'd managed to escape the execution, maybe even injure Valn. But apparently that hadn't been enough to stop his plans. "I think we should go to the Talmiran Embassy," she said slowly.

"Why there?" Lestare asked, his question mirrored in the others' expressions.

"Because that's where Valn did his planning. There still might be something there we can use to prove that Lucia and the others are innocent and that King Allence didn't violate the treaty."

"Seems a little late for that," Fredricel said. "If what you said is true, then we've got an army charging our doorstep. I doubt they'll stop killing us just so we can quibble about proof."

Naya's fingers bunched tight in the fabric of her skirt. "It isn't too late. If we can convince the other Powers this was a setup, they can still force Talmir to back down. Banen's armada is twice the size of Talmir's. Their army might not be as big, but it would be more than enough to cause trouble if the bulk of Talmir's troops have already moved south into Ceramor. Silmar won't be able to threaten Talmir directly, but they could send troops into Ceramor to protect the cities." It was the only option she could think of, but it still made her uneasy. Some part of her still thought of Talmir as home. And the people there didn't deserve to be attacked any more than the Ceramorans did.

"How are we supposed to contact anyone, much less convince them to believe us?" Marecen asked.

"The Banian and Silmaran Embassies are only a few blocks away from the Talmiran one," Naya said. "Jalance said he thought all the embassies had longscribers linked back to their own governments. If we can break into the Talmiran Embassy, maybe we can find proof of what Valn's been doing. We'll take it to the other ambassadors and they can send it out for us."

"That," Iselia said after a moment, "is a terrible plan. What's to say we'll find anything, or that the people at the embassies will let us in? Even if they do, if the Talmiran Army gets here first, they could take the city before the other Powers have time to do anything more than make threats."

"Well, I don't hear you offering anything better," Naya said.

Iselia shook her head. "I admire what you're trying to do, but last time there was trouble the other Powers sided with Talmir. What makes you think they won't do the same again?"

"That was before the treaty. Last time, the other Powers only got involved when it looked like the Mad King would conquer

Talmir. They won't support another war so long as we can make them see that Ceramor hasn't violated the treaty." Naya could see the doubt still plain on their faces. She drew in aether, trying to look confident. "I'm going to the embassy. Anyone who wants to come with me is welcome, but I won't force you."

"I'll go," Corten said.

Naya flashed him a grateful smile.

"Might as well see what's happening there," Lestare said with a shrug.

"Are you serious?" Marecen gave her brother a hard look.

"Like she said, we don't have a better plan." His expression softened. "Mar, please. I know you're scared, but we can't just sit around waiting for Valn's troops to find us."

Marecen shook her head. "I already watched you die once."

"I'm not dying again. I'll be careful. I promise."

Naya could feel the misery and uncertainty in Marecen's aether. Finally Marecen looked up and nodded. "All right. But if you get him killed," she said to Naya, "I swear there will be no safe place left for you to hide."

Fredricel rubbed his chin. "Well, if you're all intent on going, give me a few minutes to check the streets and make sure there aren't any more guards lurking nearby."

Jessin licked his lips nervously, then shook his head. "I think I should stay here with Lucia."

Iselia looked between them, then nodded. "I still think it's a waste of time, but all right. Let's see if this bastard has any secrets left to hide."

CHAPTER 37

They scavenged the apartment for anything that might be of use. Iselia found another kitchen knife for Naya and passed Corten an iron poker. Naya hefted the little knife. It wasn't very sharp, but it would still be better than going to the embassy unarmed. She tried not to sigh as she tucked it into the waist of her skirt. At least her hand had mostly stopped hurting. Lucia had warned her that severing the new bone from her bond might reopen the crack. But so far it seemed she'd gotten lucky on that count.

As the others prepared, Naya found an out-of-the-way spot in the kitchen. She leaned back against the wall and closed her eyes, trying to remember everything she could about the embassy. Valn's office was on the first floor. Would it be best to go in through the front door or to break one of the office windows? How many people would still be there? Surely Valn would have left a few guards at the embassy. Would her father be there?

"Hey," Corten said.

Naya's eyes snapped open and she found him standing just in front of her. "Hi."

Corten rubbed the back of his neck. "How are you holding up?"

"All right," Naya said, then shook her head. "No, that's a lie. I'm terrified."

"Yeah, me too."

They were both silent for a moment, and Naya realized for the first time that the rest of the apartment had gone quiet as well. "Where did everyone go?"

"Lucia's still sleeping, and Jessin is with her. Everyone else went downstairs. Fredricel checked the street. He said there aren't any patrols around, so if we're going to do this, we should leave soon."

Naya nodded and felt a blush creeping up her cheeks. The space between them seemed suddenly smaller, the air sparking with something that longed to jump from her chest to his. "About what happened earlier—" Naya began.

"I think I'm falling in love with you too," Corten said.

Naya blinked. "Oh." She paused, stunned. "I thought you said you didn't really know me."

Corten smiled. "I've seen enough to know you're a good person. You're strong and passionate, and what happened at the palace made me realize I don't want to lose you."

Naya's throat tightened. "I don't want to lose you either."

"You don't have to. When all this is done, let's go somewhere. Anywhere you want, but let's just get away from all this." Corten waved at the darkened window, a gesture that seemed to encompass all the chaos and uncertainty brewing in the city beyond.

"What about the glass shop?" Naya asked. Her chest felt like it was expanding, stretching too tight to contain the emotions trapped inside.

Corten glanced at the floor, then drew a deep breath and squared his shoulders. "Like Matius said before, it's not like it will burn down without me. Besides, I've been feeling like it was time for a change for a while. This is probably going to sound stupid, but being around you makes me feel like I'm coming alive again. I hadn't realized how much I was still hiding from what happened to me. I wasn't really trying to learn what Matius had to teach, because I still felt like none of it mattered compared with being a necromancer. Maybe someday I can go back and try again. For now, though, I just want to try being alive."

They weren't alive. Not really. But Naya's certainty crumbled when she thought back to the execution platform. For an instant she'd stood facing Valn and she'd seen the fear and shock and anger written on his face. She'd chosen to fight, and in that moment she'd felt more alive than she ever had before. That same surge of joy had echoed when Corten's lips touched her own. "You know I can't walk away from what Valn's done. I have to see this through."

Corten gave her a lopsided smile. "Then I'll help."

"Thank you." Naya tried to return his smile. By tomorrow they could both be dead, or fleeing from an army they couldn't fight. It was stupid to hope for anything, but she couldn't stop herself.

"You're welcome."

"I mean thank you for forgiving me. I still don't feel like I deserve it."

Corten leaned forward, pressing his forehead against hers. "You do."

She kissed him again, feeling his arms wrap tight around the small of her back. The world fell away. For a moment Naya thought she could feel Corten's emotions spiraling through her—hope and fear mingling in an intoxicating rush.

Someone made a loud throat-clearing noise from the kitchen doorway. Corten jerked away, turning and putting his hands behind his back like a schoolboy caught stealing cookies.

Iselia stood scowling with her hands on her hips. "Really?" she asked.

Corten coughed. "I take it everyone's ready?"

"Everyone else is." Iselia raised one eyebrow. "Of course, if you two are too busy to help us stop this little war . . ."

"No," Naya cut in. "Let's go."

Nervous energy filled Naya as she stepped into the cool night air. Her fingers brushed the handle of the kitchen knife at her waist. Hopefully she wouldn't have to use it.

The others were waiting for them in the dark street behind the house. "Right, good luck," Fredricel said to Iselia. "It's quiet here, but I'm guessing that won't be the case near the embassies. Keep your heads down and try not to get caught."

"You too," Iselia said, giving her grandfather a hug.

Fredricel smiled, though his eyes looked misty with worry. "Don't fret over me."

They watched him go in solemn silence. After he retreated inside, Naya motioned for the others to follow. They didn't speak as they slipped from one dark street to the next, avoiding the blue-white glow of the lamps. Naya felt as though the whole city were holding its breath, everyone barricading themselves into their homes until they could see what the morning would bring. She used the aether to guide them around those few people who were still out on the streets.

They were nearing Market Street when the first shouts reached their ears. Naya froze. The shouting was coming from somewhere up ahead—one voice, then more.

"Is that smoke?" Marecen asked.

Naya sniffed the air. She'd been so focused on blocking out the oppressive fear in the aether that she hadn't noticed the acrid scent on the wind. Her chest tightened. "Come on," she said.

The smoke thickened as they neared the embassy. Naya quickened her pace, and when she rounded the last corner her steps faltered and her eyes widened.

"Well damn," Iselia said.

Smoke billowed from the shattered windows of the Talmiran Embassy, illuminated by the flickering orange glow of the fire inside. A small crowd had gathered in front of the burning building. A few looked like they were trying to organize a bucket line from the nearest fountain, but most just stood and stared.

"What now?" Marecen asked. She and her brother came up beside Naya.

"I don't know," Naya said, feeling her hopes curl and crumble to ash. Any evidence Valn might have left would soon be consumed by the flames.

"We can still go in," Corten said. "It's like the glass in the furnace. So long as we don't stay too long, the fire shouldn't damage our bones."

Lestare nodded. "It could be there is still something worth saving."

Marecen looked uncertainly at the rest of them. "I can't go in," she said.

"But you could go to Velicia's shop and tell them what's happening," Lestare said.

"Or find one of the fire brigades," Iselia said with a wary look at the embassy. "The last thing we need is to have the whole city burning down before the Talmirans even get here."

Marecen looked at Lestare. "You sure you're okay with going in there?"

Lestare smiled. "I'll be fine. You go get us some help."

"Don't worry, I'll keep an eye on him," Iselia said.

"What about you?" Corten asked Naya.

Naya looked back at the blaze. Only a minute or so had passed, but already the flames looked like they were growing brighter. "If we're going to do this, we need to go now." She took a moment to describe the layout of the embassy, and then the four of them headed toward the crowd. Marecen moved in the opposite direction in search of help.

The crowd around the fire was growing slowly, and Naya had to shove with her elbows to get through.

"Hey!" someone called, trying to grab her as she broke into the open and started for the embassy's front door.

"Stay out of the way!" Iselia shouted back. "And go get some water, for Creator's sake."

Naya didn't wait to see if the stranger complied. This close she could feel the heat against her face. The flames growled like a hungry beast. She couldn't see the telltale glow of aether around the front door. If there'd been any runes there, the fire had already damaged them beyond function.

"Okay," Corten said. "Move fast, don't let your clothes catch fire, and try to keep your bones away from the flames. If they start to hurt, get out of there."

Naya flexed the fingers of her left hand. Aether sung in her bones. She concentrated the strength down to her legs, imagining the bottoms of her feet becoming hard and heavy as iron plates. With a shout she kicked the door. Wood splintered. She kicked again and felt something give.

The door crashed open and Naya stumbled into the burning embassy.

CHAPTER 38

Smoke billowed around her and heat pressed against her. Flames licked along the wall farther down the hallway. Naya ran forward, fighting a strange sense of vertigo. She could smell the smoke, taste it on the back of her tongue. Her mind was screaming that she should be choking, that any minute the flames would char her skin black.

I don't need to breathe. The fire can't hurt me. She repeated the words again and again like a prayer. Iselia and Lestare headed up the stairs to check Celia's room while Naya and Corten moved toward Valn's office. The thickening smoke seemed to swallow them as they got deeper into the building, making it almost impossible to see. They crouched low, trying to escape the smoke and the heat rising toward the ceiling.

"Your skirt!" Corten shouted.

Naya looked down and saw a tongue of flame licking up the fabric. Her hands shook as she drew the kitchen knife and slashed away the burning section.

As they continued down the hall, it became obvious that this was where the fire had started. The air was black with smoke, and the flames rolled over the right wall in hypnotic patterns. Naya wondered how long the ceiling would hold. They might survive the heat for a little while, but she doubted any of them would live through being buried under piles of burning wood and plaster.

Valn's office door was open. Something that might once have been a desk squatted near the back wall, flames licking off it and up to the ceiling and walls.

"We need to get out of here," Corten shouted over the roar of the flames. "Anything in there is long gone." Soot smeared his cheeks, and his clothes were scorched where embers had landed.

Naya shook her head. "This didn't just happen. Someone set this fire."

Corten grabbed her arm. "All the more reason for us to get out of here."

"No, wait!" Naya's eyes caught on something near the door, barely visible in the smoke. The carpet had been folded over in one corner, exposing the wood beneath. She pulled her arm free of Corten's grasp and ran into the office. The heat inside was even more intense than it had been in the hallway. Naya felt it spreading in her bones. The pain grew by the second. She fell to her hands and knees and crawled toward the exposed floor, squinting against the smoke.

It hadn't been her imagination. A thin crack ran where a three-foot section of flooring was raised a little above the rest. Naya dug her fingers into the opening. The section of floor swung up on hidden hinges to reveal a steep stairway like the one leading to Jalance's vault. A wave of dizziness hit her. She had to get out of the heat before it charred her bones.

"Come on!" she called over her shoulder, before lunging through the opening. She half crawled, half fell down the stone steps and landed in a heap on the floor. She heard Corten follow a second later.

Naya lay against the cool stone and waited for the pain in her hand to fade. Trails of smoke wisped off her clothes. She sat up, pinching out a few still-smoldering spots along the hem of her skirt. Corten crouched beside her and stared up at the orange light. "We should close that before the fire spreads." He'd managed to hold on to the heavy iron poker Iselia had given him. Naya looked around, realizing she must have dropped her kitchen knife somewhere up above.

"I don't think anything down here will burn," she said after taking a closer look at their surroundings. The tunnel was low and cramped, with walls of rough stone. Ten feet farther along the tunnel, an aether lamp glowed outside a heavy-looking door.

Corten followed her gaze. "Did you know this was here?"

Naya shook her head. "I saw the edge of the trapdoor and thought maybe Valn had hidden something here." She walked to the door, resting her hand on the knob and closing her eyes. She couldn't sense anyone on the other side. When she tried the knob she was surprised to find the door unlocked.

Beyond it was a narrow room containing a rumpled bed, a desk, and—judging from the smell—a chamber pot. There was another door on the far side, and a long metal chain was bolted to the floor next to the bed. Naya followed the length of the chain with her eyes until she found the heavy shackle at its end.

"They were keeping someone prisoner here," she said.

"Why?" Corten asked. "Valn had access to the palace dungeons. Why would he need to keep someone here?"

Excitement ran down Naya's back like a shiver. "Because it wasn't someone he arrested. I think Delence might still be alive." She ran to the door on the other side of the room. Locked. She fumbled through her pockets for her lock picks, but of course Valn's guards had taken those when they'd captured her. The door looked heavy enough that she doubted she could smash it open. She let one hand slip through the wood, feeling around on the far side, but couldn't find any way to turn the bolt without a key.

Naya took a step back and glared at the door. She didn't want to risk going back up through the fire. And when she reached out into the aether, she sensed, or thought she sensed, a faint trail of emotions somewhere beyond the door.

She crouched to examine the lock. It was fashioned from ordinary metal and wood, and when she'd reached through the door she hadn't felt the chill of even a thin salma wood plate. There had to be a way through.

"We could try breaking it," Corten said, though he sounded uncertain as he hefted the metal poker.

Naya rapped her knuckles against the door, listening to the solid thunk. "Maybe." The door outside had been weakened by fire, and out there she'd had the aether of the crowd to draw from. "I just need something that could fit in the lock. I wonder if . . ." She stared at her fingers pressed against the door. She could change the shape of her face. Why not do the same with her hands?

"What is it?" Corten asked.

"I have an idea."

She let the fingers of her right hand turn a wispy blue, then pushed one into the lock. The cold pressure as her finger reluctantly solidified was uncomfortable in a way that reminded her of jamming her toe on a table leg. The part of her that still thought of her body as a physical thing insisted her finger was being crushed. But after a moment she felt the delicate pressure of the lock's pins.

Naya clenched her jaw, ignoring the discomfort and trying to feel the subtle release of the pins sliding into place. She closed her eyes and felt one pin catch, then another. Seconds dragged by, and finally she found the sweet spot on the third. She twisted, again feeling a twinge as some part of her imagined her finger snapping from the strain. The lock clicked. Naya opened her eyes and flashed Corten a grin.

Beyond the door was a low hallway a little wider than the one on the other side of the room. "Where do you think it goes?" Corten asked.

"I don't know." Naya reached out through the aether. There wasn't much in the tunnel, but she could just sense a trace of emotions somewhere up ahead. Maybe they weren't too late after all. "There's someone down there."

Corten tightened his grip on the poker. "Delence?"

"I can't tell."

"Guess we'd better go find out."

There was no light ahead, so Naya ducked back to retrieve an aether lamp from one of the wall hooks behind them. They moved forward cautiously. The air smelled of dust and old rot mixed with the smoky stench wafting from their burned clothes. The rough stone walls looked older than the room behind them, and there were strange marks carved into the stone every few paces. After about thirty feet, a smaller tunnel branched off to their left. A little ahead, the main tunnel curved to the right.

Naya closed her eyes and searched the aether, trying to pinpoint the lingering mix of fear and anger. "This way," she said, motioning the lamp toward the tunnel to the right.

The swinging lamp cast strange shadows against the walls as they ran. They passed two more junctions and Naya used the aether to guide her decision each time, praying she was right about its source. With every turn the sensations grew stronger, twining in a familiar mix that made her palms grow cold with fear. As they rounded the corner, she spotted three people up ahead. One of them was being dragged along by the others, and all of them wore lightweight coats with the hoods pulled up. "Stop!" Naya shouted.

The three turned. When Naya saw their faces, she froze. Her father's beard looked scruffier than it had when she'd last seen him, and there was soot smeared under one of his eyes. A heavy sword hung sheathed on his belt. Beside him Celia stood holding a small aether lamp. Naya had seen their prisoner only once, but she recognized him immediately. It was Delence.

The old man's gray hair was lank with grease, and dark bags shadowed his eyes. His wrists were bound in manacles. When he moved, it was with a careful stiffness that suggested great pain.

Her father's eyes widened when he saw Naya and Corten. "Stay away!" He put a hand on his sword hilt and dragged Delence a few steps back.

"Go," Celia said, handing him the aether lamp. "I'll deal with this."

Naya's father snarled something, then dragged his prisoner farther down the tunnel. "Let me go!" Delence said. He struggled, but her father punched him hard in the gut and forced him to keep moving. The light of their lamp soon faded around the next corner.

"Turn back and I'll let you leave," Celia said. She shifted so she stood at the center of the tunnel, then drew a short club from inside her jacket.

Naya felt Corten tense beside her. Even if the fire didn't block the path behind them, there was no way she would give up and let her father drag Delence off to who knew where. She took a step forward, letting her body fall into a fighting stance. Celia smiled, but Naya thought she sensed a thread of fear in the spy's aether. "You were a better pupil than I expected. I'd rather not kill you, but I will if I have to."

"Let us pass," Naya said. "You have to see this plan is madness."

Celia paused for the space of a breath, then her expression hardened. "No. Not all of us can abandon our loyalties so easily as you."

"He's getting away," Corten said under his breath.

Naya glared at Celia. "Get out of my way or I'll make you."

In response Celia reached into her jacket with her free hand and drew out a slender knife. Runes ignited with aether as the blade slipped free of its sheath. Naya felt the tug of the wraith eater a second later and took an unconscious step back.

"What do we do?" Corten asked.

Naya watched as the glowing runes seemed to crawl along the blade. "Stay back," she said. Then she gathered her aether and channeled it into the runes of Celia's lantern, which flashed brightly before the runes cracked, plunging them into darkness. Naya rushed forward, focusing on the wisps of blue aether rushing off Celia and into the knife. In all their sparring matches, Celia had always been faster, always bested Naya before she could land more than a token blow.

This time would be different.

She kept her left hand tucked close to her body and her eyes on the knife. Celia stepped back, slashing sideways at chest level. Naya ducked under the blow, aiming for the narrow opening to Celia's left. The knife tugged at her aether and her shoulder scraped stone as she threw herself into a clumsy roll.

Celia was already turning to face her when Naya came back up to her feet. She swung the club toward Naya's head, but Naya let it pass through her. As she'd expected, Celia stabbed with the knife a half second later. Naya turned her body sideways to dodge the thrust. Then she concentrated aether into heat in her right hand and grabbed Celia's wrist. The stink of burning leather rose from the sleeve of Celia's jacket, but the spy managed to twist free, reversing her grip on the knife and stabbing downward. The tip of the blade slashed through Naya's skirt and into her thigh. Naya screamed as the knife sucked at her energy. She stumbled back, but the pain made her knee collapse. As Celia stepped forward to slash again, Naya raised her hand, snatching at what little aether she could and again pooling it in her palm.

She turned her head away and released the energy as a flash

of light. Celia cried out in surprise. Naya looked back and saw the spy take a step away, slashing wildly in front of her. Before Naya could get back to her feet, a faintly glowing figure stepped behind Celia. It raised its arms above its head, then swung down. Naya heard a muffled thud, and Celia collapsed like a puppet that'd had its strings cut.

"Looked like you could use some help," the figure said. Naya recognized Corten's voice. Squinting at his face, she thought she could just make out his features outlined in the blue glow of his aether. His hands were wrapped around something. After a moment Naya realized it was the iron poker.

"Thanks," Naya said.

Her leg felt weak as she forced herself to her feet, and she could still feel the tug of the wraith eater from where it lay on the ground a few paces away. Celia groaned, her hands scraping feebly against the rough stone floor.

"What do we do with her?" Corten asked.

Naya hesitated. They didn't have time to tie Celia up, and besides, they didn't have any rope. Naya inched closer to Celia and reached carefully for the wraith eater. The blade's hunger intensified as she grasped the hilt and twisted it the way she'd seen Celia do when she'd drawn the blade. The pulling sensation stopped and the knife's runes went dark. Naya sighed with relief, then took the sheath from Celia's belt and tucked it into her skirt pocket. She didn't like the thought of keeping it close to her, but better that than to leave it with Celia.

"Come on. Let's get going before she wakes up." She placed one hand against the wall and sought out her father's emotions in the aether. Her free hand found Corten's and together they hurried on.

They felt their way through the dark, moving as fast as they could. After a while Naya began to imagine she could sense the outline of the space around her, something halfway between touch and sight guiding her every step. Light blossomed ahead as they neared the source of the aether. They rounded a bend in the tunnel, and the walls widened to form a small room. Her father stood on the far side, the lamp on the ground beside him as he struggled to drag Delence up a narrow flight of stairs. When he saw them, he shoved Delence back and grabbed the hilt of his sword.

Naya's throat went tight, her legs shaky. She could feel her father's fear and anger, a foul smoke billowing over the cold steel of his determination. "Father," she said in a trembling voice.

He flinched from the word, stepping toward Delence. The old politician's face was twisted in a grimace of pain. His eyes darted between Naya and her father, looking uncertain about what was going on.

Naya stepped forward. "It's me," she said, the words coming out stronger. "Please, I know how you feel, but you're making a mistake. The necromancers aren't evil. Valn's just using them as an excuse to invade Ceramor."

Her father shook his head, his expression hardening. "You're not her."

"I am. Please, listen. You don't have to do this. This doesn't have to end in war."

Her father laughed, the sound bitter and echoing in the stone chamber. "My daughter would have known that war was the only way this could end. The corruption in Ceramor has spread too deep. The people here need a strong hand to guide them back into the light."

"That's the last thing we need," Corten said, surprising Naya by taking a step forward. "Besides, your plan's already failed. Give us Delence. It's over."

"No," her father said. His sword seemed to slide from its sheath in slow motion. The air around it rippled as aether rushed into the rune-scribed steel. Her father raised it above his head, then lunged for Corten. Corten's eyes widened. He stumbled away from the clumsy swing, then struck back with the poker. The blow landed on her father's knee, but even from a distance Naya could see there'd been little force behind the strike. Corten scrambled backward, tripping over Delence's leg and barely avoiding her father's next attack.

"Stop!" Naya rushed forward and grabbed her father's sword arm, trying to give Corten a chance to move out of range. As her fingers touched his sleeve, she felt his aether envelop her. It was the same as what she'd felt when he'd ordered Valn to kill her, only now the last threads of his grief were drowned out by hate. Her father threw her off with a bellow, half turning to face her. "You," he snarled. "How dare you steal my daughter's face? How dare you defile her memory?"

"I am your daughter," Naya said again, anger boosting the volume of her voice. "And maybe I wouldn't have died if you had told me what was really going on. How could you work with Valn? How could you condone killing your own people?" Behind him she saw Corten inching forward.

Her father's lips pulled back from his teeth. "Those men were sinners. They did more good in death than they ever did in life. But when this is over, Valn will answer for my daughter's death."

Naya backed away, terrified by the force of his rage. She knew she should gather aether for an attack, but her arms felt frozen in place. Corten inched toward her father, raising the poker to strike him as he had Celia. Her father noticed the shift in her attention. He turned at the last second, catching Corten's blow on his forearm rather than his head. Metal hit flesh with a wet crunch. Her father snarled something, then plunged his sword into Corten's gut and sliced upward.

Naya's scream mingled with Corten's shriek of pain. His body rippled and collapsed as the sword tore through him.

Something snapped and aether flashed as her father pulled the sword free. Corten clutched his chest. His eyebrows furrowed in a look of confusion and he opened his mouth as though to say something. Before he could, his body dissolved, his aether sucked into the wraith eater like smoke drawn to a chimney.

Naya screamed again as Corten's empty clothes collapsed to the floor with a clatter of dry bones. Her father whirled to face her. His eyes were hard and his knuckles had gone white from gripping the sword. One arm hung limp at his side.

"Stand still," he said. "Let me end your pain."

His words cut through her terror and grief. Naya's lips curled back into a snarl. Despite everything her father had done, and despite his hate and fear, she'd still thought that maybe she could make him see the truth. She'd wanted to believe there was a way to reconcile his actions, to make him do the right thing. So she'd talked instead of fighting. She'd hesitated. And now Corten was dead.

Naya drew in as much aether as she could. Her father lunged, the point of the sword aimed at her heart. She twisted sideways and stepped toward him, no longer caring if he hurt her. The blade slashed her side and icy pain nearly blinded her. Her bones strained as her fingers wrapped around her father's wrist.

She closed her eyes and reached into his aether. The sword stole nearly everything, but she found the dense ball of energy at his core and pulled. She hadn't known what she was doing when she'd drawn the assassin's soul. This time she was ready. The energy seared through her like molten glass. She imagined channeling it down into the vortex of the wraith eater.

The world twisted. For an instant her vision doubled and she saw herself through her father's eyes. He stared down at the imposter who had stolen his daughter's form. He would purge it, put her soul to rest. Then he would get Delence back to the ships. They would take Ceramor and save her people, and then all his sacrifices would be worthwhile. His daughter's death wouldn't be for nothing.

The energy flared and the vision shifted. Naya could feel her father's soul fading as the wraith eater consumed it, could feel his confusion and pain as he struggled to pull away from her. She saw her father as a boy, coming home to his mother crying. Her eyes were bleary with drink as she told him how his father had died fighting against the Mad King's army. His hatred for Ceramor's undead gnawed and grew with each passing year, his disgust doubling when the treaty was signed and his countrymen went back to their lives as though there weren't monsters lurking on their borders. She saw herself—a little girl in a doorway, too skinny by far, but with eyes that met his and didn't look away. The mother said the girl was his. He'd made her a promise, long ago when he was still young and time seemed abundant. He'd avoided that promise for years, but now as he looked at the little girl he thought it might not be so bad after all. There was something about her, a fire in her eyes.

Naya's legs collapsed under her. Runes shattered and aether exploded out from the wraith eater's blade. Pain flashed through her hand as one of her bones cracked. She gasped in aether as her hold on her father's soul faltered. She heard the lap of death's tides, but their cold was a welcome balm after the fire of her father's soul. Through a haze she saw her father's body collapse to the floor. Dead.

Silence fell as Naya stared at her father's corpse. Then a rough voice whispered from the stairs, "Who are you?"

Naya looked up and found Delence staring at her, his eyes wide with a mix of fear and fascination. She closed her eyes and drew in a shuddering breath. The pain of cracked bones pulsed through her hand. Who was she? She was a reaper. She was her father's killer. In his last moments she'd been the one to prove that the undead could be every bit the monsters he'd feared. And the worst part of it was that he'd died loving her, or at least the version of her he'd once seen.

Naya didn't lock the pain away. She let it roar through her. Then she opened her eyes and met Delence's gaze. "My name is Naya Garth."

CHAPTER 39

Naya crawled to where Corten's clothes lay. She poked through them and found the two carved ribs that formed his bond. Their runes were dead and dark, and one of the bones was cracked clear in half. Naya closed her eyes, trying to sense some hint of his presence. She pushed aether into the undamaged bone, ignoring the pain that lanced through her hand. A few of the runes glowed feebly, then faded again.

This couldn't be happening. Corten couldn't be gone.

Maybe he wasn't.

She gathered up the bones carefully. Corten had said it was almost impossible to sing a soul back a second time. But in the gap between *almost* and *impossible* there was still hope. She just had to get Corten's extra bones and find someone to make a new carving. Then Lucia could sing him back and—

Delence cleared his throat. "Do you know what's going on in the city?"

Naya looked back at the politician, irritation making her lips twitch. What did that matter? She needed to find a way to save Corten.

"Garth told me some of the plan," Delence continued. "I know they're trying to take the city, and I know they've been gathering people they thought would help them. How far has it gone? Is the king still alive?"

"I don't know," Naya said. Her thoughts reluctantly shifted as she remembered why they had come here and what Corten had died for. "Valn had control of the palace, last I heard. He's been sending lies to Banen and Silmar to keep them from getting involved. We came looking for something we could use to convince the other Powers to help us."

"Well, you've found it. Get me to the Banian Embassy. I know their ambassador. She trusts me, and if I can get her to send a runner back to my house, I should be able to retrieve a few documents that will help back up my part of the story."

Corten's bones felt impossibly heavy as Naya clutched them to her chest. Her hand ached, and just the prospect of standing up made her head spin. "It might be too late," she said.

"It will be if we don't move quickly." Delence struggled to his feet.

Naya's grip tightened on the bones. She glanced down at her father's body. Her eyes burned, though she couldn't say if the dry tears came from anger or sorrow. Standing up hurt. Delence was right, though: she couldn't help anyone if she just sat here.

The stairs led up into an empty basement, and from there onto a quiet street just a few blocks from the harbor. Naya was relieved when no one tried to stop them. With her bond damaged, it was all she could do to help support Delence.

The fire had spread to the second floor of the Talmiran Embassy, and the crowd had swelled to fill the street. Naya skirted the edge of the chaos, trying to keep her head down. She spotted Iselia sitting near the fringe, her clothes singed and her expression exhausted. "Wait here," Naya whispered to Delence, then hurried over.

Iselia smiled when she saw Naya. "What took you so long?" she asked. "We got out ages ago. We found some old letters upstairs, but that was all we could grab before the fire got too hot. Did you find anything?"

"Yes. But listen, I need you to go back to Lucia. Tell her she needs to send someone to get Corten's bones and carve a new bond."

"Did one of his bones crack? Wait, where is he?"

Naya's throat closed up. She shook her head. Iselia's eyes went to the bones clasped tight to Naya's chest. She covered her mouth with one hand. "Oh."

"Please," Naya said. "We don't have much time. I have to get to the Banian Embassy. Will you . . ."

"I'll go now. Here, take these—" Iselia handed Naya a few crumpled letters. Naya took them, then forced herself to give up Corten's bones.

It seemed to take an eternity to walk the three blocks to the Banian Embassy. When they finally got there they found the building surrounded by a mix of Ceramoran and Banian soldiers. "Let's hope they're on our side," Delence muttered before straightening his spine and limping toward them. When he was a few paces away, he called out, "My name is Salno Delence. I am requesting asylum for myself and my companion under article fifty-six of the Treaty of Lith Lor."

Whispers spread through the group. After a moment one of the Banian soldiers stepped forward to get a better look. "Way's light," the man said, "it's really him." He seemed to remember himself and snapped a quick salute. "Sir, if you'll follow me, I'm sure Ambassador Maylan will be eager to speak with you."

The edges of the world blurred as Naya and Delence were ushered inside. Naya's thoughts kept returning to Corten. Had Iselia made it back yet? How long would it take to find Corten's bones? She imagined his soul trapped somewhere in the dark waves, struggling as the tide pulled him farther and farther from the land of the living.

"Miss?" the soldier next to Naya said, her tone suggesting it wasn't the first time. "If you'll come with me?" She was dressed in a green-and-blue uniform and had the dark skin and sharp features of a Banian.

Naya blinked. She was standing in a broad hallway with polished wood floors and minimalist paintings of oceanscapes lining the walls. People were rushing all around her. "Where's Delence?"

"Lord Delence is meeting with Ambassador Maylan to discuss the situation. If you'd follow me, I'll show you to a room where you can rest."

"I don't have time for that," Naya said. "I need to . . ." She trailed off. What was there left to do? She could go back to Fredricel's house and see if anyone had gone to retrieve Corten's bones. But in her current state, even that short walk seemed daunting. And once she got there, she didn't know what she'd be able to do other than get in the way.

"If there's anything you need, I'm sure one of the staff can see to it," the guard said. Naya drew in aether, trying to sense the woman's emotions. But whatever she might be feeling was lost under the press of the city's pulse.

"All right," Naya said. Maybe a few minutes' rest wouldn't be such a bad idea. It would give her bones a chance to start healing.

The guard led her to a small room with a tea table, a couple of chairs, and a low day couch strewn with hard-looking pillows. Naya slumped onto the couch as soon as the door closed, then set the letters Iselia had given her down on a nearby chair. Naya probably should have given them to Delence, but she'd been so focused on just getting here that everything else had slipped away. Well, no matter. She could pass them on to someone before she left. She closed her eyes, telling herself she'd only rest a moment before starting out to Fredricel's house.

Next thing she knew, someone was shaking her shoulder. Naya's eyes snapped open and she found Delence standing over her. The old politician looked far better than he had when they'd entered the embassy. His face was still pale and drawn, but his skin was clean and his hair and mustache combed. He was wearing new clothes, a wide-sleeved shirt and loose pants in the Banian style. "How are you feeling?" Delence asked.

Naya blinked. The bones in her hand had settled into a steady pounding and her limbs felt weak and heavy. "I'm fine. I thought you were meeting with the ambassador."

"That was six hours ago."

"What?" Naya sat up, wincing at a fresh stab of pain. "What's going on? Did the ambassador believe you? Have the Banians sent word to Talmir?"

Delence moved the stack of letters to sit with a groan in the chair opposite Naya's couch. "We've begun negotiations. I'll be on my way over to the palace in a few minutes to address the situation there. We have reason to believe King Allence is still alive, so that's one good thing. Ambassador Maylan will want to speak with you regarding your role in all of this. There are quite a few interesting stories about you circulating." He paused, obviously expecting a response.

Naya fought the urge to shrink back into the couch. Her mind still felt sluggish, but not so much that she didn't see the danger in the question. "Valn told a lot of lies. He said whatever he needed to start his war," she finally said.

The corner of Delence's mouth twitched in a look of amusement. "I suppose that's true. Now we'll have to say whatever we must to keep the peace. Given your unique position, I'm sure you understand that better than anyone."

There was a weight to his words that sent a shiver through Naya. "I think I understand," she said. After everything that had happened, it could still be easy for someone to twist the facts against them. If they discovered she was a reaper, they might call for her execution regardless of all she'd done to try to stop Valn.

"Excellent. Then are you ready to speak to Ambassador Maylan?"

"There's something I need to do first. My friend's bond was damaged. I have to help him."

Delence leaned back in his chair. "The city's in turmoil still. We've had riots in several neighborhoods, and our current intelligence suggests the bulk of the Talmiran fleet is less than a day out from our port. If you have any information that can help us dig out the rest of Valn's allies, now is the time to give it."

Naya shook her head. "Valn hardly told me anything. The only other person I even knew in his organization was the woman you saw in the tunnel. Her name is Celia. She led Valn's spies. Those letters came from her room. If anyone knows his secrets, it's her."

Delence stood, then picked up the letters and pocketed them. "Really? That's good to know. I already have people looking for her. Do you have any idea where she might have gone?"

"No. I don't know anything else. I just want to go help my friend."

Delence stared at her for a moment. "Speak with the ambassador. Her questions should only take a few minutes. After that I'll find some guards to escort you through the city."

Delence led Naya down the hall to Ambassador Maylan's office, a small room decorated in the same style as the rest of the embassy. The ambassador greeted Naya from behind a large desk and offered her a seat. Delence quickly bid them farewell.

Ambassador Maylan was an old woman. Deep wrinkles carved her skin like the grooves of tree bark, and her thickly braided hair had faded to a steely gray. Naya struggled to keep her mind clear as she answered the ambassador's questions. She described the conversation she'd overheard between her father and Valn, and gave what details she could on the other Talmiran spies and the codes Celia had taught her. The ambassador's face gave no hint to what she thought of Naya's answers. Naya tried to read her aether, but her emotions were masked by the tug of the office's many lamps and the energy of the guards standing just a little behind Naya's chair.

"Very well," Ambassador Maylan said after what felt like an eternity.

"Will you help us stop them?" Naya asked.

Ambassador Maylan steepled her fingers. "The Banen Isles have no wish to see another war between our allies. I will contact the Six and request that they open formal negotiations with both sides."

"You need to do more than that!" Naya leaned forward despite her pain. The Six were supposedly the ultimate power on the Banen Islands, a mysterious council of rulers rarely seen by outsiders. Every account she'd ever heard of them claimed they were wise and just, but right now Ceramor didn't have time to wait while they debated the best course of action.

Ambassador Maylan pursed her lips. "I don't need to do anything. Your and Lord Delence's accounts answer several questions I had about Ambassador Valn's recent behavior, but I don't intend to make the situation worse by acting rashly. Even if I did have the authority to command the fleet, I wouldn't send it sailing off to foreign shores without having a better grasp of the situation. I will, however, suggest that the Six ready our fleet, and I will send a request to Queen Lial that she not move any Talmiran troops into Ceramor until the details of this matter can be resolved. I will also update the ambassador at the Silmaran Embassy regarding the information you've brought and request Silmar assist us in maintaining peace here."

Naya leaned back in her chair. "Just hurry," she said. "A lot of people will die if the Talmiran Army lands here."

"Believe me, young lady, I am exceedingly aware of that. But we're not yet over the precipice. I will do what I can to see this doesn't end in more blood." She nodded to the guards. "Please see Miss Garth to the door."

Naya allowed herself to be led out. At the end of the hall, she was met by two new guards, these dressed in Ceramoran colors. The taller of the two nodded as she approached. "Lord Delence says we're to escort you wherever you need to go, Miss Garth." Naya looked between them and the door. Fear for Corten warred with the feeling that she should stay here and do whatever she could to ensure the Banians defended Ceramor. She hesitated a moment longer, then stepped out into the uncertain night.

By the time Naya got back to Fredricel's apartment, Lucia was awake. The necromancer's eyes widened in alarm when she saw the guards.

"It's okay," Naya said quickly. "Delence sent them to help us."

"Delence? He's alive?" Lucia sat up with a grunt of effort. Her skin was still a little gray, but her eyes were sharp and her wounds bandaged.

Naya nodded. "Did Iselia tell you what happened?"

Lucia closed her eyes. "Yes. Corten isn't the only one we lost. Between the fighting at the execution and people taking advantage of the chaos, most of the city's necromancers are already busy. We're supposed to prioritize first deaths over attempting to restore those who were already undead in a situation like this, since the chances of success are so much higher."

"You can't leave him dead!" Naya took a step toward Lucia.

Lucia gave her a sharp look. "I won't. I sent Jessin with instructions on how to find Corten's bones in my shop. He's agreed to do the carvings. As soon as he's done, I'll attempt a singing. If we can manage it, I want to do that back at the glass shop. I think a familiar location will help."

Naya paced across the apartment as the last hours of the night wore into morning. When footsteps sounded on the stairs, she ran to the door, but the visitor wasn't Jessin returning with Corten's new bones.

"They told me Lucia was here," Alejandra said as she burst into the room. Her dress was torn and stained, and her hair had fallen out of her bun to hang like the tentacles of some dead sea monster.

"Ali?" Lucia's face lit up. She sat up and looked like she was about to attempt standing, but Alejandra reached her first. She wrapped her arms around Lucia, her movements careful and light, as though she feared she might break something. Lucia rested her head against Alejandra's neck and closed her eyes.

"I'm so sorry," Alejandra said. "I should have foreseen the trap. I should have found a smarter way to get to you. But when I heard they were going to execute you, I couldn't think." Her voice choked off.

"Shh," Lucia whispered, patting Alejandra's hair. "I'm just glad you're alive."

Alejandra leaned back a little, then planted a kiss on Lucia's lips. "Me too. I promise I'll kill the next person who tries to take you from me."

Naya tried to ignore the surge of jealousy that rose in her as Alejandra's hand slid down to squeeze Lucia's undamaged fingers. "How did you get out?" she asked.

"Delence took back control of the palace," Alejandra said. "He got a message through that the Banians had agreed to defend Ceramor. He offered amnesty to anyone who helped apprehend Valn. Most of Captain Terremont's men turned against Valn after that. They managed to overpower the remaining soldiers from the Talmiran Embassy, then opened the gates for the rest of the guard to secure the palace. They found the king and four of his advisers locked up in his apartments. Once they were safe, the guards released all the Council members from the dungeons. Most of the necromancers are performing resurrections, and everyone else is working to prepare defenses around the port, in case the other Powers can't force Talmir to back down."

"Let's hope that isn't necessary," Lucia said.

It was past noon by the time an exhausted-looking Jessin returned with Corten's bones. Naya had to fight to keep from snatching the bag from him and running to the glass shop. There were no carriages to be had, since most of the city's horses had already been requisitioned to help with the defense. Lucia was doing better, but Naya doubted she could manage the long walk up the hill and still have enough strength left for the singing. After a short conversation with the guards, they managed to get space on one of the few trams still running. As they wound up the hill, Naya willed the tram to go faster. Every rattle and bump resonated up through the cracked bones of her hand. But the pain wasn't as bad as the frustration of feeling the seconds grind past and knowing each one whittled away their chances of retrieving Corten's soul.

They found Matius waiting for them at the shop. As they stepped inside he gave Naya's shoulder a sympathetic squeeze. "How are you feeling?" he asked.

"I'm fine."

Matius nodded, then turned his attention to Lucia. "Right, well, I've shut off the furnaces and cleared some space for you in the room upstairs. I'll make sure no one troubles you."

"Thank you," Lucia said.

Upstairs, Naya paused at the door to Corten's room. It was unnerving to see it with the bed and all the clutter pushed back against the walls, like disrupting the space had somehow erased a small part of him from the world. She tried to ignore that chilling thought as she helped Lucia chalk the rune circles to contain the portal. The necromancer sat down gingerly near the center of the circle, cradling her injured arm. "You'll probably be more comfortable downstairs," she said to Naya. "The portal can cause minor disruptions to soul bindings, and with one of your bones already cracked—"

"I'm fine here," Naya said. She knew she couldn't help with the singing, but she also couldn't stand waiting downstairs.

"Then stay quiet. I need to concentrate." Lucia closed her eyes and took several deep breaths. Then she began to sing.

Naya found the necromancer's song just as eerie, and just as enticing, as the first time she'd heard it. As the notes flowed through her, the room grayed, becoming less real to her eyes. Tiny invisible hands pawed at her, and she heard the dark tides lapping at the walls. Naya clenched her jaw and stared at the bones in front of Lucia.

The longer the necromancer sang, the harder it was to judge how much time had passed. Naya could feel the tides trying to suck her in as Lucia's song grew more insistent and the connection with the other side strengthened. The strange words took on a tone of command, but still Corten's bones remained dark. Naya closed her eyes. She tried to reach out, knowing nothing she did or said could find him. *Please come back.* She thought she felt something shift. She opened her eyes. A blue glow illuminated Corten's bones. *Come back.*

Lucia's voice faltered and the edges of the portal began to waver, then to shrink.

"No," Naya whispered. She leaned forward, reaching out even as she felt the portal weakening. For just an instant a wispy figure stood in the center, reaching back toward her. Then the black tendrils enveloped it and the portal snapped closed.

Lucia cried out, then collapsed to the floor, unconscious.

Naya froze with her arm still outstretched. Her eyes locked on Corten's lifeless bones. "No," she whispered again.

Footsteps pounded on the stairs and Matius burst into the

room. He took one look at Lucia's unconscious form and his shoulders drooped. He hurried to Lucia and pressed one hand to her forehead. After a moment she groaned and opened her eyes.

Naya crawled to her. "It didn't work," she said. "You have to try again."

"Can't," Lucia whispered, then closed her eyes again.

Naya turned to Matius. "Then we have to find another necromancer to do the singing."

Matius shook his head. "Even if we could find someone able to make the attempt, you'd never convince them. If Lucia couldn't bring him back, then there's no doing it. I'm sorry, but it's over."

They laid Lucia out on the bed and Naya sat beside her. She stared, trying to think of nothing, as she waited for the necromancer to wake. A hollow ache grew in her chest. Corten couldn't be gone. It wasn't fair. People like him weren't supposed to die.

Lucia opened her eyes. She glanced at Naya, then looked away, tears brimming. "I tried," she whispered. "I'm sorry." Naya could feel the grief in Lucia's aether, the soft ache intermixed with threads of bitter anger Naya suspected were directed at her. She couldn't blame Lucia for that. Corten never would have been in that tunnel if not for her. If she'd only acted faster, maybe she could have saved him.

Matius cleared his throat behind them. "Come on. Let's get you back to your shop. You'll rest better there."

After they helped Lucia down the stairs, Matius put a hand on Naya's shoulder. "Corten was a fine boy," he said softly. "And for what it's worth, he was happier helping you than I'd seen him for a long time. I know he would have come back if he could."

Naya's throat was too tight for words, so she just nodded.

"If you ever need anything—a place to stay or just somebody to talk to—my wife and I live in the yellow house at the end of the street. You're welcome anytime."

Naya squeezed her eyes shut. "Thank you," she whispered.

The guards escorted them to Lucia's shop, then took up position by the shattered door. Naya was beginning to suspect that they were as much there to keep track of her as to protect her, but the pain in her bones and the deeper ache in her chest made her too tired to care. She put Lucia to bed, then did her best to clean up the ransacked workroom.

The sun set, and new guards came to replace the ones standing watch. They brought news that the Talmiran fleet had arrived but so far hadn't launched any troops. Apparently Delence and two more of the king's advisers were preparing to meet with the fleet's admiral under a flag of truce.

When the workroom was as clean as it was likely to get, Naya ascended the stairs and locked herself in her tiny room. She found the glass bird Corten had made waiting for her on the floor where she'd left it, its beak still frozen in the semblance of a smile. Naya picked it up in shaking hands, running her fingers over its smooth head and the lopsided curves of its wings. Then she closed her eyes and let the sobs tear their way out of her throat.

CHAPTER 40

Eventually Naya's sobs faded to hiccups, then silence. She stared at the glass bird, remembering the feel of Corten's lips on hers and the wild, wonderful hope when he'd said he loved her. After all she'd done to him, he'd forgiven her. He'd believed in her and called her strong when all she'd been able to see were her failures.

Naya remembered the glowing figure she'd seen just before Lucia's portal closed. They'd been so close. She was certain she'd felt Corten's soul struggling to cross back into life.

And now I'm going to give up on him?

"No," she whispered. "This isn't over." She set the glass bird down carefully, then stood. Her bones ached as she walked down the stairs, but she ignored the pain. They would heal eventually, and she had more important things to worry about.

She found Lucia and Alejandra in the workroom, talking quietly over cups of steaming tea. Both women looked up at her in surprise as she approached.

"What happens to a soul if it isn't resurrected?" Naya asked.

Lucia blinked, sharing a confused glance with Alejandra. "Well, that depends on who you ask," she said.

"The Dawning keepers here tell us that souls must first pass through a transition before they are welcomed into the Creator's embrace," Alejandra said. "That's the place you saw before Lucia sang you back. I've heard it described many different ways, but everyone agrees they feel a force pulling them away from life."

Naya tried not to shiver. That wasn't much different from what she'd grown up believing. Granted, the Dawning keepers in Talmir never said anything about a transition. But they'd also called the undead monsters. Who knew what else they'd gotten wrong. "Is that what you believe?" she asked, meeting Lucia's eyes. "Is that why you sometimes can't bring a soul back? Because they've already gone to the Creator?"

Lucia looked away. "I don't know. It's been a long time since I attended a chapel service. There are of course a number of other theories, but I suppose that one is the most common."

Alejandra put her hand over Lucia's. Her expression was sympathetic when she met Naya's eyes. "Sometimes even we have to accept that a death is beyond our powers. Necromancy doesn't make us immortal; it only gives us a chance to extend the time of those who die too young. I met Corten several times. He was a good boy. We all mourn him, but—"

"But what?" Naya asked. "He's gone? We tried once and now we should just give up on him? Maybe you can, but I won't. He died because of me." She stepped toward Lucia. "I felt him at the portal, just before it closed. Necromancers always say that souls come back because they still have a purpose in this world. Well, Corten belongs here." A new thought struck her, and her insides clenched. "What if he got trapped, or lost somehow, trying to make it back? I need to know what happened to him. Please, there has to be something else you can try."

Silence. Naya could feel Alejandra's pity, but she ignored it, keeping her eyes locked on Lucia. Lucia licked her lips. "No one has ever succeeded at finding a soul again after a failed resurrection. It's impossible," she finally said.

"That's what everyone said about healing a wraith's bones," Naya said. "But you found a way to do that."

She saw something flash in Lucia's eyes and felt the hungry echo in her aether. Lucia might have spent years living quietly. But before that she'd experimented with the most powerful magics of her age. "There are some theories . . ." Lucia began. "Back when I was doing research for the reaper bindings, I came across descriptions of something called a shadow walk. If the accounts can be believed, it was a method for transporting someone physically into death. I think perhaps it could be modified to search for a soul, but . . ."

"But what?" Naya asked. Her chest felt tight, her head strangely light.

"But it's possible there's nothing to search for. Also, I don't know how to perform the ritual. I made copies of the diagrams once, but they were in a separate journal from the one Valn brought me. If it was somehow spared in the purge, I don't know where it would be."

"But if you had it, could you make another attempt?" Naya asked.

Lucia glanced to the workroom door and lowered her voice a little. "Perhaps."

"Lu," Alejandra hissed. "The Talmirans already baited you into using illegal runes once and it nearly got us both killed. I know you mourn Corten. But there are limits."

Lucia didn't answer, instead watching Naya with a curious expression. Naya's thoughts raced. Lucia didn't know where her other journals were, but Valn might. And Naya could guess where Valn would be, assuming he wasn't dead.

Naya hurried to the workroom door. Outside she found two guards wearing King Allence's colors. "I want to speak to Delence," she told them. "Could one of you get a message to him for me?"

The guards exchanged a look. "Lord Delence is very busy," one of them said.

Naya tried to sound confident. "It's important."

After a pause the guard nodded. "We could pass on word that you wish to speak to him, but I wouldn't expect much. Lord Delence is helping the king identify and replace all those who betrayed him. It may be some time before he can speak to you."

It took three days before Delence's reply came in the form of a carriage and an invitation to the palace. Naya felt out of place sitting on the fine red-and-gold fabric as the carriage rattled through the city. The past three days had been torture. Her thoughts had dipped in and out of a fog of pain and grief. She tried to focus on her plan, but even hope felt fragile. The somber tone of the city's aether didn't help. Denor and Corten hadn't been the only ones to die in the chaos of Valn's coup attempt, and it seemed no one was certain what would happen next.

When Naya arrived at the palace, a servant escorted her through the empty audience chamber and to an office in one of the small side halls. There she found Delence sitting behind a desk covered in neat stacks of paper.

"Ah, Miss Garth, welcome," he said, motioning for her to take a seat. As she sat he activated a large rune-powered teakettle on the desk.

Naya put on a fake smile that she hoped would disguise the knots in her stomach. "I'm sorry to bother you. I know you're busy."

Delence smiled back. "That is what happens when one is tasked with reconstructing a government. We've already had to replace several people who accepted Valn's bribes."

Delence sounded almost cheerful as he discussed the treason. Naya reached out through the aether, but the teakettle was sucking up most of his energy. Between that and her fractured bones, she couldn't pick out his emotions from the background hum.

Did Delence know about her role in his kidnapping and his son's death? It was hard to imagine he didn't by now. Was his warm greeting just a mask, or did he not care about her past crimes?

"I wanted to talk to you about Valn," Naya said cautiously. "I know you captured him when you took the palace back. Is he still . . ."

"Alive? Yes. His injuries were severe but not fatal."

"Has he said anything?" Naya asked.

"Quite a bit. Not all of it has been useful, but our interrogators are working to extract any secrets he may still be hiding."

"Good," Naya said. But as the words left her mouth, she felt a twinge of doubt. It was good to know that someone was making sure Valn's work was well and truly over. But his plans weren't the only secrets he'd likely held. How would Delence use the information he'd extracted from Valn? Naya knew she'd done the right thing in helping stop Valn, but she didn't like the idea of Ceramor using him as a tool against her homeland.

Delence leaned forward. "Yes. But let's not waste any more time. I think I know why you've come. You must be wondering by now why we haven't imprisoned you."

Naya tensed. "What?"

"King Allence appreciates the sacrifices you made exposing Valn, and he intends to issue a pardon covering your actions spying against the people of Ceramor, and your role in capturing me. Hiding a reaper is more complicated than pardoning a few crimes, but we're doing what we can. So far I've managed to contain and discredit the rumors. Thankfully, few people knew what you were. I've convinced Lord Jalance to hand over the incriminating materials, and for now we'll keep a protective eye on Madame Laroke to make sure no one attempts to coerce any further favors from her."

Naya sat back, struggling to absorb all he'd said. She'd given little thought to her own fate with everything that had happened. King Allence and his government would be taking a risk by choosing to hide her. If she was exposed, the treaty gave them little choice but to execute her. And there were surely others like Valn who would gladly twist the situation to their advantage. In a way, that made tracking the source of the journal even more important. Lucia had thought it unlikely that Valn had acquired it during the purges. If he'd gotten it from someone else, then that person might know about her. Who knew how they'd use that knowledge.

"There's something else you should know," Naya said. "Lucia claimed Valn was the one who gave her the diagrams for my bond. Did he mention anything about that?"

Delence smiled. "In that area I do have a bit of good news. Based on my conversations with Lord Jalance, I had some suspicions about Lucia Laroke's true identity and the history of the journal we confiscated. When questioned on that point, Valn claimed that he got the journal from somewhere in Talmir. If it's true, then it puts the Talmiran government in a difficult position. If they attempt to expose you, they risk drawing attention to the source of the journal. Valn hinted that the book was part of a collection. So far we haven't been able to get any further details from him. But we're hopeful that this line of questioning may eventually reveal the identity of his other allies in Talmir."

Naya's eyes widened. "In Talmir? But that's absurd. What would runes from the war be doing there?"

Delence shrugged. "We can't dismiss the possibility of a lie on Valn's part, but the prospect is not so insane as you might think. Most of the forces overseeing the purges were Talmiran. They would have had the means to protect anything they did not want to destroy. Regardless, the source of that journal is only one small part of our investigations, and to be frank, there's another reason that I requested your presence here today." Delence bent to retrieve something from a desk drawer.

Naya tried to keep her expression calm even as her insides twisted. Talmir. If Valn was telling the truth, then any other surviving journals would be far out of her reach, assuming they even still existed.

Delence straightened, holding out a leather folder. "I have an offer for you."

Naya took the folder. She was halfway through skimming the single page within when she realized what she was looking at. "This is the deed of ownership for the *Gallant*. Why . . ."

"Consider it a gift. The Crown seized Hal Garth's assets, and it seems only appropriate that the *Gallant* should go to you."

Naya's grip tightened on the paper. "You're giving me a ship?"

"Yes, though it comes with a request. I want you to sail with me to Lith Lor and join me at the Congress of Powers."

Naya stared at Delence. Was he joking? Had he gone mad? "No," she said reflexively. "They'd never allow me back, never mind letting me participate in the Congress."

"Let me worry about that. Recent events have given me a great deal of leverage. This meeting may be the most important since the Congress was founded. I need people with me who are dedicated to forging peace. You've already proved you're willing to sacrifice to protect our peoples from another war. I don't expect you to participate in the negotiations, but your presence at the Congress would give us an opportunity to show the other delegates that the undead are every bit as human as the living."

"I'm not . . ." Naya began. Then she looked down at the deed to the *Gallant*. If Lucia's other journals still existed somewhere in Talmir, then this would likely be her best opportunity to search for them. But the thought of going back so publicly made her chest tighten with fear.

"You're the right person for this. Think about it," Delence said, leaning forward. "You understand their fears better than any other undead. Who better to help them see our side of things?"

The teakettle began to shriek, but Delence made no move to deactivate the runes. Naya met his eyes. Could she do this? She suspected there was more to Delence's offer than he was saying. She was no politician. She had to assume there were others better suited to this task than her. Yet whatever Delence's plans were, she couldn't pass up the chance to search for Lucia's missing journals. She had to find out what had happened to Corten's soul and if there was any way still to bring him back.

Naya ran her finger over the letters of the deed. "I would need a new crew for the *Gallant*. I can't trust my father's men."

"Of course."

"And I want Lucia to come with me."

Delence raised his eyebrows at that. "I suppose that can be arranged. It will be good to have someone around who can assist you if your bones become damaged."

"Good."

"Does that mean you agree to join our delegation?"

Naya hesitated. Surely there were other things she should ask for. But her head felt light with expanding hope. "I'll do it."

Delence extended his hand across the desk. "Excellent. I look forward to working with you, Captain Garth."

ACKNOWLEDGMENTS

Wow. So many people helped make this book happen. Thank you to my amazing agent, Lucienne Diver, who possesses superhuman powers of editing and time management. I don't know how you do it all. Thank you to Monica Perez and all the rest at Charlesbridge Teen. This book wouldn't be here without you, and I hope you're as proud of it as I am.

Thank you to all the family and friends who supported me along the way: my dad, for getting me hooked on *The Lord of the Rings*; my mom, for always encouraging my weirdness; my brothers, Zack and Aaron, for all the good times and humor; Tom and Lynette, for encouraging me and welcoming me into your family; and Matt, for everything. Thank you to Caroline for the edits and offers of fan fic. Your enthusiasm is infectious. Thanks, in no particular order, to David, John, Jeremy, and James, for your patience in reading drafts and providing insight. To Chelsea, thank you for years of friendship, empathy, and shared stories.

Thanks also to Brent Weeks. We've never met, but it was after reading the acknowledgments in one of your books that I finally tore up my excuses and decided to give this writing thing a try. Finally, thank you so much to everyone who's read this far. Books are weird and wonderful things, and I hope you've enjoyed mine.